Twelve Sinners

by

Henry James Kaye

Malcolm Gee Mysteries

Twelve Sinners

Cover Art by *The Wild Rose Press, Inc.*

The Wild Rose Press, Inc.
PO Box 708
Adams Basin, NY 14410-0708
Visit us at www.thewildrosepress.com

Publishing History
First Edition, 2025
Trade Paperback Print ISBN 978-1-5092-6359-2
Digital ISBN 978-1-5092-6360-8

Malcolm Gee Mysteries
Published in the United States of America

Dedication

To my father, who instilled his morals and work ethic in me.

To my writer's groups, who taught me how to write something others would want to read and encouraged me to keep going.

Last, but not least, to my wife for tolerating all of the hours I've put into my writing.

Day One—July 15th

Chapter 1

Tuesday, 2:30 a.m.

AD leaned against the wall of an abandoned gas station on County Road 360. He watched the approaching headlights and hoped they belonged to Officer Ronald Scott's patrol car. Being spotted didn't concern him, as he was clothed in black from head to toe, including a black ski mask. He absentmindedly swatted at a bug that buzzed near his ear.

The vehicle slowed and then came to a complete stop in the southbound lane of the two-lane road. The decal on the driver's door read "City of Madison" and "Florida's Deer Capital" underneath. Rotating red-and-blue lights lit the area like a disco dance floor. The car's side-mounted spotlight popped on, scanned left, then right, and stopped in the middle. It illuminated a wooden chair on its side in the center of the road.

AD's anonymous call a few minutes earlier to the nonemergency police number about debris in the roadway had produced the desired results. He glanced at the waning crescent moon. "Thank you, Jesus, for the patrol car and favorable conditions."

Most of the station's white paint had peeled off over the years. Beer cans littered the repair bays, its missing doors and windows only remembered by Madison's old-timers. The mixed stink of old beer, oil, rotting garbage, and urine didn't bother him. He only cared about the patrol car's occupant. The heel of his black sneaker bounced on the concrete in time with his heartbeat.

The car door swung open, and Officer Scott emerged.

AD felt a stirring in his stomach. Not the abdominal pain he'd experienced the last six months. This stirring came from excitement. He would soon take the first step toward immortality.

Officer Scott removed a flashlight from its belt loop, shined it on the chair, and sauntered forward. "Damn Georgia hillbillies never tie their shit right. This is the third time some redneck had something fall off his truck in two weeks." He clicked his shoulder radio. "Dispatch, Unit Six on scene at road debris. Going to remove it."

"Roger, Unit Six."

AD's left hand grasped the Remington .30-06 deer rifle leaning against the wall. When he received it for Christmas from his parents at age twelve, he'd declared, "She's beautiful." Davy Crockett had Old Betsy, so AD named his new rifle Beautiful Betsy. He did chores and odd jobs for two years to afford the custom-made felt-lined case she called home.

He raised the ski mask and exposed his pasty face. With feet spread, left foot slightly forward of the right and back straight, he raised the rifle to firing position.

The scent of the polished wood stock against his cheek gave him great comfort, a reminder of better days gone by when his parents were still alive. Butterflies stirred in his belly.

AD closed his left eye. The butterflies increased to a frenzy. His right eye peered through the rifle's scope. Its crosshairs settled on Officer Scott's head. AD waited.

Officer Scott dragged the chair to the edge of the asphalt and tossed it to the brush line.

AD slid his right index finger into the trigger guard and lightly touched the thin piece of metal. When squeezed, he knew it would mark the beginning of his mission.

The patrolman returned to his car, opened the door, paused, and looked around. He took the radio mic. "Dispatch, Unit Six. All clear at the debris on 360. Looked like another citizen lost part of his load. Resuming patrol. Show me ten ninety-eight, back in service." Scott clicked his shoulder radio.

"Roger, Unit Six."

AD squeezed the trigger.

A small black hole appeared slightly above Officer Scott's nose. The back of his head exploded outward, spraying skull and brain matter into the darkness.

AD looked to the heavens. "Thank you, Lord, for helping me make this sacrifice. As stated in Ezekial 18:26, 'When the just turn away from justice to do evil and die, on account of the evil they did, they must die.' "

Back at his dark blue pickup behind the station, AD lowered his head and fulfilled his custom of speaking to his parents each time he entered his mother's old pickup. "Hello, Mother and Father. The end is near. I hope you're proud of me. I'll be with you in heaven soon. Please keep a place warm for me.

Amen." He gently laid Beautiful Betsy in her cushioned, red felt-lined case. He ran a gloved hand over the wood stock and reverently lowered the lid. In ritualistic fashion, AD closed the left-most silver clip, then worked his way to the right until he had closed all the clips.

After a deep breath, AD redialed the Madison Police nonemergency number, which he knew was not recorded or traceable.

"Madison Police, how may I help you?"

"There's a police officer lying on County Road 360 about three miles south of town. I think he's hurt."

"What is your name and number in case we lose contact?"

He punched the red call-disconnect button.

AD pulled out and headed away from Madison. Over the next twenty minutes, he traced his index finger over the tops of the .30-06 shells that dutifully sat on the seat next to him. Each one stood at attention in its green-and-yellow holder. In his mind, they awaited their turn to act on God's behalf, just like he and the disciples.

He recalled Matthew 10:7. "As you go, preach this message: The kingdom of heaven is at hand."

He took a deep breath and let a sigh escape. A single sacrifice wouldn't get him to heaven, but surely eleven more would.

Two hours later, AD climbed makeshift ladder rungs to a hunting tree stand in preparation for his second and final oblation of the night.

****

Federal Judge Thomas Alexander Harrison liked his morning swims. Well before dawn, he'd rise, slip out the sliding door to the pool area, and close the door so he wouldn't wake his wife of thirty-eight years. He'd stretch for a few minutes, dive into the pool, and swim for thirty minutes. The cool water stimulated his senses and his mind. He did his best thinking while mechanically swimming lengths.

During this morning's swim, he pondered a sentencing decision he would hand down at 10:00 a.m. He wanted to make it harsher, but the law limited him on what he could do to the MFer who beat and robbed an elderly couple.

He stroked to the north end of the pool and glanced at the wall clock. 5:05. Time to get ready for work. He drifted to the ladder and climbed its rungs like he'd done thousands of times. At the top of the ladder, he grabbed a towel off a shelf and wrapped it around his shoulders.

****

Perched in the tree stand, AD squeezed the trigger and sent 150 grains of lead-tipped bullet on its way. The slug tore through the pool screen and slammed into the side of the judge's head, ripped through gray matter, and blew out the opposite side of his skull. Its journey ended when it pancaked into the wall separating the pool area and kitchen. The judge toppled backward into the pool, a cloud of pink forming around his head.

Butterflies swirled in AD's stomach. He'd taken another step toward eternity in heaven.

AD didn't worry about shooting close to inhabited homes. The judge's property backed up to a wildlife management area. Locals often heard gunshots in the early morning due to neighbors topping off freezers with venison, gator, and hog when the opportunity presented itself. After all, they lived in Antler County, Florida's deer-hunting capital.

Being frail from terminal cancer, AD climbed down from the tree stand, one ladder rung at a time, holding tightly to his trusted friend, Beautiful Betsy.

Back on the ground, he inhaled deeply several times to replenish the oxygen he'd used during the descent. The scent of pine refreshed him and reminded him of the cabin he inherited from his parents on the Withlacoochee River. God rest their souls.

Matthew 10:7 came to mind. "As you go, preach this message: The kingdom of heaven is at hand." Yes, indeed, with each offering, the kingdom of heaven came nearer for him.

He took a deep breath and let a sigh escape.

Two down, ten to go.

Chapter 2

6:30 a.m.

FBI Special Agent Malcolm Gee arrived in the office in Orlando two hours earlier than normal. He had a date with a woman who might be The One that evening and wanted to make sure he could leave work on time.

Sliding his six-foot, two-hundred-pound frame into the desk chair, he pressed the button to boot his computer.

He and his girlfriend, Valerie DiNardo, had plans to go out for dinner that evening, but they changed when she called the night before and said she'd rather order pizza in her place. He liked her idea. The last time she suggested ordering pizza delivery, she greeted him at the door wearing a black negligee. By the time they got around to calling the pizza shop, it had closed a few minutes earlier. The promise of a twenty-dollar tip convinced the manager to make a pizza and drop it off on his way home.

Malcolm thought he and Valerie might have a future together but wasn't sure if she felt the same. He didn't know how to broach the subject but knew he needed to, sooner rather than later. He didn't want to get in too deep if it wasn't going to work out long-term.

He leaned back and pulled up a picture of her from

his cell phone. He had caught her just as she straightened from feeding a seal at SeaWorld. She had curves in all the right places, though not an abundance. Many might consider her a bit slender, but he thought she was just about perfect. He particularly liked when she wore her hair in a ponytail. He remembered walking behind her at SeaWorld and watching it swing back and forth like a metronome. Her smooth, deep voice had a certain allure to it. If it were possible for a woman to be a crooner, he imagined she would fit the bill. Was she The One? He liked her a lot, but he had concerns, given his line of work and history with Patrice.

The laptop lights blinked, then the FBI warning screen appeared. Time to stop daydreaming and open email, review reports, attend meetings, do general paperwork, and field an abundance of phone calls. None of it important, but he did it to keep his pain-in-the-ass boss, Senior Agent Gregory Volkovsky, off his back.

After twenty minutes of reading emails, his FBI-issue cell phone vibrated and played the sound of a barking dog, the ringtone for his boss.

He took the phone and entered the FBI-mandated twelve-digit passcode. After leaning back, he tapped the speaker icon and said, "Hello, Gregory."

"Someone murdered a police officer and federal judge in Madison, Florida. It's near Tallahassee. The murders look like they're connected. I need you there, now."

Malcolm aimed at the trash can next to his desk and kicked it. Crumpled paper and discarded foam coffee cups skittered across the floor, one of them coming to rest in the hall. He didn't want to cancel his date with Valerie. He didn't want to travel to Florida's panhandle. He didn't want to stay there for the duration. He didn't want anything to do with the project. He had come to hate his job. Gregory needed to assign someone else.

"Why me? I specialize in serial killers. The cop probably arrested the guy, and the judge sentenced him. Easy. I don't think they need me. Send Stevens or Eschman." He didn't think it would work but thought it was worth a try.

"I'm sending you. The Madison police chief, Taylor Dautry, expects you at one o'clock. I want an update every day. People are dying, don't fuck this up."

The call disconnected.

"Yes, sir." Malcolm threw a salute, ending with an extended middle finger.

He didn't like Gregory and believed the feeling was mutual.

A week earlier, he had tested for promotion to Senior Special Agent. If he passed, he'd be eligible for reassignment away from Gregory. But he had learned a long time ago not to get too optimistic about anything involving the FBI. The Bureau had a way of pulling the rug out from under a person without warning.

****

Malcolm's NAV system took him across Central Florida's backroads and joined I-75 North near Wildwood. With luck, he'd have a chance to grab a burger and fries before he met with Chief Taylor Dautry.

North of Ocala, he instructed the car's Bluetooth to call Valerie.

After three rings, she answered. "Don't tell me you changed your mind about pizza tonight."

"Sorry, babe, I got a call from Gregory about a double murder in Madison, which is near Tallahassee. I'm on my way there now."

"What's he expect you to do? Pretend you're Jesus and raise them from the dead? We have a date tonight."

He stifled a chuckle. "The first forty-eight hours after a homicide are the most important. Clues disappear. Witnesses' memories fade. People get scared and wonder if they're next, so they clam up. Besides, this is what Uncle Sam pays me to do. You sell houses, I solve murders. Sorry." He bit his lip, hoping she'd say she understood.

A few seconds of silence gave him concern. "Still there?"

She sounded pouty. "I know, Gee. It's just...I had a special evening planned...now it's ruined."

His heart skipped a beat. "Can I have a rain check?"

"I'll think about it. Stay safe and get your cute butt back to Orlando, pronto."

"I will."

Her sigh prompted him to close his eyes and purse his lips, hoping she'd understand.

"Call me tonight?" she asked.

He smiled. "Sure will."

He disconnected and slammed his palm on the steering wheel. *This shit's gotta stop. I'm not losing her because of this job. I have a right to a life, just like Gregory does. Besides, what's so damn difficult those Madison people can't put two and two together?*

Chapter 3

6:47 a.m.

AD made the sharp left off Coulter Road onto the dirt track, sometimes gravel but mostly sand, which led to the front of his cabin. His parents, in an attempt to be clever, had named the track Hideout Lane. Truth be told, they didn't have a deed, just a handshake agreement with Farmer Coulter, agreeing they could have a cabin on the land. The tax assessor's website classified their cabin a "Farm Outbuilding," thus having no taxable value.

He dodged most of the water-filled ruts and bushes encroaching on the driving track. For the past three months, his trips to the cabin had become a ritual. Normally, he kept the brush cut back so it wouldn't scratch either of his trucks, but when he realized he neared the end of his time on earth, it didn't seem important any longer. No more trimming bushes. No more filling ruts on Hideout Lane. No more pushing leaves and pine needles off the roof with a broom.

Most people had weekends off, but not him. Work kept him moving from seven in the morning until well after sunset on both Saturday and Sunday. His version of a weekend, or time off, started when he left work Monday afternoon. Straight from work, he'd drive north thirty-five minutes, through Pinetta, cut off onto

Coulter Road, and arrive at the cabin he inherited from his parents.

Unfortunately, he had to be in Tallahassee every Wednesday at 2:00 p.m. for an all-hands-on-deck staff meeting, so he rarely had two full days off in a row.

He rounded a bend, bounced through a depression he'd forgotten about, and pulled the dark blue pickup to a stop within twenty feet of the front door. The dashboard clock registered 6:49 a.m. Eleven minutes gave him enough time to get inside, turn on the TV, and open a couple of windows.

With the truck's headlights off, a quarter moon, or more precisely, a waning quarter moon, provided the only light. Until he researched when the moonlight was darkest, he hadn't realized waxing and waning moons existed.

After opening several cabin windows, he settled into the easy chair and raised its leg rest. He watched the window curtains for a moment. They seemed to represent the cabin breathing. Both sets billowed in, then settled straight, billowed in, then settled straight. This made him smile.

Six months ago, the one-time kitchen table became a makeshift desk. During reconnaissance and planning for the mission, he'd accumulated yellow tablet paper galore, books, floor plans, foldout and computer-printed maps, photographs, drawings, and other stuff that ultimately joined the pile on the kitchen table. He even had to erect the card table his parents used for jigsaw puzzles to help hold the overflow. He wound up consuming most of his meals standing at the kitchen counter or seated in the recliner.

A sheet of paper blew off the top of the pile. He'd

pick it up later. The wall clock clicked to 6:59. Time to turn the television on. Without looking, he grasped the TV remote and pressed the power button. Within a few seconds, WTFL-TV, out of Tallahassee, came to life on the thirty-six-inch TV.

He didn't particularly care for Courtney, the Black lady, or Gordon, the older White male, who presented the morning news, but WTFL had the clearest antenna reception, so that's what he watched. He thought the station deliberately sensationalized the news in hopes of attracting viewers. Even the weatherman would make the slightest chance of rain sound like an approaching hurricane.

The station came back from several commercials to Courtney's dour countenance. "More terrible news to report. In addition to the murdered police officer outside of Madison, we've learned someone shot Judge Thomas Alexander Harrison in his Hunter's Reserve home, an exclusive gated community on the outskirts of Madison." She shook her head, then launched into the tabloid mode he found disgusting. "We don't know if the shootings are connected, but it sure appears that way. Ladies and gentlemen, keep your eyes peeled today for any suspicious-looking individuals. We're not sure if these shootings are an act of terrorism, a deranged killer on the loose, or perhaps someone with a vendetta against law enforcement. We have a correspondent on the way to Judge Harrison's home, and we should have a live scene report for you during the noon news. Stay tuned for all the details, and we'll let you know what kind of danger your family may face. In the meantime, especially you Madison residents, remember what the police say—if you see something, if you know something, say something."

The scene switched to Howard, the weatherman, whom AD suspected was gay, with his ridiculous bowtie. "Today, we'll see a high of eighty-two and ten percent chance of showers in the late afternoon. Now to you, Gordon."

AD clicked the remote's power button and set the device on the side table. He looked at the four-foot crucifix on the wall. "Thank you for the favorable outcome of my journeys this morning. Two down and ten to go. I don't have much time, but with your help, I'll complete the mission and be welcomed into heaven. Amen."

AD picked two oxycodone from a white ramekin on the tray table next to his chair and popped them into his mouth like peanuts. Two sips of left-over wine washed them down.

The array of pictures on top of the television caught his attention. Pictures of him and his parents, whom he dearly missed. He smiled, looking at the picture of him and his father, wearing their deer hunting outfits and flanking a twelve-point buck hanging from a tree branch. That was his first deer, all thanks to Beautiful Betsy. His eyes moved to a picture of his mother feeding him in a highchair. A tear formed and ran down his cheek. Soon, very soon, he'd be with them in heaven.

He laid his head back and thought about his life up to this point. His parents had done the best they could to spoil their only child. However, he had sinned and wandered away from the church. Fights in school, stealing cigarettes from the store, leafing through girly magazines, pleasuring himself in the woods, and a host of other sins filled his teen years. It cost his parents a bunch of money when he took his mother's pickup without permission, got drunk, and ran off a bridge into the creek. Sitting in jail for a few days waiting for a bail hearing, he met a chaplain who got him back in touch with Jesus and the Father.

Despite God's teachings over the years, he wasn't absolutely sure he'd be forgiven those childhood sins and allowed to enter heaven. That's when he decided to accomplish two things before he died: one, eliminate twelve sinners from the world, and two, ignite a movement where others would continue his crusade to eliminate sinners. These actions would make the world understand sin doesn't pay. They would also help him earn God's favor and secure a place in heaven. He smiled at the thought of passing through the pearly gates.

He set his cell phone's alarm to wake him at 11:55 a.m. He wanted to watch the noon news to see what the authorities had to say about the clues he'd left.

Chapter 4

12:20 p.m.

Malcolm strode down Madison Avenue past businesses with brick facades, a drug store, a sign shop, and a women's clothing store. He held his breath and unconsciously leaned away from the door as he passed the florist. The scent of jasmine brought memories he wished he could forget.

Once clear of the florist shop, he spotted the gray façade of the county courthouse still several blocks ahead. As expected, City Hall sat across the street.

Google had told him Madison Police Department sat next to the courthouse.

The aroma of hamburgers and grilled onions caught his attention. It seemed to come from Gram's Kitchen, whose front window advertised the "Freshest coffee in town," "57 varieties of burgers," and "Waffles like Gram's." A square sign hung in the front door, green letters on a white background, OPEN.

He wasn't scheduled to meet Madison Police Chief Taylor Dautry for another forty minutes. He had enough time to grab a burger and fries. He jogged across the street and opened Gram's door to the sound of a tinkling bell.

A woman clad in a red Gram's Kitchen T-shirt and blue jeans—Holly, from her black-lettered nametag—

held a pot of coffee in her left hand and greeted him. "There's a couple of tables open in the back. Seat yourself. I'll be with you in a minute." She continued to a table of four and refilled coffee cups.

Malcolm automatically looked toward the back of the room and spotted an open table. He wove through a maze of tables and heard pieces of conversation about the murders: "She's pregnant and a widow at twenty-four," "No one's safe in their own backyard," and "Some idiot is getting even, is what I think."

He sat with his back against the wall so he could watch the room's occupants, an occupational habit. Based on their general appearance, he pegged them to be office workers, shop owners, retirees, construction workers, and a couple of police officers.

Holly arrived with a smile, menu, coffee cup, and steaming glass pot full of black coffee. She handed him the menu. "Our specials are on the back. Coffee?" Her accent indicated a Southern Georgia upbringing.

"Yes, please. Black."

While she poured, he glanced at the lunch specials on the back of the menu.

"Do you need another minute?" she asked, nodding to a patron who raised his coffee cup.

"I'll have number three, medium-well, no pickles, fries."

She smiled. "I'll have it for you in a jiffy."

Malcolm perched his lips on the cup's rim and decided to let it cool before taking a sip.

He returned to surveilling the room. A man seated by himself four tables away, clad in a short-sleeved white shirt with a forest-green tie, rose and approached. He stopped several feet short and clasped his hands in front of an ample belly. "You must be Malcolm Gee."

Malcolm estimated him to be six three and 320 pounds. The man had bloodshot eyes, creases across his forehead, and crow's feet at the corners of his eyes. A generous chin spilled over his collar and jiggled when he spoke. The gray mustache and hair didn't appear to be premature.

Malcolm thought about the Beretta tucked in the small of his back but opted to wait. "Why would you ask?"

"I know everybody here except you. It ain't huntin' season, so there ain't no tourists in town. You don't look like none of the TV people. You look like FBI." The man spoke with confidence and a northern Florida twang.

Malcolm nodded. "And who might you be?"

"I'm the chief of police here in Madison. Name's Taylor Dautry, but everybody calls me Chief." No offer of a handshake.

"Why aren't you wearing a uniform?"

"Everyone in Madison knows who I am. Don't need a uniform or gun. My turn to ask a question. Why are you here?"

The initial thought was to be flippant and say something about his boss ordering him to investigate the murders, but less than an hour earlier, Roger had called and directed Malcolm to work with, strong emphasis on *with*, Chief Dautry and local law enforcement. The case already had high visibility, and Roger didn't want any calls from state bureaucrats complaining about Malcolm running over the local yokels, as Roger referred to them. Malcolm had received quite a tongue-lashing after his last project in

Akron, Ohio, where the locals had become liabilities because of constant confidential information leaks and in-fighting. He then had to bulldoze over, or go around, them for things such as roadblocks, putting cameras at major intersections, inclusion of the FBI evidence response team at crime scenes, and expedited forensics examinations. Progress wasn't made until Malcolm stopped playing politics, stopped sharing information, and stopped pandering to the media. He started doing what he thought was right, and they cornered the murderer three days later. Unfortunately, he chose death-by-cop as opposed to arrest. It didn't seem to matter to Roger that it ended quickly after "going rogue," as Roger called it. Instead, his boss seemed only to remember the phone calls from the Ohio governor, one of their senators, two House of Representatives members, the head of the Ohio State Patrol, the Akron chief of police, and the Akron mayor.

Maybe this project would be better; at least, he hoped so. He smiled and attempted to sound conversational. "Well, Chief, that's a very good question. My understanding is Judge Harrison is a federal judge. Uncle Sam doesn't like people hurting his employees, particularly those involved with the judicial system. The US has a special law, Title 18, Section 115, covering federal judges that states something to the effect—*The murder of a federal employee while in performance of their duties or in retaliation for acts performed in the course of their duties is a federal crime.* Thus, the Federal Bureau of Investigation is assigned to work the investigation. If you like, I can look up the exact verbiage, but that's it in a nutshell." He nodded once and smiled.

Chief Dautry had glazed over when Malcolm mentioned Title 18, Section 115. Malcolm didn't expect any questions, so he continued. "Now, if you're asking why me specifically is here, I suspect it's because I specialize in multiple murders, or serial killers. I'm just off the Akron, Ohio, suburb strangler investigation. Did you follow it or hear of it? I functioned as special agent in charge."

The big man pursed his lips and seemed to be thinking. After a few beats, he asked, "Mind if I sit?"

No answer about being familiar with the Akron investigation. Malcolm would proceed as if the Madison chief of police didn't follow out-of-town news.

Chief didn't wait for Malcolm's answer about sitting. He pulled a chair out, turned it around, and sat with his chest against the chair's back. "I ain't much on words. Always believed actions is what told you about a man, his character, his honesty, the way he lived. But some sum-a-bitch killed one of my officers. A young man married a year ago, pregnant wife, on the force a couple of years. I watched him grow up, coached his Little League team, went to his wedding, liked him. The same sum-a-bitch that shot Ronnie shot Judge Harrison. The judge supported law enforcement, a true friend. I didn't ask for the FBI to get involved, but since you here, I'll play along. You FBI people got ways of finding things and people that I don't. Me and everyone on the force, hell, everyone in this county, will help you all we can." He leaned forward and the chair creaked. "But this is my city, and I want that sum-a-bitch found. I want to be the one what cuffs him. You FBI people do your thing, but I get him when he's found. Do you understand me?"

If possible, Chief's eyes would have bored a hole right through Malcolm's skull. He seemed to snort when he stopped speaking.

Malcolm leaned back and rubbed his forehead. "What makes you think they're connected?"

"The sum-a-bitch left the same calling card at both scenes."

Malcolm straightened. Roger hadn't said anything about evidence. "What calling card?"

Chief glanced over both shoulders before answering. "Only me and the two detectives what found them know. They found a brass .30-06 shell casing at each scene, right where the sum-a-bitch stood when he shot those men."

"Could be coincidence. This being Antler County, Florida's deer capital, I imagine there's a lot of hunters around here."

"Wasn't hunters."

Malcolm sensed Chief knew more than he shared. "Why do you call them"—Malcolm used air quotes—"a 'calling card'?"

"My men found both of them sitting open end up, right where the sum-a-bitch stood when he killed them men."

Malcolm looked toward the front of the restaurant, his mind racing. "Sitting upright?"

"Upright." One nod.

"Not a coincidence?"

"Fired thousands of rounds through my own .30-06, never had a single casing land open end up. I ain't real smart, but don't think the odds are too good one, especially two, will stand that way unless put that way on purpose."

"Fingerprints? Even partials?"

Chief rubbed his jaw. "If we had prints, we wouldn't need you." He stood, looked down his nose at Malcolm. "See you at one."

The FBI agent watched Chief Dautry walk out the door and reminded himself he needed to remain unemotional, pragmatic, and detached to be able to follow the evidence and solve the murders. He also had to juggle media availability and not piss off any of the people who thought they were more important than stopping a murderer in the quickest time possible. His promotion to senior special agent in charge might depend on his performance here, so he needed to keep the locals, like Chief Dautry, from rocking Roger's boat.

****

AD watched the full thirty-minute WTFL news broadcast from the edge of his recliner. He stabbed the remote's power button. The thirty-second video of Madison Police Chief Taylor Dautry reading a prepared statement irritated him. Big deal, they had an investigation going into the killing of Officer Scott and Judge Harrison, they couldn't release any information now, and an FBI hotshot would be at the six o'clock briefing. So what?

AD rose and walked to the front window.

"No one said anything about the clues I left. They didn't say anything about witnesses, suspects, or leads, either. Is no news good news?"

He walked out the cabin's rear door onto the covered porch or veranda, as his mother called it, and settled into an Adirondack chair. The veranda ran along the entire rear of the cabin but only extended out six feet. AD loved the peace and quiet at the cabin. It gave him the opportunity to think, to analyze, to reflect.

This very veranda was where the initial idea of making sacrifices to gain favor with God first occurred to him. AD gazed at the river with its slow, methodical movement. Near the bank, there used to be a small mound. That's where he and his father had buried Rags, the family dog. Rags was short for Raguel, the archangel of justice and vengeance. It was that little dog and his namesake, Raguel, who sparked the idea of sacrificing sinners. After all, Raguel's main function in God's army of angels was to take vengeance on those who transgressed God's laws. The Book of Enoch laid it out quite clearly. Sitting on the veranda, watching the river, and remembering Rags was the exact point in time he'd decided to take vengeance against those who sinned against God.

He'd done extensive research over the previous three months, gathering data to determine those people whose sins would shock the world when their transgressions against God became known. Making a list of sinners turned out to be easy. Narrowing it to the twelve most worthy sinners presented challenges.

He hadn't arrived at twelve by random selection. Like everything he did, he had a reason behind it. The number twelve appeared prominently in both the New and Old Testaments. Jesus had twelve disciples. David had twelve tribes, the result of Jacob's twelve sons. Jesus' first recorded words were at age twelve. They had twelve baskets of leftovers from the fishes-and-loaves miracle. And the list went on. So, twelve became his chosen number of sacrifices.

Once he selected the twelve that best supported his message, he researched their habits. Four or five times a week, he'd gather information on their homes, their workplaces, what they did for entertainment, favorite restaurants, where they exercised, everything. He even spoke with some of them in the grocery store, at a restaurant, after church on Sunday, or walking down the street.

He used maps, traffic patterns, the likelihood of encountering others, and most importantly, ensuring that if he did encounter them, they wouldn't be surprised to see him. He then selected the location where each sacrifice would take place.

One of the more complex tasks required the sequencing and timing of who would be sacrificed on which nights and at what time. Driving distance, driving time, his beginning location, and his desired destination once complete were all key components in the development of the plan.

AD even consulted lunar cycles. Not because of superstition but because he wanted to minimize the possibility of moonlight giving him away. He knew a handful of his sacrifices would take place in somewhat remote spots, so light from the moon didn't concern him. However, he planned the in-town sacrifices for when the moon would be dark.

During his stakeouts, he had time to think and rethink. That's when he realized the importance of hiding in plain sight. He didn't want to be like OJ, where the authorities had found designer shoeprints and gloves that could be associated with OJ. That's when he knew he had to purchase the most generic shoes he could find, identical generic tires for each truck, and ammunition purchased in small quantities at high-volume retailers. He had to be Mr. Generic.

He even created an improvised shooting range at the cabin. The few residents in earshot wouldn't question someone shooting a varmint, or deer in a field, or any number of other reasons. After all, his cabin sat in the northernmost reaches of Antler County, Florida's deer capital. Even though he'd become pretty accurate over the years, he needed to hone his skills. He couldn't afford to miss; every shot had to find its mark and do its job.

Hours and hours of preparation went into devising the plan. Hiding in plain sight, efficiency, and secrecy became his keys to success.

He rose and walked down to the river's edge. He stared at the muddy water drifting by with hands clasped in front of his belt. He reviewed the previous night's sacrifices and smiled. He'd flawlessly executed each task. Surely, God had held His hand over him.

He'd removed two names from the list. Ten remained. He would listen to the six o'clock news to watch the press briefing. Every piece of information he could obtain would make his job easier. He looked forward to hearing the FBI agent.

In the meantime, he'd make a trial run to the next two sacrifice locations.

He walked around to the front of the cabin, past the dark-blue Ford pickup he'd inherited from his mother, and opened the door of his silver Chevy pickup.

He'd reserved the Ford for when he made sacrifices. It would be less likely to be seen parked somewhere on moonless nights. The silver Chevy served the purpose quite well for scouting and dry runs.

Even if surveillance cameras caught him driving by during the day, no one would think twice about seeing him.

After kicking sand off his shoes, he climbed in and headed to the cemetery.

Chapter 5

1:07 p.m.

Malcolm followed Chief Dautry into the police station's Seminole Conference Room. The circular table surrounded by six chairs practically filled the small room. A black wrought-iron stand stood in a corner with a multi-button phone covering the entire top. Nothing hung on the windowless walls, not even a whiteboard, wanted poster, or cheap artwork. A white foam food container had been jammed into the trash can, and the room had the distinct aroma of fish.

Chief took the chair furthest from the door. Malcolm placed a black binder in front of the chair closest to the door and eased into the seat, careful not to hit the wall. They stared at one another several seconds until Malcolm mentally shrugged and spoke. "The first topic I'd like to discuss is a war room. This is a central location that will be our command center. Everything involving the investigation will route through the war room. It'll be staffed twenty-four-seven. The 800 number will come to the war room. We will—"

"I have over thirty-five years of law enforcement, and I sure as shit wasn't born yesterday, so you don't need to lecture me about what a war room is."

Malcolm took a deep breath and leaned back. Things weren't starting off very well, but he needed to stay calm. He had one objective in Madison—to catch the murderer. The sooner he and Valerie had pizza in her townhouse, the better. He smiled. "Good, I'm glad you're familiar with them. Where is your war room?"

"You're sitting in it."

Malcolm frowned. The Seminole Conference Room certainly didn't have space or capability to be the kind of war room this investigation might require if it dragged into multiple weeks. "I think we're going to need a much larger area outfitted with cubicles, computers, communications equipment, office equipment, printers, projection units, all sorts of electronics, space for twenty or thirty resources to work, a couple of rooms for closed-door meetings, twenty or more smartboards, and the such."

Chief snorted. "In case you hadn't noticed, this is Madison, Florida, not New York City or Orlando. The sign you passed driving in here says we have 28,152 residents in Antler County. We don't have the kind of crime that needs a war room. Last time we had anything big, three high school kids went on a B&E spree. You probably have some fancy name for it, but we call it breaking and entering. Took two weeks, but we solved it, right from this room here."

Malcolm wouldn't be deterred. He hoped to solve the murders quickly, but if they needed a full-fledged war room, the type he'd seen in Akron, Philadelphia, and Atlanta, he wanted to be prepared. "Is this the largest room you have access to?"

"Yep."

"What about City Hall? Anything larger over there?"

"How much space you want?"

"It would be nice to get five thousand square feet with heavy-duty electric, multiple high-speed internet feeds, and the ability to set a satellite dish on the roof."

Chief rested intertwined fingers on his rotund midsection. "Nope, nothing over there."

Malcolm felt his face redden. He thought about his walk from Gram's Kitchen. "There's a vacant building across the street with a For Sale sign. Do you know who owns it?"

"Johnny Robertson moved his dry goods store a couple blocks away."

"Can you check to see if we can use it?"

Chief cocked his head for several beats, licked his lips, then bellowed, "Martha!"

A few seconds later, Malcolm sensed motion behind him where a woman stood, mid-thirties, wavy blonde hair, full face, and pointy nose. "Yes, sir."

"Call Johnny. Tell him we're going to use his old store to catch Ronnie and the judge's killer. We'll need a bunch of keys."

She responded, "Yes, sir," and disappeared.

Puzzled, Malcolm asked, "Don't you have to check with him first?"

Chief scowled. "I run this city. The mayor thinks she does, but I do. People around here do what I tell them. Nothing happens in Madison without me knowing about it."

Malcolm rubbed his jaw. "You might want to tell that lady we only need one key. We'll install a card reader once we have access. Besides, who is she, and what's her role?"

"Martha. My secretary. Her husband's a sergeant here, so don't try nothin' funny with her." Chief pointed a beefy index finger at Malcolm. "She's off limits, you hear me?"

Malcolm raised his hands surrender fashion. "No problem from me. I like to know the players and what they do. How confident are you Johnny will let us use his building?"

"Like Judge Harrison, he's a friend of law enforcement."

"I guess that means he'll let us use the space."

"If I say so, he will. How you going to fill it? We don't have none of the stuff you talked about. Some of that shit I don't even know what it is."

"No problem, the FBI has the resources. Once we get access to the space, my facilities people will have it usable in a day, two at the most."

"You'll have a key in twenty minutes, so you better get your hot-shot facilities people hopping. There's a murderer out there that needs caught."

"The equipment will be on trucks in a couple of hours. All they'll need is an address to deliver it to."

Chief shrugged. "If you say so."

Malcolm flipped to a new sheet of paper in his binder. "Now that that's settled, let's talk about what you and your folks have done so far."

Chief scratched his chin. "Go ahead."

"Can you bring me up to date with investigative actions Madison PD has taken so far? Searching for security video, canvassing the neighborhoods the murders occurred in, requesting subpoenas or warrants for cell phone records, researching common criminals between the officer and judge, actions of that kind?"

"It's best you talk with the boys doing the detective work. They'll be here right quick." Chief rose and left the room, scratching his head. Thirty minutes later Malcolm drummed his fingers on the three pages of notes, questions, and tasks he'd completed since last seeing the big man.

Malcolm left the conference room and wandered deeper into the bowels of the building. He passed a couple of very small offices with LEBEAU and PALMER on respective doors, then an even smaller room with a sink and coffee maker. Forced to go left or right, he chose right, remembering what a college roommate always said, "You can't go wrong when you go right."

The first open door revealed Chief Dautry at a dark mahogany desk that easily measured four feet by eight feet. Chief looked up with furrowed brow and remained silent.

Malcolm leaned against the door jam. "Why didn't you come back?"

Chief scratched his chin. "Nothing more to talk about until two o'clock."

"There's a great deal for us to talk about."

"I'll see you at two."

"Why wait until then? We're losing time."

"That's when I arranged for you to talk with the responding officers and lead detectives."

"It would have been nice if you told me that before."

"I told you, I been in law enforcement a long time. I know how things work. Now, I need to finish reviewing this. I'll be there at two."

Malcolm wagged his head. "This will get solved quicker if we work together."

"You're here 'cause someone murdered a federal

judge. I didn't ask for you, but since you're here, I'll play ball because I want to find the sorry sum-a-bitch that murdered two fine men. Don't push me, and don't treat me like I'm stupid. Do you understand?" He stared at Malcolm over half glasses perched on his nose.

"No problem. Can we move forward?"

Chief looked Malcolm in the eye, mouth corners turned slightly upward. He slowly nodded. "At two." Chief took a sip from a tall white mug with blue lettering proclaiming Madison High School State Champs 2009. He peered down at his report without saying anything further.

****

The patrolman who responded to the call about a dead policeman lying on the road had a face resembling a turkey—small, beady, close-set eyes, narrow and long face, and a great deal of loose skin along the neck. His body looked like he'd undertaken a bread-and-water diet but forgot the bread. The City of Madison shirt looked at least two sizes too big for him. Malcolm had seen wire hangers fill out a shirt better than this man. The tape on the bridge of his eyewear didn't appear to be a fix for broken spectacles but seemed intended to keep the glasses snug to his nose.

Patrolman Avery didn't look at anyone when he spoke. He had that faraway look of a person still trying to come to grips with what he saw. His voice trembled when he spoke. "When the call came across the radio, I didn't believe it, but when I couldn't get Ronnie on his cell, I got worried. It took about ten minutes to get on scene. When I rolled up, Ronnie's car sat in the southbound lane, light bar on, engine running. He lay in a heap near the rear tire. I used the spotlight and checked the surrounding area. I didn't see anything, so I got out but stayed behind my car door."

He stopped and took a deep breath and wiped his mouth with the back of his hand. The words tumbled out like water from a spigot. "It was spooky. When I radioed in what I saw, I heard my own voice coming from Ronnie's open door. I took a step toward him but saw the back of his head wasn't there." He shook his head, looked confused, and raised his hands palms up. "Just not there anymore." Avery wiped his mouth again. "I ran to the side of the road and puked. Everything else is a blur."

Malcolm wrote three pages of notes during the patrolman's report. He placed stars next to several items, check marks next to a couple, and about a dozen question marks beside others. He thanked Officer Avery and allowed him to leave.

The detective responsible for Officer Scott's investigation entered next. He looked chiseled out of black granite. The garnet T-shirt, with a picture of Chief Osceola, the FSU mascot, on the left breast, looked like someone had painted it on. Muscle cords stood out on his forearms and the backs of his hands. He had developed his lats so well that his relaxed arms remained at least six inches away from his hips. Police ID on a lanyard around his neck, thick black belt with a case for handcuffs, extra magazines, and holstered sidearm on his right hip completed the ensemble.

Chief introduced Detective Jack Palmer and pointed out this man had been an All-American running back for FSU legend Bobby Bowden. One of the absolute best who didn't get to the NFL. He had suffered a knee injury against the lowly Florida Gators.

Who, in Chief's opinion, deliberately hurt him to get him out of the game, but the Gainesville sum-a-bitches still got their asses whooped.

Jack spoke slowly but concisely and shared information. His Southern drawl made *get* sound like *git*, and *tire* became *taar*. He believed the shooter had scouted the area, practiced stopping patrol cars over the previous couple of weeks, hid beside the abandoned gas station until Patrolman Scott returned to his vehicle, then fired a single shot that killed the man.

Malcolm asked, "Why do you think the shooter had practiced stopping patrol cars?"

"It smelled like a setup to me. So, I did some quick research. First, according to the dispatcher, the voice that called in the chair on County Road 360 sounded like the same voice that called in a police officer laying on the road. Both declined to give their names. Then, I reviewed call logs over the past month and sure enough, Scott had responded twice in the past two weeks to remove items from the road. That morning became the third such call, first at that location." Jack Palmer rubbed his left shoulder with a gnarled hand.

"Why do you think the shooter only fired one shot?"

"Only found one shell casing, sitting open end up, right where I believe the shooter stood."

"Any prints?"

"Smeared, like it had been wiped. Nothing usable."

"The slug?"

"It disappeared into two hundred acres of woods. I doubt we'll ever find it, but a patrolman is walking around looking at trees."

"Prints on the chair?"

"It had been wiped clean. Smelled from bleach. Only prints were from Scott."

"Footprints? Tire tracks?"

"Lots of both. That old station is a hangout for high school kids drinking beer and smoking dope. Probably too many to be helpful by themselves. We may find a match at the judge's scene to tie both murders together. They're making casts of a couple of tire tracks in the back of the station where I believe the shooter parked. Maybe they'll give us something. Haven't had a chance yet to see if they match anything at the judge's house."

The detective remained silent while Malcolm wrote, flipped back and forth in his notes, and summarized what he'd been told.

The detective nodded with each point.

Malcolm asked, "Anything I missed, or misstated?"

"The capital *H* etched on the casing."

Malcolm straightened. "A capital H on the casing?"

"Yes, sir. Looks like he used a tiny screwdriver or awl, to mark the brass with a capital H."

Malcolm looked at Chief, expecting surprise. Instead, the police chief looked passive, almost bored. Either the man had a great poker face, or he knew about the H.

What could a capital H represent? An initial? Using his fingers to count, Malcolm determined H was the eighth letter of the alphabet. Perhaps the number eight would prove significant. Malcolm added two more items with question marks to the notepad. He also added a question about whether Chief knew about the H and, if so, why he hadn't said anything earlier.

"You think the shooter deliberately put the H there? Didn't come from the ejection mechanism, or when it fell on the ground?"

"I'm the department's weapon instructor and range master. I bet I've seen over a hundred thousand shell casings and never seen anything like that. My grandfather served in an artillery unit in Vietnam. He once told me they put the initials of KIAs on shells before they'd fire them at hostiles. My guess is the bad guy did the same thing."

"Interesting point." Malcolm added it to his notes, then asked, "What investigative actions have you undertaken?"

Palmer's forehead furrowed. "Investigative actions? Like what?"

"Things such as canvassing for security video from neighbors, collecting voice recordings of calls that resulted in Scott being dispatched, checking his—"

Palmer waived his hand. "First, the call that came in about the debris came in on our nonemergency number. We don't record nonemergency calls."

Malcolm's head jerked up. "You don't record them? Really?"

Palmer crossed his arms across his chest. "That's correct. Lets folks call about their neighbor's barking dogs, or loud music, kids running around, stuff like that without being retaliated against. If the accused wants to know who called about them…" He shrugged. "We have plausible deniability. And I was about to say I already told you what we done regarding fingerprints on the chair, footprints, tire marks, and such. The killer picked a spot more than a mile away from any buildings along that road, so there isn't any security footage."

Palmer's lips became a thin line.

"I get it, he stopped in the middle of nowhere, but someone pulled the trigger. How did they get there? There must be buildings, either residential or commercial along that road, and in today's world, I would bet at least half of them have some sort of security cameras that may have caught the vehicle coming or going. Get all of that footage."

Palmer wagged his head. "This is Madison, Florida, a small town. The security most people depend on requires ammunition. They don't have much use for security cameras. With that said, there may be footage from along that stretch, and I'll personally check every building along that road. Let me ask, how do you think that's going to be watched and analyzed?"

"I'll have video forensics specialists available tomorrow to review the data and build a database."

A slight smile creased Jack's face. "Consider it done."

"I'd like to convene a meeting tomorrow morning at eight for no more than one hour with the investigation's major stakeholders. We'll meet at my hotel and review progress, share information, sync activities, strategize, et cetera. Are you available?"

"No problem."

Malcolm thanked the detective for his time and asked to be kept in the information loop.

After Palmer left the conference room, Malcolm took several minutes to flip through his notes, added a couple of question marks, and drew multiple stars and Xs as reminders of things to be added to the war room storyboards once they became available.

He also jotted a couple of ideas for the upcoming

press conference. He placed a *PC* beside them. He had to say something but wasn't sure exactly what yet. The media hadn't endeared themselves to Malcolm over the years. He saw firsthand how they no longer dealt in facts. Facts had become unfashionable. They preferred to speculate and, worse, offer that speculation as fact, all for their own self-serving desires. Working task forces in Seattle, New Orleans, and Akron demonstrated in a painful way what the press could do. He needed to provide facts they couldn't dispute and hopefully not twist.

After underlining several points he wanted to mention at the press conference, Malcolm looked at Chief and asked, "Did you know about the H on the shell casing?"

"Yep."

"Why didn't you say something about it at Gram's?"

"No need. I know Jack would cover it. He's a good man, knows his job, his place in this department and in Madison."

Something about the way Chief said "knows…his place" bothered Malcolm. Something to be aware of going forward. "Is there an H on the shell casing from the judge's murder?"

"You'll find out when you talk with the next set of boys."

After a quick bathroom break and coffee refill, the patrolman who responded to the judge's shooting entered the conference room. Tall, skinny, forehead full of acne, the young man sat and spoke before introductions could be made. "I graduated from Madison CC two months ago with my associate degree in criminology. I ain't never seen a dead person before except at McCully's funeral home, so I don't know if'n I'm remembering right or not. It was horrible. This doesn't happen in Madison. This is not some big city. I never expected this kind of thing. My folks told me to do something else, but I didn't listen to them. Now look." He kept wringing his hands.

Chief interrupted the rambling. "Clarence. Straighten up, son. You're not helping this FBI man none. He don't have time for your whiny crybaby stuff. Be a man and answer his questions best you can."

Chief turned to Malcolm. "This here is Clarence Higgins. Like he said, he's pretty new to police work. Clarence, this is FBI Special Agent in Charge Malcolm Gee. He's come all the way from Orlando to help us. He's seen this sorta thing before, so nothin' you say is gonna surprise or upset him. Okay?"

The young man nodded and licked his lips. "Okay, sir, I'm ready."

Malcolm asked for a brief synopsis of what had happened.

The patrolman stared wide-eyed. "The judge's wife met me at the door, all hysterical, yelling and screaming. I tried to calm her, but she kept shouting and crying. When she told me Judge was dead and floating in the pool, I wanted to wait for backup or the sergeant to come, but she kept pulling at my arm. Thank God the EMT boys showed up just then. I figured they'd know what to do, so I just followed them. When we went to the pool, it was horrible, just horrible. The water was red, and Judge didn't have part of his head. I wanted to puke but helped fish the judge out of the pool. That's all I know." He wiped sweat off his brow with a finger and wiped it on his uniform pants.

Malcolm went through the same list of questions he'd asked the patrolman who found Officer Scott. The rookie patrolman's eyes darted from Malcolm to Chief and back to Malcolm before answering anything. Most of his answers were "I don't know. It was horrible."

Chief thanked Clarence for coming back in and instructed him to tell Audrey he would approve the overtime and to clock out right away. The patrolman scurried out the door muttering about this being horrible.

Malcolm stood and stretched. "That man is shaken. Do you have a mental health person for him to see?"

Chief frowned. "Like he said, this ain't some big city. I gave him the next two days off. He'll have to get over it if he wants to keep his job."

Malcolm wanted to respond but decided against it. "I'm ready for the detective working the judge's murder."

An overweight man carrying a leather-bound portfolio filled the conference room doorway. He wore khaki slacks, and a light-blue polo shirt with the Madison City logo embroidered on the left chest.

Chief waved him in. "This here is the other detective, Robert LeBeau. In addition to doing investigations, he oversees the evidence locker and serves as our senior instructor." The man had curly blond hair the consistency of steel wool, which was evidently impossible to comb or brush. "Detective LeBeau also played for the great Bobby Bowden. One of the best offensive linemen to ever wear a uniform there."

Seeing the man's width, Malcolm could easily

imagine him protecting a quarterback on Saturday afternoons. It appeared the man had stopped exercising at the end of his playing days but kept the same eating habits. His polo fit so tight the seams looked ready to burst. His cheeks had the blushed appearance so many obese men had.

After shaking hands and exchanging pleasantries, Robert took a seat, which creaked when he sat. Malcolm's first question was the same as he asked Detective Palmer. "Please bring me up to speed on your activities."

Several times during his recitation LeBeau verbally patted himself on the back due to his cleverness in discovering information. In Malcolm's opinion, LeBeau had only noted the obvious, but he didn't want to burst the man's ego balloon.

LeBeau seemed delighted with himself for finding the shooter's tree stand. He went into great detail about sightlines, angles, observation, and thinking like an assassin, which is exactly what the shooter was, a "Goddamned, murdering assassin." He then went on a rant about how low a man could go to use a deer stand the judge himself had built, to assassinate a much-beloved man, a supporter of law enforcement, a benefactor of high school sports, and a terrific daddy. According to LeBeau, "The world has begun to fall into the outhouse faster than it could be pumped out."

Malcolm had no idea what this last statement meant but nodded anyway. He raised his hand. "Sorry to interrupt. Can you tell me if you found anything in or on the tree stand?"

LeBeau puffed out his chest again. "I climbed the ladder and used my high-intensity MagLite XL50 flashlight to scour the tree stand's walls. I saw lots of writing on the walls. Just normal tree stand stuff like 'Kilroy was here' and a drawing of the guy with the big nose. My cell phone pictures are in my report. Then, as I was backing down the ladder, I saw something shiny. I knew it wasn't a diamond or anything, so I shined my light on it. That's when I discovered a brass shell casing sitting in the middle of the floor. It sat on end. Pretty peculiar if you ask me. There wasn't anything else there, but I thought I detected the smell of recent gunfire. I made sure to put that in my report." He reached into his portfolio and pulled out a stack of paper that looked to be at least forty pages. "By the way, here's two copies, one for your file and one to carry for quick reference." He slid both copies across the table to Malcolm. The chair creaked when he leaned forward.

Chief Dautry remained stoic, not looking at either man.

The cover page had Malcolm's name printed on it, and LeBeau had signed it in blue ink.

Malcolm pulled the documents toward himself. "I'll review this in detail a little later. Thanks." He slid both copies under his notepad. "Back to the tree stand, did you say you saw a lot of writing on the walls?"

"Yes, sir. Probably bored hunters or kids playing around. I took pictures that are in my report."

The writing on the walls of the tree stand gave Malcolm an idea for the press conference. He placed a PC next to his note. One of his favorite ploys was to plant a red herring, and LeBeau gave him a whopper to use. "Okay, detective, did you check the casing for fingerprints?"

"Clean as a brand-new bowling ball. But the shooter marked his initials on the casing." LeBeau donned a smug smile.

"Marked his initials?"

"He wrote HH on it. Like his name is Hubert Humphrey, or maybe Howard Hillmer. One of them was vice president a long time ago, the other is a guy I played ball with, but I don't think the assassin was either of them; they're both dead, I think."

Malcolm glanced at Chief, who stared at his coffee cup.

Now they had twin Hs. Eighty-eight. He remembered from a case early in his career where men with shaved heads equated HH with eighty-eight. HH also represented "Heil Hitler." He made a note to consider the murders as hate crimes. Scott, being Black, qualified. But Judge being an older White male didn't fit any of the known hate group profiles.

LeBeau continued. "Yep, the way I look at it is all you need to do is run a Google search for anyone with the initials of HH and you'll have your list of suspects. Easy as making pie."

Malcolm made a note—*LeBeau...detective?* "Detective, has the slug that killed the judge been found yet?"

LeBeau puffed out his chest. "Absolutely, I found it"—he poked himself in the chest—"stuck in a concrete block wall next to the pool. I didn't want to destroy evidence, so I requisitioned the department's forensics man to bring some tools and get it out. It's already on its way to Tallahassee for testing. I work efficient. No wasted time or motion." He smiled. "Oh, and by the way, I included a copy of the forensics' request and tracking number in my report. I have it memorized, so I can give it to you if you want to note it somewhere. I got a close eye on it. Paper seems to grow legs and wander off sometimes, if you know what I mean." He grinned like he had revealed the answer to an extremely difficult question.

"Thanks for the thoroughness. Did you see any footprints or tire tracks that might be of value in determining the shooter's identity?"

"I did." Detective LeBeau leaned back in his chair, looking very proud of himself.

Malcolm waited for LeBeau to continue, then said, "And?"

"I saw lots of tire tracks and shoe tracks. I told the forensics guy to get pictures. They're here in my report. There was a lot of footprints, even mine. Found truck tires where I think the shooter parked. Riley's still trying to figure out what kind of shoes and tires. There's a bunch of both, so it'll probably take time."

"Who's Riley?"

"He's my cousin on my mother's side. I think it's twice removed because his parents got divorced because his daddy couldn't keep his zipper up."

"Besides being your cousin, why's he looking at forensics evidence?"

" 'Cause he's our forensics guy. Teaches chemistry at the college part-time, knows a lot of chemical stuff."

Malcolm made a note to have his own team contact Riley and help however they could, maybe just take it over. He went through his notes, asked a couple of clarifying questions, and summarized what the detective had reported. Satisfied, he said, "I have confidence you'll notify me should anything of significance be found. I'm out of questions. Is there anything else you can think of that would be important for me to know?"

LeBeau straightened. "You're FBI, so you probably already figured this out, but I'll mention it anyway. After you Google all the HH people, compare them against perps who Ronnie arrested, or the judge put away. That'll be your man. Easy." The detective wiped his hands together as if he'd explained $E=MC^2$ in record time. "It'll be like the stink from finding yesterday's catfish still sitting on the dock on a sunny day. You won't be able to miss it."

Malcolm set his pen on the notebook and wondered for a few seconds how this man became a detective.

Remembering his conversation with Palmer earlier in the afternoon, who appeared to be sharp, he carefully phrased his next question. "Other than what you've mentioned, what other investigative actions have you undertaken? I'm interested in things such as canvassing for security video from neighbors, asking to see the judge's work and personal computers, submitting a request for phone records, and the such."

LeBeau leaned back, his eyebrows rose. "Wow, you're good at this stuff. I've never done that kind of stuff before. Can you show me how to do it?"

Malcolm felt his face become warm. "Sure, I'll have an FBI resource work with you tomorrow morning. Speaking of tomorrow morning, I'd like to have a meeting with all of the major stakeholders at eight. We'll meet at my hotel and review progress, share information, sync activities, strategize, et cetera. Are you available?"

"Absolutely, this is some exciting stuff. The whole

FSU offensive line couldn't keep me away."

"Thanks for the information, detective. I'll see you tomorrow morning. Stay safe out there."

The detective stood. "I already done most of the heavy lifting, but if you want to brainstorm this some more, I'll make myself available." He pointed at Chief. "Dad, er, I mean Chief, knows how to reach me. I'm at your disposal." His eyes seemed to twinkle when he mentioned "Dad."

Malcolm added *Dad?* to the list of questions on his pad.

LeBeau continued, "You know, it could be a win-win situation if we worked real close. If I were deeply involved in what's going on, I could add a ton of help with the area, the people, and how we do things here. That way, we'd solve this sooner, and you could get back to Orlando sooner."

"I'll keep that in mind. Right now, I'm just gathering information to formulate a game plan."

The detective shrugged. "Okay, let me know." He had a cold smile when he left and swung the door closed with a wrist flip.

Chief squirmed in his chair.

Malcolm looked at Chief. "Dad?"

Chief's face reddened. "He didn't come from my loins. I married his mama when he was six."

"I see."

"Dumb as the day is long. I got no idea how he has that big house with a pool in Judge Harrison's community. His wife must have money that I don't know about is all I can say."

"Convenient that your stepson is one of two detectives. Oh, and your forensics guy is a relative too.

Must make for interesting conversation when you get together for family cookouts."

"I suggest you not spend much time on that. You got a press conference coming up. Hope you're ready."

Malcolm's press conference strategy had evolved over the past three hours with a big assist from Detective LeBeau. It would be unorthodox, but worth a try. "I have a couple of ideas of what to say. I'd like you on board, Chief. It's important both of us be on the same page."

"I don't really want to talk. I only want to catch this sum-a-bitch. Like I told you, I want to be the one to cuff him. Other than that, you go ahead and say whatever you want."

Being conciliatory seemed the best way to handle things for the moment. "Okay, I'll do my spiel, and I won't answer questions."

Chief shrugged. "It's your show."

Malcolm shook his head. "It's *our* show."

Chief stood and muttered, "Sounds like you got it all under control." He walked out the door, wagging his head.

Malcolm reminded himself to remain unemotional and maintain a pragmatic attitude. If he followed the evidence, he would be out of Madison in no time.

Chapter 6

5:50 p.m.

The "Halleluiah" chorus from Handel's *Messiah* erupted from AD's cell phone. He snatched the phone and stabbed its face with an index finger. The music stopped.

He loved the "Halleluiah" chorus soundtrack so much he'd made it his wake-up alarm. It was so beautiful, reverent, and full of joy. He wished the choir at his church could sing that well, but God didn't give everyone the same gifts.

Normally on Tuesdays, his day off, he napped in the afternoon and didn't set an alarm, but today, he wanted to watch the six o'clock news. They had stated on the noon news that the FBI special agent in charge would brief the media on their investigation. This would be AD's opportunity to observe his main adversary. Sure, that clown Dautry remained involved, but he didn't seem to be much of a threat. He hadn't considered the FBI becoming involved. This could now be a totally different story. They had resources, technology, and, most importantly, experience in this kind of investigation.

He shuffled to the window and closed the curtains to block the setting sun. With a bottle of red wine in hand from the refrigerator, he plopped into the chair and used the remote to turn the TV on.

An empty podium materialized with over a dozen microphones attached to it. Each mic identified its owner—CNN, *New York Times*, all the local affiliates, NPR, FSU Radio, and several AD had never heard of. A mixed group of men in police uniforms, suits, and casual attire formed a semicircle around the podium facing the audience. One of two Black female city councilwomen stood amongst the other city council members.

AD's heart beat a little faster than normal. He finished the last of the wine in his goblet and refilled it. He gazed at the crucifix on the wall and wondered how much pain Jesus endured having nails driven through his palms and feet. If He could endure that, AD could certainly endure his own malady and complete the mission.

Mayor Brenda Perez, the other Black female on the city council, entered the picture, placed a piece of paper on the podium, and straightened her dress. She smiled as if about to give a campaign speech, then seemed to remember the purpose of her appearance and frowned. "Ladies and gentlemen, thank you for being here today. As you know a pair of barbaric murders has wracked Madison. Our police department is working hand-in-hand, cooperating in every way possible, with the FBI. Before Special Agent Malcolm Gee comes to the podium, I want to unequivocally state that you are not in danger. Our police department along with the sheriff's department, state police, and numerous FBI personnel are working round the clock to find and apprehend this murderer. The governor informed me he's ready to send National Guard troops to our beautiful city at a moment's notice to protect you, our precious citizens. Rest assured, we are here for you, you will be protected, and we love you."

AD squirmed and drummed his fingers on the chair's armrest as the mayor continued her phony song and dance.

The mayor smiled and nodded. "I'm confident this heinous villain will be apprehended shortly. We have the best of the best working on this." She stepped aside and swept her hand across the semicircle like the models on *The Price Is Right* when revealing what's behind door number two. After a few seconds, she returned to the podium and, like a good politician, looked into the camera. "Now, I call FBI Special Agent Malcolm Gee to the podium to provide an update on the investigation."

AD leaned forward and rested his forearms on his knees.

Malcolm Gee's appearance disappointed AD. Instead of a John Wayne lookalike, he saw a rather nondescript man. He guessed Malcolm's height to be six feet, about two hundred pounds, with short brown hair. He appeared to be in his late thirties. He looked like a boring man no one would look at twice in a store or on the sidewalk.

"Thank you, Mayor Perez. First, let me reiterate the mayor's statement, the residents of Madison and Antler County are safe. The Madison Police Department, the Florida Department of Law Enforcement, and the FBI are being utilized to identify the killer and find him, which we will. Let me give you a synopsis of what's happened today."

AD quickly bored with FBI Special Agent

Malcolm Gee's monotone rehash of what he'd already seen on the news. His rubber-soled shoe bounced.

"I'm not at liberty to reveal everything we know, but I can share with you we found white chalk markings at each crime scene. They appear to be a signature, or calling card, or message of some sort."

AD jumped to his feet, knocking over the TV tray table next to his easy chair. Sheets of paper, pills, ramekins, and the remote scattered across the floor. "You're lying."

Gee continued. "These markings suggest the murders may be connected. Both appear to be well-planned crimes against targeted individuals."

Malcolm stared straight at the camera. "We are in the process of establishing an 800 number where the good citizens of Madison and Antler County can anonymously report anything they know, or even suspect. Also, we're offering a ten-thousand-dollar reward for any information leading to arrest and conviction, so don't hold back, call the hotline."

Reporters shouted questions, but Gee exited the screen.

AD rubbed his stomach, then threw his index finger at the TV. "I left shell casings. You didn't mention them." Spittle flew with another finger jab.

After two gulps of wine, AD retrieved the remote from the floor and pressed its off button. He couldn't believe they hadn't said anything about the casings. He had placed them in clear sight.

And what could the FBI be talking about? Chalk markings? If there were markings, he surely would have seen them.

First things first. Before he reviewed the plan for

the next set of sacrifices, he'd have to figure out how to tell them about the shell casings.

Chapter 7

8:35 p.m.

The skinny hotel room desk wasn't the most comfortable place for Malcolm to work, but it was the only surface available until the war room became accessible. At least the desk chair offered comfort and lumbar support. Malcolm flipped the desk light on and spread out his handwritten notes from the day's meetings at the Madison police station.

He had been the lead agent on several multiple-murder investigations before. Still, this one was different in that he had to work with a police department void of experience investigating a single murder, much less multiple murders. To compound the difficulties, Madison had minimal technological infrastructure and no experience working with the FBI. Most of what they knew about murder investigations might have been learned while watching TV.

He knew it wasn't uncommon for the top local cop to be reluctant to allow the FBI to take control. But if Chief Dautry continued to drag his feet, it would create a significant issue. He couldn't let the investigation bog down, and he couldn't be the cause of the governor or other bigwigs calling Roger. It would be a fine balancing act.

At the moment, his most important task was to

identify and itemize the major investigative efforts that needed to be done and who to assign them to. He knew several senior FBI resources would arrive in the morning, and he needed to be ready to have them hit the ground running. Nakul Datta, a top forensics analyst, had already arrived from Atlanta and would be raring to go. Beverly Choo, an electronics expert, and Danny Petrowski, second-in-command, were on their way.

Fortunately, Roger appreciated the complexity of running a serial killer investigation and made resources available to Malcolm. However, with appreciation comes expectation. As long as progress was being made, resources would be unlimited. Once progress stalled, which it always did in these kinds of efforts, Roger would be a pain in the ass. They needed results and fast.

No time to waste. The notes he took during his meetings with the Madison PD people would be the basis for a list of tasks and who would be responsible for each. Once the information started to roll in, the tasks would be expanded, resources would be added, and the plan would be modified to follow the evidence.

He tore the twelve pages of notes out of his notebook and taped them to the wall above the desk. He leaned back and looked at the four columns of three sheets each. Twelve. That number seemed significant, but he didn't know why. He mentally played with groupings: An even dozen, three groups of four, four groups of three, two groups of six. He scratched his head and pondered the significance of twelve for several minutes. Nothing came to mind.

The clock read 10:07. Less than ten hours before the morning meeting. Malcolm stretched and flexed his hand in expectation of the task ahead. He cleared his mind to focus with as much pragmatism as possible.

With pen in hand and a blank sheet of paper in front of him, Malcolm looked at the top left page on the wall. He jotted three items to the investigative to-do list:

1. What suspects had MPD identified? Chief, Palmer, LeBeau.

2. Request public to share all video—Palmer & LeBeau teams canvass within five-mile radius of shootings, announce at press conference, post on all social media.

3. Increase patrols, two to a car, between midnight and dawn…periodic roadblocks at random intersections and along frequently traveled roads…MG talk to Chief…MPD key here.

He wished Danny were there and the storyboards active. It was going to be a long night. At least storyboards would be created for this once the war-room equipment arrived and was installed, which should be the next day. He had no choice other than to do it the old-school way, pen and paper.

After three trips to the lobby for stale coffee and one new pen, his handwritten list of major investigational tasks covered three pages and included

* What prison releases occurred in the past year involving Scott or Harrison? Martha pull info

* Need to talk to businesses, see who didn't come to work the day after the murders, or reported late…check alibis…MPD & FBI

* Talk to Chief about putting cameras up at major intersections, at least twenty, to record traffic, especially midnight to dawn…MG & Chief

* Talk with everyone who Scott has arrested or ticketed in last two years…establish alibis…MPD, FBI

* Review cases Judge ruled over, particularly those resulting in incarceration, interview defendants & check alibis…MPD, FBI

* Find and question those individuals who were out and about between midnight and dawn…delivery drivers, shipping dock workers, UPS, FedEx, truckers, produce delivery, trash collection, UBER, taxis, restaurant workers going to/from a shift, twenty-four-hour restaurant and convenience store workers, bar workers and patrons, medical personnel, fire and EMS, hunters(?), etc. Use security footage to identify possible interviewees…MPD, FBI

* Speak with Roger to request subpoenas and/or warrants for cell phone records of anyone within five miles of either murder between midnight and dawn…MG

* Speak with Roger for subpoenas or warrants for cell phone records, both personal and professional, for Scott and Harrison…MG

* Speak with Roger for subpoenas or warrants for laptops, both personal and professional, for Scott and Harrison to check emails, search history, etc.…MG

* Collect and investigate all radio dispatch recordings involving Scott…MPD

* Collect all 911 recordings and dispatch logs for the past six weeks…put special attention on anything Scott had been dispatched to…MPD

* Accelerate reward bonus as donations and

contributions come in...target of $100K after one week...MG

* Request senior profiler be added to team...MG
* ???
* ???
* ???

In cases like this, he often awoke in the middle of the night with a new task in mind and would replace a set of ??? He had read a business book in college, *Think and Grow Rich* by Napoleon Hill, where the author stated the brain continues to work even while we're asleep. Hill went on to say that if a person has a problem, they should think about it while drifting off to sleep, and the brain will continue to focus on that problem while the body rests. At first reading, Malcolm didn't believe it, but a professor challenged him to try it. He soon became a believer and practiced it every chance he could.

If the empty slots weren't filled during the middle of the night, then surely, more tasks would be required as soon as information came in. This investigation, or project as he liked to think about it, wasn't his first rodeo, and he knew the next three days would be critical data-gathering days. That data typically formed the base of everything moving forward.

The clock now read 1:52. Four hours until he'd get up to prepare for the day. He knew it wouldn't be much time for his brain to work while he slept but hoped he'd prove Napoleon Hill correct once again.

Day Two—July 16th

Chapter 8

Wednesday 5:45 a.m.

Malcolm woke with a start, panting and covered in sweat. He threw the sheet off and draped his legs over the edge of the bed. For half a minute, he hugged himself and rocked back and forth. He'd dreamt about a project early in his career involving kidnapping, assault, and eventually death.

He frequently had nightmares about previous projects while working on a new project. Most people used sleep to rid themselves of bad thoughts and feelings. Instead, horrendous thoughts and feelings would resurface for him. He had the uncanny ability to envision, in color and with sound, the killer's activities. It became an incredible asset when working on a project, but he couldn't forget about it once he envisioned it. While those visions were often invaluable in stopping a serial killer, they came at a post-project personal cost.

Once he stopped rocking, he lay back, feet on the floor, and pulled the sheet over his now cold body. After a couple of deep breaths, he glanced at the bedside clock. Almost six o'clock. With a sigh, he rose to finish preparations for the meeting scheduled at eight.

Before falling asleep, he had typed the

investigative to-do list into his laptop. After showering and dressing, he hurried to the hotel's business center and printed more than enough copies for the expected attendees. The young lady at the front desk volunteered to collate the copies and staple them while he grabbed a makeshift sausage biscuit and coffee at the hotel's breakfast buffet.

The hotel conference room had been arranged exactly as he requested: Tables formed a square, or at least as close to a square as they could make it, twelve chairs with plenty of room between them. Chief and Robert, both larger than normal men, needed the extra space. Several Madison sergeants would be in attendance, plus Nakul Datta, and a couple more FBI specialists would arrive during the day. Extra space never resulted in problems, but tight quarters often did.

The hotel staff had already placed small water glasses and pens with the hotel's name and logo. A quick trip around the nearly square table and dropping the three-page document in front of each chair made the room look ready.

A new voice broke his focus. "Excuse me, are you Malcolm Gee?"

The voice belonged to a man wearing a Madison PD uniform standing in the doorway. He had large bags under his eyes, suggestive of not sleeping much the past couple of nights. A little pudgy around the middle, a slight pull of two buttons on his long-sleeved white shirt, and ruddy complexion gave him the look of an Irish cop Malcolm knew in Philadelphia. The man's white shirt displayed the stripes of a sergeant.

"Yes, I'm Malcolm, and you are?"

The man smiled. "I'm Jeremy Osgood, second shift

desk sergeant." He looked to his left, presumably down the hall, and motioned with his head. "This is it, boys, come on in."

Two more Madison PD uniforms followed Jeremy into the room, Charlie and Kevin. More introductions and handshakes occurred. The men seated themselves along one side of the table.

The next man to appear wore tan slacks, white polo shirt, and dark frame glasses. His dark skin and black hair contrasted with the white shirt. Malcolm thought if he had only worn a tennis sweater around his neck he could have passed for an Ivy League student.

He looked at Malcolm. "You must be Malcolm Gee."

Malcolm smiled and responded, "You must be Nakul Datta."

He flashed a perfect set of white teeth. "Guilty as charged. My friends call me Goose."

The two men shook hands and Malcolm asked, "Where does Goose come from?"

"Nakul translated to English is mongoose, and Datta is gift. So my American associates call me Goose for short." A round of introductions and handshakes followed.

Jack Palmer and Robert LeBeau entered last, followed by a hotel staff member pushing a cart with several coffee pots and a tray of donuts.

Malcolm waited a couple of minutes while coffee was poured and donuts on small paper plates were added. At 8:05, he clapped his hands. "Gentleman, let's get started."

He looked at Robert. "Where's Chief?"

A sheepish grin appeared for a second. "He's busy.

He asked me to take good notes and pick up an extra copy of whatever handouts you use. I'll brief him later this morning."

Malcolm tried not to show his surprise. The chief of police should be here, not expect his stepson to take good notes and brief him later. What could he be doing that was so important he couldn't attend? This needed looking into, later.

Forty minutes later Malcolm had completed his seventeen-item presentation. Several questions had been asked and answered along the way. He collected cell phone numbers of the three MPD sergeants and stated several other FBI resources would be arriving today. He glanced at his watch, 8:57, then looked around the table and asked, "Any last questions before I let y'all go?"

Robert raised a hand. He waited until Malcolm nodded, then asked, "Have you reviewed this stuff with Chief?"

"No, I expected him to attend this morning."

Robert scratched his head. "Um, I'm not sure he's going to be too happy about you assigning tasks to his folks. He gets pretty protective."

Did Chief want to catch the killer, or did he want to be some pompous fool protecting his turf? He wanted to get snarky with Robert but knew he couldn't shoot the messenger. He offered, "I understand, but I'm of the belief that catching the killer is his top priority. If I'm wrong, please ask him to contact me and I'll be happy to discuss things."

"Okay, he'll probably call."

Malcolm made sure he smiled. "No problem. I'll be talking with each of you as the day progresses, but we meet again tomorrow morning, in the war room. It's being put together in Johnny Robertson's old storefront across from the station." Blank faces around the table. "Okay, gentlemen, no one's catching the bastard sitting here. Get out there and good luck."

****

AD kneeled in the rear pew of St. Hubertus Catholic Church and stared at the stained-glass window towering above the altar. Jesus on the cross took center stage. The crucified thieves stood on either side of him. AD wanted to be like the thief whom Jesus told, "I tell you the truth, today you will be with me in paradise." He too wanted a place in heaven for all eternity.

He liked the church's atmosphere when he could sit alone—no kids crying, no one coughing, no cell phones going off, no one present, just God and him. Being alone with God in a holy place brought a peaceful and comforting feeling. He prayed to St. Hubertus, the patron saint of hunters and woodsmen:

St. Hubertus, I beseech thee for assistance, for guidance. How do I make the authorities aware of the clues they've been provided? Once they recognize the clues, they will follow them and uncover the sins perpetrated against God by those who I've already sacrificed. The world must become aware of those sins. The world is full of doubting Thomases. They won't believe until they have proof. They must see and recognize the punishment sinners receive. The world needs to repent, to join the crusade to turn sinners away from evil and to the rewarding love of God, our Father. How do I ensure law enforcement recognizes, then follows, the clues? I will now be quiet, empty my mind, open my heart, and listen for your guidance.

AD closed his eyes, bowed his head, and listened.

His thoughts circled time and again to the FBI's 800 number, but he didn't trust it to be truly anonymous. He couldn't take a chance on them uncovering his identity too soon, otherwise, he'd never complete his mission, and not get to heaven.

AD rose, slid from the pew, genuflected, and approached the white marble statue of St. Hubertus in the church's narthex. He sank to his knees, made the sign of the cross, and prayed. "St. Hubertus of Ardennes, help me find a way to point the FBI in the right direction. I need your guidance and wisdom. If it is your will, please help me make the world aware that sin is punished."

AD bowed his head, lowered his clasped hands, and tried to empty his mind so he could hear St. Hubertus whisper to him. Saints only whispered, so they required silence to be heard. He strained to hear a response.

Several minutes later the answer came, full of encouragement and promise.

AD wiped a tear from his cheek and looked at the statue above him. "Thank you. You never let me down. May this be done in God's name. Amen."

He held on to the statue's pedestal and struggled to rise. He shuffled to the door, slowing only to dip his fingers in the holy water dish and make the sign of the cross. He felt refreshed and had work to do before his meeting in Tallahassee that afternoon.

Chapter 9

1:46 p.m.

The weekly all-hands meeting held by AD's boss in downtown Tallahassee seemed like a giant waste of time. However, today's meeting provided a wonderful solution to how AD could mail a letter to Chief Dautry without it being traceable.

AD entered the meeting room fifteen minutes early, placed his notepad on the table closest to the door, and took a seat.

Normally he walked in ready to be bored for two hours, but today he had entered full of anxiety. His heart beat faster and palms sweated.

He needed to make a quick escape at the meeting's end, and everything needed to go right for his plan to be successful—mail the letter to Chief Dautry, pick up his oxy and alprazolam, and get back for the six o'clock news briefing on TV.

At 1:55 p.m., Patrick Michael O'Connell arrived and shuffled directly to the podium. Many in the organization secretly thought the old man's diminutive stature made him look more suited to decorating someone's lawn than leading a meeting with almost a hundred attendees. He had to stand on a wooden box to see over the podium.

At precisely two o'clock, the old man spoke with

the slightest hint of an Irish accent. "Good afternoon, ladies and gentlemen. We will follow the agenda I emailed Monday. I hope everyone came prepared to engage in a lively conversation about the discussion item: attire." He looked over the half-glasses perched on his red bulbous nose. A lopsided grin revealed a substantial gap between his two top teeth. "Before we begin discussion, let's have each department head provide their weekly report so everyone is current."

The meeting had dragged on for over an hour. For about the tenth time, AD lifted the pages of the notepad and verified the plain white envelope sat wedged between the last sheet of paper and the cardboard tablet backing. Amazing that writing forty words could be so time-consuming and nerve-racking. How could authors write novels? They must be very gifted individuals.

The old man prattled on about proper office attire. AD could care less. If someone didn't adhere, then the old man should talk with that individual, not waste everyone's time.

AD's heel bounced. He hoped—no, prayed—that Billy, the autistic mail boy, wouldn't be early gathering the day's outgoing mail and wouldn't notice the lack of a return address on the envelope.

The clock ticked to 3:59. AD straightened and eyed the door.

The seventy-eight-year-old man at the podium paused and looked at his audience. "Questions?"

A few of the attendees shook their heads, two others muttered, "No."

Another crooked smile. "If there are no questions, the meeting is over. Go and serve the people."

****

AD shifted into drive and moved his gray Chevy pickup into downtown Tallahassee rush-hour traffic. With the state legislature in session, politicians, their staff, and the distasteful lobbyists, Tallahassee's secondary roads always seemed clogged. The men with their expensive suits, big cars, flashy jewelry, and constant preening seemed slimy. The couple of times he'd met a lobbyist, he immediately wanted to bathe. He couldn't stand the sight of the women showing cleavage or wearing short skirts and high heels that made them walk like they had something stuck up their rears. The whole bunch would surely be damned to hell when Judgement Day came.

After almost twenty minutes of stop-and-go, he entered I-10 eastbound and settled into a comfortable sixty miles per hour. If traffic remained steady, he'd arrive right on time to pick up his two-week supply of medication. This would probably be his last pickup. If he were alive in two more weeks, his jail keeper would provide his oxy and alprazolam free of charge. Otherwise, he'd be dead, and medication would no longer be a concern.

AD recollected his visit to the mail room. He had arrived in the nick of time to slide the letter out of his notepad into Billy's sack. He heaved a sigh of relief when Billy cinched the sack's drawstring without question.

His smile grew to a grin. Once the news media learned his true purpose, surely others would adopt identical missions. Imagine what a wonderful world would remain if all the sinners were removed, twelve by twelve.

But he couldn't get ahead of himself. He'd only

removed two so far, ten more to go. First, he needed to meet the man who supplied his medication, then get home to see what the chief and FBI had to say at their six o'clock news briefing.

Arriving home, AD set a goblet and half-empty wine bottle on the end table next to his recliner. He plopped into the recliner amid a squish of air. He preferred the recliner at the cabin but wouldn't need either of them in a couple of weeks. A well-practiced point and click of the remote brought the TV to life.

Chief Dautry stood at the podium and pointed his index finger at the camera. "One of you knows something that will help us catch this sum-a-bitch. Tell us. There's a lot of folks out there who are on tough times. Think what a twenty-five-thousand-dollar reward can do for you and your family. Tell us what you know. Don't trust the FBI? Hell, talk to me, I know most everybody in Antler County. I'll keep your name quiet." He tapped his chest three times in unison with "talk to me." Chief grabbed the sides of the stand and stared into the camera. "He killed two of our own. Help us get him, and I'll make damned sure the SOB don't do it again."

AD shook his head and tsked. "Taylor, I've told you before, God doesn't like that kind of language."

Chief took a deep breath. "Here's FBI Special Agent in Charge Malcolm Gee. He'll give you some information, then answer questions."

When Agent Gee moved to the podium, AD leaned forward, elbows on knees, and counted the microphones. Twenty-one. Six more than the last time. He grinned. Word had gotten out, which gave testimony to his actions.

The FBI man nodded to someone off camera. "Thank you, Chief Dautry. I echo the chief's comments. If you know something, say something. We don't care who you talk to, just tell someone. Call the 800 number, talk to Chief, or someone in law enforcement. But tell someone.

"We've received several leads, and we thank you. We're looking into each and every one. Also, our handwriting experts are examining the chalk markings found at the scene. I'm not at liberty to release pictures yet but hope to soon."

AD threw his hands in the air. "Chalk markings? I would have seen them." He poured wine into the goblet so fast a little sloshed out.

"A preliminary profile of the murderer suggests it's a male, possibly ex-military, possibly has an issue with law enforcement and the legal system."

A quick swipe of the finger cleared the spilled wine and carried it to AD's mouth. Waste not, want not.

"We have an entire team of investigators looking into possible connections of someone Patrolman Scott encountered who made an appearance in Judge Harrison's courtroom."

AD pulled back on the recliner's side handle and raised the footrest with a *thud*.

"That's everything I can share right now, other than to encourage anyone who may know anything or may have seen anything this past Tuesday morning to please contact law enforcement. Oh, and the reward is now up to fifty thousand for information leading to the arrest and conviction of the killer. Questions?"

After fifteen minutes of listening to ridiculous questions and the FBI man talking in circles, AD pointed the remote at the TV, and pressed off. The house settled into silence. It brought peace and calm, two of his favorite things.

He selected an oxy from the refilled white ramekin and a well-practiced flip of the wrist sent it into the air. The little white pill followed a familiar arc and floated into his mouth. A swig of wine washed it into his stomach where it would perform its magic in a few short minutes.

AD stretched, and the chair reclined to an almost prone position. The back of his right hand ran across his mouth and settled onto his abdomen. He'd lost more weight; he could feel his ribs easier than before.

He closed his eyes in his favorite and most comfortable position for sleep. These days he rarely slept in bed, but there would be plenty of time for slumber in heaven.

Maybe he had given the police and FBI more credit than they deserved. Ex-military? Run-ins with the law? They sure had him pegged wrong. Maybe the letter would put them on the right track. The world needed, no deserved, to understand what happened when they knowingly sinned.

Enough about that. He needed to rest for tonight's sacrifices. First the kid in the rock band, then the lady at the nursing home three hours later.

Day Three—July 17th

Chapter 10

Thursday, 1:52 a.m.

AD moved through Oak Ridge Cemetery in a crouch. He didn't expect anyone to be around at this hour, but no sense taking chances. Once at the chain-link fence separating the cemetery and Mockingbird Trail, he took a knee. The prior week he'd attended a burial about thirty yards away. Sad day, but he thanked the Lord for ending the woman's suffering. Her pain and loss of control during the final seven or eight weeks had been brutal for her and her family. AD refused to dwell on those who had gone to be judged by God. There wasn't anything he could do about them, but he certainly could help Timothy Kurtz meet the creator, very soon.

A quick glance at his watch warned that Timothy and his bandmates would emerge from the rear door of Rock Bottom, a grunge bar near the community college, within a few minutes.

Based on prior recon, the band quit playing at 2:00 a.m., shut down their electronics, and paraded out the bar's rear door between 2:10 and 2:15. Timothy always led the short caravan across the driveway to the white van advertising his father's business, Tri-County Auto Parts.

It was now 2:01—soon, very soon.

Deuteronomy 5:11 kept running through his mind. "You shall not invoke the name of the Lord, your God, in vain. For the Lord will not leave unpunished anyone who invokes his name in vain."

How could anyone name his band the Jesus Jerks? The intentional and blatant disrespect was beyond belief. The young man's parents took him to mass, enrolled him in religious education, ensured he made his First Holy Communion, and was confirmed. Timothy Kurtz had been given every opportunity to learn and to love God, but he threw it all away. God willing, tonight, the world would find out you can't take God's name in vain. You can't disrespect the name *Jesus* and not be punished for it.

AD slid Beautiful Betsy's barrel through a diamond-shaped aperture in the chain-link fence. With cheek nestled against the cold stock, peering through the rifle's scope, he found the bar's rear door handle. A slight twist of the scope's adjustment knob brought the handle into focus. With the scope now zeroed in, he took a deep breath to calm himself and focused on steady deep breaths.

When he took the shot, he needed to be very careful he didn't hit any of the other band members. AD refused to allow collateral damage, as Oliver North once called it. The other boys needed to witness the carnage a .30-06 slug inflicted on the human head. They needed to witness it so they could provide testimony to the news media. Hopefully, it would shock them enough to stop their own sinful ways and repent in an effort to save themselves.

The back door of the bar banged open, and light spilled out.

They had changed routine. AD caught his breath.

The kid with severe acne exited first, followed by the grossly overweight kid. Timothy came out third with his arm around the waist of a person AD hadn't seen before. He couldn't tell if Timothy's friend was male or female, but it really didn't matter. The tall skinny kid came out last and swung the door closed. Timothy and his friend stopped at the driver's door, arms still around each other's waist.

AD couldn't carry out the sacrifice lest the newcomer be harmed.

Timothy opened the driver's door, his friend slid in, then Timothy. It all happened much too quickly for AD to risk a shot.

AD looked to heaven. "Your will be done."

Timothy had gotten lucky, maybe in more ways than one. AD wouldn't risk sacrificing or injuring someone he didn't know for certain had committed a severe enough sin. No need to hurry this sacrifice. The band would be at the bar again on Friday.

He carefully withdrew the rifle's barrel so he wouldn't scratch Beautiful Betsy. Once the scope's lens caps had been placed, he stood. After brushing off the right knee of his black slacks, he maintained a crouch and worked across the cemetery to Washington Street. A sigh of relief escaped his lips when he didn't see any police cars, and his Ford sat exactly where he'd parked it earlier. His next oblation didn't get off work until five a.m., so he didn't need to hurry.

****

Allison Newton rolled away from her desk and stretched, arms extended, legs straight, feet off the floor, and yawned. Her dark-blue scrubs top, already tight across the midsection, threatened to pop a seam. The long sleeves of the white sweater she wore under the top rose to mid-forearm. She rubbed the back of her neck and gazed at the clock above the nurse's station. Another five minutes and she'd be able to leave.

Being the pharmacy tech on the night shift at Pine View Assisted Living Center meant she also functioned as the completer of paperwork and became a nurse's aide when needed. The residents kept her busy at the start and end of each shift, but the middle four to five hours were normally quiet.

The staff kept sixty memory-care patients highly sedated at night so they didn't create any issues. Three little pink pills at ten and they slept until six or seven the next morning, well after her shift ended. The 250 other residents had an odd assortment of medication needs: pain pills, relaxants, sleeping pills, baby aspirin, ibuprofen, and the list went on. There always seemed to be one or two who had a test the next morning, which required something special. If medication needed to be inserted via suppository or taken orally, she had responsibility for making sure it happened at the appointed time. If injected, that responsibility rested with someone else.

Her shift replacement, Linda, sauntered to the desk and shook her head. "Good morning. How have things been?"

Allison smiled, said, "Typical night," and rose from the desk chair.

"It's amazing, you always seem happy."

Allison nodded. "If they ever took this shift away from me, I'd probably have to look for another job. I leave here, get home, pack lunches for the kids, get them up, feed them, and get them to school. I sleep while they're in class and pick them up when school's over. Having my mother move in after Jim died makes it possible for me to leave them overnight. I'm pretty lucky." Allison walked over to the file cabinet and lifted a cloth purse with a daisy pattern out of the top drawer.

Linda took Allison's chair and wiggled the mouse. "Enjoy your long weekend. Who knows, maybe you'll get lucky and meet a guy."

"I wasn't looking for a husband when I met Jim, but we had four years and two kids before he died. You never know what may happen. Life's one huge surprise after another. See you Monday." She waved, slung the purse over her shoulder, and sauntered down the hall to the time clock.

Allison clocked out precisely at five a.m. and exited the side door next to the time clock. The fresh air felt good when it hit her face. She hummed while she walked, then the hair on the back of her neck stood up. Something didn't feel right. A pivot back toward the building and all seemed quiet there. She turned to scan the tree line at the end of the parking lot.

****

Punctuality was important and valued by AD. His day job, as he called it, required him to be exactly on time. Early or late were not options. According to his prior reconnaissance trips, he knew Allison Newton would walk out the employee-only door within the next three to four minutes.

He leaned against a tree and recalled the day she told him she'd let a patient die instead of trying to save the man. She claimed it was okay because he wanted to die, he wanted to end his suffering, so she stood there and held his hand as he took his last breath. It didn't seem to matter to her that Deuteronomy 5:17 stated, "You shall not kill," and Ecclesiastes 8:8 warned, "No one is master of the breath of life so as to retain it, and none has mastery of the day of death."

It wasn't for her to decide that the man should die at that instant; it was up to God and God alone. Only God had authority over people's lives, and only He can extend or end them.

On the other hand, if she were working on God's behalf, like the angel Raguel did, or himself, then that would be an entirely different matter. She would have been working with God's blessing, but by her own admission, she had chosen inaction and allowed the man to die. She didn't work on God's behalf but on the wishes of a mortal, which was not God's way.

The slam of a door caught his attention. He saw Allison Newton walking across the parking lot toward her car. Always the same: purse slung over her left shoulder, flowered lunch box dangling from the right hand.

AD quickly straightened and reached for Beautiful Betsy. Leaves on the tree he'd been leaning against rustled.

Allison paused and looked in his direction.

AD froze. His heart thumped in his chest. He felt perspiration on the back of his neck.

She leaned forward and stretched out her neck.

He hoped his black outfit, complete with black ski mask, allowed him to blend in with the surrounding bushes and trees.

After a few seconds that seemed like an hour, she

shrugged and continued toward her car.

AD hurriedly assumed firing position, thankful he had removed the scope's lens cap earlier.

Approximately five steps away from the car, she pressed a button on the key fob. The car headlights and interior lights illuminated.

Standing, his left foot slightly in front of the right, he centered the scope's crosshairs on her forehead, exactly like he had the past three times he scouted her.

A look of worry, or confusion, washed over her face, and she looked straight at him again.

A gentle squeeze of the toothpick thin trigger sent the .30-06 lead slug straight to her forehead.

AD paused a few seconds and recalled Matthew 10:7. "As you go, preach this message: The kingdom of heaven is at hand." Yes, indeed, with each offering the kingdom of heaven came nearer for him.

He took a deep breath and let a sigh escape.

Three down, nine to go.

Chapter 11

6:22 a.m.

The sound of a siren woke Malcolm. He tried to ignore it.

The siren wailed again, a few feet from his head. Chief Dautry's ringtone.

He twisted and pawed at the nightstand. The TV remote hit the floor with a clatter.

Another siren howl.

He snatched the phone a split second before he fell off the bed with a *thud*.

With his lower half still wrapped in the sheet like a mummy, Malcolm swiped an index finger across the phone's face. "This can't be good."

"He got another. Nursing home worker, shot above the left eye. Found in the parking lot, single mother of two."

Malcolm closed his eyes. "Same guy?"

"Bet your ass it's the same sum-a-bitch."

He knew the answer but asked anyway. "How do you know?"

"Same calling card, 'cept this one has three Hs scratched on it. I don't need to be FBI to know it's the same bastard."

"Shit. Text me the address. I'll get there right away."

"I don't text. Be out front in ten minutes."

****

Special Agent Malcolm Gee marched to Chief Dautry's table in Gram's Kitchen. "When you said you didn't text and to be outside in ten minutes, I assumed you would come by, not one of your officers."

"Well, Mr. FBI man, didn't your mama ever explain what happens when you assume something?"

Malcolm gritted his teeth and stared. He didn't need Chief busting his balls but didn't want to make a fuss in public. "Did you visit the scene?"

"Didn't need to. I seen the pictures. Besides, my mama stayed there her last couple weeks. I'm real familiar with it."

Of course, Chief would be familiar with the scene. He probably knew the victim too. "Does the victim have a connection to law enforcement like the judge and Officer Scott?"

"Two parking tickets is all. One went away, she paid the other."

"There's got to be something in common between her and the other two."

Chief leaned back, his eyebrows rose a split second.

Malcolm had a gut feeling his words had triggered something in Chief's mind. "What do you think connects them?"

"They're all dead. That's your connection." He wiped his mouth, balled the napkin, and dropped it on the plate. After a few seconds, he rose and tossed a twenty on the table. "I got breakfast. Make sure you leave Holly a damn good tip. She's got two kids at school in Tallahassee."

"What are you? Her benefactor?"

Chief paused and glared down his nose. "I take care of mine, and mine take care of me."

Malcolm stiffened. "Have any of yours stepped up and given us any useful leads?"

"At least they've called and given information. What has the FBI given?" Chief raised a hand. "Just so you don't assume again, I'll tell you. Not a goddamned thing, that's what the FBI brought, 'cept some bullshit about chalk letters that hasn't fooled anyone. Wanting to put cameras at intersections and other nonsense." Chief raised his hands palms up. "I'm beginning to think the only fool here is you."

Malcolm peered up into Chief's bloodshot eyes. "I don't know why you're busting my balls, but I'm getting pretty damn tired of it."

Chief scratched his head. "You're the high and mighty F, B, I, but I ain't seen you bring anything to this investigation. Your all-knowing, super-experienced profilers offered the same thing my bunch had already said. I got three dead citizens." He raised a thumb. "A police officer"—he added his index finger—"a law enforcement friendly judge"—his middle finger went up—"and now a single mother with two little kids. Some sum-a-bitch is killing my folks, and I'm getting pretty pissed about it. You and your fancy war room with its writing boards, computers, and brand-new furniture ain't found shit. If you can't help, then either you, or the F, B, I, need to get the hell out of town…maybe both. I promised the mayor I'd cooperate, but I didn't promise not to call bullshit when I see it, and I'm surely beginning to smell it."

Bert Parks singing, "There She Is, Miss America,"

came from Chief's cell phone. "Speak of her highness." He stabbed the phone and put it to his ear. "Yes, Madam Mayor." He listened for a couple of seconds. "Yes, ma'am, I'll be there in fifteen minutes." He slid the phone back into a shirt pocket. "Now, if you don't mind, I got to get my ass chewed." Chief turned toward the door.

"I'll delay the morning briefing until you arrive."

The tall lawman stopped in mid-stride and turned back. "You can go ahead and start the meeting whenever you want. I won't be there." The corner of his lips turned up, but he didn't smile.

Malcolm straightened and pulled his shoulders back, then reminded himself of his instructions—no, orders—not to piss off any of the main players, not to do anything or say anything that would result in a phone call to Roger. "I understand, you have other pressing items. Please know you have an open invitation to join us each morning at eight in the war room."

"Hmmpf. Robert does a fine job keeping me up to date. You can proceed however you want. Like I told you before, all I want is to be the man what puts the cuffs on the sum-a-bitch. Do you understand?"

Malcolm nodded in unison with one-Mississippi, two-Mississippi, three-Mississippi. "I understand. I would offer for your consideration that you carry handcuffs. You may need them sooner than you expect."

Chief's face reddened. "Don't you worry about me carrying cuffs. You had best worry about finding the killer before your boss decides to put somebody here who knows what they're doing."

Malcolm watched Chief weave through the tables and exit. He took a deep breath and tried to relax. A clear head would solve these murders, not being pissed at the Madison chief of police, who certainly knew which buttons to push.

Focus and pragmatism would solve this, not emotion. There had to be something in common. His gut told him these weren't random killings. A common thread ran through all three of them, and Chief knew what it might be, but what?

****

Malcolm swiped his badge through the war room's card reader. The door clicked, and he hurried to the huge bull pen where almost twenty people sat around the large table. He marched to the head of the table. "Sorry I'm late. I had an impromptu meeting with Chief. He won't be joining us."

No one said anything. Robert looked pleased, while Jack looked at the notepad on the table in front of him.

"We have a lot of new people here this morning, so let's get ourselves introduced."

Robert waved a hand. "We did all of that while we were waiting for you. I was curious who some of these people are and what they do, so I kinda started asking questions, and, abracadabra, we've all met one another." He donned a smug smile.

Malcolm wasn't sure whether to be grateful or confused. "Great. Thanks for getting the ball rolling. As promised, this meeting will not go beyond nine o'clock. Here's how I'd like this meeting to go. Each team lead will speak for a couple of minutes, giving us the highlights of what you've unearthed since our previous meeting. You'll also identify any areas where you need assistance from another team. You will be expected to huddle with that team leader directly after this meeting and discuss what you need. If you can't agree or need additional resources, find me. Danny, my second in command and project scribe, will update the storyboards and follow up to ensure those cross-team items reach resolution. Any questions?"

Robert raised his hand shoulder height, then lowered it.

The detective didn't speak, so Malcolm continued. "I want to state this plainly, and you'll hear me say it multiple times. I don't need to be involved in everything, but I do want to be informed. Questions? Everyone understand?"

Several Madison PD folks muttered, "Yes, sir," several heads nodded, and someone responded, "Okay." Exactly as he expected.

"Goose, any news from the tip line?"

Nakul "Goose" Datta rose halfway out of his seat but seemed to think better of it and stayed seated. "Just before I came in here someone called in about a strange person was camped at Secret Lake Park. Anyone know where that is?"

"It's northeast of town, kinda secluded," Jack offered.

Malcolm looked at Jack. "Can you have someone check it out?"

"Consider it done." He wrote something on a pad.

"Anything else from the tip line?"

"Nothing worth getting excited about." Goose shook his head.

"Robert, please update us about your tasks, specifically, installation of cameras at major intersections and cases where Judge Harrison and Officer Scott may have overlapped."

"Chief said he wouldn't allow cameras to be installed; it would anger the residents if they knew they were being watched. He also said it would be a waste of time, money, and potential damage to poles and wires and shit like…er…excuse me…stuff like that. There was no overlap between Judge and Scott. End of report."

Malcolm wanted to scream at Robert, but he couldn't shoot the messenger. "I'm sorry, I may not have heard you correctly. You said Chief won't allow cameras at major intersections? I didn't know he needed to approve that."

Robert nodded like a bobblehead. "I don't know, but he said he wouldn't allow it. Chief is Chief and does what he wants. If you want to talk to him about it, go ahead, no skin off my nose." He leaned back and crossed his arms.

For the third time in less than an hour, Chief had managed to become a stumbling block. This couldn't go on.

Chapter 12

9:30 a.m.

Malcolm, Detective Robert LeBeau, Detective Jack Palmer, Goose, Danny Petrowski, the task force scribe, and Beverly Choo, an FBI agent who specialized in electronics, remained at the oblong conference table after everyone else left. Due to his two decades of experience and vast background in intelligence analysis, Danny functioned as the assistant special agent in charge in addition to his role as the project scribe.

Danny had multiple cell phones in front of him along with a wireless keyboard and laser pointer. Paper coffee cups and a half-empty donut box from Darlene's Delicious Donuts sat in the middle. The four men and one woman stared at the data displayed on the smartboards.

LeBeau pulled closer to the table, the wheels on his chair squealing in protest. "This is some fancy setup you have here. Are you going to leave all this stuff when we solve this, and you go back to Orlando? I could conduct some great training with all these ceiling-mounted projection systems and smartboards and comfortable chairs. Reminds me of a couple of my FSU classes."

Everyone, except Jack Palmer, looked at LeBeau.

Danny opened his mouth, then seemed to change his mind and remained silent.

Malcolm rose and approached the left-most smartboard. "Let's start at the top."

LeBeau's chuckle sounded like a kid who saw one of his friends do something stupid.

"Detective LeBeau, was there something I said that you wanted to comment about?"

"I'm sorry, it just sounds funny to say 'let's start at the top.' Only grave diggers start at the top. Everyone else normally starts at the bottom and works their way up." He looked around at the others, and no one smiled. "I guess it's just my strange sense of humor. Please continue...at the top." He chuckled again.

Officer Ronald R. Scott

Anonymous 911 caller reported a police officer lying on County Road 360...approx 3 miles south of Madison

Killed approx 2:35 a.m. while responding to call of debris on roadway

COD—Gunshot to bridge of nose...high caliber...probable deer rifle based on caliber of shell casing

Shooter apparently hid next to an abandoned service station

Evidence—.30-06 brass shell casing standing on end...south side of gas station...probable location where shot fired

Slug not found...MDP searching wooded area

No prints...streaks suggest wiped clean

Capital letter H etched on casing

3rd time in 2 weeks responded to debris in roadway

No hair, fibers, blood, or other biologics found...no DNA available

No witnesses

No video

Shoe and tire imprints noted...being researched...being cross-checked with other scenes

No motive...no one claimed responsibility

Possible connection to Judge Harrison and Allison Newton murders

The smartboard to the right contained information for the judge:

Judge Thomas Alexander Harrison

Found floating in pool by wife

Shot approx. 5:00 a.m. after leaving pool for morning exercise...between left eye and ear...fatal

COD—Gunshot wound to the head...high caliber...probably deer rifle

Slug dug out of concrete wall...sent for analysis

Shooter fired from deer hunting tree stand behind house—casing found there

Evidence—.30-06 brass shell casing standing on end on floor of tree stand

No prints...streaks suggest wiped clean

Capital HH etched on casing

Hair found on tree stand...probably animal...being checked

No other biologics found...no DNA available

No witnesses

Neighbor has security camera, but out of town, trying to contact

Shoe and tire imprints noted...being researched, being cross-checked with other scenes

No motive...no one claimed responsibility

Possible connection to Scott and Newton murders
Allison S. Newton
Found by co-worker in parking lot outside Pine View Assisted Living center
Shot approx. 5:10 a.m. after leaving work...right-center forehead...fatal
Shooter fired from group of trees at end of parking lot
Evidence—.30-06 shell casing standing on end behind bushes where he probably stood
No prints...streaks suggest wiped clean
Capital HHH etched on casing...eliminate white supremacy?
Slug not found...MPD looking
No hair, fibers, blood, or other biologics found...no DNA available
No witnesses
Nursing home security video being reviewed
Shoe and tire imprints noted...being researched and cross-checked with other scenes
No motive...no one claimed responsibility
Possible connection to Scott and Harrison murders

Malcolm waved his hand across all three boards. "Okay, folks, let's build a board for the murderer—what we know, identify similarities, build a profile. The media people are calling him the Madison Murderer, so we'll call him the same."

Danny pulled the wireless keyboard onto his lap. "Ready when you are."

Malcolm talked, Danny typed, and words appeared on the board.

Madison Murderer
All victims shot between 2:00 a.m. and 6:00 a.m.

High-powered rifle....30-06...probable deer rifle based on caliber

All shot in head from distance...65-100 yards

Shell casings stand open end up...H, HH, HHH...would HHHH be next?

What do the Hs represent?

No hair, fibers, blood, or other biologics found...no DNA available

No witnesses...MPD and FBI teams continue to canvass neighborhoods and businesses looking for witnesses, security video, employees getting to work late

No apparent connection between victims

No apparent motive

No one claiming responsibility

No prints on shell casings...streaks suggest wiped clean

Possible neighbor and assisted living center video being reviewed by forensics video techs

Multiple sets of shoe and tire prints...may or may not belong to MM...being researched and cross-checked...apparent matches and similarities exist

MPD and FBI teams canvassing businesses within twenty-mile radius for possible video or witnesses or purchases of similar items

Malcolm stepped back and looked at the list. "Did I miss anything?"

They shook their heads.

"Danny, pull up the map of Madison County. Let's see where the three murders took place."

Robert raised his hand with index finger extended. "I just wanted to mention I worked really hard with Danny to create this map in a clear and concise manner, so it's easily recognized and understood even by those who don't have the knowledge I have."

Danny cleared his throat. "Yes, I was about to mention that. Thank you, Robert." He tapped his keyboard a couple of times and each image shifted to the right until the outline of Madison County appeared along with roads drawn in. Danny spoke. "The four-lane roads are in blue. The two-lane roads are in black. The green ones are primarily residential streets. You'll notice the red number one south of city center on Route 360. It corresponds to Officer Ronald Scott's crime scene. The red number two several miles west of town is Judge Harrison. The red number three on the eastern edge of downtown is Allison Newton. There's a legend in the lower right corner in case you're not familiar with Madison."

Beverly Choo leaned back and pointed at the map. "With all of the video cameras in the world, it doesn't seem possible there's no video from the first murder. To add to that, there's only one 'maybe' video from the second and that's still being reviewed for possible value. Do we feel comfortable all of the neighbors and businesses were canvassed properly?"

Malcolm looked at Jack.

"There's no buildings or structures within a mile of Scott's murder that would have video."

Beverly nodded. "Okay, your local knowledge is an asset to you. I'll give you that Scott was in the middle of nowhere. What about the judge's house? Only one possible video? Really? I thought he lived with rich people. Those people have lots and lots of toys, including cameras."

Jack responded, "Judge lives at the rear of a small,

gated community."

Robert interrupted, "I live there too. I been to his house, so I can attest to what Jack's saying."

"As I was saying, his home backs to a wildlife area," said Jack. "There were no entries into the community after 11:49 until our officer arrived at 6:13. The first exit occurred at 6:21 by a resident. We've spoken to twenty-four of his twenty-five neighbors. Nothing. The one we've not spoken to is in Europe on vacation."

Beverly shook her head. "Come on, I'll bet a steak dinner that more than one of the judge's neighbors has a security camera."

Jack continued, "The murderer fired from a tree stand in the wildlife area behind the house. No one points their cameras back there. The only way to get there is by entering the wildlife area three miles away in a truck or jeep. You have to know the area to do that. This is someone who lives, or at least hunts, here. He's planned well."

Malcolm enjoyed the back and forth. Both participants had good points and weren't afraid to present them.

One of Danny's phones vibrated. He snatched it and looked at the message. "The nursing home security video got the gun flash, but not much else. They tried to enlarge it, but the pixel ratio isn't sufficient. They think the shooter either wore a mask, is dark-skinned, or could have painted his face. They're not certain."

Malcolm pointed to the evidence board. "That's not much, but it's more than we had ten minutes ago, add it."

Danny raised an index finger. "Wait, there's more.

Oh, Goose, your folks have come through. The video review technicians estimate the shooter to be between five seven and five nine. Thin build."

Robert spoke. "That's cool. I imagine there's a lot of geometry involved in that."

Goose took the initiative. "Comparative analysis is used. They take the dimension of something they are absolutely positive of, then compare it to the subject matter. They then apply an algorithm that's been proven accurate to one one-hundredth of an inch and extrapolate the size of the subject matter. In this case, they probably measured a tree trunk, its proximity to the subject, the shooter, and made multiple calculations to derive an approximation of the shooter's size. It's all math."

Danny set the phone down and took the keyboard. "I'll get this added to the storyboards. It'll be ready for remote viewing within ten minutes."

LeBeau straightened. "What's remote viewing?"

"Give me a couple minutes, then I'll show you how to access all of this from your cell phone or laptop, so you can see it without being here."

LeBeau's eyes got big. "Wow, that's really cool. I sure hope you leave all this equipment when you guys go home. I can do remote learning for our guys, maybe even other departments. Who knows, maybe I could earn a couple extra dollars. Sure would help out with clothes for the girls."

Malcolm clapped his hands a couple of times. "We don't have much to go on, but we have a start. Jack's right. The killer planned his executions and knows the area. A cartoon I saw a couple of years ago comes to mind. The caption stated, 'We have met the enemy and he is us,' or something similar. Jack, this guy lives in or around Madison. I want you to focus on locals. Reach out to all of your contacts, see what they know. Revisit people, question them again, see if anything new comes to mind."

He pointed at Robert. "Study this map. Figure out the driving time from the police station to each of these locations. Figure it for the middle of the night. Time the driving from one location to another, especially from Scott to the judge's crime scenes. Feed all of that information to Danny so he can add it to the boards.

"Then I want you to join our canvass team. They're charged with going to every house, business, church, and anyplace else that might have a video camera. Get copies of their videos for four hours before and two hours after each killing. Get that data to Goose. Goose, review every second of the footage, track passing vehicles, in either direction, for that time frame. Look for commonalities and report back to us. Got it?"

Robert grinned. "This is cool the way you guys work. You sure know what you're doing."

Jack rolled his eyes.

Next, Malcolm pointed at Beverly. "Get your electronics stuff unpacked and set up. I have a feeling we're going to need it sooner than later. Danny, keep the boards updated. We meet tomorrow at eight."

Everyone left the area except Malcolm. He plopped into a chair, put his feet on the table, and studied the boards. His gut, which hardly ever failed him, told him the three victims had a common connection. Once he knew the commonality, it would be downhill from there. He couldn't get it out of his head. Did Chief know the connection and want to keep it to himself? To make himself look good? Maybe he knew the killer and wanted to protect one of his own?

Chapter 13

3:10 p.m.

Malcolm's phone sounded like a barking dog. He didn't need to look at the display. "Hello, Roger."

"You passed the senior agent exam." Typical Roger, right to the point.

Malcolm fist-pumped at the news. He'd worked hard, studied hard, did everything required to earn the promotion. "Thanks for the good news. When does it become effective?"

"You'll be transferred to the Dallas section when the shit-show in Madison is wrapped up. Promotion and pay increase become effective first of the month following transfer. Now go find this bastard so the governor and director will get off my back." The call disconnected.

Malcolm massaged his forehead. Dallas? He'd be transferred to Dallas? The Big D! Huge city with lots of opportunities. Away from Roger. Maybe he'd get a boss he could have a conversation with, exchange ideas with, who might actually help with career planning, and look for opportunities to showcase his talents. Maybe they could have a beer after work and get to know one another.

Dallas, what a break.

He'd never been to Dallas other than to change

planes at DFW or Love Field. He'd always heard Texas girls, especially those in Dallas, wore the tightest jeans. The future looked good. Once they captured the murderer, he'd be able to mosey his way to Dallas, and away from Roger. Maybe he'd learn to wear cowboy boots, line dance, eat Tex-Mex and BBQ. "Look out Dallas, here comes Malcolm." He fist-pumped again.

Then his thoughts shifted to Valerie. He rubbed his jaw. He didn't want to leave Valerie. Would she relocate to Dallas with him? Was it too early to even think about them being a couple? Now what?

****

Chief Dautry's secretary, Martha Osgood, approached his desk holding a white number-ten envelope in a gloved hand. She held it up for Chief to see. "Came in today's mail. No return address but says confidential."

He extracted forceps from his desk and took the envelope by its corner. A twist of the wrist allowed him to eyeball both sides, then raise it to the light. He sniffed it for good measure. "I'll take it. Thanks, Martha."

"I looked and sniffed, too. Nothing."

"I'm sure you did. I certainly don't know what I did to deserve someone like you." He winked.

She flattened the skirt over her stomach, which resulted in her ample breasts sticking out. "Didn't look suspicious, so I brought it to you instead of calling Riley to do his forensics thing. Happy reading."

Chief watched her walk away and thought she had a little extra to her giddy-up.

Before entering the hall, she glanced back and winked.

"Damn. Some days it's good to be Chief." His attention returned to the envelope. He inserted a pocketknife blade under the flap and opened it with a *zip*. He shook the envelope and a tri-fold sheet of plain white paper slid out and hit the desktop. He used the forceps and knife to unfold it. After a quick read he leaned back. "Damn, my luck is running good today."

This letter could be exactly what he needed to show up the FBI prick, or, if he didn't handle things right, it could blow up in his face and cause all sorts of harm for his election bid. Things needed to be handled very smartly, and he was just the guy to do it. But he'd need help so he'd have deniability.

After about twenty minutes, he sat up, nodded his head a couple of times, and smiled. He knew just the man to help him, Detective Robert LeBeau.

Chapter 14

3:51 p.m.

Chief looked in all the spots he could think of but couldn't find Robert. He walked into Martha's office and asked if she'd seen him.

"On my way back from Grumpy's Barbecue, I saw him walking toward that new war room. You might want to check there."

Chief grumbled a "Thanks." He thought about calling but hadn't seen the war room yet and decided to check out all the fancy stuff he'd heard about from Robert. He left police headquarters, his leather-soled shoes slapping the concrete with every step as he crossed the street.

An Authorized Personnel Only sign adorned the top panel of the war room's door. Chief patted his shirt pocket, then pants pockets. He hadn't brought his access card.

He pulled the door handle, it didn't move. He pushed. The door didn't open. Realizing he couldn't get in without a card, he cupped his hands on either side of his face and looked in through the door. He saw an empty desk in a smallish foyer surrounded by eight-foot-high partition walls, nothing else.

He stepped back and peered to the left, then right. The windows had been frosted from the inside. Only the top foot or so remained clear, but a person would have to be on a ladder to see in.

Chief knocked on the door, waited a few seconds, then banged on the door. A man wearing a short-sleeved white shirt, open at the collar, and dark slacks came to the door but didn't open it. "Can I help you?"

"I'm the chief of police here in Madison. I want in."

"Use your card key."

Chief threw his hands in the air. "If I had a card key, don't you think I'd have used it? Go tell Gee I'm at the door."

The man gave a thumbs-up and disappeared. Chief waited in the sun. Perspiration trickled down his chest and back. The white shirt stuck to him. He used an index finger squeegee fashion to remove sweat from his forehead and flipped the resulting liquid to the side.

After what seemed like ten minutes, Malcolm appeared and tapped a button on the wall. The door clicked.

Neither Chief nor Malcolm moved.

The door clicked again.

Malcolm chuckled. "You need to grab it." He hit the button again and the door clicked.

Chief quickly yanked it open. Once the big man made it through the door and it closed, Malcolm said, "Welcome to my world. What can I do for you?"

"I came to talk to my step-s…Detective LeBeau."

"Come on in, Robert's in bullpen two, right this way."

Chief followed Malcolm, rounded the eight-foot partition, and stopped after two steps. He had never seen such an arrangement, not even on TV.

Three of the largest TV screens he had ever seen hung from the ceiling in separate corners. They appeared to be tuned to three different news networks. Some sort of whiteboards with printing on most of them covered two whole walls. Two men and one woman huddled around one of the boards. At least six projection units hung from the ceiling and pointed at segments of the whiteboards.

Four-foot cubicle walls created three large areas each with oval tables in the middle. Detective LeBeau sat at one of the tables with four others Chief didn't know. Coffee cups littered the table.

Chief brushed past Malcolm and approached the table. "Robert, I need you in my office."

LeBeau, eyebrows raised, looked at his table mates, then Malcolm.

Chief cleared his throat and nodded toward the door.

LeBeau bit his lower lip. "I'm kinda busy here. I'm helping these nice FBI people understand where things are located in Madison and calculate travel times. This is critical work."

Chief shook his head. "I need you for something critical, too. Now."

LeBeau hesitated a few seconds then pushed away from the table and stood. "Having me in your office instead of here is like having a bucket of fat, juicy worms sitting on the dock. They don't do any good unless they're in the water." He turned to Malcolm. "I hope to be back quickly. But, just in case, keep my number handy. I'll be like the Minutemen from the war a long time ago. You call and I'll be ready in a minute to lend my expertise and knowledge in catching this murderer." He glanced at his table mates. "I'll be back just as soon as I can." Robert pivoted on a heel and followed Chief out.

Chief led the way across the street, into police headquarters, and down the hall to his office. Chief entered and sidestepped to allow Robert to enter. He pointed to a sheet of paper on his desk. "Got that letter from the murderer." Chief closed the door.

Robert walked around the desk, leaned forward, and placed his hands on either side of the single sheet of white paper. He read aloud:

"I sacrificed those men. They held positions of responsibility and respect but weren't what everyone thought. They sinned and deserved to be stopped before they hurt others again. I don't know anything about chalk markings. Look at the shell casings."

He paused a few seconds, then read it aloud again, this time much slower. When finished, he settled into Chief's chair and looked up. "Was it addressed to you?"

Chief pointed. "That's the envelope."

Detective LeBeau eyeballed the envelope. "I would guess it's from the killer. He knew there weren't any chalk markings, and about the shell casings. But he said *men*. One was a woman."

"It was postmarked yesterday in Tallahassee. Allison Newton was killed this morning."

Robert leaned back with hands behind his head. "This guy went all the way to Tallahassee to mail it? Or maybe he lives there and commutes here for the murders. Which do you think?"

Chief swiped his hand like shooing a fly. "Get outta my chair."

LeBeau bolted out of the chair like he had been

ejected from a fighter plane. They almost collided when both men chose the same side of the desk to move around. Robert settled into a guest chair and crossed ankle over knee, exposing about six inches of skin above white socks. "I guess Gee was right. He said the killer would take the bait and tell us there weren't any markings. Pretty smart of him. Now that the killer's hooked, I wonder how Gee figures to reel him in."

"Forget the FBI. What do you reckon he means when he says they weren't what everyone thought they were?"

"Maybe he thought they pretended to be someone else. Like on Halloween, everyone dresses like someone else. Dracula. Spiderman. Sleeping Beauty. I remember one year I wore one of Mother's dresses and put lipstick on. But I don't think Judge Harrison or Ronny wore dresses, but I'm sure Allison did."

Chief wondered if he had made a mistake talking to his stepson about the letter. The boy followed direction about the same as a good hunting dog but wasn't nearly as smart. Thought he knew it all, but most of the time the jackass didn't have a clue what he was talking about. Right now, he needed Robert to follow directions and keep his mouth shut. "I gotta think on that some more."

Robert nodded in agreement. "Want me to find Gee and tell him?"

"No!" After the ass-chewing the mayor gave him earlier, he felt like he needed to make something happen and make sure everyone knew Chief Taylor Dautry provided an important piece of information. Besides, he wanted to be the one who captured the SOB. He wanted everyone to see him on TV cuffing the murderer and reading him his rights. Not only would it show Madison is his city, but free TV advertising was worth its weight in gold when running for office.

"Robert, you keep your mouth shut. I don't want no one but us Madison boys to know about this. Get these bagged"—his index finger wagged between the letter and envelope—"take them to that Riley kid in forensics. Have him check them over. He's only to tell *you* what he finds."

"Don't you think it would be better to have the FBI do this? They have a lot of neat tools Riley don't have."

Chief straightened. "Look, I told you I want Riley to do it. And keep your mouth shut. You report back to me." He pointed at LeBeau. "Understand?"

Robert shrugged. "You're the chief."

"Damn right I am. Now get this evidence bagged, pronto."

"I'll be back in a jiffy with a couple of evidence bags." LeBeau stuck his head out the door, looked both ways, twice, then exited.

Chief reread the letter and scratched his head. Maybe the FBI man had finally brought something to the party.

Robert returned with several evidence bags and sat in the same chair he'd occupied a minute earlier. His brow furrowed. "Chief, shouldn't this go to the FBI to check? They have a lot more cool stuff than Riley and can probably do it faster. Don't we want fast to stop the murderer?"

Chief gritted his teeth and took a deep breath. "Look, son, Riley will do it fast too. He'll do it right here in his lab. He has the lab at the college if he needs it. The FBI will send it to Washington, D.C., and it may get lost. Riley won't lose it. I know you're concerned about other murders, but I'm confident in our own abilities. Do you understand?" Chief nodded with the expectation it would also make Robert nod.

The detective's brow smoothed, and he nodded. "I see what you're saying. That's why you're Chief. I'll tell Riley to rush it and to put tape over his mouth."

"That's why I made you detective. Now git."

Once alone he pondered the possibilities and devised a pair of plans to suit either scenario that the forensics report could present. Both options made the FBI man look bad. He leaned back and smiled.

Chapter 15

5:47 p.m.

Malcolm knew he'd have to hustle to make the six o'clock press briefing on time. He left through the rear door of the war room, bounced down the steps to the sidewalk, and saw Detective Jack Palmer headed in the same direction.

Madison Avenue had gotten crowded the past two days. For two solid blocks, TV trucks lined both sides of the street with their telescoping satellite dishes and colorful logos…CBS eye, NBC peacock, white ABC letters on a black dot, and at least two dozen other trucks, all with their generators running.

Malcolm quickened his pace until he pulled even with the detective. "All these media people must make the merchants happy."

Jack smiled. "You'd think. But the media people are like locusts, they only eat and shit. The restaurants are happy. Locusts don't buy flowers, insurance, antiques, or clothing. The rest of the shop owners are bitching up a storm."

"If you wrote a couple parking tickets, the trucks would move."

"Can't. Mayor says to play nice with them."

"Play nice?" Malcolm waved at the trucks. "Heck, I'd think she'd be more interested in making her constituents happy. They're the people who voted for her."

"She has her eye on Johnny Robertson's state Senate seat in Tallahassee, with an eventual run for governor. He's retiring, and she fancies herself made for politics: Black, female, married to a Hispanic, looks good on TV. She checks a lot of boxes. She needs the locusts on her side to win Johnny's seat. Problem is, she don't know Chief's gonna run for Johnny's seat. Mayor and Chief will square off."

"Johnny? The same Johnny who loaned us his empty store?"

"Yes. He's a"—Palmer used air quotes—"a 'friend of law enforcement.' "

"How do you know all this?"

Jack snickered. "Chief told me in confidence 'cause he wants to name me interim chief until I run for the permanent seat."

"Do you want to be chief?"

"Not sure. Got its ups and downs. I'd do the interim thing though, just to help out, be a team player."

"He must like you."

"All he wants is to fracture the Black vote enough to get him elected. He's a card-carrying member of the good old boys club. No minorities. You figure it out from there."

"Didn't realize that about Chief."

"You ain't been around enough to see how nasty this city can be." Jack nodded to a man passing by. "Chief and Johnny are two of a kind."

Malcolm stepped over a dog turd. "You seem cynical."

"I know what I see. Johnny is a businessman and a

politician. Can't get much worse. He'll do anything to make money or get attention."

"So Johnny's going to retire, and Chief will run for Johnny's state Senate seat, against Mayor Perez?"

"Gonna be one hell of a battle with lots of money and mud. Just the way small town politics works in the panhandle."

A reporter with a *Press* placard stuck in the band of his fedora appeared from a storefront alcove. He walked backward in front of them and shoved a miniature recorder out. "Skipper Bradford, Noteworthy News. Any progress on finding the Madison Murderer? Suspects?"

Malcolm raised a hand. "Sorry, no questions other than at the briefing."

The reporter stopped in the middle of the sidewalk, forcing the two law enforcement officers to also stop. "Did you find more chalk markings this morning? What did they say?"

Malcolm took a deep breath. "The briefing starts in ten minutes," then shouldered past the reporter.

Once Jack caught up, Malcolm glanced back to ensure the reporter remained out of earshot. "Can you believe that guy wearing a fedora and the simple questions? Is he for real?"

"I guess he likes hats. Overheard him talking with Chief earlier. He's a crime blogger. Sounds like a new one, trying to get traction for his blog. Chief told him to talk to you."

"Just what I need, a wannabe reporter. Can you help me with something else?"

"What?"

"Why's Chief busting my balls? I'm gone once the

murders are solved."

Jack shrugged. "He don't like anyone who might show him up. He's part of the good old boy network. He has to look strong. All of them think their shit don't stink. Plus, he got the mayor riding his ass. She needs to look strong, too. Having citizens get shot in the head don't look good for either of them." Jack stared straight ahead. "I don't want to say no more. Don't want to bite the hand that feeds me and the family."

Malcolm liked Jack Palmer. The man spoke his mind and seemed to be able to reason things out.

They reached the city council building's rear door, and Malcolm pulled it open.

Chief stood in the small foyer. Jack turned sideways to slide by. Malcolm stopped.

Chief hooked thumbs in his belt. "What're you going to say?"

Malcolm straightened. "We found more chalk markings, portions of them are making sense, and there's enough residue we're checking for the manufacturer, distribution, and where the killer purchased it."

The police chief looked off with a blank stare. "And you think this is gonna cause the bastard to contact us?"

"You got any other ideas?"

Chief turned and disappeared through a door marked Staff Only.

****

5:59 p.m

AD carried a bowl of mac-n-cheese in one hand and kneaded the lower right quadrant of his abdomen with the other. The frequency, intensity, and duration of the pain suggested the cancer continued its quest of his liver. Two weeks ago, prior to putting his plan for eternal life into motion, he figured he had four, possibly six weeks of mobility left. Not much, but doable. With the pain's progress, he'd reduced his estimate to two to three weeks. He said a silent prayer he would remain strong enough to complete the crusade.

With a *squish* of air, he plopped into the recliner and snatched the TV remote off the end table. He perched the mac-n-cheese on a knee and stabbed the remote's buttons several times. FBI Special Agent in Charge Malcolm Gee standing at the podium appeared on the screen. AD leaned forward and counted the microphones. Nine more than yesterday, but a new one excited him more than the others. The name tag stated Central American News. His message would now be heard internationally. "Yes, God is truly good."

Pleased a foreign media representative had joined the ranks, AD straightened and looked at the crucifix that matched the one in his cabin. He offered a prayer to Jesus, asking for good news from the FBI agent. His letter should have arrived today, which would put the investigators on the right track to find out why those sacrificed had been chosen, to learn what sins they had committed.

Special Agent Gee pulled a sheet of paper from the inside pocket of his blue sport coat.

AD slid to the edge of his chair.

In a somber tone, Malcolm read, "Ladies and gentlemen, as you know, we had another shooting this morning."

AD's heel bounced. "Tell us about the letter."

"As with the other murders, the crime scene

investigators found an odd set of chalk markings where we believe the shooter stood when he fired the fatal shot."

AD threw the remote against the back of the couch. The bowl of mac-n-cheese clattered to the floor. "You're lying."

Gee continued, "Unlike the previous two crime scenes, we've secured enough of the chalk to send it to the FBI lab in Virginia. We're getting closer to this heinous villain. It's a matter of time. We advise residents of Madison and those who live in the local area to remain indoors between midnight and 7:00 a.m."

AD listened for another fifteen minutes, but there was no mention of the letter, only an increase to seventy-five thousand for the reward.

Surely the letter had arrived today. Maybe Taylor Dautry hadn't checked his mail. Or maybe his floozy secretary hadn't given it to him.

The thought of the chalk markings brought the heels of his hands to his eyes. "There weren't any markings. I checked. What's he talking about?" He massaged his temples with his fingertips. There couldn't be markings. He'd looked. There wasn't anything suitable to write on: no trees, no rocks, no buildings, just leafy bushes.

He'd had a tough two days, but the white bowl of oxy and black bowl of alprazolam sat within arm's reach. He chose one of each, popped them into his mouth, and washed them down with a gulp of wine. He raised the footrest, reclined, and closed his tired eyes. Tomorrow would be better. A smile curved his mouth at the thought of sacrificing Timothy Kurtz, and possibly another later that night. He drifted off, wondering if perhaps Chief Taylor Dautry and his hussy should be moved up the list.

Chapter 16

9:38 p.m.

Malcolm left the war room, paused on the sidewalk, and took a deep breath. His mind needed to rest. He'd studied the storyboards for hours, had spoken to every major stakeholder, and hadn't come up with a connection between the victims, who the murderer might be, or what drove him.

The scent of pizza reminded him of Valerie, his girlfriend, and their canceled date several nights earlier. He'd called her every day, sometimes twice, since being in Madison, but today he'd been busy and hadn't called her yet. Girlfriend? It sounded good, but would she agree with the term?

He missed spending time with her. She allowed him to be himself. She didn't seem to mind his analytical and inquisitive nature. She liked going places where she could do things. He on the other hand preferred to sit and watch. He considered her a life participant, while he considered himself a life voyeur. When they went to SeaWorld one Sunday afternoon, she absolutely delighted in feeding the sting rays, the seals, and the dolphins. She screamed like a kid when a dolphin splashed her. He preferred to stay back and watch her toss sardines to the animals. They went to the Strawberry Festival in Plant City where she spent almost an hour in the petting zoo while he stayed outside and watched. They had a strange relationship, but it worked for him. He hoped it worked for her, too.

He knew he passed Pete's Pizza Parlor to and from his hotel, so he decided to stop there for takeout. Then he'd go to the hotel and give Valerie a call.

The building looked like an old 7-Eleven someone converted into a pizza shop. Bright lights from inside illuminated the upfront parking spaces. A single car occupied the far left spot.

There weren't any customers seated at tables or the counter. However, he spotted a middle-aged couple behind the counter. The man bent over a large stainless-steel sink washing something. The woman presided over an army of glass salt and pepper shakers, lids off. She held a miniature funnel in one hand and a cylindrical box of salt in the other.

When he pulled the door open, the sweet aroma of pizza, oregano, and cheese greeted him. If the pizza tasted as good as it smelled, he'd be in for a treat.

The woman looked up and smiled. "Just in time, we close at ten." She set the funnel down and moved to the computer screen. Her name tag proclaimed NANCY in handwritten letters. The man wiped his hands on a towel and slid over to what looked like the pizza-making station. His name tag stated PETE.

Malcolm eyed the overhead menu a few seconds then said, "I'd like a medium meat lover's pizza, add onion and anchovy. To go, please."

Pete grabbed a dough ball from the refrigerator and threw it onto a butcher block board with a *thud* and *splat*. The woman tapped on her computer screen, then pulled a small white slip from the printer and placed it in front of Pete.

Malcolm sat at the counter and watched the man roll out the dough with an old-fashioned wooden rolling pin. After a few swipes, he thrust the flattened dough in the air, spinning it at the same time.

It soared almost to the ceiling and then descended into Pete's hands.

Malcolm pointed at smudge marks on the ceiling directly above Pete. "Looks like you were exuberant a couple of times."

"That happens when I'm pressured, like when we have a lot of orders. I don't do pressure very well. That's when I make mistakes."

Malcolm straightened. Of course. Ramp up the pressure on the murderer. Make him make a mistake.

Pete continued work on the pizza dough. He deftly laid the now-formed pizza shell on the floured tabletop. His hands blurred when he added the pepperoni, sausage, ground meat, bacon bits, and ham slices. "Do you like a lot of onion or just a little?"

"I'm going to an empty hotel room, so pile on the onion and anchovies."

Nancy looked up from filling saltshakers. "You know, that's a hefty pizza. Shame you don't have anyone to share it with."

"I'd like to share it with Valerie, my girlfriend, but she's in Orlando. She's a great gal. Not sure why she spends time with me, but I sure am thankful she does."

The salt box in Nancy's hand hovered over the funnel. "Aw, that's so nice of you to say. Despite being FBI, you got a good heart."

"How did you know I'm FBI?"

She chuckled. "I saw you on TV."

Pete asked, "You going to get him soon?"

Malcolm nodded. "That's the plan. We're getting closer. It won't be long." He hated to lie to such nice folks, but he couldn't tell them he was at a loss as to what to try next.

"Sounds like the pressure's on. Glad it's not me. I'd be a stumbling, bumbling fool."

Pete's remark reinforced Malcolm's thought that more pressure, new pressure points, needed to be applied to put the murderer on the defensive. He just needed to figure out more ways to ramp up the pressure. He turned around and stared toward the parking lot.

Before he realized it, Pete had opened the oven door and used the spatula paddle to lift his pizza out of the oven and then slide it into an open box. Four whacks with a cutter, and Nancy flipped the lid closed to reveal "Pete's Pizza and Pasta—Best Pizza in Madison" on top. She taped three sides and set it on the counter.

Malcolm reached for his wallet.

Nancy raised her hand like a crossing guard stopping traffic. "No charge. You're doing all of us a big favor by being here, away from your girlfriend, trying to return our city to the way we like it. You call Valerie, and remember to tell all your FBI friends we got the best pizza in town."

He thanked them, wished them continued success, and assured them he'd spread the word about what a great place they had.

He carried the hot-bottomed pizza box to his car. He sat the pizza box on the seat next to him. Valerie and Dallas nagged at his mind. Should he mention the transfer when they spoke tonight, or keep it to himself until he returned from Madison and could talk to her face to face?

What if she was *the one*? After Patrice, he swore he'd never get close to anyone again. His training stressed that he be cautious of people. His past history warned him to be concerned for the well-being of those he was close to. He didn't want to repeat history. His investment advisor always told him, *Past history of this product is not indicative of what will happen going forward.* Could that same philosophy be applied in the case of Valerie?

With the pizza box secure on the passenger seat, Malcolm started the car and pulled to the street, prepared to make a right toward his hotel. A pickup passed headed toward downtown. Malcolm's headlights illuminated Jack Palmer driving.

Why would Jack be out at that hour instead of home with his family?

Jack's truck pulled into a parking space at the police station. The lights went out, and Jack exited. Instead of going into the station, he crossed the street toward the war room.

Malcolm rubbed his jaw and decided to make a left instead of right toward his hotel. He drove to the police station and parked next to Jack's truck. Malcolm looked in his rearview mirror and saw the lights go on in the bullpen and storyboard section of the war room, one row at a time.

Malcolm exited his car and approached the war room. Light from the top of the windows dimly illuminated the sidewalk. An obscure FBI edict stated natural light needed to be allowed into FBI facilities to foster creativity, productivity, and a feeling of oneness with nature. It all sounded like a bunch of BS to Malcolm, but he didn't have a choice. The facilities manager from the Jacksonville regional office, who oversaw the makeover, ensured adherence to FBI policy. Malcolm mentally recited the old mantra, Mine is not to reason why, mine is to do or die.

He extended the magnetic card key toward the reader but paused. He hurried back to his car, retrieved the pizza, and returned.

Malcolm passed his card key over the reader. The door unlocked with a loud click, and he pulled it open. When he exited the small vestibule, he immediately spotted Jack at the same table they occupied that morning, drumming a pencil on the tabletop, looking at the storyboards.

"Hey, Jack, what are you doing here so late?"

Without turning around, Jack responded, "This whole mess really bothers me. Thought I'd come here and go over things again, see if I've missed something. See if any of the new information Danny added sparks a thought."

"Me, too. I hope you like pizza." Malcolm slid the box onto the table. "I'll get napkins, plates, and cups."

They ate in silence for several minutes, staring at the storyboards.

Jack slid another slice of pizza onto his plate. "You know, the only thing that would make this pizza better is a very cold beer."

Malcolm raised his paper cup of diet soda. Jack did likewise and they touched cups.

Jack looked at Malcolm. "Doesn't seem right without the clink."

"I learned in training that successful people do what they can with what they have. Whatever works." He smiled.

Jack cocked his head. "Why do you do this? Chase killers?"

Malcolm leaned back and sighed. "The easy answer would be someone needs to, so why not me? Truth be told, I took one of those personality tests in high school, and it said I should pursue a career in technology or law, where logic could be applied. I pride myself on being logical, analytical, even-keeled, so law enforcement seemed a logical choice."

"What about the death? Doesn't it bother you? It's tearing me apart."

Malcolm rubbed his forehead. "It bothers the hell out of me. It's the worst part of my job. Some days I question why I do this. Since I typically don't know the victims or the families, you would think I'd treat it as part of the job. But I don't. I have this sense, and you're going to think I'm crazy, but I have this sense that I speak for the murdered."

"How so?" Jack cocked his head to the side.

"Serial killers really piss me off. They normally don't know their victims, but yet they wantonly take another human's life. It's not like the victim can tell you who did what, like a shopkeeper who was robbed or a wife who was battered. They can describe the bad guy. A serial killer's victims are dead; they can't tell investigators shit. They're silent, voiceless. They need someone to represent them. So, I take it upon myself to avenge the voiceless. Am I making sense?"

Jack nodded.

"It's like this. I have a talent that allows me to

stack the building blocks to figure out who the bastard is and track him down. It's the best feeling in the world to know I stopped some sick, demented motherfucker from killing innocent people. In all honesty, I don't give a rat's ass if they die during capture, or if they spend the rest of their life in jail. All I care about is stopping them from murdering more people.

"So, to answer your question, hell yes, it bothers me. That's why I do what I do."

Jack pinched his nose between the eyes then looked at Malcolm. "There's more to you than meets the eye. I'm glad we're on the same side." He extended a fist.

Malcolm touched his fist to Jack's. "Thanks. Do you understand what I mean when I say 'building blocks'?"

The detective shook his head back and forth.,

"Those are the building blocks." He pointed and swept his index finger left to right pointing at the storyboards. "What we need to solve these murders is right up there. If it's not there now, we need to keep adding to the boards until we know who the bastard is, then we figure out where he's at. From there, it's all tactical logistics."

Jack smiled and nodded. "It all makes sense. Thanks. Okay, so you're the expert. What's it going to take to figure out who this bastard is?"

"That's an excellent question. We have over one hundred people working on this. At least thirty are doing research. The FBI is very good at research. But looking into people's backgrounds, reviewing video, interviewing, and re-interviewing is time-consuming and isn't going to get it done this time. I believe we need to figure out ways to apply pressure to him, put him in situations he's not prepared for, and make him make a mistake. At the moment, other than increasing patrols and visibility, I don't know what to do. That's why I'm here." Malcolm turned to look at the boards.

"What have you done in past cases? How did you get the break you needed?"

He smiled. "What I'm doing now. I study the storyboards looking for commonalities, trying to connect dots, identify patterns, anticipate what the bad guy's going to do next."

Malcolm stood and walked to the Madison Murderer evidence storyboard. "Typically, criminals who do big things like this are either the brains or a laborer. In this case, it appears there's only one person involved, so that person is both. There's a great deal to be said for a one-person show, particularly if the criminal is more brains than brawn. No one to argue with you, secrecy is absolute, command is simple. On the other hand, the brains person typically isn't good at the physical things needed to be carried out. For instance, maybe they don't know how to pick locks, apply makeup for a disguise, or aren't willing to torture, and the list goes on. You with me?"

Jack nodded.

"It actually plays to our benefit when it's a one-man show and that person fits the brains aspect of the equation. He'll eventually get into a situation he's uncomfortable with, or isn't experienced enough to handle, or doesn't know how to do something."

Jack raised a finger. "So, what you're saying is this guy hasn't encountered anything unfamiliar yet. We need to wait for a mistake."

"You're right but wrong. This guy has done his homework and created a plan that utilizes the skills and knowledge he has. The crime scenes haven't revealed anything of value except the shell casings, and we're confident those were deliberately left there for us to find. But we're not sure why he left them. Otherwise, we have nothing.

"Normally, in murder cases, the body yields the greatest number of clues and hence information. Unfortunately, in this case, we're dealing with long-range gunshots, so the killer is nowhere near the victim. But the second most prolific source of clues and information is the crime scene itself. In this case, we have two crime scenes, which we call victim crime scene and killer crime scene. The victim crime scene is the victim's location when he or she was murdered. The killer crime scene is where the murderer triggered the event, the shot, or the explosion, for instance. Unfortunately for us, the shooter is smart, picked his spots well, and cleaned up after himself." He paused for a second. "Am I making sense?"

Jack, sitting on the edge of his chair, nodded.

"We've collected helpful information. At all three killer crime scene locations, we found matching shoe prints. Size eight and a half athletic shoe. Manufactured overseas, imported by Universal Sports Shoe, sold in every big box retailer in the country. We found the same tire tread near all three killer crime scenes. Once again, very generic, sold in every Walmart, Costco, tire wholesaler in the country. Either this guy is smart and knows he's likely to leave clues, or he's plain lucky. My guess is he's smart and planned it out."

"Agreed. But a minute ago you said I was right and

wrong, we needed to wait for him to make a mistake. Where am I wrong?"

Malcolm grinned and pointed at Jack. "You're listening and you're smart. I love it. Okay, here's where I disagree. We're not going to wait until he makes a mistake. We're going to put him in situations he didn't plan for; we're going to force him to do things he doesn't want to do, or know how to do."

"Aw, now I get it. That's why you dreamt up the bogus crap about chalk markings."

"Exactly. We need to find his pattern and disrupt it."

Jack massaged the back of his neck. After about thirty seconds, the detective threw his pencil against the wall. "Goddamnit, who would kill these people? They were all good, church-going folks. It doesn't make any sense. It really pisses me off."

Malcolm nodded. "It pisses me off, too. For people like you and me, it's in our nature to try to understand why and bring normalcy to a chaotic situation. That's what we do. It's our job to stop people when they go off the deep end."

Malcolm's cell phone vibrated a split second before it played the lyrics from "Walking On Sunshine." Without looking at the phone's display, he knew Valerie was calling. "Damn. I've gotten so wrapped up in all of this, I haven't called my girlfriend yet today. I need to step away and take this."

Malcolm plopped into a chair in a small cubicle. He poked the green phone icon and smiled. "Hello there."

"This voice sounds familiar, but I can't place it."

He tipped his head back and grinned when he heard

Valerie's voice. "I know. I haven't called. I'm sorry. I've been consumed with the murders, dealing with personalities, communications, press briefings…"

"I get it." He heard the smile in her voice.

They had talked about his job and how it occasionally would require him to leave Orlando to work a project. "I warned you this may happen."

"Yes, you did. I guess the first time is the toughest."

He enjoyed her company and wanted to spend much more time with her. Unfortunately, someone had gone off the deep end and decided to kill people in Madison. He rubbed his jaw. "I'm really sorry. Things are pretty tense. But enough about me. How was your day?"

"Busy. I went back and forth with a buyer to submit a strong offer on a house in Osteen we saw this morning. My listing presentation this afternoon went well. I think I'll get the listing. I just wrapped up some research and comps for another potential seller. Some time off sure sounds good."

Malcolm swallowed hard. "Guess I need to apologize again. There's no way I'll get back to Orlando this weekend. Sorry." He massaged his jaw again as he contemplated the possibility this might be strike three. His stomach tightened when she didn't respond. "Still there?"

"What if I came to Madison?"

He straightened. "Um…really? You'd come here?"

"I'd think about it." He heard the smile again.

Malcolm fist-pumped. "If Moses can't go to the mountain, then the mountain should go to Moses."

"I don't think that's quite what Francis Bacon

wrote about Mohammed, but I get your point. There's one condition."

"Name it."

"Your hotel allows pizza delivery, right?"

"Absolutely. And I know a place that makes a great meat lovers." He fist-pumped again.

"You men with your meat pizzas. Veggies are much healthier."

"I bet they can make a half and half."

"If I drive all the way to Madison, you better not say you're too busy to spend time with me."

He paused for a second. They had only been dating for a couple of months, but he didn't want to lie to her either. "Look, I have to be honest. This is my work, and it's not a regular eight-to-five job. The only promise I can make is I'll spend as much time as I possibly can with you. You're important to me, I enjoy your company, and I'm motivated."

"If I get there, I'm going to hold you to that."

Day Four—July 18th

Chapter 17

Friday, 4:55 a.m.

Malcolm rolled over and peered at the clock, 4:55. He'd woken at one thirty and hadn't been able to return to sleep. Twice he got up, checked emails, reviewed reports and forensic data, and remotely reviewed the storyboards, only to eventually sit and stare at the wall. Finally feeling drowsy, he returned to bed both times but couldn't fall asleep. His mind kept analyzing the murders, trying to view them from every possible angle, trying to think like the murderer. What did the murderer know that linked the victims? The little red light on the ceiling smoke detector didn't offer any answers. He massaged his face, concentrating on the jaw muscles.

Could someone be losing their life while he stared at the little red light? He threw off the sheet again and padded to the window.

The only happy thought he could muster in the past three hours involved Valerie and her visit this weekend. He could certainly use a break from the project, Chief being uncooperative, and the lack of progress. Maybe taking a break would allow his mind to reset and look at things from a different perspective. Unsure how much time he'd be able to spend with her, he planned to make every minute count.

He wandered to the desk, sat with a *whoof* from the

chair, and wiggled the mouse. When the laptop lit up, he connected to the Storyboard system and added a new board.

Madison Murderer—Questions?

1. Motivation for killing?

2. What criteria used to select victims?

3. Why hasn't murderer contacted us?

4. Why only strike between two a.m. and six a.m.?

5. What did the Hs mean? Would the next victim have HHHH?

He picked up the eight-by-ten color photographs of the shell casings from the desk corner. The brass shined, maybe even sparkled. It certainly didn't give the appearance of partaking in the murder of innocent people. What did the *H*s mean?

The sound of a barking dog, his boss's ringtone, interrupted his thoughts. It couldn't be good news at this hour of the morning.

"Hello, Roger."

"Did I send you to Madison to work, or be on vacation?"

Good old Roger, no-nonsense, direct, and to the point. "It's 5:00 a.m., Roger, what can I do for you?" he asked through clenched teeth.

"Find the murderer so frickin' Mayor what's-her-name will stop calling me. She's a royal pain in the ass. Now she's threatening to have the governor send in National Guard troops to protect her citizens. I don't need this shit."

"I'm working on it." Malcolm paced the room.

"For Christ's sake, three people in four days. What the hell's going on? You have forty agents doing interviews, checking backgrounds, reviewing video, and a shitload of other things. On top of that, you have another fifty support personnel working on research, fielding phone calls, checking and cross-checking all sorts of shit. But your sorry-ass reports sound like you don't have shit to go on. What the hell's going on?"

Malcolm spun on a heel at the window and paced toward the door. "Chief Dautry's not been the most helpful. He shoots down any idea requiring his department's involvement. I have a feeling he's holding something back, but I don't know what and certainly don't know why he would do that."

"For shit's sake, Agent. This isn't your first rodeo, and you've run into people like him before. Handle it. What the hell do you have? Anything?"

"Our knowns are pretty sparse. The best we have is a mixture of footprints with a size eight and a half being common at all three scenes, but I'm not ready to claim that's the killer. There's a broad assortment of tire tracks with four of them being truck tires common across the three scenes. This town is full of pickup trucks, so that doesn't help much right now. We also have three .30-06 shell casings with Hs on them. No fingerprints, no fibers, no hair, no blood, no trace of anything, nothing that would provide DNA. No witnesses. No motive. Nothing."

"Video show anything?"

"The nursing home had video surveillance of the parking lot, but all we got was the gun flash. It looked like the shooter wore a mask, or may be Black, and appears to be average height."

"What about the baiting with the chalk markings?"

Malcolm reached the door and turned for the window. "Nothing yet."

"If that's not working, find something else. I sure as hell don't need the governor calling. And I don't think you want the National Guard showing up. Get this fucking thing solved. I don't know if the station chief in Dallas will want you if this continues much longer. Find the motherfucker and end this." The phone went silent, the screen blank.

Malcolm tossed the phone on the bed. "Thanks for the encouragement, Roger."

The barking dog ringtone sounded again.

He grabbed the phone and stabbed the green phone icon. "Yes, Roger." He felt his face redden.

"It appears you've not accomplished anything except allow the body count to rise. I've made arrangements for Rachel Brock to be there at noon Saturday. Be ready for her." The phone went dead.

Malcolm glanced out the window. Being a foster child, he often found himself without anyone to talk with, so he developed the habit of speaking to himself when troubled. "Damn! Shit! Fuck! The vaunted Rachel Brock coming to town can't be good. And on Saturday while Valerie is here. That screws up the entire day. How am I supposed to continue building a relationship with her when I'm dealing with Rachel? Oh, and then he threatens me with not going to Dallas—that was pretty low. I worked hard and earned that damn promotion. Now he's holding it like a carrot in front of a jackass. The son-of-a-bitch said it himself; this isn't my first rodeo. I know what I'm doing, and I certainly don't need his threats. I already have enough to worry about."

He kicked the trash can next to the desk and scattered cardboard coffee cups across the floor. "To make it worse, he never said whether he got the goddamn subpoenas for the cell phone companies. That's critical evidence, and we're losing time. Maybe he's the one sitting around with his thumb up his ass. Maybe that's why he's such an asshole."

After picking up the kicked-over trash can, he entered the bathroom and turned on the shower. "Maybe we'll hear from the murderer today. Maybe hell will freeze over."

Chapter 18

8:00 a.m.

Malcolm wished he could whistle like so many other men, but that skill had escaped him so far in life. He clapped his hands twice to get everyone's attention.

The men and women in the bullpen quieted.

"Let's get the show on the road. We have a murderer to catch. Who followed up on the guy in a tent at Secret Lake Park?"

Charlie Wilcox, Madison PD sergeant, raised his hand and looked at Jack.

Jack nodded, "Go ahead."

"I'll make this brief. I found the guy sitting in a palmetto thicket taking pictures of bugs. He teaches about insects at some college in West Virginia and is doing research, complete with pictures. He let me search his campsite and car. No guns. Big guy, probably six two, at least two fifty. Sneakers are size thirteen. Nothing about the guy fits what we're looking for. His only weapon, other than a pocketknife, is two cans of pepper spray he plans to use if a bear or panther threatens him. Otherwise, he's harmless and clean."

"Thanks, Charlie." Malcolm turned and looked at Beverly. "I spoke with Roger this morning, no news on the subpoenas. I'll let you know as soon as I get word."

"For Christ's sake, it shouldn't take this long,"

Beverly said. "All I want is cell tower data for four hours prior to each murder and one hour after. How frickin' hard can it be?"

Jack asked, "Help me understand what data you're looking for and why four hours?"

"That'll tell us who was in the area, if they were stationary, or passing through like a mailman or garbage truck."

He nodded. "I get it. If they were passing through, then not much interest. But if they were stationary, it could mean they were scouting the victim, or possibly setting up an ambush."

"Ding, ding, ding. That man wins the large stuffed animal. Data from the cell towers are the power. Even when someone's not using their cell phone, the device is still registering a location. As long as a cell device is turned on, it'll latch on to the best signal it can get, not necessarily the closest tower. So we need data dumps from all of the local towers so we can parse through looking for someone who lingered."

"Why's a subpoena needed?"

She snickered and blew him a kiss. "Aren't you the innocent one. Cell companies don't easily give up that data. If their customers knew they turned over the data without a fight, their customers might not be happy. The companies make a judge weigh the value of catching a murderer and the public's privacy. Some judges are easier than others. I guess Judge Harrison was pretty supportive of law enforcement, but not all of them are. Some are just dickheads who want you to know they're so powerful."

Malcolm cleared his throat. "Thanks for the education, Beverly. Let's move on. Goose, anything from social media or the tip line?"

"Nothing worth talking about. There's a lot of people talking on social media, but no one has jumped out as a suspect. Mostly people sympathizing with the victim's families and the rabble-rousers who hate law enforcement. No one taunting. No one threatening. No one taking credit. The tip line? Things have slowed down, we only received fourteen calls yesterday. Madison PD ran three of them down, the others were people complaining they're scared to come out of their houses and want us to hurry up and catch the guy. It might be helpful if you remind people at this evening's press briefing to call in anything they see."

"Will do." Malcolm proceeded around the table. Each key stakeholder spoke about progress and high points of the investigation, but none of them had any suspects.

A glance at his watch showed 8:58, time to wrap things up. "Stay on it. We're going to get this guy sooner than later. See you tomorrow at eight."

One of the Madison PD sergeants spoke. "Tomorrow's Saturday."

Malcolm felt his face redden. "What's the point?"

The sergeant's eyes darted to other members of the PD. "Most of us have families, baseball, scouts, soccer, errands to run, family stuff to do. Is it necessary we meet?"

Malcolm tapped the side of his head as if thinking. "Is it necessary we meet?"

Jack opened his mouth as if to say something but closed it. He looked at the tabletop and slowly wagged his head.

After the ass-chewing he received from Roger

earlier, Malcolm wasn't in any frame of mind to condone this asshole's whining. People were dying, families were being torn apart, and he was worried about running errands. He must have been another of Chief's relatives. He leaned on the table and stared at the PD rep. "Really? Let me ask you this. Do you think the killer will take the day off?"

"Well, I don't know." He licked his lips, then frowned.

"I'm sorry to be so blunt, but tough shit! There's someone out there killing Madison residents, your neighbors. I don't know if he's going to take time off or not, but we're not. People are dying. It's our job to stop him, and we're going to do that with, or without you. If there are no other questions, meeting adjourned. Go find the sum-a-bitch."

****

Chief Dautry heard *tap-tap-tap* on his office door. Without looking, he knew who knocked. Only his stepson, Robert, was damn fool enough to knock on an open door. God only knew how his three daughters would turn out. They looked cute as angels, but he prayed they wouldn't be as slow as their father. Of course, Momma's elevator didn't run to the top floor either. She must have met Robert on one of the lower floors. No telling how both of them graduated from FSU on the same day. Certainly not one of his alma mater's better days.

When Chief looked up from the newspaper, open to the Gulfstream Downs racing results, Robert, still in the hall, raised a multi-page document between thumb and index finger. "Gee was pissed, and I got the forensics report on…"

"I don't give a shit about Gee. Don't be standing in the hall talking about something I told you to keep quiet about. Get in here and close the goddamned door."

Eyebrows raised, Robert stepped into the office, then closed the door. "No one in the hall, so we're safe." He sat on the edge of a chair and handed the evidence pouch and report to Chief. "Riley didn't find anything. No prints. No telltale marks. Nada. The envelope and paper can be bought at any big box retailer. Mailed from Tallahassee at the main post office on West Park yesterday."

"Did you check the security footage at the post office to see if someone from Madison visited there?" He cocked his head.

"Thousands of people go in and out of there every day for all kinds of stuff."

"I didn't ask how many people went into the God-damned post office. I asked if you pulled their surveillance video and looked for Madison people."

"But Madison has over five thousand residents. Antler County has over twenty thousand. I don't know them all; I might miss someone."

"You didn't even try?"

"No." Robert's shoulders slouched, and he hung his head.

Chief didn't give a rat's ass if he'd hurt the boy's feelings. Besides, the kid needed to grow a set. "Look, I got the mayor raggin' my ass. She's threatening to call the governor, who's threatening to send in the National Guard. Three citizens are dead, and you're telling me about thousands of people going into the friggin' post office. I don't want excuses, I want information." He slammed the desk with an open hand.

Robert jumped. "I'm sure they have cameras there, but I got no idea what to look for, but I bet the FBI—"

"I don't give a shit what you think about the FBI. I told you this needs to stay with us Madison boys. Give me the frickin' evidence pouch and report. Now, go get their security video and tell me when you got it. Understand?"

"Yes, sir." Robert stood, opened the door, and looked back at Chief. He opened his mouth as if to say something but shrugged and exited.

Chief thought his stepson rolled his eyes but didn't want to pursue it. If he were connected by blood, Chief would have backhanded the idiot, but his momma protected him. God only knew what would happen to the boy when Chief won the state Senate seat and resigned as chief. He hoped to be there when Mayor Brenda Watson found out she'd be running against Chief. The look on her face would be priceless. The election would be a landslide in his favor. He already had plans for the extra money he'd be making from those appreciative of his position and influence. The Madison residents could only afford so much, but he'd have a much larger pool to draw on once he joined the state legislature.

That stupid bitch mayor would probably have Robert fired, but it wouldn't matter one bit to him. His stepson didn't deserve the job. He couldn't do it and didn't have any chance of ever being able to do it. She'd probably do the city a favor firing his ass. Save the city a bunch of money and maybe get someone in that position who could actually do something.

He needed to figure out how to use the letter to his advantage. He leaned back and stared at a dark spot on the ceiling. He needed to look in charge and make it appear the FBI took direction from him. Within a couple of minutes, a plan took shape. It would piss off the FBI man, but he didn't care, he needed to look strong. This whole thing could work to his advantage come next election. It felt good to be Chief.

Chapter 19

5:48 p.m.

Despite hurrying along Madison Avenue to attend the six p.m. media update, Malcolm couldn't help but notice the flower boxes dotting the sidewalk. They contained wilted, drooping flowers. Even the couple of grass patches around tree trunks appeared scorched after a full day of the sun's heat. Their fresh appearance that morning had vanished as the day progressed, much like his own energy and attitude. The pressure of things not going well made him feel agitated, tense, and on the defensive. Everyone expected him to stop the murder of innocent people, but he didn't have anything to work with. He needed a break.

His attitude got worse when he noticed the fedora-wearing reporter leaning against the squat blue mailbox in front of Rutherford's Drug Store. The reporter held a rolled-up sheet of paper in one hand and the ever-present miniature tape recorder in the other.

Malcolm thought about crossing the street, pretending to go to Gram's Kitchen, but suspected the reporter would know the press conference started shortly, so he didn't have time to waste. He'd march forward and try to ignore the locust.

When he got within ten feet, the reporter thumbed the side of the recorder and pointed it toward Malcolm.

"Special Agent Gee, any news on a suspect?"

"What's your name?"

"Same as yesterday. Skipper Bradford with Noteworthy News."

Malcolm recalled Jack saying the locust was a wannabe crime blogger and wore the fedora to attract attention. In an odd way, it made sense. The more people who recognized the blogger, the more people would probably subscribe to the blog. If that was his schtick, then so be it, but it really didn't matter; he didn't have time to verbally dance with this guy. "Come to the press conference and you'll hear what I have to say." He stepped to the right.

The reporter stepped to his left and blocked the way. "What are you doing to find the Madison Murderer?"

"Once again, you'll have to attend the press conference. Speaking of which, I need to get there, so please excuse me."

Malcolm stepped to the left.

The reporter thrust out the scroll. "What are your thoughts about this letter from the murderer?"

Malcolm brushed aside the paper and attempted to walk, but the reporter blocked his path.

"The letter says there aren't any chalk markings. Is that true? And the murderer talked about sinners and shell casings. What's special about the casings?"

Malcolm stopped and stared at the reporter for several seconds, unsure what to say. Either someone with inside knowledge of the case leaked confidential information about the shell casings and chalk markings, or the murderer actually did write it. He didn't like either option.

Malcolm grabbed the paper. A quick scan confirmed that whoever penned it knew pertinent facts. His stomach flip-flopped, and he felt trapped. Who in the hell leaked this information? Despite his insides being in turmoil, he smiled. "Clever attempt to get information, but you obviously have no idea what you're talking about." He continued his walk toward the city council chambers, but slower.

Skipper scurried to fall into pace. "The letter accused the victims of being sinners. Do you suspect a religious zealot is responsible? Have you found out what sins they committed?"

Malcolm stopped and faced the reporter. "That's one of the oldest tricks in the book. You, or someone in your organization, wrote it trying to get information from me. Come to the press conference, and you'll hear what everyone else will hear."

"Nice try, Special Agent. We both know the murderer wrote it. He's the only one, besides law enforcement, who would have all the information."

Let's turn the tables, see if I can get some information from the reporter. "If the murderer wrote it, why would he give it to you?"

"I got it from someone inside the police department. They said it came in yesterday's mail."

Damn, that sure is discouraging news. Malcolm looked the reporter in the eye. Skipper didn't blink. "Look, pal, if you don't have anything of value to say, then get out of my way."

"It's going to be asked about at the press conference."

Malcolm continued his march. His mind whirled like a carnival ride. He remembered Jack saying he had overheard Skipper talking with Chief yesterday. If someone in the investigation had a letter from the murderer, why didn't he know about it? Who would withhold this kind of information from him and why? What else might they be withholding? If the letter really arrived yesterday, then someone wanted to make him look bad.

The same name kept coming up, and he didn't like it. The rear door to the city council chambers hit the wall with a thud, courtesy of FBI Special Agent Malcolm Gee. "Where's Chief?" he barked at Detective Robert LeBeau.

"Said he had something to do, and you should go ahead without him." Robert shrugged.

"What the hell's he doing?" Malcolm knew he stood a little closer to Robert than he should but didn't care. "Call him, I want to know."

"You call him." Robert nodded with a half smile. "But Chief is Chief. Maybe he'll answer, maybe he won't. Chief does what Chief wants." Robert backed against the wall.

Malcolm snatched his cell phone out of a pants pocket, but before he could do anything, the phone vibrated and the lyrics of "Walking On Sunshine" played. He paused to let it roll to voice mail but after the fourth ring stabbed the green talk button and forced a smile. "Hi there."

"Are you busy?" It sounded like she purred the question.

He turned to the wall. "I'm about to go into a press conference. Do you have something quick?"

Robert slid out the door without saying anything.

"I wanted to tell you I'm in Madison. Actually, I'm

in your hotel room."

His heart skipped a beat. "Really?" He glanced at his watch. "It'll be a couple hours before I get there."

She giggled. "Are you in position to FaceTime?" She giggled again.

The city's public relations officer tapped Malcolm on the shoulder and held up two fingers.

The FBI man gave a thumbs-up, licked his lips, and glanced around. "That wouldn't be good right now."

"That's a shame. I think you'd enjoy it."

"It'll have to wait." He took a deep breath to avoid saying things that might be overheard.

Silence reigned for several seconds.

"Malcolm, why's there Roman numerals scratched on the bullets?"

"What are you talking about?" He leaned against the wall and closed his eyes.

"The pictures of the bullets on this desk show Roman numeral one, then two, then three. Is that how you keep track of which bullet is which?"

He felt like someone had punched him in the gut. Roman numerals. Why hadn't he, or anyone else, thought about that? "Those are pictures of evidence no one knows about. Please put those down and don't say another word about them."

"I'm bored. You better get here soon." He heard the pout in her voice.

"Make yourself comfortable. I'll get there as soon as I can."

"I have. You should come and get comfortable, too." She purred again.

"I promise, just as soon as I can. Gotta go. Bye." He poked the red end button and kicked the bottom of the wall. How did he miss it? Turn the shell casings ninety degrees and what everyone thought looked like H's were actually Roman numerals. "Damnit!" But what did they mean? Time's up. He had a press conference to run and needed to be ready for Skipper Bradford to ask about the friggin' letter.

****

Malcolm walked out the front door of the city council building. Three steps brought him to twin podiums with an array of microphones jutting at him like porcupine quills. He scanned the line of cameras pointed at him. He doubted he'd ever stood in front of this many cameras before. Had to be at least thirty, and that didn't count the photographers who sat cross-legged on the concrete plaza.

He scanned those assembled but didn't see the fedora. That didn't mean the locust wasn't lurking somewhere. With a little luck, maybe he had dissuaded Skipper. He could only hope.

The sooner the briefing started, the sooner he'd be able to see Valerie. Malcolm extracted a sheet of paper from his sport coat pocket, unfolded it, and smoothed it with deliberation. He didn't need it but wanted a moment to compose himself. His mind still swirled about the supposed letter and Chief Dautry being absent without notification. He remembered an FBI instructor saying, "There's no such thing as coincidences."

****

AD leaned forward, elbows on knees, and peered at the TV. He tried to count the microphones but couldn't see all of them. He smiled. The unwitting media appeared to be helping him get the message out—Don't mess with God.

Was the FBI man holding his letter? What else could it be? He rubbed his hands together in anticipation of what would be said.

****

After a deep breath, Malcolm looked at the assembled media. "Ladies and gentlemen. Thank you for attending. I'll keep this brief, then open the floor for a few questions." Time to sling some BS and misinformation.

"First, I'd like to thank everyone for the tips and information they've shared. Several have provided information that's proven to be very useful. In fact, before I came out here, I received news of an evidence breakthrough. I'm not able to divulge it currently, but it's a significant revelation. We're getting closer."

"If you see something, say something. Please be particularly vigilant from midnight until sunrise. If you don't have to be out, don't go out. If you're out and can wait until sunrise, stay where you are, stay safe. If you see something, or suspect something, or overhear something, but aren't sure if it's worth reporting, report it. Let the professionals decide its value."

****

AD chuckled. They'd never see him and know he was the Madison Murderer. No one who knew him would ever suspect such a thing.

If they knew his plan for tonight, they'd realize how much they didn't know. He lifted his goblet of red wine in a mock toast and took a big gulp.

He looked at the crucifix on the wall, made the sign of the cross, closed his eyes, and uttered a prayer asking God to allow him to fulfill his destiny, to give him the strength and days necessary to glorify the loving and benevolent Almighty. He'd completed three offerings. Only nine more, with two planned for tonight. "In your name, I pray these things, sweet Jesus. Amen."

****

Malcolm pointed to a tall, thin, bald reporter wearing a tan polo shirt.

"Richard Head with WCTV. Chief Dautry's not here. Have you taken the lead and sent him packing?"

"Chief and the entire Madison PD are integral to this investigation. They bring a wealth of local knowledge. They continue to contribute to our eventual success."

Malcolm looked left and pointed to a female reporter in heels and dark-blue business suit with white blouse. She nudged the cameraman next to her and pushed a string of blonde hair behind an ear. The squat cameraman spun around, dropped to a knee, and flashed fingers, three, two, one.

She smiled. "Dorothy Abrams, America's News Network. Has anyone looked into a possible connection with local vampire cults or worshippers? With your warning about being vigilant between midnight and dawn, it seems this would be prime hunting hours for vampires."

Where did the network get her? Vampires? Is she serious? People are being shot, not having their blood sucked out. Vampires? Let's move on to someone more reasonable. "All options are being explored."

Malcolm scanned to the right edge of the crowd. Skipper Bradford leaned against a lamppost, arms crossed, seemingly watching without any intention of becoming involved in the Q & A. Perhaps he'd gotten upset over nothing.

A hand rose toward the center of the group. Malcolm pointed and nodded.

"William Hillard, I live over on Prescott Lane, have for over forty years. Ronnie Scott was my nephew. I'm pretty damn pissed you ain't found the bastard doing all this killing. I don't think you're being honest with us. I saw on the internet a letter that the killer sent to the po-leese. I don't want no BS. Is that letter real? Yes or no?"

A silence settled over the crowd. Several cameras shifted their attention from Malcolm to William.

Malcolm had prepared for reporters, not family. "I have not seen any such letter on the internet." Malcolm immediately pointed to a reporter in the front row.

"Have you had any communication with the murderer?"

"No." He lifted his paper off the podium. "Thanks, folks. Remember, if you see something, say something."

He spun around, trotted up the steps, and entered the city council building. He exited the rear door, out of sight of the assembled crowd, and hurried to his car. He'd track down Chief later. He needed to get away from the bullshit for little, clear his mind. With a little luck, he'd be in Valerie's arms within fifteen minutes.

****

AD slapped his knee. "Halleluiah. Someone finally mentioned the letter." He selected an oxy from the white ramekin and a pink alprazolam from the black bowl. Tossing them in the air, they settled into his mouth like popcorn did in his childhood. A swig of wine washed them down. "Ah, that feels good already." A pull of the chair's lever raised the footrest, and he reclined. "Time to rest. I have the Lord's work to do tonight."

Day Five—July 19th

Chapter 20

Saturday, 1:52 a.m.

Lack of moonlight made AD's navigation through Oak Ridge Memorial Garden difficult. He carried Beautiful Betsy's case in one gloved hand and often used the other hand to steady himself on a tombstone.

Since leaving his blue pickup under oak trees almost a mile away, his head and eyes moved back and forth, like a radar dish, looking for movement or anything out of the ordinary. He didn't expect to encounter anyone crazy enough to wander around a cemetery at this hour, but vigilance had to be maintained. Discovery would almost certainly jeopardize earning eternal life in heaven.

The cool nighttime air made the trek across the cemetery more bearable than the previous attempt. His path required a diagonal cut across the cemetery's grid. Across a column, down a row, across a column, down a row.

Halfway to the western fence, his ear caught the noise many of the younger generation called music. It undoubtedly came from the Rock Bottom Bar, where Timothy Kurtz and his band played. Circumstances had kept him from offering Timothy two nights ago, but, God willing, this time would be different. He smiled at the thought.

Positioned at the chain-link fence once again, AD dropped to a knee. He released the silver snaps of the black leather case, each with a soft click. A lift of the lid revealed Beautiful Betsy, ready to do her job: kill. The band's noise would end soon, and about ten minutes later, its members would exit the bar's rear door. Another scan of the area didn't reveal anything unexpected. He used a thumb to slide the ski mask slightly above the eyes. The cool air felt good. A drop of sweat into an eye at the wrong moment could cause unnecessary complications.

AD allowed himself to settle back, legs crossed lotus style. He had instructed a young person once to sit Indian style, but a mother wagged her finger at him and said, "Indian style is demeaning; you should say lotus position or crisscross apple sauce. Please be correct."

Off to the left, near the cemetery's southern fence, he noticed the silhouette of the backhoe used to dig graves. Its extended arm probably protected an open grave.

Thoughts of Ronald Scott came to mind. The man who sinned against God would be interred later that morning in this same cemetery. Of course, AD would be in attendance. If Scott's pregnant wife knew her husband had sex with other men during his softball weekends away, she'd be humiliated. It was disgraceful for a good Catholic girl like her to have a husband, soon-to-be father, lying with other men. The shame that poor woman would feel when her husband's sins became known. Some of her friends and family might ridicule her and say she couldn't keep her husband satisfied, so he went looking for men. Leviticus 18:22 said, "Thou shalt not lie with mankind, as with womankind: it is an abomination."

What was the politically correct word for her husband? Gay? Faggot, queer, or homo better suited Scott, but those words weren't permitted any longer.

A few days from now, Judge Harrison would also be buried here, and AD would again be in attendance, hiding in plain sight. Sacrificing the judge wouldn't undo any of the bad things he'd done, but it would certainly prevent him from continuing to wrong the innocent. Deuteronomy 10:17-18 stated, "For the Lord, your God, is the God of gods, the Lord of lords, the great God, mighty and awesome, who has no favorites and accepts no bribes, who executes justice for the orphan and the widow." Judge Harrison gained wealth to the detriment of the innocent. Money was more important than the lives he ruined with his sentences, or sometimes, lack of sentences. God would certainly punish him in proportion to the crimes he committed.

The music stopped; the night became still. Time to prepare for the fourth offering. It took most of his forty-six years of life to realize it, but his destiny required he rid the earth of unsavory, sinful individuals and give God another reason to smile. AD's reward would be eternal life, free of cancer, free of pain, free of dealing with the brown-nosers and hypocrites he encountered all day, every day. But he couldn't expend any further thoughts of them. In a few minutes, he'd smite another sinner.

He repeated the steps from several nights ago: insert Betsy's barrel through a diamond-shaped opening in the chain link. A quick twist removed the caps protecting the scope. He rose on one knee, hunched over the rifle, and inhaled the beautiful scent of the wooden stock's polish. With bare cheek and chin on the rifle's stock, he peered through the scope. With practiced care and a couple of twists of the scope's adjustment knobs, the bar's rear-door handle came into focus.

AD remained patient even though his legs and back ached from the crouched shooting position. His current discomfort had to be minuscule compared to the pain Christ felt during the scourging and brutality of his final hours. He asked Jesus for the strength to persevere.

Without warning the Rock Bottom's rear door flew open and half a dozen people spilled out, but no Timothy Kurtz. AD's stomach tightened. He wiped his eyes and peered through the scope at each of the six young men standing next to, and behind, the van. They milled around.

After what seemed like an hour, but surely only twenty-five or thirty seconds, Timothy Kurtz appeared and weaved his way to the van. With key in hand, the young man stabbed twice at the keyhole on the driver's door but missed both times.

The kid with severe acne pushed Timothy aside. "Give me the fucking key, you fucking clown. You're so fucking high, there's no fucking way I'm letting you drive."

Timothy straightened and leaned precariously. He'd probably have fallen over if not for propping a hand on the van's fender. "Fuck you, asshole. You're jealous 'cause you didn't get any of Andy's stuff. You shouldn't be so fucking cheap, you fucking asshole." Timothy swiped a hand across his mouth. "Here." He shoved the key toward acne-face. "I'll go home with Andy. Don't hurt my dad's van or he'll kill me. I feel too good to die." He burped, then giggled.

Acne-face unlocked the van and popped the locks. The other five piled in.

Maintaining the crosshairs on Timothy's nose proved to be a challenge. The kid swayed like he stood on a boat in moderate waves. First this way, then that. He extended a hand to the wall, which settled his movement. He flipped off the van as it rounded the building's corner.

AD took a deep breath, held it, and squeezed the trigger.

Timothy Kurtz's head snapped back, then he fell backward, just like in the movies, except no one caught him before he hit the ground.

A quick check through the scope revealed Timothy no longer had a face. AD knew the forensics people would work for hours gathering bits and pieces of the kid's face and brain matter splattered against the building's wall, garbage dumpster, and parking lot.

AD paused a few seconds and reflected on Matthew 10, Verse 7. "As you go, preach this message: The kingdom of heaven is at hand." Yes, indeed, with each offering the kingdom of heaven came nearer for him.

He smiled, took a deep breath, and let a sigh escape. Another successful offering. Four down, eight to go.

He pulled the rifle's barrel back through the diamond aperture, careful not to scratch the weapon he'd owned since the age of twelve. His dad, God rest his soul, would be proud of the marksman his son had become. Soon, he expected to see his father and mother in heaven.

With well-practiced movements, he ejected the spent shell casing and caught it midair. His gloved thumb and index finger set the casing, upright, next to the fence where it certainly would be found.

He sensed, more than saw or heard, something behind him.

"Did you just shoot that man?"

AD recognized the voice and couldn't breathe.

Chapter 21

7:06 a.m.

Malcolm sat on the bench across the street from Gram's Kitchen. The tinkle of the bell alerted him every time someone opened the door, coming or going.

The majority of the patrons looked to be middle-aged and older. He recognized a couple of Madison shop owners. Probably stopping for breakfast and to hear the latest town gossip before opening their businesses.

The aroma of bacon made him want to enter and order breakfast, but he needed to maintain watch for Madison Police Chief Taylor Dautry. Six unanswered, unreturned phone calls the last ninety minutes took Malcolm to the limit of his patience. His teeth hurt from the constant clenching they had endured for over an hour.

It seemed unlike Chief to not stop at Gram's for at least his usual large coffee, triple sugar, no cream. When he dined in, the servers knew to rustle up a bowl of biscuits and gravy, three eggs over easy, four bacon, and hash browns. But so far no Chief.

Malcolm checked his watch—7:11. He massaged his jaw. He'd give it another twenty minutes then march to Police HQ and search for the big man.

Malcolm didn't see Skipper Bradford until the

reporter sat on the bench next to him.

Skipper tipped his fedora. "Waiting for Chief?"

"Maybe."

"He'll be along in a few minutes. Had to go home, get cleaned up, and dressed for Scott's funeral this morning."

Malcolm had forgotten about the funeral. "How do you know Chief's schedule this morning?"

"I saw him at Rock Bottom earlier this morning. I didn't see you there."

"What's Rock Bottom, and why would I be there?"

"Rock Bottom's a grunge bar near the college. It's where the Madison Murderer killed Timothy Kurtz a little after two this morning. I thought the FBI would be anxious to do their investigation thing. I know your girlfriend is in town, but I thought at least one of your people would have gone to the scene."

Malcolm closed his eyes. "How did you find out?"

Skipper placed his recorder on the bench between them. "Based on your red face, it appears you and Chief aren't on the same page."

"We're fine."

"Seems like there's a communications rift between the two of you. Care to comment?"

"I can't comment on something that doesn't exist, but I still want to know how you found out about the murder."

"Maybe Chief will comment." Skipper nodded past Malcolm down the street. "Here he comes."

Malcolm swung around and spotted Chief passing Daisy's Flower Shop. He had never seen him in a dress uniform before: jacket, long-sleeved white shirt, dark blue tie, shiny badge above his left breast pocket, embroidered patch on sleeve, dark-blue slacks with a red vertical stripe on the side, and polished black shoes. Except for the pot belly and graying hair, he could be featured on a recruiting poster.

Special Agent Gee took a deep breath and held it for a couple of seconds. Being in public he needed to stay calm. A confrontation between the local police chief and the lead FBI agent would certainly hit the news in a very negative and ugly fashion, especially with Skipper the Locust nearby. Malcolm rose and moved to the center of the sidewalk in front of the State Farm Insurance agency, arms crossed.

Twenty paces away they locked eyes. Chief slowed for a second, then continued his march forward. Two paces away he said, "You're lookin' chipper this morning like all the stress has left you."

Malcolm wouldn't be distracted. "Why wasn't I informed about a letter from the killer?"

"The detective didn't want to bother the"—Chief's index finger tapped Malcolm's chest with each letter— "F, B, I. Besides, our forensics guy is right here to check for prints and stuff. I'm sure it only took a couple of minutes to get it to Riley. I agree with his reasons. I figured once the forensics report came back, we'd look at things together, like a team." He hooked his thumbs into his belt.

"Riley? According to Detective LeBeau, he's what, a cousin on your wife's side?"

"I told you before, I take care of mine, and mine take care of me. Riley's a fine young man, local Madison boy, well-educated. There's nothing wrong with him or what he does."

"According to my team, Riley can check for prints

but doesn't have the ability to check for DNA. He has to send it to Tallahassee, and it'll wait in line. We have the means to do a preliminary check in the war room, and the rest will be expedited in Jacksonville."

"DNA is no big deal if the guy's not in the computers anywhere." Chief donned an I-gotcha grin.

Malcolm wagged his head. "DNA doesn't have to be in a database. We can get all sorts of information from DNA. We can determine eye color and racial makeup, and at the very least we'll be able to reverse the mitochondria and search for family members as well. All of this is critical evidence, could be used to find the killer, and stop the murders. We can do all the tests we need within two blocks of here. It doesn't have to go to Tallahassee. Do you realize you've delayed the analysis?"

"I ain't delayed nothin'. I tried to get things checked real quick."

Malcolm felt his face redden. "Did you know we can match our combined DNA index to international profiles through Interpol, Mossad, New Scotland Yard, and over a dozen other similar entities?"

"What's that got to do with my citizens getting killed?"

"It's simple." Malcolm knew he was talking louder than he should, but he didn't care. "We don't know who the killer is, maybe he's in some database somewhere. So, why not check? Any information we can get on him, like a name, or nationality, could prove to be useful. Why not turn over all the rocks to see what's under them?"

Chief waived a dismissive hand. "The only rocks are in your head if you think some international bad guy would come to Madison, Florida, and kill our citizens. You go ahead and look under rocks. I'll do my own thing, and we'll see who finds and cuffs him first. Go to Riley and get the goddamned letter and wave your damn magic wand. See what you get."

Malcolm threw his hands in the air. "I'll do that. Even a copy of the letter might have helped some. At least my linguistics people could dissect the words, phrases, sentence structure, and a ton of other things to help the profilers. That letter's important, and it should have been shared. People could die because of your stonewalling."

"Don't you try and lay that shit on me. You're the high and mighty leader of all these F, B, I people. But no one could find you after the press conference. You disappeared. Poof. Someone even called your boss trying to find you, but he didn't know where you were either." Chief threw his hands in the air like a magician.

"You called Roger instead of me?" Malcolm waved his phone.

"I don't know why they didn't call you. I'll make sure I tell them the next time. By the way, my forensics guy didn't find anything, so I'm sure if you send one of your guys over, he'll give you the letter as soon as he gets in this morning. Oh, I think he's teaching a class this morning, so it might be a while."

Chief stepped to the right. Malcolm stepped left.

Malcolm raised on his toes, but still fell several inches short of being eye-to-eye with his nemesis. "Not so fast. Why wasn't I informed about this morning's murder?"

Chief, hands behind his back, rocked back and forth and leered. "I sent an officer to your hotel a little after three this morning, but he said it sounded like you and your girlfriend were involved and he wasn't sure about interrupting. I told him not to bother. You could visit the scene during daylight, and I'm sure you'll get LeBeau's report."

Malcolm waved his cell phone. "Someone could have called."

"I told you. I'll suggest that next time. You'll get copies of the photos and crime scene data, but you're welcome to visit the scene if you want."

"You're sure the same guy did it?"

"Yep."

"Why?"

"They found two shell casings but only one body and he was only hit once."

Malcolm held up two fingers. "Two casings?"

Chief nodded once and looked down his nose.

"Etchings on both?"

Chief nodded once. "Thanks to Robert keeping me informed, I knowed they were Roman numbers four and five. Now, if you don't mind, I'm hungry and have a very busy morning."

"Okay." Malcolm took a deep breath and blew it out through pursed lips. He looked up into Chief's eyes. "We're not working very well together. You can be very beneficial to this investigation if you'll participate. At times I feel like you're standing in the way of progress."

"Son, I'm not standing in the way. I'm trying to keep you from wasting time and taxpayers' money. Your foolhardy ideas may work in the big city, but they ain't what's needed here."

"If we don't try, we'll never know if they'll work

or not. What do we have to lose?"

"These are my people you're talking about here, digging up their phone records, tracking where they're at, or where they been, recording them driving down the street. What if they don't want no one to know where they was? That ain't right and ain't what these folks are used to. Hell's bells, if they knew I agreed to all of this, they'd lynch me from the oak tree in Four Freedoms Park."

Malcolm wasn't going to take any more of Chief's attitude and bogging things down. "If you don't want to be part of the solution, then get the hell out of my way. There are innocent people dying, and I'm going to find the murderer and put him in jail."

Chief folded his arms across his chest. "You go ahead and find him, but I better be the one who puts the cuffs on him, if he's alive. Some of my boys may just do the government a favor and save the expense of a long trial. These people what been shot are friends and neighbors. We tend to take care of our own and punish those that need it. Your big city ways don't work here, so I suggest you stop pushing your crap on us and get to finding the murderer. I think I've said everything I have to say. I'm going to get breakfast and try to reassure my citizens this sum-a-bitch is gonna be caught real soon."

"Why did I have to find out about the letter and another murder from a reporter?"

Chief pointed over Malcolm's shoulder. "Ask him. Then you can tell me what he says. Oh, and Officer Scott's funeral Mass is at ten, at St. Hubertus, with interment immediately following. Please show him the respect he deserves and be there." He shouldered past the FBI agent and entered Gram's with a tinkle of the bell.

Malcolm turned to follow, but Skipper blocked him. The reporter had what Malcolm's boss would call a "shit-eating grin." He also held the miniature tape recorder at chest level.

"Special Agent-in-Charge Gee, it appears there's an inability for the FBI and Madison PD to share information. Is that why the Madison Murderer is still loose?"

"I have no comment."

"Will you attend Patrolman Scott's funeral today?"

He took a deep breath and forced a smile. "If you're there, you'll find out." Malcolm spun on his heel and marched toward his car muttering about two shell casings, but only one body. What happened and what could that mean?

Chapter 22

9:50 a.m.

Malcolm took one of the remaining three parking spaces in the St. Hubertus' sand-and-rock parking lot. He had never liked funerals, but since Patrice's death, he absolutely hated and avoided them whenever possible. It angered him a police officer like Officer Scott, who seemed to be loved by everyone, had lost his life in the line of duty. Billy Joel certainly hit the nail on the head when he sang "Only the Good Die Young."

He rolled his head around to the left, then to the right. It didn't relieve the tension. Not only did he have the funeral to deal with, but Rachel Brock was due in town at noon and would probably require his presence for five or six hours. It would be a long day, but Valerie would be at the hotel when he finally wrapped up. He smiled, thinking of Valerie working on her tan at the hotel pool. He'd try to make it up to her with a good dinner tonight, maybe in Tallahassee.

Malcolm turned off the ignition and swung his door open. The July heat and humidity smacked him in the face like a sauna. Heat already shimmered off vehicles. In a couple of hours, it would be unbearable at the cemetery if there were no breeze.

The ground under his leather-soled shoes crunched when he stood. He scanned the now full parking lot and counted seventeen law enforcement vehicles scattered amongst an assortment of trucks and SUVs. At least a dozen vehicles lined Washington Street waiting to pull into the full lot. Officer Scott's family would be proud of the turnout.

His gaze followed the line of people parading toward the church. Chief Dautry stood at the bottom of the building's steps and spoke or nodded to each person that passed. Of course, the man would be there, front and center, where everyone would see him. He often seemed more like a politician than a law enforcement officer. The way he recognized everyone parading by, Malcolm wondered if the man knew everyone in Madison. If so, did he also know the killer?

The Madison Murderer knew the area and how to move around at night without being noticed. Transiting an area in the dark proved difficult for those unfamiliar with the surroundings, but this person arrived, shot, and vanished without anyone seeing him. Only a local could do that. The murderer had to live in or very near Madison. If that hypothesis were correct, then the odds were very good Chief knew him. And the odds were equally good the killer would be at the funeral, too.

Serial Killer 101, Malcolm thought with an inner grimace. Study after study proved serial killers, like the Madison Murderer, would often be in the crowd at a murder scene. They also liked to attend funerals and memorials. If being in attendance wasn't viable, they watched intently on television, or via news clips. In small-town Madison, a stranger near a murder scene or at this funeral would be noticed.

The FBI forensics experts offered a mundane physical description of the suspect that could fit hundreds of individuals: Male, five feet seven to five feet nine, 140 to 160 pounds, slight of build. Not much to go on, Malcolm decided as he surveyed the crowd. But it didn't take much to rule out the majority of males this morning: too tall, too short, too heavy, too old.

He had read a rather detailed explanation of how they determined the height. It referenced the video from the nursing home and included multiple pictures of the fence separating the cemetery and Rock Bottom's back parking lot. The pictures, enlarged twenty times, showed where something had worn away the dark coating of dirt and mold inside one of the fence's diamonds. They believed that's where the shooter rested his .30-06 rifle. The distance from the ground fit an approximation of someone five seven to five nine on one knee. This was supported by an indentation in the soil, suggesting the shooter knelt for his shot. In addition, they melded together two partial footprints that made a size eight and a half.

His forensics folks also showed pictures of crushed leaves at Allison Newton's shooting. Once again when they blew up pictures the image of an eight-and-a-half shoe print could be seen. The athletic type of tread was sold in most big box retailers, manufactured in the Philippines, and distributed in the US by Universal Sport Shoes.

The forensics team supported every suggested profile item with facts and figures. No guesswork for those folks.

Malcolm zigzagged through the parked cars. Each step brought a crunch until he reached the concrete sidewalk.

He had walked only twenty yards, and already

sweat dripped under his arms and perspiration formed along the middle of his back. Fortunately, the suit coat covered the wet spots.

Malcolm didn't extend his hand when he reached Chief. "Gonna be another hot day," the agent said.

"Glad you made it. Officer Scott deserves your respect."

Neither man looked at the other.

Agent Gee continued scanning the attendees for someone who fit the suspect's physical description. He knew it might be a long shot but didn't have anything better to do at the moment. "Quite a turnout," he remarked, just to say something.

Chief nodded to a couple walking by. "Not surprising. People liked and respected Scott. I wonder how many will show at your funeral."

"Not sure." He paused a split second and looked at Chief out of the corner of his eye. "I wonder how many will celebrate at yours."

Chief opened his mouth, but a couple, probably in their eighties, approached. The man carried a black suit coat over his arm, and his well-worn black pants showed about two inches of white socks. The woman, slightly stoop-shouldered, clutched a black patent leather purse to her white blouse. The black skirt extended to six inches above black patent leather shoes. A hint of mothballs accompanied their approach. The woman craned her neck to look up at Chief and scowled. "Taylor, I hope you catch the bastard that's killing all these people. I taught two of them in third grade. I taught you too. We used to have such a nice, safe community here. You could leave keys in your car, doors unlocked, walk the dog at night, all without being worried someone would get you." She pointed an arthritic index finger at him. "You have to stop this nonsense."

To his credit, he managed not to look like a scolded schoolboy as he replied, "We're doing everything we can, Mrs. Stevens. I've got the FBI here." He pointed to Malcolm. "I have state police from the governor who are helping. Every man and woman on our force is working on this. We'll get him."

"Taylor, you don't need the FBI or that sleazebag governor, or anyone else. Whoever is doing this lives right here in Madison, and you better get him before he kills someone else."

Her comment piqued Malcolm's interest. Another person, not involved in law enforcement, had the same thought as he did. "Why do you think he lives here?"

"Don't either of you watch *Dateline*? That's what happened last night. It wasn't the husband this time; it was a neighbor. He knew his way around, knew where people lived and worked. That's exactly what's happening here. The bastard lives among us, and you two need to stop him. What if he comes after Henry and me?"

Her husband rolled his eyes. "You watch too much TV. That was in California, where they're a bunch of fruitcakes anyway. Let's go so we can get an end seat in the back. Never know when we'll need the bathroom."

Mrs. Stevens wagged her finger back and forth between Chief and Malcolm. "Get to looking at the people who live here." She took her husband's arm with one hand and the railing with the other. They took the steps one at a time, like a toddler learning to deal with steps.

Both men nodded to another couple passing by. Malcolm said, "She's right, and since you know everyone in Madison, I bet you know the murderer and how the victims are connected. Anything you want to share?"

Before Chief could respond, the sound of Morse code being tapped came from his pocket.

In one smooth motion, Chief extracted the phone and raised it to his ear but pointed it outward, presumably for Malcolm to listen. "Palmer, this better be important. You know I'm at Scott's funeral Mass."

Malcolm edged a little closer and heard Jack Palmer say, "We got a dead body at the cemetery."

"Is this some kind of sorry-ass joke? They're all dead."

"This one ain't buried. It's Crazy Kenny, the homeless guy."

Chief's forehead wrinkled, and he glanced at Malcolm. "Just a sec." He moved several paces away from the steps and put the call on speaker. Malcolm followed him. "The guy who doesn't wear a shirt, no matter how cold it is?"

"Same one. Nice little bullet hole in the center of his chest."

"What's his back look like?"

"He's lying on it."

Chief tossed a hand in the air. "Well, duh, roll him over."

"That's not an option without violating the scene. Riley's gotta do it."

Chief's face reddened. His head nodded in unison with his curses. "Shit. Shit. Shit. Is there a shell casing anywhere around?"

"I asked the cemetery workers who found him. Negative. Crime scene tech's ten fifty-two is thirty minutes."

Chief looked at his watch, then turned his back to the parade of people marching to the church. "Keep them away until after Scott's burial. Put a tarp or something over the body so no one sees it, and keep everyone away. No crime scene tape, no one standing around. Keep Riley and his forensics van out of sight."

"But Chief…"

Chief stiffened. "Don't but me, listen to what I'm saying. I don't want anyone the wiser we had another murder. Do you copy?"

"Yes, sir, but…"

Chief's face became even redder, and his eyes bulged. He moved the phone to the front of his face and spoke as if using a microphone. "Shut up and listen. Cover it and keep everyone away so any evidence isn't destroyed. We gotta bury Scott, then work the scene. Am I clear?"

"I can't cover it where it's at. Scott can't be buried this morning."

"Why the hell not?" Spittle flew from Chief's mouth.

"Kenny's at the bottom of Scott's grave."

Chapter 23

Noon

The war room was eerily quiet. Only Malcolm, Danny, and Beverly Choo were present. Robert, Jack, and several other members of the Madison PD were expected, as well as Rachel Brock, but none had arrived yet.

Danny looked at Malcolm with raised eyebrows. "No kidding? At the bottom of the officer's grave?"

"Yep. According to the cemetery workers, they dig the graves the day before the burial, then the morning of the funeral, they place the casket-lowering thingy over the hole, erect the canopies, set up chairs, and whatever else is needed. They noticed something wasn't right when they were placing the casket-lowering thing. We had to postpone the burial until tomorrow so the scene could be worked. Let's get what we know so far on a storyboard."

Malcolm's focus was so intent on the Kenneth Murchison storyboard, he didn't notice a very tall female enter the war room and approach their table. She stopped and watched words appear on the storyboard.

Kenneth Murchison, aka Crazy Kenny

Saturday

Found at bottom of Officer Scott's grave by cemetery workers

Shot approx 2:00 a.m. (same approx time as Timothy Kurtz) entry center of chest, exit upper back, upward trajectory...shooter kneeling while victim standing? close proximity, fatal, high caliber, weapon consistent with other murders

Slug not found...Madison PD scouring cemetery with metal detectors

Initial investigation suggests victim shot near where shooter positioned himself for Timothy Kurtz shooting...drag marks to Scott's grave...blood splatter where standing

Question—If same shooter, why in the chest? Possibly surprised shooter while in the act.

Appears the suspect dragged the victim approximately sixty yards to Scott's grave...heel marks and drops of blood mark the path

Killer tried to hide body by pushing dirt on top of it...cemetery workers noticed hole not deep enough

Evidence—one .30-06 brass shell casing found in victim's pants pocket

No prints

Streak marks suggest deliberately wiped

Roman numeral (letter?) V etched on casing

No hair, fibers, blood, or other biologics found where shooter knelt

No witnesses

Security video from college across the street being reviewed...report not available yet

Shoe and tire prints being researched/cross-checked with other scenes

No apparent motive

Probably connected to the killing of Scott, Harrison, Newton, Kurtz

Danny typed almost as fast as Malcolm talked. When done, the FBI man stared at the newest storyboard.

When the tall woman spoke, Malcolm spun around and Danny stopped typing. "Impressive collection of information. You're following your training well."

Malcolm looked up, way up, into the face of the newcomer. He judged her to be mid-forties, based on a hint of a wrinkled forehead and crow's feet spreading from the corners of her eyes. Her hairstyle covered more of the left side of her face than the right. She wore a white blouse, black sweater, black slacks, and black sandals. No makeup. No jewelry except a long strand of purple beads. The rumor mill warned to never reference Van Gogh within her earshot.

"You must be Rachel Brock." He and Danny stood, Danny's mouth slightly agape.

"I am." She extended her hand to Malcolm. Her arm looked ten feet long, and her hand engulfed his. He guessed her to be at least six foot seven. "Pleased to meet you."

She shook hands with Danny, nodded to Beverly, then pulled out a chair.

Once seated Malcolm asked, "Would you like something to drink?"

"I'll take a Diet Coke or Diet Pepsi, whichever you have."

Danny rose. "Our machine's not stocked yet. I'll run out and get some." He left the bullpen, and Malcolm heard the front door click.

She set her briefcase on the table, extracted an ultrathin silver laptop, opened the top, and pressed the power button.

"That's a nice laptop you have there. It doesn't look like FBI issue."

"It's my personal machine. I'm pretty good at what I do, so they look the other way regarding my equipment." She smiled, smoothed the hair on the left side of her head, then curled it inward with her index finger. "But I don't believe I'm here to discuss my laptop."

"Of course not." The rumors he'd heard about her being a ball-buster seemed true.

She looked at the designer watch on her wrist, then at the front door. "I don't have all day, so let's discuss something germane to why I'm here. I've read the reports, which don't say much. I need information. So, I want you to walk me through the facts of each victim's story. I'll want to hear about the evidence. Do not, and I repeat, do not tell me any opinion, conjecture, guesses, or anything else not supported by facts. Do you understand?"

"Absolutely. The facts and nothing but the facts, ma'am." He smiled.

She didn't. "If I had a dollar for every time someone used that old *Dragnet* line, I'd be lying on a beach instead of sitting here. Are your boards in the sequence of the murders?"

"Yes, ma'am." He bowed his head slightly in the hope of showing contrition.

"Stop with the ma'am bullshit. Call me Rachel or Ms. Brock, whichever you're comfortable with. Stop wasting my time. We have a lot of ground to cover."

The lock on the front door clicked. Instead of Danny returning with drinks, Jack Palmer, Robert LeBeau, three men in PD uniforms, and a short, chubby man with a crewcut entered.

Malcolm waved them over. "Gentlemen, please join us. I'd like you to meet Rachel Brock, one of the FBI's top profilers. She's from the FBI's Behavioral Analysis Unit. She's here to help flesh out the murderer's profile."

She rose and extended her hand.

Jack took a step backward and gazed from head to toe.

Robert seemed unfazed and accepted her hand. "Robert LeBeau, Madison PD, lead detective on three of the murders."

Jack accepted her hand. "Jack Palmer, Madison's other detective."

Introductions of the three shift sergeants and Riley, the department's forensics technician, were made.

Malcolm continued, "Rachel, these men are key members of the investigation."

"I was told the police chief would join us," Rachel stated, looking around.

"I imagine he'll show any minute."

Robert shook his head. "Chief said he was busy and wouldn't make it, that we should go on without him. He wants me to brief him when we're done here."

"Busy doing what?" Malcolm asked.

"Chief does what Chief wants." Robert shrugged.

Jack looked away and slowly nodded.

"I brought my notebook." Robert lifted it for everyone to see. "I'll brief him when we're done."

"Okay. Let's take seats," Malcolm said.

Jack and Robert circled the table and took seats on either side of Malcolm. Riley and the three sergeants sat at the ends of the table. Rachel had empty chairs on either side of her, while everyone else sat shoulder to shoulder.

Danny arrived with two twelve-packs of cold Diet Pepsi, set the cartons in the middle of the table, and pulled the wireless keyboard onto his lap. Normally, when things needed to be added to a board, his fingers danced over the keyboard like a master pianist playing Tchaikovsky's Piano Concerto No. 1. Malcolm felt confident the same would happen today.

After a sip of coffee, Malcolm began. With sporadic input from Jack and Robert, Malcolm spent the next three hours going through each murder. Then they spent forty-five minutes going through the map board, the evidence board, and Malcolm's questions board.

Rachel grilled Malcolm, Jack, Robert, and Riley on details regarding distances, elevation differences between the shooter's position and his victims, and forensic techniques used when analyzing evidence.

Rachel straightened and wagged her head. "Come on, guys. This is not some game we're playing here. For Christ's sake, people are dying, and you're supposed to be the ones to stop it. You've only done half the job." She broke them into two groups. One group she demanded research weather conditions such as temperature, humidity, wind speed, and direction during each killing and the data be added to the storyboards.

The second group was ordered to consult a lunar table for moon phases. She moved around the boards, pointing, cursing, throwing her hands in the air. "I'm really disappointed in this group, especially the FBI people who should know better. The Madison people, you get a partial pass, but for Christ's sake, most of this shit is just common sense. My grandmother would have done more preparation, and she's been dead twelve years."

She clapped her hands. "Come on, guys. Let's get our asses in gear, but maybe you'll want to get your heads out of the way first. Danny, make sure you get all of this shit on the boards."

By the time they finished the last storyboard, Malcolm felt drained. On the other hand, he admired Rachel's thoroughness, focus, and desire to understand every detail. It amazed him that after more than five hours of intense work, Rachel still looked fresh, ready to keep at it. Maybe the caffeine from fourteen cans of Diet Pepsi kept her from showing any signs of slowing down. To his surprise, she only excused herself once to use the restroom. Most of the group used the occasion to visit the restroom themselves and/or refill coffee cups. No one drank Diet Pepsi except Rachel. Throughout the entire exercise, she remained animated, hands waving, fingers pointing, hands on hips when staring at someone. Malcolm could tell, based on the faraway or glazed-over expressions on the faces of other attendees, particularly the Madison PD members, they were also exhausted.

Rachel remained standing with hands behind her back. She paced the bullpen area, approached boards, and studied them for a few seconds, then moved on. Several around the table exchanged looks resulting in shoulder shrugs. No one said anything.

Rachel eventually sat and looked from one person to another. "Let's review the Serial Killer 101 textbook. Danny, you'll want to start a new board for this. Title it,

Serial Killer Educational."

Danny shifted everything to the right.

She sighed. "If I talk too fast, slow me down. Danny, it's going to be important you capture everything I say. You'll need it for reference later on. I don't know what my accessibility will be once I leave today, so you'll be on your own. Everyone else, buckle your seatbelts."

One of Danny's phones vibrated and skittered across the tabletop. He grabbed it with a sheepish grin and made a T with his hands.

Rachel pursed her lips and wrapped the necklace's purple beads around her finger.

Malcolm looked at Danny. "What's up?"

Danny scrolled through the message on his phone. "Security video from the college across the street shows a thin man, dark clothes, wearing a ski mask…approximately five seven, walking in a crouch across the far end of the cemetery. He's carrying a case that could hold a .30-06 rifle." He slid a finger on the screen. "He came into view at 1:41 a.m. for six seconds walking toward where Timothy Kurtz was shot from." Danny paused. "There's more coming, hold on."

Malcolm straightened. "We finally have a visual on the bastard."

Danny continued. "At 2:53 a.m., he appeared for seven seconds walking away from the fence. They believe his entry point was the far corner of the cemetery. Wait, there's still more."

Malcolm leaned forward. Rachel popped the tab on another Diet Pepsi and drummed her fingers on an armrest.

"The corner he likely came from and went to is

bounded by trees on the north and Washington Street on the east. Several of our agents and Madison PD uniforms were dispatched to canvass for witnesses, video, tire tracks, anything. That's it." Danny set the phone on the table.

Malcolm grinned. "Danny, update the Kurtz and Murchison storyboards as soon as we're done here."

"Will do."

Malcolm turned to Rachel. "Sorry for the interruption. This helps confirm what we suspected from the nursing home. This is a big step for us. Please continue."

She nodded once, rose, and walked to the blank "Serial Killer Educational" board.

"Here's a quick synopsis of the Serial Killer 101 training at Quantico. Criminals, especially killers, are like old dogs, they don't learn anything new. They operate the same way through their entire crime spree. We catch them because it becomes so repetitious, they lose focus, or they're forced into something new and don't know what to do and make mistakes.

"Perhaps you've heard of Ted Bundy, John Wayne Gacy, Jeffrey Dahmer, the D.C. Sniper, the Green River Killer, and Richard Ramirez, the original Night Stalker, just to name a few. If Ted Bundy had changed his MO, I can tell you that he'd probably have died from old age. He, like all the others, carried out their crimes in the same manner over and over. It helped us establish a profile and a modus operandi. In ninety-four percent of cases, if a serial killer left their victim out in the open the first time, they did every time. If they knifed the first one, they knifed all of them. If they tortured or sexually assaulted the first one, they did it to every one of them. In this case, your guy uses a rifle and shoots from hiding, that's how he'll plan to do it every time. Knowing this gives you a huge leg up. It might sound cruel, but you're fortunate you don't have to worry about molestation, dismemberment, torture, or any of the other gruesome things that occur. Your guy is pretty cut and dried, very predictable. Any questions so far?"

Malcolm had heard comments similar to these before, during training, but no one had ever stated them so matter-of-factly. Jack seemed enthralled. He sat on the edge of his chair with his mouth slightly open, wide-eyed, focused on Rachel. Robert and several of the Madison PD personnel appeared in a daze. Beverly appeared to be soaking it all in. Danny kept his head down, fingers dancing across the wireless keyboard with amazing speed.

Danny pointed to the board and stretched his fingers. "All good?"

She glanced at the board. "Looks like you have the salient points. Now, create a new board titled *Madison Murderer Profile*."

The scribe shifted everything to the right and titled the new board. As Rachel spoke, he typed fast and furious.

Madison Murderer Profile
Name—Unknown
White male
Age: Forty to Fifty
Single...time of murders indicate the killer has freedom of movement...not currently in a relationship
Kills early morning, before the sun comes up, probably has a job requiring him to start early...somewhere between 6:30 and 7:30...darkness

helps hide him from being seen or recognized...almost certainly a local resident with prominent position...must kill when dark because he's easily recognized by locals

Intelligent...scouts his victims, looks for occasions when they're at the most vulnerable to a long-range weapon

Planner...methodical planner suggests he has a list of victims and sequence in which they will be killed...has at least two escape routes planned for each shooting

Long barrel rifle suggests he has issues with one-to-one contact...mildly antisocial...tries to avoid direct face-to-face...may be proud of his rifle and shows it off to others...he CHOSE a rifle, it's not a random weapon or one of convenience

He doesn't like getting his hands dirty...his job is likely white collar or where personal sanitation is important, but probably not medical...medical personnel typically save lives, not take them

Probably undersized and uses a rifle to eliminate the possibility of a physical confrontation with victims...using a rifle also supports antisocial attitude

Being antisocial probably either stems from the people around him or he was raised as a single child and spent large amounts of time by himself...he probably sees people as hypocrites, problems, time suckers...people bring him their problems and want him to fix them and he can't fix all of them, so he tries to avoid them

Killing is a ritual for him...hence shell casing with Roman numerals etched...same weapon each time, no variation...kills from distance...probably mutters a prayer before or after each killing

Educated...so able to overcome his antisocial desires and being standoffish...supports being able to study his victim's habits and plan their execution along with escape routes

Communication conducted via mailed letter...no phone contact via cell or landline...further support of being mildly antisocial

Robert raised his hand. "He's smart. He probably knows it's called a 'cell' "—he used air quotes around cell—"because criminals who use them normally wind up in a cell." He donned a satisfied grin and crossed his arms over his chest.

Rachel's mouth fell open, and her eyes widened. Jack and Malcolm looked at the tabletop.

"Sir, if you're going to interrupt me again with such an asinine comment, I suggest you save it for the assholes you hang out with at the bar. It's not needed, nor appreciated." She pointed at him. "Don't you dare waste my time again."

Robert straightened in his chair, grabbed the chair's armrests, eyes widened, and he frowned. "Of course, please carry on."

After pinching the bridge of her nose, Rachel continued:

Doesn't like to get his hands dirty, avoids the blood and spatter that come from knives, handguns, baseball bats, and such...being rifle distance away avoids seeing the gore associated with his attacks

There doesn't appear to be a demographic angle of any sort since the victim's ages, races, and sexes vary...whatever the commonality is, it's not demographically related

Trying to tell law enforcement something with the shell casings...He wants the world to know what he's doing and why he's doing it

Given that he's concerned about sinners, the Roman numerals suggest a religious connection such as the Ten Commandments or Popes...sporting events, kings and queens, building erection dates, and others use Roman numerals, but that doesn't seem to fit here

His letter refers to the victims as sinners...investigation of the victims in comparison to the Ten Commandments has merit

Seems to kill without remorse, like he's on a mission or quest

Exhibits sociopathic traits

Has familiarity with Madison and the ability to move around without anyone taking note of it suggests he's a resident...this also suggests he's known by many in the community, or they know of him in his nonkiller mode

Despite being accurate with his shots, he's probably not had military training...Uses a .30-06 rifle...not a military type weapon...suggests he's hunted quite a bit

With his ability to scout and research, it'll be difficult to catch this guy, unless he makes a mistake. Or you get lucky and he's gotten all of his targets and will drift off into the sunset. I don't believe that's the case

Likely to keep killing until he makes a mistake or dies, either by suicide or suicide by cop.

Shell casings with Roman numerals and mailed letter are definite signs his mission is so important he's willing to take risks at insuring his mission is publicized...he wants the world to know what he's doing and is challenging law enforcement to piece together the clues to determine why he's doing it

He may have a death wish, or be impervious to the thought of dying...probably made his peace with his version of God...a desire to help, impress, or serve that God could be the motivation

Killed two people the first night...Killed one person the second night...probably planned for two, but the second victim did not present itself in the manner in which he prepared for

Whomever the murderer slated to be the second victim (fourth total victim) on the second night, probably Timothy Kurtz, remained at the top of the list

If he isn't able to kill a scheduled victim, he won't take them off the list...he'll try again and again until he's successful

He'll have an escape strategy in place for each victim

If he senses someone is aware of him and what he's doing, that person, or persons, could be added to his list

When you get physically close to him, you'll have to act quickly and decisively or else he'll disappear or possibly kill himself

He's on a mission, so if he suspects he's about to be captured he'll go someplace else and resume

He's a methodical planner and doesn't seem to do anything haphazard or quickly, it's all well thought-out.

She waited until Danny added the last couple of items, then said, "There you have it, that's the guy you're looking for. Questions?" She used both hands to smooth the hair on the top and back of her head, then smoothed the sides by dragging the hair forward.

Jack straightened. "Other than what we got from the college surveillance video, do you have a physical description? Eye color? Hair color? Hairstyle? Potential scars? Anything?"

"I provide the psychological profile. What you're looking for is physical evidence. I'm not qualified to offer that information, nor am I inclined to offer an opinion."

Jack had more questions. "Do you have a gut feel for what his profession might be? What kind of business he's in that requires he start work early?"

She smoothed the hair on the left side of her head and dragged it forward. "I'm not familiar with Madison and your industries. Whatever the killer's profession, it'll be structured, orderly, have an obvious leader, possibly require a uniform, have a definitive start time the killer can't be late for."

Rachel looked around the table. "If there are no other questions, I'll be on my way." She pointed at the soda box. "Would you mind if I took a couple with me?"

Danny shrugged. "I'm not a Diet Pepsi person, so you'd be doing me a favor by taking it."

She slid the laptop in her briefcase and grabbed the half-empty twelve-pack.

After she left, Jack spoke first. "Wow, that lady's intense and knows what she's doing."

Danny flexed his hands and fingers. "She can talk, too."

Malcolm sighed. "Dang, that's a lot of information. I need time to get my head wrapped around it. Let's take a ten-minute break."

Everyone except Malcolm left the area. He leaned back and propped his feet on the table. He mulled over the profile she'd developed. His gut said she was close, but something didn't set right. She was off somewhere, but his gut didn't tell him where. He'd learned over the years to trust his instinct, and this would be no exception.

Almost twenty minutes later, the investigators had taken their positions around the table.

"Okay, she's given us a lot of good information. Despite it being incredibly detailed, the odds are it's not one-hundred-percent accurate. I have a feeling her information will get us into the ballpark, but we still need to find where our seat is. So, we need to be flexible with the information and not take it as absolute gospel."

Malcolm glanced around the table, no one looked puzzled. "Robert, you've lived here all your life. Take Jeremy Osgood and put together a list of all the businesses that even remotely fit the employer profile with emphasis on those requiring a uniform and require an early start."

Robert and Jeremy nodded.

Malcolm pointed at Jack. "Work with Charlie to schedule patrols. Stay visible during the day, but I want someone on every road within ten miles of downtown at least once an hour between midnight and dawn. I want the murderer to know we're out and about. I'd also like you guys to put together a plan for random roadblocks between sunset and sunrise. Figure out the best place to put them, so he can't see them up ahead and turn off on another route. You know, around bends, just over the top of a hill, in a valley where there's no way he could cut off or turn around without creating suspicion. Let me know how much manpower and any other resources you'll need."

Jack smiled. "Good ideas, consider them done."

Charlie gave a thumbs-up.

"Beverly, I know this is outside your expertise, but I want you to work with Kevin." Malcolm pointed at the third Madison PD sergeant. "Go through all their call logs, patrol logs and phone recordings looking for mention of a vehicle parked on the side of the road, or in a parking lot, anyplace it shouldn't be. Look for parking tickets on the days in question. Contact tow operators to see if they had any calls between midnight and dawn on the days of the murders. Check with ride-share companies to see if they had any pickups or drop-offs near where the murders occurred. Follow up on anything, and I do mean anything, that seems even one-percent suspicious."

Kevin glanced at his watch then looked at Beverly. "I go on duty shortly. If you don't mind coming to the station, we can work there."

She smiled. "Give me a minute to pack up my stuff, and I'll follow you over."

"Danny, go through the new information. Put together a profile sheet that can be given to everyone, especially the Madison PD folks. We'll begin canvassing tomorrow morning. Teams of one agent, one uniform. Work with Benjamin to get the duty roster from whoever's on desk at the PD and put together the pairings. Contact all of our agents and have them at the PD roll call in the morning so they get the game plan."

Danny gave a mock salute. "Copy that."

"Lady and gentlemen, we're going on the

offensive. We're going to pressure the SOB from directions he never even knew existed. Let's get him before he strikes again."

Chapter 24

4:35 p.m.

The overhead sun baked the sky and everything under it. Even the grass seemed wilted, and the trees drooped on the St. Hubertus property. The church's cornerstone stated *Commemorated 1920.* Chief Dautry climbed the concrete steps for the second time that day. His jaw hurt, and he had a headache. He knew Ray, the parish gossip, would be inside preparing the church for the upcoming five p.m. Mass. Most people didn't realize it, but quite a bit of effort happened prior to Mass—doors unlocked, lights turned on, A/C turned down, wine poured, hosts counted, candles lit, selection of the offertory family, usher assignments, preparation of the Bibles and lectionary, and many other tasks.

Chief paused at the front door. He had always admired the carving of St. Hubertus, the patron saint of hunters and woodsmen, in the wooden door. It depicted a magnificent twelve-point buck and St. Hubertus, sword strapped to his belt, wearing a Robin Hood hat. It seemed ironic that he came to the church now with the intent of seeking help finding the person who hunted Madison's residents.

The instant he opened the church's main door, the lingering scent of incense from Officer Scott's funeral mass greeted him. It brought back memories of when he served as an altar boy in this very church. The priest then was a gentle soul, a grandfatherly type, beloved by everyone. Not many people liked the current pastor, Father Davidson. Many thought of him as an ornery SOB, but being the only Catholic Church for almost thirty miles didn't give Madison and Antler County's residents many choices for Mass on weekends.

Taylor Dautry followed the same routine he'd followed for over forty years. Enter the church, dip his fingertip in the holy water cup, make the sign of the cross, sit in the third pew from the rear. Years ago, a previous pastor had identified three as a biblical number, a good number, one all Catholics should remember and observe. The Holy Trinity. The Three Wise Men. Three were crucified together. Christ rose on the third day. And the list went on. Ever since then Taylor Dautry always sat in the third pew from the rear.

After entering the pew, he knelt and recited the same prayers he'd said since childhood. He then turned his attention to the confession box along the church's back wall. The sight of the illuminated red light above the penitent's entrance meant the pastor sat available to hear confessions, and Ray, the five p.m. sacristan, would probably be in the sacristy by himself.

Chief stood, genuflected upon exiting the pew, and made the sign of the cross. He nodded at two women in line for confession as he passed them on his way to the sacristy.

He paused at the doorway and saw Ray standing at the counter with a handful of unconsecrated hosts. The man used thumb and forefinger on a gnarled hand to drop hosts, one by one, into the ciborium. "Sixty-seven, sixty-eight, sixty-nine."

He'd already half filled the glass pitcher with red wine. The four extra wine goblets, or chalices, sat at attention next to the pitcher. He'd neatly arranged everything on the dark wood tray that would transport these essentials to the altar after the Prayers of the Faithful.

Chief Dautry waited until the seventy-four-year-old man stopped counting. "Hello, Ray."

The old man flinched and turned toward the door. His weathered face gave testimony of working the cotton fields for over six decades. His lips formed a half smile, revealing a missing lower tooth. "Hello, Chief. Father's still hearing confessions."

"I saw. I wanted to speak with you. Have time for a quick question?"

"Of course."

"I'm sure you're aware of the murders."

The sacristan frowned and nodded.

Chief continued, "It dawned on me this morning that all of the victims belong to St. Hubertus."

Ray's forehead wrinkled. "I hadn't realized that."

"Have you seen any strangers hanging around, or maybe a new parishioner the past month or so?"

"Not that I noticed."

Chief nodded knowing Ray made it his business to know everything going on in the church and about its members. "Do you know of any St. Hubertus connections between the victims? Choir? Bible study? Lectors? Committees? Fall Festival? Anything?"

Ray slowly wagged his head. "Nothing comes to mind. Ronnie Scott served as an altar boy and later an usher. Judge sat on Parish Council. The lady killed at the nursing home, I'd call her a Chreaster, you know, someone who only came on Christmas and Easter. We only saw that Kurtz boy when his father made him come, played on his phone the whole mass, didn't even take communion. Kids and phones these days, going to be the ruin of this country." He wagged his head again. "Don't think there's anything in common, Chief. Half of the people who live in Madison attend St. Hubertus, some more than others. Maybe it's coincidence."

"St. Hubertus is the only common thread."

"I understand what you're saying, but I don't know. I'll ask around and see if anyone knows anything." He shrugged. "I know you and Father don't get along. So, if you want, I'll ask him and see if he has any ideas."

"The sooner the better."

"I'll talk with some other folks after Mass too. And I'll keep an eye open for strangers."

"Thanks, Ray. I appreciate it. We have to stop him before he kills again."

"Staying for Mass? I'm short an usher, could use the help."

"Sorry, I got a murderer I gotta find." He gave a wave, turned, and left.

The walk to his car made him feel like a salmon swimming upstream, everyone else walking toward the church while he walked away from it.

Once in his car with the AC blasting, he inhaled deeply and blew the air out his mouth, making that motorboat sound children liked so much. He leaned a little to the right so the cool air would blow directly on his face.

He'd had a tough week. The mayor on his ass, the FBI prick not being any help, threats of the governor appointing a special investigatory task force, threats of the National Guard coming in, and now the murder count up to five. His backers for Johnny Robertson's state Senate seat had bluntly stated he needed to resolve this pretty damn quick. He felt the pressure to catch the bastard.

He smiled at the thought of the look on the mayor's face when he told the bitch he had decided to throw his hat into the ring for Johnny's seat. That would really piss her off, but there wouldn't be anything she could do about it. He'd have the most powerful men in the state, and more importantly their money, behind him. She'd have a bunch of hourly workers and her fellow darkies behind her. Nobody in her camp had the smarts to run a district-wide campaign. Sure, she'd won the mayor's seat, but only because her opponent had an IQ in the moron range. That dipshit couldn't find his way out of a one-stall bathroom, and everyone knew it. This time, she'd have an opponent who had experience, a sterling reputation, name recognition, power, and money behind him. Most importantly, the man who had caught the Madison Murderer. He'd be the obvious winner. No contest.

Time to arrange a little stress relief. He slid the phone out of a pocket, tapped *Lenny* from the contact list, and waited.

The familiar sound of Lenny's voice, thick and muffled from years of smoking, answered. "Twin Pines Motel."

"It's me. I'll be using the end room tonight."

"Damn. I got the swingers group coming tonight. They've reserved the whole place."

"I don't give a shit who you got coming to your

fleabag motel. I want the end room. And don't forget to block off the two parking spots out the back door."

"Come on, Chief, these people keep me in business. I really need the money from that room. The organizer likes it. If he gets pissed, he might take all those people someplace else next time."

Chief took a deep breath and exhaled slowly, making sure Lenny heard it. "Look, asshole, if you want to stay in business, you need to worry about law enforcement first. Piss me off and I'll have your swinger hangout shut down tonight. Hear me?" Chief waited for the answer he knew would come.

"Okay, you win. Can you be gone by midnight like the last time?"

"Her husband's shift ends at midnight, so we'll be gone by eleven thirty."

"That'll work. The swinger's group starts some sort of game at midnight where the women get half naked. That's the signal for them to pair up and head off to rooms. Let me know when you leave, and I'll hurry down, change the sheets, and tidy up. If you're gone by midnight, I should be able to make my money and keep everybody happy."

"I don't give a shit about the swingers, asshole. Leave the key on top of the coach light and put the cones in the parking spaces. I'll be there by eight." He punched the red disconnect icon and smiled. *Some days it's good being Chief.*

Chapter 25

6:10 p.m.

Malcolm drummed his fingers on the desk. He expected to hear Chief's voice mail but instead heard, "Calling me on Saturday night, this sure as shit better be important."

Malcolm stiffened and rose to his feet. "Damn straight it's important. You've been dodging me for two days. Haven't shown up at any of the meetings or press conferences. What the hell's going on?"

"I have other things to do." Malcolm had to move the phone away from his ear. "I have an entire city to worry about. You're the vaunted F, B, I. You're the hotshot that's supposed to solve these murders. So, don't bust my balls because you're not making any progress. Queen Mayor told me to play nice with you, so I'm following directions."

"It's bullshit and you know it. I think you know you're in over your head and won't admit it. You can't keep up with the investigation and all the activity. So, you send Robert as your proxy. Do you think your people don't notice?"

No response for several seconds. Malcolm could picture the big man, red-faced, eyes bulging. "Look, Gee, I don't give a shit what you think. Chasing after me is barking up the wrong goddamned tree. You need to be chasing the killer. I already told you this, and I'll say it just one more time, all I care about is cuffing the sum-a-bitch when he's found. I want lots of reporters around. I want lots of pictures, and I want you to disappear."

Malcolm shook his head and made his voice conversational in hopes of getting Chief to talk with him as opposed to screaming. "What's so important about cuffing him that keeps you away from our meetings and strategy sessions?"

"Don't you worry about me. Robert's doing a fine job keeping me posted on what you're doing. Just find the sum-a-bitch. I'll be there then."

Was this the time to mention what he'd learned from Jack about Chief running for the state Senate seat? Perhaps it would be best to not betray that confidence. He valued the relationship he'd built with Jack, especially the man's potential as the investigation continued. No sense taking the chance of burning the bridge between them.

With a nod, he responded, "Okay. You go do whatever you wish, and I'll do my best to keep Robert up to date. But I want you to know I've taken command, no more sharing the lead. I'm going to drive this thing to a conclusion. I'll do what I can to honor your desire to put the handcuffs on him, but I'm not making any guarantees or promises. Do you read me?"

"I been telling you that I have just one thing I want to do here. Put the cuffs on him. I ain't going to say it again."

Chief disconnected.

****

AD plopped into his recliner and raised the leg rest

with a *thud*. He washed down a pink alprazolam with a gulp of red wine to calm the jitters.

His brief conversation with Ray and several other men after the five o'clock Mass caused his stomach to flip flop, like when the nun in school caught him cheating on a test. Hearing that Chief Dautry visited the church and asked about a St. Hubertus connection took him off guard. He wanted to puke but controlled himself. However, continuing nausea required he cancel his customary Saturday evening supper at Denny's and head straight home.

He couldn't be caught yet. He'd only achieved four of the planned twelve sacrifices and hadn't gotten to the most eye-opening ones. Maybe starting with the most notable would have been the way to organize them. Making a big bang right away instead of building momentum to a grand finale now seemed like a better approach. Too late to do anything about it now. He had his plan, and he needed to continue working it.

He couldn't have avoided the unfortunate sacrifice of Crazy Kenny in the cemetery. It took all his energy to drag the body to the open grave and shove dirt on top of it. He certainly didn't expect anyone would notice the grave wasn't as deep as normal. But they had.

To compound the problem, the grave had been dug to receive Ronald Scott the next morning. That also helped derail his plan. Regardless, what was done was done. Just the thought of it brought on nausea and the beginnings of a new headache. He rubbed the back of his neck with one hand while the other rubbed his stomach.

While he didn't know of any particular sins the homeless man may have committed, AD knew he had to have sinned sometime over his lifetime. After all, only two sinless people had ever walked the earth, Jesus Christ and the Virgin Mary. Surely, Crazy Kenny wasn't worthy to wash the feet of either. So, instead of the twelve on his list, he'd make it a baker's dozen. He raised a half-hearted thumbs-up.

With Scott's burial rescheduled for tomorrow, his plan of getting much-needed rest at the cabin no longer seemed possible. He'd have to somehow pull together the strength to carry on. He didn't have much choice. Christ had Simon of Cyrene to help carry his cross. However, AD knew he would have to carry his own cross.

He loved his time at the cabin. Peace, quiet, the ability to think and converse with God helped him keep moving forward even in the darkest of times. He sighed at the thought.

The cabin is where the idea first formed. Luke's Gospel 10:2 stated it best. "The harvest is abundant, but the laborers are few." The verse went on to state the master of the harvest should be asked to send more laborers. Well, AD saw himself as the master of the harvest and would do his best to recruit others through his actions. If he could only get the authorities to look at each victim and reveal the sins, the recruiting process would take care of itself.

Now he needed to figure out what to do about Chief Dautry. Pretty smart of the lawman to connect the sacrifices and St. Hubertus. Something needed to be done to throw law enforcement off track, but what?

AD downed the remaining wine in two gulps and refilled the goblet. After a hearty belch, he swiped the back of a hand across his mouth. The other hand continued to rub little circles over the burning pain in his lower abdomen.

Maybe he should write a letter warning Chief to stay away. After thinking about it for a minute, he decided it didn't seem practical. Chief had always done whatever Chief wanted to do. He'd see it as a challenge and become like a drunken boxer—swing at anything and maybe get a lucky knockout.

It reminded him of what Mike Tyson once said, "Everyone has a plan until they're punched in the face." AD had a well-thought-out plan, but he'd been punched in the face. Time to float like a butterfly and sting like a .30-06 slug. He chuckled at his own cleverness.

A wince crossed his face when he reached into the magazine rack next to the chair. The manilla folder wasn't heavy, but he caught his breath, nonetheless. He pulled out a single sheet of paper with twelve numbered names listed. Numbers one through four had already been crossed out. Using a pen given to him by a Realtor at church that evening, AD added "#13, Crazy Kenny" to the bottom of the list then drew a line through the name.

Eight more sacrifices before his mission would be complete.

He looked to the four-foot crucifix on the wall for inspiration. With closed eyes, he made the sign of the cross and prayed out loud. "Heavenly Father, all loving, please hold your hand over me while I honor you. Give me the strength and days necessary to glorify you, to expose these sinners for all the world to see and understand punishment is swift and sure. May the world not follow in the ways of the offenders lest they also be punished. Instill in others the passion to undertake their own crusade, to be examples to the world. Lastly, dear Father, if it pleases you, bless me with the wisdom necessary to carry out the remaining eight oblations before I'm called home to be at your right hand. These things I ask in the name of your son, Jesus."

AD calmed himself and waited to hear what words, what thoughts, what solutions God would impart. It didn't take long before he had the draft of a plan.

"Matthew 18:20, 'Where two or more are gathered…' " He let it trail off. He circled the names next to number eleven, Chief Dautry, and number twelve, Martha Osgood, Chief's secretary. "Yes, this will work quite well." He then drew a line from the circle to below the crossed-out name of number four, Timothy Kurtz. He added an arrowhead with a flourish and uttered a gentle, "Thank you, Lord, for a solution and tonight's opportunity."

Chapter 26

10:45 p.m.

For forty-five minutes, Malcolm sat in the hotel room chair, focused on his laptop, reviewing the war room storyboards. His knee bounced the entire time. He scrolled from one to another to another. He'd mumble to himself, read lines aloud, ask questions aloud, scratch his head, but mostly read aloud.

With Valerie in the shower and unable to hear him, he felt comfortable reading each entry out loud. He seemed to process verbal information better than written information, one of the reasons he talked to himself in odd situations. Kids used to make fun of him in school for it. It took time, but he eventually decided to stop being concerned with what others thought. As a small concession to potential ridicule, he more whispered than spoke in a normal voice when talking to himself.

He didn't know what he searched for, but search he did. His gut told him something important had been buried in a storyboard and he had to find it. When he'd completed review of the thirty-third and last storyboard, he returned to the first, *Officer Ronald Scott*, and resumed whispering each line to himself, again.

The opening of the bathroom door interrupted his recitation. Valerie, clad in white bathrobe and towel wrapped around her hair turban-like, came out.

A cloud of hot, humid air wafted out and washed over him. Other than a small, ragged patch of clear glass, the bathroom mirror had fogged over. He leaned slightly to the side and checked his toiletries on the counter. Hairbrush, shaving cream, shaver, floss, toothpaste, toothbrush, mouthwash, and deodorant were all there and in the proper sequence. Thankfully, Valerie hadn't disturbed anything. Their first, and only argument as far as he could remember, was that she disturbed his items. She didn't see it as a big deal, but it was to him. Being bounced around in foster care for so many years, he didn't have many items that were his own, but he had become possessive of his toiletries. They were personal items that no one should mess with. However, some of his foster brothers thought it funny to hide his items, or worse, use them without his consent. Foster care had also taught him to be prepared to pack quickly. Three sets of clothing were all he needed and all he had. His clothing and toiletries would fit in a grocery store plastic bag. Even as an adult with a good paycheck, he found it difficult to have more than three of any article of clothing.

Valerie stepped into his view and waved her hand. "Hey, are you okay? You look sad."

Malcolm's heart flip-flopped when he focused on her. She looked so pure and clean, so lovely, so beautiful. He wanted to take her in his arms and hold her, claim her as his. She made him happy, the happiest since he lost Patrice many years earlier. The more time he spent with Valerie, the more potential he saw in a long-term relationship with her.

But what about Dallas? His stomach felt empty.

Should he bring up the topic now or wait? He didn't want to throw a wrench in their developing relationship, but she deserved to know. Addressing problems immediately, not letting them fester into larger issues, had always been his philosophy. Better to find out now than later. He licked his lips and took a deep breath.

She interrupted his thoughts. "What's that on your computer screen?"

He turned back to the laptop. "Storyboards of the murders. I've been looking for anything we may have missed, anything that will help figure out who the bastard is. I'm convinced something important is hidden in there, but I don't know what."

She pointed to the screen. "Can I help? I promise not to tell anyone about it. I want you back in Orlando." She grinned.

Her comment caused him to pause. Was she also thinking they had potential for a long-term relationship? Perhaps now would be a good time to broach the Dallas subject.

With hands on hips, she interrupted his thoughts again. "Well, can I help?"

At first, he wanted to say, "No," but remembered she'd figured out the Roman numerals on the shell casings, so, maybe she could help. "Sure, pull that chair over."

"Can you read it to me? I think a lot better when I hear things than read them."

His heart skipped a beat. A kindred soul.

She took his face in her hands and peered into his eyes. "Gee, are you okay? You don't look right."

He cupped his hands over hers. "I'm fine. A thought hit me."

She bent and pecked his lips with hers.

Malcolm reached into the fold of her robe, but she backed away. "There'll be time for that later. Tell me about your storyboards."

"Only if you insist." He worked through the boards and answered her questions until he came to the Madison Murderer board. "This one's about the killer and the letter he wrote. The linguistics folks haven't found anything special about it. His words are typical for high school graduates. They don't give any clues to his location, identity, upbringing, nada. Nothing special about the paper or envelope. The envelope and stamp were self-seal, so no DNA from saliva or fingerprints on the sealant. The only piece of useful data is it had a postmark from the main post office in downtown Tallahassee. No telling how it got there. Someone spoke with the head guy and found out thousands of people come and go every day, and over one hundred trucks bring mail there for sorting and distribution. That letter could have been dropped off there, or dropped in a box forty miles west of the city and brought there for processing. In case you're not sure, we're about thirty miles east of Tallahassee."

She straightened and rocked her head side to side. "I'll have you know my Florida geography is pretty good. I know exactly where we are and where Tallahassee is. So, what's the letter say?"

"It was sent after the first two killings, Officer Scott and Judge Harrison." He read it aloud:

"I sacrificed those men. They held positions of responsibility and respect but weren't what everyone thought. They've sinned and deserved to be stopped before they hurt others again. I don't know anything about chalk markings. Look at the shell casings."

She stood, cinched the bathrobe tighter, walked to the window, and stared out. She tap-tap-tapped the side of her face with an index finger.

Malcolm leaned back, crossed his arms, and remained silent.

"Weird message." She turned to face him. "What sins is this guy talking about?" Her forehead wrinkled and she frowned. "Sin against who? A god? Mankind? Mother Nature?"

He shrugged. "All are possible."

She extended her hands palms up. "Assuming the victims did commit a sin, how does this guy know what they did?"

"You know…" He pointed at Valerie. "That's a damn good question." He stood and kissed her lightly on the lips. "You keep reminding me that you're as smart as you are beautiful."

"I bet you say that to all your girlfriends." She grinned.

"Only the ones I love." He winked.

"So, how would this guy know people sinned? Do you think he knows what their sins were? If so, how?"

He snapped his fingers. "He's gotta be a counselor, or therapist, or something like that. Someone people feel comfortable talking to."

He straightened and raised an index finger. "Or maybe he's bugged someone's office." The heaviness he'd felt the past couple of days lightened. "We have a new investigative track."

She gazed up at the ceiling. "I wonder how many of those kinds of people operate in Madison?"

He shook his head. "We can't limit it to just

201

Madison. We have to look at therapists and counselors probably for twenty miles from city center. I'll free up Goose in the morning to lead that effort." He opened his arms wide and engulfed Valerie in a bear hug, lifting her a couple of inches off the floor. "You're amazing. I'm so glad you're here."

"Me too." She squirmed away and uncinched her robe.

Chapter 27

11:20 p.m.

Dressed in black, including the black ski mask, AD peered through the 20X scope and scanned the line of vehicles along the rear of Twin Pines Motel. He stopped when he came upon Chief's car with Martha Osgood's parked next to his. He looked to heaven. "Thank you."

With his right eye peering through the scope he searched until he found "119" on the motel room door, the room they always rendezvoused in. A couple of clicks of the adjustment dial made the numbers nice and crisp.

Despite it being slightly over one hundred yards away and dim lighting, he had confidence he'd hit the targets; he had God on his side.

According to the book of Samuel in the Old Testament, David, the Israelite, slew the giant Philistine, Goliath, with a mere sling. David's weapon initially appeared to be inconsequential to the mighty Goliath's arsenal of spear, lance, and sword. However, the world found out David, with God watching over him, used the sling to achieve victory. Likewise, AD, with God watching over him, would use Beautiful Betsy to achieve victory. Victory over sin and teach the world even the smallest of the small can achieve great victories in the name of God.

When he initially planned the sacrifices, he intended Madison Police Chief Taylor Dautry and his hussy girlfriend to be the last sacrifices. But the police chief had become too smart for his own good. So, he needed to be moved up the list. No longer numbers eleven and twelve, they became numbers five and six.

Accepting bribes to look the other way, disadvantaging others for personal gain, and fornicating with a married woman were more than enough reasons for having Chief on the list. Hebrews 13:3-5 pretty much summed up Chief Dautry's sins against God and mankind. "Be mindful of prisoners as if sharing their imprisonment, and of the ill-treated as of yourselves, for you also are in the body. Let marriage be honored among all and the marriage bed be kept undefiled, for God will judge the immoral and adulterers. Let your life be free from love of money but be content with what you have, for he has said, 'I will never forsake you or abandon you.' " And Exodus 20:14—"You shall not commit adultery"—supported his married girlfriend being on the list.

Both of them had earned their spots on his list. They deserved to be there. And, God willing, he would make an example of them. When it became known to the world how these two sinned and duped their spouses, the message would be clear: Not even the mighty Chief of Police, Taylor Dautry, could avoid God's wrath and punishment. Sin against the Lord and be prepared to suffer the consequences, be prepared to suffer eternal damnation.

AD reviewed his plan. He expected Chief to be standing when he fired the first shot but had no idea how she would react. He hoped she would freeze, thus giving him time to fire the second, and final, shot. If she didn't freeze, he had twenty more shells he could pepper the car with.

He'd overcome challenges before, and tonight would be no different. His time on earth ran short, so he couldn't fail.

AD recalled the day Chief Dautry explained how he manipulated things so the affair could bring him more enjoyment. The man bragged about promoting Martha Osgood's husband, Jeremy Osgood, from patrol officer to second-shift desk sergeant. Since then, Sergeant Osgood worked from three thirty p.m. to midnight. This allowed Martha to rendezvous with Chief at Twin Pines on nights her husband worked to protect the citizens of Madison. Chief would tell his wife he had a stakeout, or meeting, or surprise inspection, or poker game with the boys. The head of the Madison Police Department completed the story with a chuckle and said, "It's good to be Chief." What a horrible thing for him to brag about.

When these two were found dead outside a seedy motel room, the truth would be out for everyone to know. No sense writing any more letters. Within the next few minutes, Chief wouldn't be able to receive mail unless he checked the dead letter file. AD chuckled at his cleverness.

****

Chief sat in the straight-backed chair and watched Martha Osgood's breasts jiggle as she shimmied into her black thong panties. He told her, "Richard Burton once said of Elizabeth Taylor, 'Her breasts are apocalyptic. They would topple empires.' If he'd seen

205

yours first, he would have said it about you."

"You say the nicest things, but you're not getting any more tonight. Look at the time, it's eleven thirty. I need to get home before Jeremy does." She used her foot to move clothes around on the floor until she uncovered the bra that matched the thong. She leaned forward, lifted the demi bra cups to her breasts, stood, and hooked the clip separating the cups.

Chief rose. "Damn, woman, you sure look sexy."

"Taylor Dautry, you stay right there. I said no more." She looked around the floor again. "Where's my top? I need to cover these puppies before you get me into trouble with my husband."

****

AD knew they'd be coming out any minute. He lifted Beautiful Betsy and peered through the scope. He found the "119" and shifted slightly to the left to see the curtained window. He could see shadowy movement behind the motel room's drapes. Soon, very soon.

****

Martha dropped the hairbrush into her purse and glanced in the mirror for the umpteenth time.

Chief took a couple of steps toward her but stopped when she spun on a heel and pointed a finger at him. "Don't you dare. We don't have time for any more."

"Okay. We need to get out of here anyway so the swingers can use it."

She smiled. "I'd like to go to a swinger party sometime. I think it would be fun. You're pretty big where it counts, but I heard some of those guys are hung like horses." She rolled her eyes. "God, I'm getting horny."

"We'd have to drive a good distance, maybe

Orlando or Tampa. Can't do that anywhere in the panhandle, too many people know me here."

She grinned. "We could do something next month when Jeremy's at that opioid conference in Miami. It runs Friday to Tuesday, so we could make a weekend of it. Drive to Tampa Friday night, maybe go to a beach Saturday during the day, then a swinger party Saturday night. Gosh, I wonder what they wear at those kinds of parties. I'd have to buy some new clothes."

"I don't think they wear much. That's kinda the idea of the party, isn't it?"

"I bet I could find something on the internet. Anything you could want can be found there." She turned and looked in the mirror again.

He reached around, cupped her breasts from behind, and kissed the side of her neck.

She squirmed away. "Stop it." Martha checked the floor on one side of the bed, then sidestepped to the other side. "Looks like I got everything. Can't leave any evidence."

They both laughed.

****

AD waited patiently in the brush slightly over a hundred yards away. A glance at his watch showed Chief and his Jezebel secretary Martha would be leaving any minute. Her husband got off work in twenty minutes. She needed to get home and change into something more appropriate for a wife of almost fifteen years.

He reminded himself to be careful walking through the cow pasture on the way back to his blue truck. He couldn't afford the possibility of stepping into something that would leave a recognizable footprint.

When Chief stuck his head out the door, AD straightened, then pulled the Remington .30-06 to shooting position. He steadied his breathing and nestled his cheek on the rifle's stock. Left eye closed, right eye perched behind the scope.

He clicked the safety off and smiled.

****

Chief didn't see anyone on the sidewalk or parking lot. "Coast is clear. Get your beautiful booty moving."

Martha slid past him and scurried to her car.

Chief flipped the light switch off, swung the door closed with practiced ease, and placed the key on the coach lamp next to the door, right where he found it.

Four quick steps and he stood next to Martha. She turned and leaned back against her still-closed car door.

Chief placed both hands on Martha's hips and leaned in.

They kissed. He squeezed her rump as if checking a head of lettuce in the grocery.

She moved his hand away and bit his lip.

****

AD waited until they separated to get clean headshots. He wanted to take Chief first, but because of their positions, he switched his plan. He didn't like change but had no choice.

His right index finger lightly touched the trigger. Crosshairs centered on the side of Martha's head. He held his breath.

She pushed her lover away.

Flame shot from the rifle's muzzle as the slug sped to Martha Osgood's head.

AD ejected the spent cartridge and jammed a fresh round into the chamber. He found Chief's face in the crosshairs. Chief's expression morphed from confusion to understanding.

AD held his breath and squeezed the trigger a second time.

Chief disappeared.

AD searched with his scope but couldn't see either of his sacrifices.

He recited Matthew 10, Verse 7—"As you go, preach this message: The kingdom of heaven is at hand." Yes, indeed, with each offering the kingdom of heaven comes nearer.

He took a deep breath and let a sigh escape.

God willing, their bodies wouldn't be found until morning. That truly would be a blessing if the Lord so willed it.

He ejected the spent shell and caught it in his gloved hand. He delicately placed both shells at his feet. They stood erect, like soldiers standing at attention.

He hummed "Soon and Very Soon" as he wound through the cow pasture to his mother's old, blue pickup a half mile away.

Six down. Two more in the morning and he'd be ready for a rest.

Day Six—July 20th

Chapter 28

Sunday, 6:30 a.m.

Malcolm opened the hotel room door and caught sight of a Madison PD officer sitting near the elevator. Instinctively, he extended his arm to stop Valerie. He stuck his head out the door and looked both ways but didn't see anyone else. He turned to Valerie. "Something's not right, stay here."

"But where…"

Malcolm looked her in the eye. "No buts. I don't know why that officer is there, but it's not right. I'm going to find out, you stay here." He didn't want to tell Valerie, but his first thought was somehow Madison PD had become aware that he, Malcolm, was a target of the Madison Murderer.

He slid out the door, hand on the 9mm Beretta tucked in the small of his back. He glanced over his shoulder and saw Valerie watching him through the partially open door. He motioned for her to close the door, then turned his attention to the officer sitting next to the elevator.

The police officer sat on a metal folding chair with a book in his hands. He appeared to be reading *Jessop County Murder*.

"Officer, why are you here? What's wrong?"

The officer flinched, then squinted. "Agent Gee,

you're supposed to call Detective Palmer."

"Why? What's going on?"

The officer closed the book, tapped the elevator call button, and wagged his head. "I don't know, I'm just following orders. He wants you to call him." The man gave a dismissive wave.

The elevator door opened with a *clang*. He entered the waiting car and the door closed with a matching *clang*.

Malcolm jumped when someone touched his arm. He spun around, one hand reaching for the Beretta and the other hand rising to ward off any strikes that might be coming.

Valerie took three steps backward with her hands raised, palms out.

"Goddamn it. I thought I told you to stay in the room."

"I'm sorry, I saw you talking with him and then he pressed the button, so I thought it was okay. I'll not do it again."

"You could have gotten hurt."

"I know. I said I won't do it again. So, what did he want?"

"I'm supposed to call Jack."

"Why?"

"The officer didn't know why, he was just following orders." Malcolm found Jack Palmer's name in his phone and poked it.

Within seconds "Palmer" roared in his ear.

"Jack, this is Gee. What's up?"

"The murderer struck again last night. He shot Chief and his secretary, Martha Osgood."

Malcolm took a step backward and leaned against

the wall. "Damn, Jack, I don't know what to say. He's taken it to a whole new level."

"Can anyone hear what I'm saying?"

Malcolm put his arm around Valerie. "No, why?"

"Only a half dozen people know this…Chief's still alive, but barely."

"That's great. How is he?" Malcolm responded louder than he intended.

"Chief's in the neuro-intensive care unit at Tallahassee General. He's there as a John Doe, but there are two unis guarding his room. Gee, only six or seven people know Chief's alive. Everyone else thinks the shooter got them both. Not even the mayor knows. She made me acting chief. You gotta keep it quiet. If the murderer knows Chief is still alive, he may try to finish the job."

"I get it. What's Chief's prognosis?"

"According to the doctors, the slug took a chunk of his skull off and a portion of the brain. They're not able to do any testing yet, but it doesn't sound good. His wife had Father Davidson from St. Hubertus give him the final blessing. He and Father didn't get along, so I give the priest props for putting aside their differences and doing the right thing."

"Damn, that's three from the PD. What's this guy doing?"

"There's something you need to know. Chief and Martha had a thing going."

"Isn't…er…wasn't she married to the night desk sergeant?"

"Long story, maybe over a beer sometime. Regardless, almost everyone in the department knew. The killer shot them coming out of a cheap motel a little before midnight."

"You sure it wasn't her husband or Chief's wife?"

"The husband was still on shift when the motel manager called it in. Mrs. Dautry was drunk as a skunk at a garden party. Twenty of the city's most upstanding citizens will alibi her. One of our guys found two .30-06 shell casings about a hundred yards away. They had Roman numerals six and seven etched on them."

Malcolm leaned against the wall and blew out all the breath he had. His mind raced with possibilities and questions.

Valerie shook his arm and whispered, "Gee, you okay?"

He held an index finger to her lips. "Update me on where things stand."

"Riley and a couple of your people have covered the murder scene, plus the spot he shot from. They didn't recover anything other than the shell casings and a few probable shoe prints. The mayor alerted her favorite reporters, and the news has already hit the media. The governor called twice. I'm ignoring the mayor right now. There's a news briefing at 1800 hours, that's six o'clock for you city folks. I hope we'll have something to tell them. Oh, and Patrolman Scott's interment is at 1300 hours today. I plan to be at the cemetery, but observing from a distance. Rachel said killers liked seeing the aftermath of their work, so maybe we'll spot him at the interment service. That's it for now."

Malcolm remained silent for a few seconds. He welcomed Valerie's closeness and tightened his arm around her shoulders in a half hug.

"Gee, you still there?"

"Sorry, lost in thought. Question: why the uniform next to the elevator?"

"Well." The acting chief of police drew this word out. "I tried calling, but no answer. Got concerned and sent a uni to make sure the murderer hadn't visited your hotel. He said it sounded like you didn't want to be interrupted, so I told him to get comfortable and wait for you."

"But…"

"No, there's no but. There's not a damn thing you could have done that I didn't handle. Get pissed at me if you want, I made the decision."

"Damnit, Jack, he should have knocked. I would have gotten my ass dressed and made it to the scene. My evidence response team should have been there to process the scene."

"I told you a couple of your guys were there. What would you have done at one thirty this morning? They had already pronounced Martha dead. Chief lay in an ambulance, a portion of his head missing, unable to talk, on his way to Tallahassee. The shooter had disappeared. There wasn't a goddamned thing you could have done. I was awake and at the scene. Besides, when I hit the wall this afternoon, someone needs to take the reins and do the press conference."

"I don't give a shit. This is what I do for a living, and I'm damn good at it when I'm kept informed and involved. Pictures and statements are great, but they're not the same as being there and seeing it with my own two eyes. I want to form my own frickin' opinions based on what I see. I'll then weigh my thoughts against what I see in reports. You small-town boys deal with shit like this maybe once in a lifetime, but this is what Uncle Sam pays me very well to do."

"I just don't see the point in getting you out of bed in the middle of the night when I'm already here. Maybe you don't trust me?"

Malcolm threw his free hand in the air. "Oh, for Christ's sake, Jack. Trust isn't it. This is the second time I wasn't notified, wasn't given the chance to see the scene fresh, undisturbed. When a pro, a real frickin' pro like myself, sees the unblemished scene, complete with carnage, I see the crime itself. I often recreate it in my mind's eye and see exactly what the bad guy did and what the victims did. My mind wraps itself around what happened, looks at it from multiple angles, and can imagine every goddamned millisecond of it. Once the processing starts, once the bodies are moved, once pieces of potential evidence are moved, the scene is gone forever, never to be recreated again. You, in your omnipotent wisdom, have deprived me of doing what I do best. This is twice now enormous mistakes were made. Who knows how far we may have been able to move forward? It's lost, that's two frickin' opportunities flushed down the shitter, never to be seen again."

"Okay…okay. Point made. I won't let it happen again even if I need to take a battering ram to your door."

"If that's what it takes, then do it. Don't give this bastard any more advantage than he already has." Malcolm paused for a few seconds while he took a deep breath and counted one-Mississippi, two-Mississippi, three-Mississippi, all the way to ten-Mississippi. "I'm going to cancel this morning's debrief. If you'll contact your folks, I'll let mine know."

"That'll make a couple of the guys happy."

Louder than he wanted, he responded, "I don't give a shit who's happy and who isn't. I want this asshole caught. If your guys get pissed, so be it. They'll get over it when I'm gone. I'm canceling because there's a lot we need to do right now."

"Ten four. I'll call mine."

Malcolm took another deep breath. "Where are you?"

"At the station."

"Stay there. I'll see you shortly."

"No need to hurry. Get yourself some breakfast. And I wouldn't mind if you'd stop by Gram's and pick up an order of biscuits and gravy along with the biggest mug of black coffee she serves."

"I'll get breakfast for both of us. I'll be there in thirty minutes. Oh, and I'm going to want to see what kind of progress your team made canvassing for video near the previous crime scenes, and they better be out around the motel right now looking for video, Sunday or not. Bye." He disconnected and looked at Valerie. "How much did you hear?"

She wrapped her arms around his waist, resting her head against his chest. "I heard about Chief and his secretary. I also heard we're delivering breakfast."

"Not us, me."

Her forehead creased for a second. "Okay, but I'm not sitting by the pool again today, I'm at least going to the cemetery with you. It wouldn't be appropriate for you to go to the interment by yourself. You need a woman on your arm."

His eyes moistened. "I'm so sorry about all this work stuff and not being able to spend more time with you. This is just…a really, really busy and tense time for me. I hope you understand. You're important to me, and I don't want this to screw up what we have going."

"I understand. Stopping a murderer is pretty important, too."

He kissed her forehead. "You're too good for me. I don't deserve you."

She looked into his eyes, smiled, and winked. "I know."

Chapter 29

12:35 p.m.

The folks at the hotel told Malcolm the best way to get to Oak Ridge Cemetery was to follow Route 53 north. They warned him not to pay any attention to street names, follow the route signs, and he'd see Oak Ridge on the left.

Living in Orlando for the past ten years, he'd become accustomed to roads having a number as well as a name. Route 50 was called Colonial. His condo complex sat off State Road 436, aka Semoran. So, why shouldn't Route 53 in Madison be called Duval, then Base Street, then something else?

The town dozed on this hot Sunday afternoon. Everything fit his perception of a small southern town. Many in Madison referred to it as a city, but he thought of it as another town whose better days were in its rearview mirror.

They passed Four Freedoms Park with its monument dedicated to President Roosevelt's four freedoms: freedom of speech and expression, freedom of worship, freedom from want, and freedom from fear. Jack had given him a quick lesson over pizza about the park, its messages, and commemoration to the first hero of World War II, a Madison resident.

He glanced at the cloudless sky. His next-door

neighbor, a graduate of the University of North Carolina, would have said, "Look at that sky. Carolina blue. God surely loves us to provide such a beautiful sky." Then she'd sigh.

The car's digital temperature display read ninety-six.

Malcolm reached over and patted Valerie's leg. "Damn, it's going to be hot out there. Are you sure you want to do this?"

She continued to look out the window. "It wouldn't be proper for you to attend without a woman with you."

"What makes you say so?"

She paused for several beats. "My momma always told me you can tell the true worth of a man by whether he has a woman with him when things ain't so good, like funerals, or money's tight, or someone's sick. Any man can have a woman with him at a party, or he's flush with cash, or when times are good. But a woman only goes through tough times with a good man. And Malcolm Gee, you're a good man."

His heart fluttered for a second. Her words deepened his feelings for her. She might be *the one*. He mentally crossed his fingers. She seemed to understand him and accept him, warts and all. He'd had girlfriends before, but they wanted to change him, make him "better." Better for who? Him or them? So far, Valerie hadn't told him he should do this, or not wear that, or say something different. She allowed him to be himself. She allowed him to be comfortable.

"That's cool that you have such good memories of your folks. Mine died in a car accident when I was thirteen. I wound up in foster care."

"Why am I just finding out now?"

He nodded. "I don't like talking about my past."

"I understand, but that's a pretty important part of who you are. It makes me wonder if there's anything else about you I don't know."

"Look, it's behind me, I prefer to look forward. Besides, in this job it's easier, well, maybe better, to not divulge much about yourself. There's a lot of really bad people running around that could use little pieces of information to do bad things against me or others."

"I understand. There weren't any family members who would take you in?"

"My mother's sister was an alcoholic and gave me up after a couple of months. Guess she really didn't want me. I was passed around from one foster family to another. I hadn't been the best kid, bit of a troublemaker, hated school, and actually, people in general. One of my foster families tried to get me interested in church and God, but that didn't work. I told them if God really existed and loved everybody, why did he put me in this mess, why did I feel unwanted instead of loved, cheated out of having real parents? If their God loved everyone so much, why didn't he fix my life? Two days later, the lady from the state came and took me to a group house. I guess that ended the love-your-neighbor bullshit the minister talked about during his speech.

"Most of the foster families I lived with only seemed interested in the stipend they received from the state. They didn't give a rat's ass about me. It took time, but I finally realized that being one of the thousands of foster kids that no one really looked after meant that I needed to suck it up and deal with it. I had a biology teacher with a sign in his class saying: *If it is to be, it is up to me.* It took a couple of months, but it finally dawned on me what it meant. I needed to take responsibility for me." He slapped himself in the chest.

Valerie twisted in her seat, straining against the seatbelt, to look at Malcolm. "Don't stop there. So, what did you do? How did you get to be an FBI agent?"

"In high school, I met another foster kid. We agreed that we needed to take responsibility and make something of ourselves. The Marine recruiter sounded pretty good: Join the Corps for four years, learn a trade, or go to college afterward on the GI bill, easy. That sounded good until Alex said he didn't see any reason to spend four years in the Marines when we could get endless student loans and spend those four years going to college. College had to be better than boot camp. It made sense. We graduated high school, found jobs, got an apartment together, and enrolled in the local community college. Fast forward five years, after we transferred to Penn State in Happy Valley, drank too much beer, partied too much, even attended a few classes, we both graduated with law enforcement degrees. Even before commencement, we had jobs lined up as deputy sheriffs. They sent us to the academy, we graduated and hit the streets. We became detectives in five years." He paused and looked off to the left. "And here's the cemetery."

Waiting for an oncoming car to pass, he flashed back to the two previous times he'd been in cemeteries. Both times it had been for people he dearly loved and missed: his parents and his fiancée Patrice. The guilt of not paying his respects since those memorable days began to rise. *Man, I'm not looking forward to this. I gotta control my emotions. I'm here because of work, not because I lost someone I cared about. Focus on the project.*

"Malcolm, it's green. Are you okay?"

He heard the concern in her voice. "I'm fine, just spaced out for a second."

He made the left onto the cemetery's single-lane entrance, dodged a pothole, drifted between a pair of rusty wrought-iron fence posts, and entered the cemetery proper. Valerie pointed across the grounds to a line of parked vehicles with several law enforcement vehicles interspersed. Off to the right, near a large tree, three canopies, approximately ten-by-ten feet each, sat like huge purple umbrellas. One of the canopies straddled a brass casket. An amazing number of flower baskets were arranged in a horseshoe shape around the casket. The other two canopies provided shade for about thirty folding chairs, the majority of which were occupied.

If the interment had happened the day before, as scheduled, he would have expected a much larger presence of family, friends, and especially law enforcement.

He pulled up behind the last car, turned the engine off, but didn't open the door. Valerie, with hand on door handle, looked at him with raised eyebrows.

He cleared his throat. "I prefer to stand behind the last row. You can sit if you like."

"I get it, you don't like funerals." She smiled and cocked her head.

"They're not my favorite way to spend a Sunday afternoon, but I'm here to show respect for a fallen law enforcement officer. We work for different branches, but he's a brother, and I want to respect the sacrifice he made. The closest seats should be for those who knew him best, had a connection with him, and will miss him."

Malcolm didn't want to scare Valerie, so he didn't mention serial killers often revel in the aftermath of their kills. The bureau referred to this as schadenfreude. He recalled the definition—the malicious enjoyment of someone else's misfortune, suffering, or unhappiness. To stoke their enjoyment, they become obsessed with television coverage, newspaper coverage, online blogs, as well as funerals and memorial services. They liked it when the media showed distraught family members, body bags, and physical carnage. At events, they typically stayed in the back, almost voyeur-like. Thus, it wouldn't surprise him if the Madison Murderer were in attendance or at least watched from afar.

"I get it. Can we leave the car? It's pretty warm without AC."

"Of course." He put his hand on her forearm. "I appreciate you coming along."

"My momma trained me well."

Her smile made his heart feel full. "Yes, she did."

He exited his car and smiled at the number of marked law enforcement vehicles in attendance. Not as many as at the church the day before, but plenty to thwart any shenanigans by the murderer, if he was in the area.

They walked, hand in hand, to the rear of the gathering. The shiny brass-colored casket drew their attention. The priest, wearing a full-length white robe, cinched at the waist, Bible in hand, stood on the opposite side of the casket from where the mourners sat.

Malcolm leaned over and whispered, "Why's that guy wearing white? Shouldn't he be in black?"

She nodded and rose on tiptoes to whisper in his ear. "From what I remember about my Catholic school upbringing, the white robe is called an alb. It normally has thirty-three buttons. Three, and multiples of three, are important biblical numbers. Priests can wear one of three colors for funeral ceremonies. White represents ascension to heaven. Black is a symbol of mourning and death. Purple suggests penance and reflection. Purple is worn a lot during Lent, which is a sorrowful time in Christ's life. Besides, given the heat and sun today, I wish I had worn white instead of this black dress."

He wrapped an arm around her waist. "You make that dress look good."

"Do you men ever think of anything else?"

"Not sure. I'll have to give it some thought." He winked.

She poked him in the ribs.

"I don't remember you mentioning going to church. How do you know so much about all this Catholic stuff?"

She frowned. "I thought I told you."

"Oh, you're right. You wanted to be a priest and studied about priest stuff but found out women can't do that, and you became disillusioned and your family left the religion when your dad couldn't do something because of an age restriction."

"I guess you were listening after all."

"Okay, enough chitchat, I need to pay attention here." He straightened and perused the assembly.

Officer Scott's wife, along with two older couples,

probably parents, along with three females about the same age as the wife, occupied the front row.

The priest looked at his watch and straightened. "I see a couple more cars arriving. We'll give them a few minutes, then commence."

Several heads turned toward the late-arriving vehicles, and faces frowned.

****

AD watched the last-minute arrivals settle into chairs or stand along the back. He counted sixty-eight in attendance, plus the cemetery crew seated under the tree. He didn't count himself because he was neither a mourner nor worker.

The count would have been higher, but the local police stopped all the TV and media people at the gate per the family's request. All those people were assigned an area approximately a hundred yards away. It looked like there were twenty or thirty of them and at least six cameras on tripods. He wished there were more, but given the interment was postponed due to his faux pas of depositing Crazy Kenny in Scott's grave, the numbers seemed satisfactory.

He took particular attention of the FBI agent and his female friend. They made an attractive couple. She blessed herself and bowed her head when they arrived. A sign of Catholic upbringing. The agent did FBI things like standing toward the back and scrutinizing each person as if checking for a flashing red arrow and sign stating "Madison Murderer." His plan to hide in plain sight appeared to be working.

****

A slight breeze brought the scent of jasmine, undoubtedly from the mountain of funeral baskets behind the priest, to Malcolm. He stiffened, his heart began to thump, and his stomach felt hollow. Akron, eight years earlier. He could see a woman's big brown eyes, just like Valerie's. But the woman's eyes were filled with confusion, knowing she was about to die, but didn't know why. He tried to clean the memory before another victim flashed into his mind, before even darker memories took over. He held his breath and tried to refocus on the scene around him. Then, the jasmine scent dissipated in unison with the hair prickling on the back of his neck. Someone was watching him. His gut instincts, honed by normally being the outsider in someone else's world, were almost always right. Some son of a bitch was watching him and doing a damn good job hiding it. He couldn't pinpoint who or where and didn't like it.

He scanned those in attendance, even checking the cemetery workers under the tree. He even scrutinized the backhoe a respectful distance away. Nothing looked out of the ordinary, but he still felt someone watching him.

Unable to shake the feeling, Malcolm wondered where Jack was. He extracted his cell phone and looked at the display. Several messages, but none from Jack. He texted —*Where are you?*—

Within fifteen seconds, Jack responded —*150 yds 2 your 6*—

—*Anything of interest?*—

—*Nada…you?*—

Malcolm typed —*Nothing yet.*—

A man hurrying away from the mourners toward the line of cars caught Malcolm's attention. He typed —*Man headed to car…know him…concern?*—

—Conrad...embalmer + anatomy teacher at college...he's good—

Malcolm returned to scanning those in attendance.

The officiant glanced at his watch, then the parked cars, and said, "Please stand."

While the priest droned on about ashes to ashes, and resurrection of the soul, Malcolm continued to study those in attendance. He looked for anything out of the ordinary. Nervousness. Trying to hide taking a picture. Writing notes. Anything.

His gaze systematically proceeded from one person to another. Standing behind the last row of chairs didn't allow him to see many faces, but he watched for posture, fixing or playing with their hair, massaging neck or shoulders, fidgeting, looking around, and the list went on.

The possibility the Madison Murderer could be in attendance, or somehow viewing the ceremony, kept him focused on the people and their mannerisms. He trusted Jack to cover the perimeter and outskirts.

Malcolm didn't pay attention to the priest. He had more important things to focus on. As the priest droned on, Malcolm drifted about ten feet farther away from the casket to observe even those who stood in the rear. He spent several seconds focused on each of the sixty-or-so attendees. Two warranted further scrutiny.

One of the men sat at the end of the fifth row. He appeared to be there by himself. Every minute or so, he'd glance at his watch or cell phone, then wipe his hands on his pant legs.

The second man of interest stood behind the last row, far right. He had a rigid stance. Feet shoulder width apart, hands clasped behind his back, the way military personnel stood when at ease. Also, the man seemed to be smiling. Who smiles at a funeral?

Malcolm slid his cell phone from a pants pocket and texted Jack.

—Man behind last row, far right…know him?—

—Smiley Johnson—funeral director—

The hairs on the back of Malcolm's neck rose again. He got the distinct feeling someone watched him but couldn't tell where the watcher was. Malcolm wondered if it were Jack but quickly dismissed the thought. It had to be the murderer, but where was he? How could he see Malcolm, but Malcolm couldn't see him?

Malcolm turned back to the priest who bowed to the wine bucket next to him, said something too soft for Malcolm to hear, then passed the edge of his hand over the bucket in the shape of a cross. He did it three times.

Father Davidson slid a metallic wand with a bulbous head out of the metal bucket as if extracting a knife from a wooden block. The priest turned to the casket and shook the implement which sent water droplets onto the top of the casket. He stuck the water wand in the bucket, pulled it out, and shook it at those present. Most of the attendees touched their forehead, belt buckle, left shoulder, and right shoulder, including Valerie.

The priest slid the water sprinkler back into the bucket with a metal clang. He turned and faced those in attendance. He looked pale, and his face shined from perspiration.

After opening his Bible, the priest scanned those assembled. "My brothers and sisters. Before I conclude Ronald James Scott's service, I'd like to share a passage from the New Testament, Romans 5: 5-8." He read, "And hope does not disappoint, because the love of God has been poured out into our hearts through the Holy Spirit who has been given to us. For Christ, while we were still helpless, died at the appointed time for the ungodly. Indeed, only with difficulty does one die for a just person, though perhaps for a good person, one might even find courage to die. But God proves his love for us in that while we were still sinners Christ died for us."

He closed the Bible. "Despite death, there is hope, and hope comes from the love of God through the Holy Spirit. God has done so much for us. So, when it's our turn to do something for Him, we need to do all we can. As scripture states, 'only with difficulty does one die for a just person.' Ronald James Scott's death happened for a reason, for a greater purpose. God is great and He is good at all times. He is all-knowing and all-powerful. His favor is to be sought. Any and all help we can provide will always be recognized and appreciated by God."

The priest turned around, laid his hand on Scott's casket, and bowed his head. Those in attendance rose in unison and bowed their heads.

Malcolm couldn't see him, but heard the priest say, "May the Lord Jesus Christ, our savior, bless you in the name of the Father, the Son, and the Holy Spirit."

The assembly responded in unison. "Amen."

"The service is ended. May you go in peace to love and serve the Lord."

"Thanks be to God," the assembly responded.

The priest cleared his throat and spoke. "After you've processed by and said a few words, please join the family at the American Legion post on Cherry Lake Circle for light refreshments and beverages, courtesy of the Legion Family organization."

Scott's widow led the procession. She held the arm of a stocky man who had the same squarish face and flat nose as her. She wailed and threw her arms around the metal coffin.

Malcolm could feel her pain. It resonated through his entire body. His arms trembled, legs no longer felt sturdy. He placed a hand on Valerie's shoulder to steady himself.

Valerie's own tears wetted her cheeks.

Malcolm had never attended a victim's funeral before. He avoided them. Always sent another agent to watch the crowd and report back. For the first time in memory, he stood within a few feet of someone grieving the loss of a loved one. The woman's pleas tore at his soul. She keened, "Ronnie…Ronnie. Oh my God, no. God, how could you let this happen? He'll never see his baby. This isn't the way life is supposed to be."

Family members tried to raise her off the casket, but she clung tight, nails scratching the bronze surface. The priest motioned for them to let her go. Malcolm agreed it might be best to let some of it out; she had to grieve, she had to release the emotion. Otherwise, it would cripple her in the days and weeks to come. Malcolm had learned the hard way about the negative effects of keeping emotion pent up.

She took great gasps of air and banged her fists on the casket.

Malcolm's chest tightened; his breaths came in quick, shallow pants. Pain stabbed his stomach, and his heart raced. He clutched Valerie's shoulder when he became lightheaded.

When the widow slid to the ground and wailed that she wanted her and the baby to be buried in the same hole as her Ronnie, Malcolm couldn't take it any longer. He had to walk away.

Valerie caught up to him after a few steps. "Honey, what's wrong?"

He sobbed and steadied himself on a tombstone. "It hurts to lose someone you love for reasons you can't understand. That poor woman."

"Yes, she's suffering, and will for a long time. But, as the Good Book says, 'This too shall pass.' "

He had never told anyone, not even Patrice, but more than anything in the world, he wanted to have children he could raise and take on camping trips, coach their soccer team, and tickle so much they cried from laughter. If heaven actually existed, Scott might see his child there. Perhaps they would then have an opportunity to interact, play ball together, hug one another. Maybe Scott would be able to tickle his child until the kid cried from the enjoyment.

Malcolm couldn't catch his breath, like when he'd rung the doorbell at the McMullen house and run away. He tripped and fell onto a baseball. It only knocked the wind out of him, but he thought he would die. Today he had the same feeling. He clutched his chest with one hand and Valerie's arm with the other.

Anger welled within him…the unfairness of it all. He had never felt this way before when dealing with work-related death. He had always approached his job with the victims in mind, as a representative of them, the voice of the murdered. He worked hard to remain emotionally detached, treat it as a job, as a challenge. His skills of logic, pattern recognition, hard work, and research to solve cases had kept him at arm's length. But this one got to him.

Emotions he had buried fifteen years ago tore through his chest. He slid to the ground and leaned against a tombstone. He struggled for air, fought to regain control. He knew Valerie knelt beside him and spoke, but he didn't understand a single word.

He shook his head to rid himself of the picture of Officer Scott's wife embracing the casket. A husband, a son, a soon-to-be father, a law enforcement officer lay inside that casket, ready to be lowered into the ground. Officer Ronald James Scott would not wake up, would not return home after work, and his wife would never see him again. His child would never see him, hold his hand, or hug him. That child would never feel his father's love.

Malcolm didn't believe in God or heaven. However, he did believe in the Golden Rule. And some asshole motherfucker with a rifle had violated it.

He straightened his legs, placed both palms on the grass. He forced his eyes open and looked at fluffy white clouds. His therapist had taught him to mentally count one-Mississippi, take a breath, count two-Mississippi, take a breath, for ten full breaths. Once again it worked. He regained control of his emotions and his breathing. He turned to Valerie and smiled.

She smiled back, wiped tears from his cheeks.

He wiped his wet cheeks with the backs of his hands and jacket sleeves. He looked around the slab of granite toward the casket. The same casket he previously decided to not parade by. "I want to pay my respects to Officer Scott. He deserves it."

After a couple of deep, cleansing breaths, he stood.

Valerie held his arm. She looked like she'd seen a ghost. "Are you okay?"

"Long story. Memories I try to forget." Each step he took became easier, and his posture gradually straightened.

They joined the end of the line of those waiting to say a few last words to Ronald James Scott.

Some touched the casket with fingertips, others put their entire palm on the casket. Two young men, possibly softball teammates, did fist-bumps with the casket.

When Malcolm reached the casket, he placed both palms on the top, surprised it felt cold on such a warm day. With eyes closed and head bowed, he muttered, "You don't know me, and I don't know you. I don't know why this happened to you, but I swear I'm going to find the motherfucker who did. I'll stop him so no other wife, mother, or child has to go through this sort of thing again. Rest in peace, officer."

Valerie and Malcolm, arms around each other's waist, walked to the car, their steps in perfect unison. Once inside Malcolm started the engine, adjusted the AC vent to blow against his face. He sat in silence, eyes closed, head against the headrest. After about a minute, he opened his eyes, looked at Valerie. He marveled at how their emotions had somehow spiderwebbed together.

Her presence brought a sense of comfort, a calming influence, a clarity. He wondered if she would become the security blanket most kids have, but he never did. In one of his foster homes, all three biological kids had blankets they carried everywhere. Each child had his own color—blue, green, and yellow. As long as they had those blankets, everything seemed good in the world. He wanted a blanket, something to wrap himself in, something that would protect him. Unfortunately, no one saw fit to give him one. Maybe Valerie would become his blanket.

She broke his thought. "Feeling better?"

He looked into her eyes and flashed a smile. "You make things better."

"Glad I can help."

"I'm going to ramp things up. Chief never liked the idea of the chalk markings. In fact, he didn't like any of my ideas, but I don't have to worry about him being a stick in the mud. I'm going on the offensive. I'm going to put pressure on the bastard. When people are pressured, they make mistakes."

"What are you going to do?"

"Come at him from every angle I can think of."

Chapter 30

2:05 p.m.

AD hadn't walked through any particularly sandy areas during Scott's funeral, but his father's teachings stayed with him. If he'd heard it once, he'd heard it a thousand times, "Son, take care of your truck, respect it, and it'll take care of you."

Before placing his feet on the silver pickup's floor mat, he kicked the heel of his right shoe against the running board three times, *thunk-thunk-thunk*. He repeated the process with the left shoe, *thunk-thunk-thunk*. He did things in groups of three as much as possible. After all, the number three appeared in extremely important places and ways in the Bible. For instance, the Holy Trinity, the Father, the Son, and the Holy Spirit. Three apostles followed Christ into the garden at Gethsemane. The three wise men who followed the star. The list went on. The number three could be found over 460 times in the Bible. Granted, fewer times than the number seven, but the number three played a prominent role in the Bible, the greatest book ever written. So, the importance of the number could not be overstated.

He liked routine, habit, repetition, process. It made life so much easier than constantly having to react. A great deal of his job turned out to be reactionary.

Initially he considered his job a calling to help people, to minister to them in their time of need. But, as the years went on, the calling turned into work, and now he classified it as a job.

He drove out the cemetery's west exit, made a right onto Mockingbird Trail, rolled past the community college, then stopped in the shade of a stand of oak trees. He took a deep breath and leaned his head against the headrest. He hadn't expected to see the FBI man at Scott's funeral. Could Gee be on to him? Could his attendance be serendipitous? Did they have him under surveillance? Was this part of Chief Dautry showing up at the church last night? Would he be able to carry out his next offering unhindered? Perhaps he should lie low for a couple of weeks, let law enforcement become complacent. But his methodically constructed plan didn't have the flexibility to take time off. Twelve sinners in twelve days summarized his mission statement, and he needed to fulfill it. Without knowing how much time remained before the cancer rendered him unable to function, he couldn't waste time. Six days gone, six more to go.

The spot in his lower right abdomen flared and reminded him the cancer progressed. The pain became worse with each passing day. He figured he only had a couple of weeks, at best, before he'd no longer be able to care for himself. Lying low for two weeks didn't seem to be an option. Every day brought him closer to dining at the Lord's table. Only God in heaven knew the day and hour when AD's spirit would leave his body and ascend to heaven. He couldn't disrupt God's plan.

He needed to think, to parse through everything

that happened the past couple of days. Chief snooping around the church, the unfortunate interaction with Crazy Kenny, moving Chief and Martha up the list, the FBI agent present at the funeral, the increased pain. Surely all of this meant something and required adjustments to the plan, but what adjustments? He needed time to think, to listen for God's voice.

AD had a typical Monday planned, meetings, teaching, and dealing with the things that occurred over the weekend. He couldn't take the day off...or could he?

He prayed aloud to God, asking for deliverance, even a temporary one. He couldn't die yet, he had a mission, a crusade to complete. His eternal life may depend on it. The future of mankind could depend on it. He needed to ignite the crusade in other believers. He couldn't fall short, he needed to make an example of the twelve. He made the sign of the cross, bowed his head and prayed:

How long, O Lord, will you allow me to do Your work?

How much longer will I be able to carry on?

I beseech thee, oh Lord, to allow me to fulfill my self-appointed task.

Through Your generosity give me the necessary time to honor You.

Please, do not let me see your face until I have provided warning and proof.

Permit me to demonstrate sin is not the way to heaven.

If it pleases you, Lord, consider and answer me, O Lord my God.

Jesus chose twelve, I also have chosen twelve.

Give me the time needed to ensure all twelve sleep the sleep of death.

Enlighten my mind, my entire being with the ability to carry out the sacrifices, sacrifices that please You, O Lord my God.

I trust in Your loving kindness.

My heart shall rejoice in Your salvation.

I will sing to you my Lord and my God.

I thank you for what you have provided.

I ask that you deal bountifully with me and my remaining time.

In these things, I ask Your will be done, not mine.

Amen.

AD made the sign of the cross, scrunched his shoulders, and took a deep breath, then exhaled. He felt better.

He couldn't be caught, at least not yet. He couldn't run out of time before he sacrificed the twelve. He had researched each one. He found each person guilty of wantonly sinning, of disregarding the commandments Moses had brought down from Mount Sinai. They had to pay the price. As Newton stated in one of his laws, for every action there is an equal and opposite reaction. It only made sense that if people sinned for pleasure, they paid the price afterward.

He had seen it so many times with parents and children. The parents would threaten the kids, "If you do that again, I'm going to ground you, or spank you, or take away your cell phone, or not give you your allowance." Well, if the parents didn't carry through with their threat, the kids never learned that their behavior wasn't acceptable. Well, he, AD, God's soldier, wouldn't repeat the error. He would dole out appropriate punishment. Not only would he administer it, but the entire world would hear about it so they could repent and straighten their path. Unfortunately, AD had only completed a fraction of the offerings. Also, the world hadn't learned yet why he had chosen the first six. He needed to resolve that. There had to be a way, but how?

AD leaned forward, chest against the steering wheel, and looked to the heavens. "Lord, my savior and redeemer. I am in need of guidance. What do I do? Give me the wisdom, the knowledge, the foresight necessary to complete the mission I have set upon. Allow me to help you to my fullest." He leaned back, closed his eyes, and listened with his heart.

Nothing.

He needed uninterrupted thought, and most importantly time to listen. He didn't know of any other place than his cabin where he would be left alone and not bothered by people's wants. The Withlacoochee River represented serenity, in a way his own version of the Jordan, where so many great events took place. He had never heard of anyone performing a baptism in the river, like John the Baptist did in the Jordan, but it was a special place. So, it made sense to go to the cabin, maybe for the last time, to sort things out.

He would call off tomorrow, for personal reasons, and spend time next to the river, searching for answers and guidance. He wasn't expected in the office on Tuesday, his day off, so he'd have a couple of days all to himself. Plenty of time to recharge and replan for the final push.

He shifted into drive and pulled away from the shade. To ensure the FBI didn't follow, he took State

Road 53 north, then cut across northern Madison County on Country Road 150, then Route 145 north. That route had plenty of sharp curves where he pulled over and paused for a minute or two.

On the drive, he decided to use his mother's old, dark-blue Ford truck to return to Madison and make one more offering. If the FBI did suspect him, they certainly wouldn't be looking for an old, faded, blue pickup.

Rounding a curve on Route 145, AD saw flashing red-and-blue lights ahead. His heart and mind raced.

Had they figured out he was the Madison Murderer? But how would they know he was on this road? Had they bugged his car?

His chest tingled and he became aware of taking shallow breaths. He licked his lips.

He couldn't turn around in the middle of the road without attracting attention. There was no place to turn off. The only option was to join the three cars in line in front of him.

When it came his turn, he eased forward. The police officer leaned forward and peered through the windshield. He smiled and waved him through.

AD recognized the man as someone he would occasionally see at St. Hubertus Sunday mornings. God must truly want him to succeed. He had put this man, who seemingly recognized AD as a fellow St. Hubertus attendee, in this spot, at this time.

As AD drifted by, the officer waved and said loud enough for AD to hear through the rolled-up window, "Have a good day."

AD returned the wave, pulled away, and monitored the rearview mirror. He took a deep breath when the officer stopped the next car in line and motioned for the driver to roll the window down.

AD stayed five miles an hour under the speed limit until he reached Coulter Road. That was when Psalm 116, verse 12 came to mind. He recited it out loud:

"How shall I make a return to the LORD for all the good he has done for me? The cup of salvation I will take up, and I will call upon the name of the LORD. To you will I offer a sacrifice of thanksgiving, and I will call upon the name of the LORD. My vows to the LORD I will pay in the presence of all his people."

Who needed Dave Ramsey, or Tony Robbins, or all those other supposed motivational experts? He had the opportunity to earn eternal life—what a wonderful gift God offered us. Not only would he earn a seat at God's right hand, but he'd also show the world they needed to straighten up, otherwise they'd suffer the same consequences as Holt Steadmyer soon would.

That lying, cheating, stealing mailman deserved his spot on the list. Stealing packages from rightful recipients was a despicable thing to do. He bragged that the people would eventually complain to Amazon, Walmart, or their prescription company, and the sender would resend. None of them was smart enough to figure it out.

Exodus 20:15 and Deuteronomy 5:19 both stated very clearly, "You shall not steal." Corinthians 6:10 went on to state, "nor thieves nor the greedy nor drunkards nor slanderers nor robbers will inherit the kingdom of God."

Even mail carriers weren't exempt from following God's commandments.

Chapter 31

6:02 p.m.

This Sunday evening felt no different from any other July evening he'd experienced since being in Madison. Hot. Humid. Sticky. Malcolm stood in the shade, at the top of the county courthouse's steps. Judge Harrison's wife stood next to him. Her eyes darted around, she licked her lips every few seconds and wrung a flowered kerchief in bone-thin hands.

Malcolm knew she didn't want to be there, didn't like the limelight, but he convinced her the investigation needed her to speak to the populace, to implore them to continue turning in tips.

He honestly told her the investigation had run into a stone wall, and they needed something to crack it. Her reaching out might be what's needed. It could be critical in solving her husband's murder.

He cleared his throat and looked at Mrs. Harrison. "Ready?"

"No, but I guess we need to get this over with." Her smile was not convincing.

Together they would take the next step in putting pressure on the murderer. Malcolm cocked his arm so the seventy-year-old woman could take it to descend the five steps to the plaza and side-by-side podiums.

He wondered how the podiums stayed erect with

the multitude of attached microphones. He didn't know how much a microphone weighed, but he imagined the amassed group constituted a significant weight.

The assembled cameramen and reporters quieted to total silence by the time Malcolm and Mrs. Harrison reached the podium.

Malcolm gazed at the locusts, sitting, kneeling, standing in the blistering sun. Dark, damp stains under arms, around necklines, appeared to be the uniform of the hour. With less than a minute in the sun, he felt sweat trickle down his spine.

"Ladies, gentlemen, citizens of Madison and Antler County, thank you for being here and watching on TV." He looked into a TV camera straight ahead. "Thank you also for the tips you're calling in. We sincerely appreciate every one of them. Keep them coming."

He took a deep breath and paused for dramatic effect. "As a result of those tips and review of security footage you have shared with us, we are now looking for an older model dark pickup truck, possibly a Ford. It has been spotted in the vicinity of several of the murders, and we'd like to speak with the driver to see if they have any information that could lead to the capture of the murderer. If you're the owner of that vehicle, please come forward, you could be in line for part, or all, of the reward. You could be the key to stopping these senseless murders."

He paused again to let it sink into those listening. He didn't expect the owner to come forward, but he did expect someone to call in about a neighbor, the guy down the street, or someone they work with.

"Earlier today I attended the interment of Officer Ronald Scott. I saw his grief-stricken pregnant wife and parents. We laid a fine young man to rest today, never to see his unborn baby. Tuesday, Judge Harrison will be buried in the same cemetery. It seems quite unfair. Two fine men who served the people of Madison, who loved their communities, whom others loved and respected. Brutally murdered for no apparent reason."

****

AD leaned forward in the recliner and threw an index finger at the TV. "You're a bunch of idiots. If they looked below the surface, truly investigated, they'd see those sacrificed had made fools out of Madison residents. Those people wantonly sinned and took advantage of those they were responsible for serving and protecting. They're sorry excuses for human beings." He threw his index finger at the TV again as if poking it in the chest to emphasize his point. "They deserved what they got." He untwisted a wine bottle's top, and instead of refilling the goblet raised the bottle to his lips and took two long swigs.

"They deserved to die and will proceed directly to hell, where they belong. They sinned against God, the people, and their families. Hypocrites. They're all a bunch of hypocrites. Every one of them." Another swig of sweet red wine.

By the time AD reseated himself, Judge Harrison's widow, Joan, stood at the podium. She dabbed her forehead and cheeks. Makeup didn't hide the bags under her eyes. She had a faraway look. He could see tears ready to flow from moist eyes. AD put his hand over his heart and felt sorrow for the poor woman. Everything he knew about her told him she lived life as a good, caring, and loving woman. She deserved better than the low-life husband she married forty years ago.

Joan Harrison licked her lips. "I have no idea who would kill my loving husband, a father and grandfather. My Thomas has lived in and served this community for over sixty years, everyone loved him, respected him. He always had a smile and good words to say about people. Even the criminals he sentenced to jail mostly said they deserved it. Why anyone would kill him is beyond me. Madison and Antler County have lost a wonderful member of the community. My family has lost the pillar of our existence. I don't know how we'll move on, but we must. We can't let everything Thomas held sacred be wasted. Whoever did this to him, to us, must be caught. I and my entire family need to understand why someone murdered our Thomas. We need closure. Will you please help us? I'm begging you from the bottom of my heart, help find the sick and demented person who did this. Help put them behind bars where they belong so they'll never hurt another person again." She paused and steadied herself on the podium. "I know nothing will bring my Thomas back, but we need to know why, and we need to prevent this senseless murderer from continuing to inflict so much pain. My Thomas was a good man, a good provider. We are offering another twenty-five thousand dollars to the reward money. It's now one hundred thousand. Talk to law enforcement, talk to the FBI, call the tip line. Please, please, help me, help my family."

Her lip quivered and eyes got big and round. A hand reached in from the side and took her elbow.

AD pointed at the TV. "Stupid woman. Be careful what you wish for. Soon, very soon, you'll find out why I took your dear Thomas away. He'll never sin again. He'll never break the ninth commandment again. Or any other commandment. When the world finds out he took money to let off criminals, took money to put innocent people in jail, looked the other way to protect the rich, you'll be embarrassed to even admit you knew him, much less married him."

AD crossed himself, closed his eyes, and muttered, "Please Lord, God of mercy and love. Her husband was not the man she thought him to be. Once her eyes are opened and she realizes the reason he was sacrificed, give her strength to carry on. She didn't know what he did. She didn't know his sins. She wasn't part of his sinfulness. Please look mercifully on her and help her accept that Judge Thomas Harrison deceived her, had wantonly and deliberately sinned, and deserved to receive the punishment delivered to him. In the name of your son, Jesus Christ, I ask this of you. Amen."

****

Malcolm stepped to the array of microphones and gazed over the assembly. He used an index finger to wipe sweat off his forehead.

He stared again into the Fox News camera almost directly in front of him. Here comes the next item to pressure the bastard. "The person who killed Officer Scott, Judge Harrison, Allison Newton, Timothy Kurtz, Kenny Murchison, Martha Osgood, and Chief Dautry is obviously a coward. They hide in the shadows like a thief. Instead of stealing your wallet, they stole people's lives, inflicted incredible stress and pain on families. Shooting innocent people from a distance without rhyme or reason is sick. The press has dubbed you the Madison Murderer. I'm confident you're watching. I'm confident you think you're so much smarter than the rest of us." He grabbed the edges of the podium.

"Leaving chalk markings at each scene, taunting us. Yes, we received your letter, the way you carried on about the victims. Why? I don't know what you think you know about these victims, but you're wrong." Malcolm rose onto the balls of his feet and leaned forward. "You're not God, you can't judge them, you can't punish them for whatever reason your demented mind may conjure. We've investigated and didn't find anything that would even come close to reason to execute someone. Respected, loved, and solid citizens of the community describe each person you murdered." Malcolm pointed into the camera. "Look into these eyes." He used two fingers to point at his own eyes. "You will be caught. You will be punished. You're not God, you don't get to decide who lives and dies. You're mortal like the rest of us. Your time is coming to an end, real soon."

****

AD massaged his lower right abdomen. He nodded and spoke aloud. "You're right, Mr. Lawman, Special Agent in Charge Malcolm Gee. My time's coming to an end, real soon."

Several weeks ago the pain pulsed, but the past few days it had become steady. The ramekin of oxycodone tempted him, but he needed to keep a clear head. He needed to think.

Chief Dautry had come way too close to uncovering the Madison Murderer's true identity. As long as he lay in a coma at Tally General, he didn't present a threat, but should he come around and be able to speak, it could bring unwanted problems. If he eliminated Chief now, would they figure out how he knew where they hid him? If they figured it out, they would know who he was and possibly end his crusade early.

AD had only accomplished half of his objective. He needed the selected twelve sacrifices. Not six, but twelve. Twelve was so very significant in the best book ever published, the Bible. Twelve appeared at the Last Supper. Twelve stars above her head in Revelation symbolized the twelve patriarchs of Israel. Twelve gems in the breastplate of the high priest. Even the carving on the front door of St. Hubertus church depicted St. Hubertus, the patron saint of hunters, with a twelve-point stag. There was no getting around it, the number twelve played a prominent role in biblical history.

Yes, twelve was the correct number, and he would tally that many.

He needed to focus on other matters. They evidently had some video of his mother's Ford truck. If he had been in the blue pickup, would that officer have stopped him? Maybe he needed to use the silver Chevy when going out to sacrifice sinners. Would that work for the remaining six? What kind of issues might arise?

He also realized that if the world didn't know why he'd selected the twelve, then his message wouldn't get out. If taken alive, he'd have a chance to tell everyone, to list the sinners and their transgressions. But if killed during capture, or if the cancer got him before completing the mission, then how would the world know? In all his planning this possibility had never occurred to him. What should he do?

****

Malcolm turned the ignition key, and a flick of the wrist twisted the air conditioning knob to max cool. The air wasn't cool yet, but the breeze on his face brought relief from the heat and humidity. Valerie sat in the passenger seat and waved a homemade paper fan in front of her face. It reminded Malcolm of the kind the kids made in school out of a sheet of paper folded multiple times. Despite her glistening face, he thought she looked beautiful. He didn't think there could ever be another Patrice, but this woman sure came close.

She must have sensed him looking at her. Valerie turned but kept the fanning action going. "What?" She smiled.

"You're amazing. I think I love you." The words shocked him, but he didn't regret saying them. He had spoken the truth.

She blushed and leaned over.

They kissed.

She gazed into his eyes, stroked his face. "I do love you."

The sound of a barking dog sprang from his coat pocket. "Damn."

Valerie leaned back and made that little giggle he liked so much. "Your boss?"

With a nod, Malcolm raised a finger to his lips, then stabbed the green accept button on the car's display screen. "Gee here."

"What's this shit I hear about you being shacked up with some bimbo and not available to visit active scenes? If that's true, I'll yank you out of there so fucking fast it'll take your tonsils four hours to catch up with the rest of your body. You better have a damn good explanation."

Malcolm glanced at Valerie. Her eyes bulged, and her mouth flew open. He shook his head. "My girlfriend surprised me with a visit, but she's not a bimbo and she's not the reason I didn't visit the scene. The Madison PD somehow didn't think to call and tell me. I spoke with Acting Chief Jack Palmer. That won't happen again."

"How long is your girlfriend going to be there? Never mind, just tell me she's already gone."

"She'll be leaving shortly."

Valerie stiffened and shook her head, then extended her middle finger to the phone and mouthed the words *No fucking way*.

"I don't know what was going on between you and Chief Dautry, but I'm tired of getting phone calls. Speaking of which, I expect another half dozen about your press conference. What the hell are you doing? Calling the murderer a coward, a low-life, and a scumbag? Are you serious? And, you had the judge's wife there? Jesus H. Christ, what the hell is the matter with you?"

Malcolm closed his eyes and took a deep breath. "Look, Roger, we're at a dead end. We've got nothing to go on. I've got to do something to get him to reach out, make contact with us. Write another letter, slip a note under my wiper blade, something. Right now, he has the upper hand. He's not a spur-of-the-moment guy. He's orchestrated every moment so far. If I can throw him a curve ball, get him angry, react out of emotion, he'll make a mistake. I don't think he's taunting us, I think he's on a greater mission or quest. That's why he wrote the letter. He's telling us something, but we're not sure what. I'm hoping he'll reach out again. Maybe he'll give us a clue as to who he is, where he is, what he's planning next."

"And what if he doesn't?"

"We still have the possibility of Chief Dautry helping us somehow."

"He's in a coma, and the doctors aren't sure if he'll ever wake up."

Malcolm massaged his forehead, trying to prevent a headache. "Correct, but we have to look under all the rocks, around all the bends, and follow up on every possibility. In the meantime, we continue digging."

"What if the police chief doesn't come around, or can't help?"

"We're no worse off than we are now."

"You're playing a dangerous game. Plus, you're going against training and bureau policy. I hope to hell you're right. I'm getting a lot of pressure to make progress, to get this solved. Your ass is in a vise, and I'm turning the crank. You better do something real fucking soon."

Silence.

Malcolm looked at the phone. Roger had disconnected.

The press conference had riled Roger up, hopefully the Madison Murderer would be even more riled.

"If that pompous fool of a boss of yours thinks I'm leaving after him calling me a bimbo, he's got his head stuck where the sun don't shine. I'm staying, and I'm going to help you solve this. Bimbo. Humpf."

Chapter 32

7:28 p.m.

The afternoon sunshine had given way to dark skies toward the west. Gray and black clouds this time of year generally brought storms. They certainly seemed to foreshadow the stormy situation AD had on his hands.

He made a right off SR 145 onto Coulter Road. If he'd gone another fifty yards, he'd have crossed the Withlacoochee River and entered Georgia.

Coulter Road contained numerous ruts and puddles, but AD knew their locations and maneuvered around them with ease. Jerimiah Coulter, the farmer who lived at the end of the road, only ventured out on Sunday to take his wife to church and then to feast at Reynold's All-You-Can-Eat BBQ. Otherwise, he stayed home to tend his cattle and crops. When the road got too bad, he'd drive his tractor, grading blade on the back, back and forth from one end to the other until the road surface leveled out.

AD made a left onto Hideout Lane. Those who didn't already know would never suspect a cabin sat behind the brush and trees, a mere twenty yards from the river.

Driving with the window open allowed him to inhale the beautiful scent of fresh pine. In the shade the air felt cool and reminded him of Christmas when his parents would harvest a fresh tree and put it in the corner of their living room at home. They would take an entire day to festoon it with ornaments handed down from one generation to another. Each ball, each statue, each figurine would be carefully placed on the tree and a story accompanied each one—Aunt so-and-so brought it from the old country, or they bought that one in Atlantic City on the boardwalk, and the stories went on until they had placed each item in the perfect position on the perfect limb. The ritual ended with their traditional supper of stuffed duck, boiled red potatoes, and hot apple pie with cinnamon ice cream for dessert. It saddened him to think those ornaments might be taken to the garbage dump when he died.

He couldn't let nostalgia get to him now. Bigger and more important things demanded his attention. He'd reunite with his folks very soon, as long as he earned eternal salvation. Eternal salvation, he was committed to earning it.

AD wound through the bushes and around trees until he arrived at the cabin. It wasn't much to look at: one story, gray metal roof, screened porch across the front, faded green siding, white trim, sagging gutters. The downspouts had disappeared years ago. A single electric line extended from a telephone pole to the corner of the cabin. No phone line. No cable TV, no internet. Electricity was all his parents needed, and that's all he needed.

After entering the front door, he made a beeline for the back porch where his father's wooden rocking chair waited. He turned it slightly to face southwest and the approaching storm clouds. Another forty-five minutes and the cloud line would reach him. He loved rocking on the back porch; it had a semi-hypnotic effect on him. The rhythm of forward and backward allowed his mind to empty and stress to escape.

The Withlacoochee River meandered past the cabin about twenty yards away. The bank on the other side of the sixty-five-foot-wide river belonged to Georgia. When the bushes along his bank were kept low, he could see the brownish water. With it being the rainy season, the river flowed instead of the more typical ooze it had during the dry season. As a kid he'd often dreamt of building a raft and floating with the current all the way to the Gulf of Mexico.

Water in general provided a wonderful therapy for him. It seemed to wash away all the stress, anxiety, and worry he accumulated during interactions with those he served. No wonder Christ baptized with water. It too washed away bad things, such as original sin.

Normally, when at the cabin, everything seemed good with the world. But at the moment, things weren't too good. He had a lot on his mind.

He leaned back and thought about his parents. Neither of them was pushy or ambitious. They'd loved being teachers and loved most of their students. They just wanted a happy life, with minimal stress. They certainly enjoyed their time on Hideout Lane. Peace and quiet were all they wanted when there. They took good care of him, said their only regret was they had never been able to give him a sibling, someone to play with, someone to grow up with. However, they spent time with him, both individually and as a couple. His father probably spent more time with him because they did what Mom called boy things, hunting, throwing a baseball, working on the trucks, cutting firewood, and generally working outside. He wanted to recreate that time. Holding hands and praying before meals. Trips to the store. Rocking on the porch. Walks in the woods. If everything went right, he'd be reunited with his parents in heaven, soon, very soon.

This evening the river's current leisurely moved a palm tree log along. At the age of ten, he would have thrown stones at it. At the moment that log reminded him of how he felt, aimlessly drifting, going wherever the current took him.

Chief Dautry, the FBI, and Crazy Kenny had certainly interrupted his plans. He had devised such a beautiful plan, born from hours of prayer, planning, scouting, and dry runs. Everything moved along nicely in the beginning, then unexpected things changed. He saw change as the devil rearing its ugly head. But, with God on his side, he'd overcome the devil's obstacles and complete the mission.

The tactical objective of his mission remained intact—sacrifice twelve worthy individuals before the cancer rendered him incapable of functioning on his own. The purpose of his mission remained the same: provide proof positive that sin would not be tolerated, sin was not your friend, sin would be punished. Due to unexpected complications, the plan for completing the mission needed to be adjusted, but how?

Long after the floating log had drifted out of sight, AD continued to rock. Eyes closed, head back. He emptied his mind and prayed to St. Hubertus, asking for guidance in sorting through all of the issues.

So many things to think about, so many problems to solve, and time continued to disappear. Each day the abdominal pain grew. The discomfort now appeared in his chest, a sure sign the cancer spread.

St. Hubertus seemed to whisper that it would be best if he looked at the challenges one at a time.

Do the easy one first. Crazy Kenny. No sense spending time on him. That couldn't be avoided. It's what Oliver North called collateral damage. Forget about him and move on. Issue resolved.

Chief Dautry created an entirely unexpected problem. AD had not considered, not even once, the possibility of anyone connecting the sacrifices to St. Hubertus. Nor had he considered the possibility of only wounding a sacrifice. Chief's sacrifice needed to be completed to ensure he kept quiet about the St. Hubertus connection. Issue two now had a resolution but needed a plan for execution.

He decided to postpone pondering a plan, and the FBI, until he ate. Perhaps a can of soup would help with the pain.

AD shuffled inside to the small kitchen. He popped the top on a can of chicken noodle soup, poured its contents into one of the few pans saved from his mother's estate, and added a can of well water.

When he didn't feel good as a child, Mother made soup in this very pan for him. Coupled with a few soda crackers, as she called them, it always helped his stomach as well as his spirits. He found something about the combination comforting, and he certainly needed comforting. Alprazolam wasn't an option until he sorted through and developed resolutions for the challenges he faced.

He wandered to his easy chair to enjoy a goblet of wine and wait for the soup to heat. He filled the goblet and licked a drop off the bottle's mouth. "Waste not, want not." When he set the bottle on the table next to the recliner, it clipped the remote control's on button. The *60 Minutes* ticking clock materialized on the dusty TV screen.

After a few seconds, the female host, Eleanor somebody, appeared with a simple-looking cell phone superimposed on the screen behind her. She perched on a stool and spoke. "Cell phones. It seems as though we can't live without them. We communicate with them. We use them for music, to receive news, navigation, pay for items, and so much more. We can even use our cell phones to find someone else's location or their lost cell phone. Law enforcement also likes that we use cell phones, particularly when criminals use them. They often joke, 'Do you know why it's called a cell phone? Simple, when bad guys use one, they normally wind up in a cell.' Tonight's story focuses on a particular type of cell phone called a burner. Police don't like them, and Clifford Rubin tells us why."

He hit the record button simultaneously with Clifford's image coming into focus and eight different cell phones evenly spaced on the table in front of him. "Burner phones. Quite ingenious. Criminals use them because law enforcement can't readily identify who owns the phone. No one owns the number. It's not registered to anyone so the police don't know who's using it. Unlike the phones we have through AT&T, Verizon, T-Mobile, and the other large carriers where the phone number is associated with an individual or corporation, a burner phone's number isn't associated with anyone. Law enforcement may be able to trace a burner's use, but not necessarily who used it. Besides, it takes three minutes or more of live use for them to track where the call originates from. Burners are almost always plain phones, small screens, no fancy cameras. Criminals don't want flashy phones that attract attention. Hence, most burners are plain black, no colors, not even silver. Because there's nothing flashy about them, they are very inexpensive. For the most part, criminals use the phone once or twice and then dispose of it. Many times they'll toss the phone into a fire that destroys fingerprints, DNA, and anything else the authorities could use to identify who used it, hence burner."

When Clifford completed his story, AD clicked the power off button and wandered to his now hot soup. He added a lot of salt and a little pepper to make it taste just like Mother's soup. Each slurp warmed his stomach and brought comfort.

The more he relaxed, the more his mind worked. Being the only one who knew the sins that warranted individuals to be included on his list created an unforeseen challenge. No one had talked about Officer Scott's infidelity with another man, or Judge Harrison finding criminals innocent for a pay-off, or Allison Newton letting nursing home residents die instead of saving them. Timothy Kurtz called their band the Jesus Jerks; how could they insult Jesus Christ, who died a nasty and painful death on the cross, like that? Crazy Kenny, well, he had become an unfortunate victim.

Unfortunately, he had only wounded Chief. Why had the FBI agent lied and said Chief had been killed? Maybe they wanted to protect Chief's wife? Maybe they wanted to protect Chief from another attempt. After all, who would look for, and shoot, a dead man?

But the FBI continued to underestimate him. They didn't know he knew Chief lay in Tallahassee General Hospital.

It didn't matter why the FBI lied. They had wrested control from him, and now he needed to take it back. Completing Chief's sacrifice would make law enforcement reactionary again. He would be in the driver's seat.

With the soup consumed, he hand-washed the dishes, dried them, and put everything away. He never saw clutter in Mother's kitchen and wouldn't allow it in his either.

He needed a plan to complete Chief's sacrifice. The man had a twenty-four-hour guard. How could he get past the guards, offer Chief up, and get away?

He refilled the wine goblet and returned to the wooden rocking chair on the rear porch.

The more he relaxed, emptied his mind, and asked St. Hubertus to continue whispering to him, a three-pronged approach took shape in his mind. With twenty minutes of relaxation and clear thinking, he had all the details worked out.

First, he needed to drive the forty minutes north to Valdosta and visit several stores. He'd then swing through Tallahassee, say hello to Madison Chief of Police Taylor Dautry, then get his plan back on track with a sacrifice of Holt Steadmyer in Madison, then return to the cabin. It would be exhausting, probably without return to the cabin until sunrise, but he'd be right on schedule to make twelve sacrifices in twelve days.

Chapter 33

Malcolm stood in front of Gram's Kitchen and peered through the front window into the restaurant's dark interior. The sign on the door, red letters on white background, plainly stated CLOSED. He glanced at his watch. The pesky reporter should arrive any time. Despite being a pain in the butt, he seemed the type to be punctual.

Malcolm remembered Nancy at the pizza shop saying, "My husband makes mistakes when he's under pressure." If he could put pressure on the murderer about the chalk markings, perhaps the man would make a mistake, do something out of the ordinary, do something out of anger. In a few minutes, he'd take another step toward pressuring the murderer into making a mistake.

Another check of the time and sidewalk, both ways. No Skipper.

Being in a small southern town on Sunday evening, it didn't surprise him to see a Closed sign hanging on Gram's door. They'd probably have to drive to Denny's or Dairy Queen down by I-10 for dinner. He hoped Valerie would pick Dairy Queen. He loved their grilled hot dogs with ketchup, mustard, sweet relish, raw onion, and kraut. A side of fries and a double chocolate milkshake sounded really, really good.

Valerie sat on the bench in front of Madison Insurance. Its window advertised home, auto, boat, life, and health insurance. "Tell me again why we made that goofy document with the squiggles and strange symbols."

"I'm going to"—Malcolm used air quotes—"leak it."

"You're going to give it to the pain in the butt reporter. Okay, and it's supposed to be the chalk markings you found at the murder scenes, except there weren't any chalk markings. Is that right?"

He smiled at her. "You're as smart as you are beautiful."

She wrinkled her brow. "I'm not sure how to take that."

"We can discuss it later. Here comes Skipper."

The fedora-wearing reporter, still more than a block away, seemed to swagger as he approached. About ten feet away, the short, round man pulled out the mini tape recorder, thumbed it on, and held it in front of his mouth. "Special Agent Gee, any new murders to report?" He then extended the recorder toward Malcolm.

"No comment." Malcolm rolled his eyes, then frowned. He pointed at the recorder and drew his index finger across his throat.

Skipper's eyebrows rose, then scrunched together. After a few seconds, he pressed a button, and the little red light extinguished. "Okay, it's off, what do you want to talk about?"

"Take the cassette out. You can hold it in your hand, but I want it out of the recorder."

"You're not very trusting. I told you it's off."

Malcolm shook his head. "Cassette out or no conversation. I'll go to another reporter."

Skipper looked at Valerie. She stared back at him with a smug smile. "I know what he wants to talk about, and knowing everything I know, I'd play along if I were you."

"Okay, okay." He ejected the cassette and slid it into his pants pocket. "Instead of meeting on the sidewalk, why don't we meet in that war room you've built?"

"Nice try. Look, Skipper, everything I tell you is off the record. If you attribute it to me, I'll deny every word and make your life a living hell."

"I would think you had plenty on your plate without worrying about making my job any tougher than it is."

Malcolm nodded. "You're right, that's why I want your help."

Skipper took a step backward. "You want my help?" He pointed to his chest, eyebrows raised.

"One of the ways serial killers are caught is to get them communicating with law enforcement. It happens through emails, cell phones, lots of different ways. In our case, the murderer felt compelled to send a letter to Chief, and Chief gave you the copy you showed me."

Skipper smiled. "Nope, didn't get the letter from Chief, God rest his soul. But what's this got to do with me?"

"I don't know you from the man in the moon, but evidently Chief chose you to leak the letter to. I have something I want leaked. Interested?"

The smile faded, he crossed his arms, and his

eyebrows drew together almost forming a unibrow. "You want to leak something to me? Do you have another letter? Do you have it with you?"

"It's not a letter, but it is from the murderer. I have a composite of the chalk markings we've found at several of the locations where the shooter stood. Our experts can't make heads or tails out of them. Someone out there may know what they mean, what message the murderer is sending us. For political and career reasons, I can't send an email to the press and ask for help. We're the FBI, and we're supposed to have all the answers. But in this case, we don't. So, what I'm hoping is if a copy of the markings somehow became available to you, you would share it with your audience and colleagues. Then, as a result of the world getting a chance to see the markings, we're hopeful someone will come forward and tell us what they mean, or possibly the murderer will send us another letter. Or, if things go really right for us, he'll call our tip line."

"Serious, you want me to help the vaunted FBI?"

"You can help us, or I'll go elsewhere. There are a couple of reporters here with national organizations who may have further and quicker reach than you. I'm talking to you because Chief thought you worthy with the letter. I like continuity, but I'm not afraid to switch. I want this bastard caught."

Valerie extracted several folded sheets of eight-and-a-half-by-eleven white paper from her purse. She unfolded them with a flourish and looked at the top sheet. She then rotated the page a little to the left, then a little to the right, tilting her head with each shift of position. She looked at Skipper. "I see this stuff but have no idea what it means."

Skipper squinted at the paper. Fortunately, the pest stayed in place, but his eyes focused on the gyrating white paper in Valerie's hands.

He then smiled and wagged a finger. "Hey, wait a minute. The letter said there weren't any chalk markings."

"You're right. That's one of the things that puzzle us. We believe he put them there, but why would he claim they weren't there? He also told us to look at the shell casings. We didn't find any shell casings. Maybe he's confused. Maybe he's delusional. Maybe he's trying to throw us off his scent. Bottom line is we're at a dead end, and I'm asking for your help. If you won't help, I can always talk to one of the national people, or even find a local Tallahassee reporter to help. It's your choice."

"Give me a minute to think this through. Don't go to anyone else."

"Like I said, you had the letter, so obviously you have a source within the investigation. No one would be surprised if you have more leaked information. It makes sense and is consistent with what's already happened. But, if you're not willing to play along…"

Skipper removed the fedora and scratched his mostly bald head. The little bit of hair that circled the sides and back of his head hung like thin curtains. "Ummmmm, I don't know. Can I see them?"

Malcolm looked over his shoulder at Valerie. "Show him one page." He placed his hand on Skipper's chest to make sure he didn't bolt forward to try and snatch the page.

Skipper leaned forward and squinted. "It looks like something a little kid would draw."

"At first glance, it does, but when you study them, there's a pattern. They seem to go from Hebrew to Cyrillic, to a four-year-old finger painting."

"I didn't know Hebrew had its own letters, and I don't know what Cyrillic is." He shrugged.

"I didn't know much either. Hebrew does have its own alphabet, used mostly with the Yiddish language. Cyrillic has multiple variations, but supposedly Russian comes closest to what those markings are. One of our linguistics people explained that Russian has thirty-three letters, twenty consonants, ten vowels, a semivowel, and a couple of characters that are pronunciation signs. I don't understand it, but that's what she said."

Skipper straightened and scratched his head again. He nodded, then a smile formed. "Okay, I'll do it. But I get to post it on my blog two hours before I share it with others. Deal?"

He didn't think much would happen over the next two hours anyway with it being Sunday evening but didn't want to cave to Skipper's demand. "You have one hour. Agreed?"

The reporter took a step toward Valerie with his hand out, but Malcolm grabbed the man's outstretched wrist and twisted.

"Hey, what the hell are you doing? That hurts."

"Agreed?"

"Of course. Give me those papers."

Malcolm shook his head. "We can't be seen giving you papers. Buy a candy bar at the Rexall. When you come back, the papers will be stuck between the slats."

"Damn, is that what you call a dead drop?"

"You've seen too many movies. Now go."

Malcolm pointed to the Rexall.

Malcolm sat next to Valerie and watched the reporter until he pulled the drug store's door open, looked at them, shook his head, and disappeared inside.

"Stick the papers between the slats. When he comes out, we'll leave."

He felt relief, another part of his pressure campaign would soon be put into action, and Valerie helped make it happen. Sitting next to her, his thoughts went to Patrice and how they could sit on a park bench for an hour without speaking. Being together, touching one another, not in a sexual way, but being close, brought comfort and a feeling of togetherness, a sense of peace. The more time he spent with Valerie, the more he fell in love with her. Maybe she was the one.

Valerie poked him with her elbow. "Here he comes."

She inserted the papers between the bench back's slats and stood. "You know, I could go for a hot fudge sundae."

"That sounds heavenly. What a great way to end a day. I've put a lot of bait in the water, now I need something to take it. The pressure's building. I'm anxious for tomorrow."

Day Seven—July 21st

Chapter 34

Monday, 1:50 a.m.

Malcolm stood at the hotel room window lost in thought. He wondered if the Madison Murderer planned to strike tonight. How many other victims would have a hole in their head when the sun came up? He wanted to do something but didn't know what.

The Madison PD had every available officer, plus sixteen sheriff's deputies from surrounding counties, out on patrol between sunset and sunrise. Collectively, they traveled all paved roads within twenty miles of the city center every two hours.

According to the Welcome To Madison sign, the city's population consisted of 5,843 residents, and Antler County had a little over twenty thousand residents. Why would a serial killer choose small-town America to kill people? Why?

Earlier in the evening, when he and Valerie ate dinner at the DQ, he felt pretty good. Instead of being reactive, wondering what the murderer would do next, he felt as though they'd taken the necessary steps to force the murderer's hand, to pressure him into making a mistake.

Only a handful of people knew Chief still lived. Granted, he was in a coma, and the doctors didn't know if, or when, he'd come out of it, but the man still lived.

Malcolm's gut told him Chief knew something he hadn't shared. Hope existed the lawman would come around and share what he suspected. He seemed to know everything that happened in Madison and even Antler County. The odds seemed good that he had already determined the commonality between the victims. Knowing the commonality would be a huge boost to the investigation and to stopping the Madison Murderer.

Another item to the task force's advantage involved the relatively small area the murderer operated within. Every victim had been within seven miles of the city center. Unlike the D.C. Sniper who hunted in a much larger area, their killer stayed local. This gave a great deal of credence to the thought the killer lived in the area. Another item in their favor.

Under the direction of Goose, Beverly, and Danny, more than one hundred resources sifted through crime scene clues, reviewed videos, chased down tips, and conducted research. Every hour that passed resulted in more information being learned. It was great work when the video review team verified an older-model Ford pickup had been in the vicinity of three of the murders at the approximate time the killings took place. It could be a coincidence, or it could be valuable. Unfortunately, the team couldn't read the plate, but they continued reviewing video, now intent on finding that truck.

The noose had begun to tighten around the killer's neck, and the SOB had no idea the FBI was this close. Malcolm smiled at the thought. However, they needed a break, something to happen, a clear fingerprint, an eyewitness, video showing the murderer in action or revealing features, law enforcement accidentally stumbling on the guy, something, anything, to move them along.

Taking the initiative had buoyed Malcolm's confidence they would soon capture him. But now, standing at the window, a low-grade dread built inside of him about the bastard. Something told him another victim would soon be ambushed. An unseen countdown clock ticked in Madison, one that when it reached zero, another resident would die.

Malcolm eventually crawled into bed, lay on his back, and listened to the hotel sounds. The ice machine dropped another batch of ice, the elevator dinged, a car door in the parking lot closed with a *thud*. He stared at the smoke detector's red light and wondered if anyone would notice if it burned out.

Valerie stirred, turned her head. "Why aren't you sleeping? I thought you'd be tired after our workout."

"I have a lot on my mind."

"Like what? You can't do anything in the middle of the night."

The sheets rustled when he pulled them up. "I'm worried. Am I doing the right things? Am I missing something? Should I be out there riding around, looking for the son of a bitch? People are dying, and I'm responsible for finding and stopping the killer. I feel like I'm stuck in neutral."

She raised an elbow. "You've done this before. What was it like on those other projects?"

He rocked his head back and forth. "Every project is in a different city, different person, different clues, different reasons. None of them are the same."

She touched his arm. "I get that, but have you

269

always been able to find the killer right away? Or did it take time to figure it all out?"

A deep breath and slow exhale. "Chief knew."

"Chief was in cahoots with the killer?"

"Not connected, but he knew, or at least had a suspicion of the commonality amongst the victims. Hell, he may even have had a suspicion who the killer is. My gut tells me he was on to something, that's why the killer went after him. Maybe Chief was added to the killer's list, or maybe he was moved up the list. I don't know, but somehow there's a connection. I just don't know what. When he comes around, he'll have motivation to share what he knows, to get the guy who shot him."

"That's the second time in two days you've mentioned a gut feeling."

He nodded. "My gut's normally right. Something about my brain, it makes connections, but they're not always apparent. It's like they're in the shadows, but I can't bring them into the light."

Valerie rolled onto her back, clasped hands laid on her midsection. "So, how do you get those thoughts to the front of your mind?"

"They surface when they feel like it. Normally, when I'm talking about something else, they just sorta pop to the front of my brain." He shrugged.

She rolled to her side and placed a hand on his cheek. "Well, I have something I'd like to talk about, if you're up to it."

"Sure, I'm wide awake, might as well be productive."

"Um…you know…I…uh…I meant what I said earlier today, or yesterday, or whenever. I do love you."

He put his hand over hers. "I know, and I believe I love you too."

"Can I ask you a personal question?"

"Sure, go ahead."

"Why aren't you attached to someone? You don't talk much about yourself. You're a good man, one that a smart girl should have snagged a long time ago. Why are you single and unattached?" She paused a second. "You are unattached, aren't you?"

Sensing she held her breath waiting for an answer, he chuckled. "Yes, I'm unattached. No wife. No girlfriends. No significant others."

She released the breath and inhaled, maybe a little louder than she intended. "Anyone from your past I should know about? Anyone I should worry about?"

He sighed. "No one to worry about. I had a serious relationship at one time. We had gotten engaged, but she died before we got married."

She remained silent for a long minute then rose on an elbow. "That's it? You're not going to tell me what happened?"

"Babe, I really don't like talking about it. There's a lot of bad memories there."

She snuggled close to him, laid her head on his shoulder, straddled a leg over his. They lay in silence for several minutes.

"What was her name?"

He sighed. "Are you really going to do this?"

"I'd like to know."

He paused a second. "Patrice."

"How long did you know her?"

"Eighteen months before I proposed. She wanted to be a June bride. I didn't want to wait that long, but to make her happy, I agreed."

"What did she die of?"

He sighed again. "Is it important for you to know?"

"Yes, I don't know where our relationship is going. I don't know if we have a future or not. I want to trust you, but I don't know if I should. You don't talk about yourself much. I get it. It's part of being an FBI agent, I guess. But I need to know more about you to know how much more I want to invest in this relationship. I want to trust, but I need reasons, too."

He nodded. "I hadn't told any woman I loved her since Patrice. I didn't plan on saying it to you, it…it…came out. It's like my heart took over my mouth."

"Aw, that's so sweet. You're such a softy. You're like a big old teddy bear. That's one of many things I love about you."

"Thanks. I appreciate you saying that. Sometimes I wonder about how I come across to people. I can be pretty hard-nosed at times. You've only seen the soft side of me so far." He kissed her forehead and gave her a hug as best he could.

After almost a minute of lying in one another's arms without speaking, she tapped him on the chest. "I gave you a well-deserved compliment, but I'm not letting you off the hook. Tell me what happened between Patrice and you."

"Don't you want to go back to sleep?"

She rose on an elbow and peered at him. "Okay, if you don't want to talk about it, I'll not nag." She flopped down, rolled to her side of the bed, and faced the closet.

He waited a few beats. "Is this our first fight?"

"No."

Silence for a couple of minutes. Her breaths seemed too strong for her to be asleep. He slid over, placed his chest against her back, draped an arm over her arm, and rested his hand on hers. "What are you thinking?"

She took a deep breath and sniffed. "I'm thinking about us, whether there really is an us, or if it's you and me, two people enjoying time with one another, but that's as far as it's going."

"Your conclusion?"

She sniffed again. "I'm afraid of getting punched in the gut, told I'm not good enough at being a partner. I want to believe in you, I want to trust you, I want there to be an us. But I don't know enough about you. Just because you said you think you love me doesn't mean there's a future for us. I need more before I allow myself to take that giant leap of faith and allow myself to move to the next level."

"Okay. I'll tell you about Patrice, but it's kinda complicated."

"Is there a *Reader's Digest* version?"

He inhaled deeply, and slowly exhaled. "I lived in Philadelphia at the time. Brand new to the bureau. She worked part-time in a coffee shop while in nursing school. I became a regular at the coffee shop, we would chat when things got slow. I wanted to ask her out, but quite honestly, I didn't think I belonged in the same league as her. She was gorgeous, smart, had a loving family, knew where she wanted to go in life, really had her act together. I think she sensed I couldn't muster the courage to ask her out, so she said she had a couple of tickets to a movie premiere at an artsy-fartsy theater I'd never heard of. Her sister couldn't go, so if I wasn't doing anything, would I like to go with her. I pretended to check the calendar on my phone, which, at the time, I didn't even know how to look at, and told her I'd be happy to as long as I could buy her an ice cream afterward. That turned out to be our first date. Her family didn't much care for me. They thought I had a dangerous job, unpredictable work schedule, I carried a gun, and a handful of other things. I think they wanted her to meet and marry a rich doctor. Things went downhill quickly when I went to her father's workplace one day at the end of his shift. I asked his permission to propose to Patrice. He went ballistic, said he'd never permit it, she could do much better than me, and…well, you get the picture. He went home and told his wife. She called, cussed me out in Russian, and told me never to call their daughter again. Well, that sorta pissed me off, so I proposed that night at a restaurant around the corner from where they lived. She said yes, couldn't believe it took me so long, and she had always wanted to be a June bride. When she said yes, I jumped up and did the silliest dance anyone ever saw. The people around us in the restaurant must have thought I was crazy. I tried to explain I had found someone who loved me, warts and all. Several of them toasted us and wished us luck. Just talking about it now makes my heart thump."

She turned over and stoked his face. "That's a beautiful story, like a fairy tale. What happened? Did the family put a stop to it?"

He shook his head. "They tried, but Patrice refused to listen. We planned to elope to Las Vegas, get married on June first in one of those wedding chapels. It wasn't romantic, but it would have legally made us husband and wife. Only two more weeks. I had the plane tickets, hotel reserved, wedding rings. Her best friend since second grade and her husband agreed to be our witnesses. We had it all set up. We needed two more weeks. Then, my world fell apart."

Malcolm could feel Valerie tense. She didn't say anything, as if waiting for him to collect himself.

He teared up and his voice cracked. "They assigned me to a team charged with taking down two bad guys suspected of extortion, racketeering, and murder. Someone saw them going into a tobacco shop that fronted for a brothel upstairs. We were supposed to grab them when they came out. If they took off running, me and another new guy had the job of running them down. Since this is right smack in the center of downtown Philadelphia, on Broad Street, we needed to avoid gunfire. I hid in the alcove of a men's shop next door. The other guy hid on the other side of the tobacco shop. That's where things got kinda weird for me. We believe Patrice happened to walk by on the other side of the street, saw me, and intended to surprise me. She didn't know I was on a stakeout. She got near, the bad guys came out. One of our guys shouted at them to put their hands up. They pulled guns, all hell broke loose. I couldn't shoot because I knew the other chaser would be in a bad spot if I missed. He didn't think the same as me. He opened up, hit one of the bad guys, but also hit Patrice in the throat. She died in my arms, on the sidewalk, in the center of Philadelphia, with a top-notch trauma center four blocks away."

She wiped tears from his cheeks.

"Oh, God." He sobbed openly. "Her parents had

warned her, and they didn't let me forget it. They wouldn't allow me anywhere near. I couldn't even go to the funeral home, church, cemetery, nothing. They wouldn't allow it. They wouldn't even allow me at the funeral. I couldn't believe it. I loved Patrice as much as they did, only in a different way." He beat his legs with clenched fists a couple of times.

Valerie put her hand on his hands and held them down. She whispered, "I know it hurt, probably more than anyone could imagine."

He rocked back and forth and moaned.

She kept whispering, "I know…I know."

When he settled down, she used the sheet to wipe his tears.

He muttered, "Thank you." After a couple of deep breaths, he continued. "I had to bribe the funeral director to be allowed in after hours to spend time with her. The day of her funeral, I had to watch from across the street with binoculars from half a mile away as they buried her. Only after all of the mourners had left did I dare approach the grave. I haven't been back since then and feel guilty as hell. I loved her, and I can't bring…"

His words became unintelligible. Huge tears streaked Valerie's face. She held him as tight as she could.

"They had already lowered her into the hole, and the machines had pushed dirt in on top of her. I stood there. I didn't know what to do."

They lay in one another's arms for a long, long time. They cried together.

He watched her enter the bathroom and take the box of tissues from the counter, careful not to disturb his arrangement of toiletries. He realized she remembered how upset he'd become when she swept his stuff into a pile against the wall to make room for her hair straightener, combs, brushes, and makeup. He couldn't believe it when she tried to make light of it, and he sputtered, "What does it matter? I don't like it. Just leave my stuff alone." He wasn't prepared to explain about the cruelty of foster care then, and he certainly didn't want to get into it now.

Tissue box in hand, she sat on the side of the bed next to Malcolm, pulled several tissues out and handed them to him. She took a couple and used them herself.

She sat, hand resting on his chest. She remained silent as she wiped his tears with the other hand.

Somehow, he sensed she knew she shouldn't say anything. Her being there was what he needed, not a bunch of words. He loved her all the more for it.

Chapter 35

2:13 a.m.

AD pulled the silver Chevy pickup truck into the shadow of a construction trailer behind the Panhandle National Bank building. Downtown Tallahassee felt different in the middle of the night, almost peaceful. Minimal traffic, no pedestrians, cool air, darkness hid the trash and dirt. He liked it.

The building housed offices for Fitzgerald, Ferguson, and Riddler personal injury attorneys, two accounting firms, Sunshine Retirement and Investment Planning, Corcoran Insurance, the Capital City Technology Incubator, the Diocese of Tallahassee, and about twenty other business entities.

As on all other missions, he wore black shoes, socks, slacks, and a long-sleeved shirt. Coupled with the trailer's shadow and his black clothing, he felt confident no one would see him. With Beautiful Betsy in her case, he scampered to the delivery dock in a crouch. If the security guard were watching the camera and if he saw anything, it would just be a blur not warranting investigation.

From prior visits, AD knew how to get to the west stairwell without being observed. His only sound came when the stairwell door closed on Beautiful Betsy's protective case with a dull *thump*.

He climbed to the second-floor landing, then stopped for a full two minutes to catch his breath. To breathe easier, he pulled the ski mask off and tucked it in his belt. Endurance had become an issue over the past six months as the cancer continued its relentless march. Now, as in the cemetery, he struggled to do what used to be easy.

After a couple of deep breaths, he climbed nine steps, pivoted, ascended another nine steps, then paused on the landing for several minutes to rest and catch his breath. He followed this routine until the sixth-floor landing. He sat on a step, sucked air, and allowed quivering muscles to quiet. A glance over his shoulder revealed stairs leading to the door marked Exit To Roof. He pulled out a black handkerchief and dabbed sweat on forehead, cheeks, and chin.

During research for this crusade, AD read about a man in Iowa who accidentally left a tissue at a crime scene. The FBI used DNA from the tissue to identify him. As a result, AD carried a black handkerchief with one corner pinned to his pants pocket. He had taken every possible precaution to avoid leaving evidence.

After normal breathing returned and his muscles recovered, AD grabbed the handrail with one gloved hand, held Beautiful Betsy's case in the other, and trudged the twenty stairs to the roof door.

At the top of the landing, he leaned the rifle case against the wall and gulped air with his hands on his knees. He had almost caught his breath when he saw little dark spots on the landing floor. His sweat.

He collapsed into a sitting position against the wall, head drooped until chin rested on chest. Sweat dripped off the tip of his nose and made a damp spot on the black shirt.

The fatigue had become overwhelming. He looked to the ceiling and whimpered, "Why, Lord? Why are you making this so difficult? I'm trying to help you. Why?"

He closed his eyes and thought he must have sounded like Jesus in the Garden of Gethsemane, the place where Jesus revealed his humanity at its most basic level. Luke, in his description of the Passion, recorded that drops of sweat from Jesus resembled blood. Jesus knew he'd be crucified and die a painful death. AD knew he would surely die, but it wouldn't be painful. He already had drugs masking his pain and surely would receive more the closer he got to the end. Unlike Jesus, he would eventually pass quietly and peacefully. Compared to God's only begotten son, whom He had sent to earth to die for our sins, AD really didn't have anything to complain about. Jesus knew the betrayal and brutality that would befall him. If Jesus could endure it, AD certainly could with the aid of an arsenal of drugs. He knew the path he'd follow when he decided to undertake the mission. He wanted to sit at Jesus' right hand. He remembered what the robber who had been crucified next to Jesus said, "Jesus, remember me when you come into your kingdom."

AD's mind remained strong, but his body faltered. He mumbled, "Jesus, my redeemer, please give me the strength to carry out the mission of sacrificing sinners, those who purposefully sinned, with premeditated intent, and did it time and time again. They won't have remorse until they receive their punishment."

AD inhaled, held his breath, then released it slowly

through his nose. He did it once again and smiled. The black handkerchief dabbed his face, then he used it to wipe the floor in broad sweeping strokes.

Another deep breath and he seized the handrail. An involuntary grunt escaped when he rose to one knee. A groan louder than he expected accompanied the struggle to stand.

He grabbed the door handle, and a thought caused him to stiffen. When the door opened, he'd be bathed in light from the overhead bulb. Someone might see him. AD released the handle and looked up. "Thank you, St. Hubertus, for alerting me."

With reluctance, he took the rifle case with both hands and hefted it, six inches at a time, until it came within reach of the bare bulb overhead. With a final thrust, the case shattered the bulb. Its tiny pieces rained down on him and made tinkling sounds when it struck the floor. Glorious darkness enveloped him.

Beautiful Betsy's case slowly slid through his hands until it settled to the floor with a dull, muffled sound.

Once his arms ceased shaking, he made the sign of the cross. "Jesus, I need your help to fulfill this task. If it pleases you, give me the strength to continue. Your will be done. Amen."

He now felt stronger, energized with hope and ready to tackle the next challenge, cross the roof, and find the right window.

A tug down on the ski mask and a twist aligned the eye holes.

Ambient light from the sixth-floor landing made the door handle visible. He opened the door a couple of inches, cocked his head, and listened. No alarms. No sound of doors opening into the stairwell. No sign of the rooftop door being alarmed or monitored. It appeared God continued to ride as his copilot so far.

Tallahassee General Hospital towered above the rooftop. Dim light, like the last minutes of dusk, bathed the rooftop. He pushed the door open another couple of inches and paused. All senses operated at their fullest, listening, searching, even smelling for any sign someone had become aware of him.

Satisfied his presence remained unnoticed, he nudged the door open to its limit.

After one last check, AD stepped onto the gravel roof with a crunch. He laid the rifle case down and knelt next to it. Starting at the leftmost clasp, he opened each one while saying a silent prayer to St. Hubertus, the patron saint of hunters. The raised lid exposed Beautiful Betsy surrounded by her red velvet cocoon. He wanted to run his fingertips over the rifle's stock but didn't dare remove a glove. He knew he'd lay his cheek on the polished wood shortly. With a slight nod of reverence, both hands lifted Beautiful Betsy and held the rifle chest high as if offering it to a deity as a gift.

The twenty-four-story Tallahassee General Hospital loomed straight ahead. Dark windows dominated the building with dim, blue hues flickering in a few, signs televisions remained on in patients' rooms. A handful of windows had lights on inside. He knew that anyone in those rooms looking out wouldn't be able to see him due to glare. However, he didn't know if anyone in dark rooms sat, or stood, at their window and looked out. He could be noticed, but trusted God would continue to support his mission.

Finally convinced no one would see him at this

hour, AD duck-walked to the edge of the roof with Beautiful Betsy in one hand. He peered over the parapet at the hospital's sixth-floor windows. Two were fully illuminated. He knew they cared for the most serious cranial cases on the east side of the sixth floor. He had learned this visiting Chief the morning after the shooting.

After a couple of minutes to catch his breath, AD lifted the rifle's wooden stock to his nose and inhaled. The aroma of polished wood relaxed him, like his younger days hunting deer. His father had conditioned him that when the stock touched his cheek, it would slow his breathing, reduce his heartbeat, and focus on the target. He couldn't see his target yet, but he expected to soon see Chief Dautry's forehead bisected by the scope's crosshairs.

From his earlier visit, AD knew Chief had a private room with two police officers stationed outside the door. He also knew the room had a window, one floor below the Panhandle National Bank building's roof.

Fortunately, AD wouldn't need to interact with the guards. He'd only have to interact with Betsy. She'd take care of interacting with Chief.

He raised his head above the parapet and scanned the hospital's sixth-floor windows. Only one window showed light. That one had to be Chief's room. Due to his angle, he couldn't see Chief, so he once again duckwalked to the left, with Betsy held securely in both hands in front of him.

His hamstrings burned from the exertion. Once at the new location, he sat, back to the wall, feet extended beyond the safety of shadow. He gulped huge amounts of air and massaged his thighs at the same time.

An unexpected loud and whirring sound caused AD to cringe and duck. He looked for the noise's source and realized a roof-top air conditioner had kicked on. He remained motionless while catching his breath and allowing his heart to resume normal function.

When breathing returned to normal, he peeked over the parapet once again. He had stopped at the perfect spot. He raised to a kneeling position, lifted Beautiful Betsy to his shoulder, and peered through the scope. A couple of clicks of the scope's adjustment knob brought Chief's torso into focus.

Chapter 36

4:08 a.m.

The sound of a cheering crowd woke Malcolm. He looked around, not sure where the crowd had come from. He saw the red light on the smoke detector, and light seeped in around the window curtains, nothing else.

The roar happened again. Very close.

This time he realized it came from his cell phone on the nightstand. He did the best he could to slide away from Valerie without waking her. The crowd cheer erupted again.

She stirred. "What's that noise?"

"Jack Palmer."

"What time is it?"

"A little after four." He stabbed the green phone icon. "This can't be good."

Jack's voice roared from the speaker. "The motherfucker got Chief. He's dead."

"How? What happened to the guard on his door?"

"Looks like the motherfucker shot from the roof of the building across the street. He hit Chief twice, once in the chest, once in the right eye. Two kill shots, probably within a second of one another. This whole goddamned thing reminds me of Kennedy and the school book depository, the assassin shooting down at a sitting duck."

Malcolm rubbed his temples. "How'd he know Chief survived? We put a lid on it."

Jack exhaled sharp enough to extinguish a candle across the room. "Damned if I know. The unis at the door didn't know who they guarded, just some John Doe that someone thought was important. Even the staff thought they had a John Doe."

"What about his wife?"

"Wife won't have anything to do with him. Told Father Davidson to give him the final blessing. If he dies, bury his sorry ass in the garbage dump, that's where he belongs. She may have hated his guts, but I know the woman. I don't think she'd tell anyone he was still alive. If she had talked to anyone in Madison, we would have known."

"Maybe Robert leaked it?"

"Naw, Robert's not the sharpest knife in the drawer, but he follows instructions well. He was told to not say anything, and I'm confident he didn't."

"Any witnesses or evidence?"

"A couple of uniforms found a pair of .30-06 shell casings on the roof. One says they stood upright, the other thought they lay on their sides. They're rookies with a combined four months on the job. One of them picked up the casings to give to their sergeant, so we'll never know for sure if they stood or not."

"Prints?"

"Don't know yet. Since this happened in Tallahassee, a Tally forensics team is on the way. They're in charge. Can you pull strings and get us in the driver's seat?"

Valerie joined Malcolm on the edge of the bed and

wrapped her arm around his waist.

"I'll call my boss and see what he can do. Any etchings on the casings?"

"Negative."

"Witnesses?"

"Tally PD has uniforms canvassing the area looking for anyone who might have seen anything. Mostly homeless and drunks out at this hour, probably won't help much. Too early to get any surveillance footage from surrounding buildings, most workers don't come in for another four or five hours."

"Does the building he shot from have security cameras?"

"We're waiting for the building manager to arrive to check the surveillance footage. There's a rent-a-cop on duty overnight. He eats at two thirty, which is when the shit happened. He didn't hear or see anything until the police knocked at the front door."

Malcolm's stomach felt hollow. "Anything I can do?"

"Negative. I'm here, not able to do much. Tally PD is all over this."

"Okay, stay there, do what you can. I'll get my boss to contact the Tallahassee chief of police to establish communication and cooperation. They'll probably resist letting an outside organization in, but the FBI can be very persuasive when it wants to be."

"I'll keep the press away as long as I can, but I bet someone puts two and two together and figures out the Madison Murderer struck in Tallahassee."

"You're probably right, but tell your liaison to keep Chief's name quiet."

"Ten four."

"Jack, we're getting close, damn close. I feel it in my bones. The killer was scared of Chief or something he knew. He needed to keep Chief quiet. He's panicking. We've got to keep the pressure on."

"I bet you're right. Gotta go. Talk later."

Malcolm tossed the phone on a pillow and massaged the back of his neck.

"Gee," Valerie said as she put her hand on Malcolm's arm, "assuming the murderer knew Chief survived, how did he know Chief lay in that specific room?"

He looked at the smoke detector's red light. "You know, that's a damn good question. Someone must have leaked it, but according to Jack, only half a dozen people knew. Looks like we have another line of investigation now…who knew Chief survived and lay in that exact hospital bed? And, maybe more importantly, how did they know?"

****

Holt Steadmyer, splitting headache and queasy stomach, pulled into his usual parking space behind the post office. He sat in the Cadillac SUV for a minute, regretting drinking with Sheamus after bowling the night before. One drink led to another and another until the place closed at two o'clock. Holt and Sheamus felt too good to go home, so they went to the VFW where Sheamus volunteered as a bartender. The Irishman had a key, so he opened the place for the two of them. They continued to drink until a little after four o'clock when Holt had to go home and change clothes for work.

Holt and his wife didn't exactly get along any longer, so they slept in separate bedrooms. He liked the separate room idea because he could take care of his

288

own urges whenever he wanted without listening to Carol bitch and moan about him being a pervert, and he avoided his wife's ugly face and fat body in the mornings. If he had known thirty years ago what she would turn into, he'd have gone after one of the Gallagher twins. Those two turned out to look really good in their yoga pants teaching other women to exercise. He looked forward to delivering mail to their aerobics studio. On days they looked especially nice, he'd only deliver half of their stuff, then swing by a second time later in the day for another opportunity to check out their yoga pants stretched tight across well-formed cheeks. More than once a week, he'd go home afterward to handle an urge.

The alcohol in his stomach from the night before gurgled.

A knock on the driver's window drew his attention. He recognized a rifle muzzle. He looked beyond the rifle's scope and recognized the face smiling at him. "Holt Steadmyer, you've sinned against God and despite repeated warnings, you've continued to sin."

Holt raised a hand and pressed it against the window as if it would stop a bullet. "But…but…"

"There are no buts."

He saw his nemesis' index finger slide into the trigger guard. Then nothing.

Chapter 37

6:06 a.m.

AD waited for his secretary's voicemail greeting to finish, then spoke. "Angela, it's me. I have a personal issue to take care of. I won't be in this week. Please make the appropriate arrangements for coverage. Thanks. Oh, and I probably won't be able to take calls."

He exchanged his cell phone for the TV's remote and pressed the power button. With one hand, he raised the footrest of the recliner and took another gulp of red wine with the other hand. The wine didn't help him feel better. The cancer seemed to have increased speed over the past couple of days. The greater his activity level, the greater and more consistent his pain. Climbing all those stairs, running down the stairs to his truck, and sacrificing Hold Steadmyer had intensified an already excruciating situation.

He glanced at the TV screen and didn't see anything about the night's sacrifices. He wanted—no, needed—to take a couple of pain pills but wanted to see what the news had to say about his endeavors.

AD felt pleased with himself for persevering through the pain for the most recent sacrifice. He deliberately thought of himself as being pleased as opposed to proud. Pride, being one of the seven deadly sins, and perhaps the worst of them all, was the opposite of humility. Pride, after all, is why the devil became the devil. Being pleased with something is not the same as pride. He would never allow himself to cross that bridge.

His plan for Holt Steadmyer had him conducting the sacrifice from the end of an adjacent parking lot, but a parked truck interrupted his line of fire. Initially he thought he'd wait until tomorrow morning and try again, but he knew his time on earth was limited. He couldn't afford any delays. Walking half a mile each way, through brush, to get to and away from Holt's vehicle was his only option if he were to stay on schedule. Somehow it seemed ironic that Holt would die in the SUV the postal worker bought with money made selling goods he had stolen from people along his mail delivery route.

The city's forensic nerd, Riley something-or-other, and the FBI people would have to deal with puke along with Holt's brains and skull spattered all over the inside of the fancy, and way too expensive, car. Those people would certainly deserve a raise when they finished.

AD knew he needed to rest, regain his strength, but didn't have the time. His days grew fewer and fewer at an unexpected pace.

When the station returned from a commercial, they simply stated, "There was an overnight shooting at Tallahassee General. We don't have any details yet, but our reporter is on scene. We'll continue to monitor the situation and bring any updates as they become available."

So far, the news crew hadn't mentioned anything about Holt. They may not have found the body yet. Give it another hour and all the local stations would be interrupting regular programming with breaking news about the Madison Murderer striking again.

When he'd wounded Chief a couple days ago, AD anticipated Special Agent Malcolm Gee would rise up, take command, and gradually uncover the sins committed by those who had been sacrificed. Unfortunately, no such thing happened.

With his usefulness on earth close to the end, he didn't have time to send any more letters. He needed to get information to them sooner rather than later. Without the world knowing sin would be punished, the expected army of people to follow in his footsteps would never materialize. What would be the easiest and quickest way to make known the true reason behind the oblations?

He glanced at the TV and saw Special Agent Malcolm Gee in front of the post office.

"This is Patti Wilkens with WTFL-TV—" She flashed a smile, appeared confused for a split-second, then frowned. "—your Tallahassee news source. I'm here with FBI Agent Malcolm Gee to find out what's happening behind the Madison post office. If you look behind me, you can see the building. The road leading to the back of the building is roped off with yellow crime scene tape. Agent Gee, what can you tell us? Has the Madison Murderer struck again? What's the victim's name? Do they work here? Any idea who did this?"

Malcolm's eyebrows pinched together as the reporter rambled on.

A voice from off-camera called, "Agent Gee, can you step this way?"

Malcolm looked left, and his eyebrows rose.

"Excuse me a moment, Patti."

The camera followed him to a man wearing a fedora. He raised a miniature tape recorder and asked, "Has the Madison Murderer struck again?"

Patti's microphone joined Skipper Bradford's recorder.

"Yes, the coward has taken another Madison life. A man coming to work. A postal worker two months short of retirement. Over my years, I've seen some pretty pathetic characters. But this murdering lowlife beats them all hands down. This man's a scumbag of the worse kind. He hides in the darkness, then springs on unsuspecting and innocent people." Malcolm looked into the WTFL-TV camera and pointed his finger at the lens. "I know you're watching. Every hour that goes by we get closer to you. We've almost unraveled the chalk markings. It won't be long, and we'll be paying you a visit. You can count on it, you sick son of a bitch. There's a hundred-thousand-dollar reward on your head. It won't be long before someone collects it. You can count on it." Malcolm walked out of the camera shot.

The camera moved back to Patti, eyes wide, mouth open, apparently not sure what to say.

Skipper Bradford stuck his head into the shot and took Patti's microphone. "That's one angry man. Madison Murderer, whoever you are, your days are numbered. The whole world is looking for you, and it's a matter of time before we find you. If you're a praying person, you better drop to your knees and pray."

AD pressed the remote's power button. He struggled to catch his breath. Looking at the crucifix next to the TV, he screamed, "You have the gall to call me an SOB? Really? Me? An SOB. You stinkin' sinner, you never knew my mother. She was the sweetest person who ever walked the earth. God needed more angels, that's why He took my parents. You…you—fornicator. I'll show you and your slut girlfriend. I'll add both of you to my list. It'll be fifteen. I'm going to save you, Special Agent Gee, for last. I want you to see your tramp die and know it's because of you. You both will rot in hell, and I'll enjoy every minute of it."

He wanted to dump the bowl of oxy into his mouth but knew he couldn't. That would have devastating effects. He knew from experience that taking more than two would knock him out for twelve or more hours. He couldn't afford to sleep that long. He had work to do, the Lord's work.

He chuckled for the first time in weeks. A hundred-thousand-dollar reward for his capture. Judas got thirty pieces of silver for the greatest person to walk the earth. How stupid are these people to offer a hundred thousand dollars for him, a past sinner, a mere mortal.

Perhaps, once he completed all of the sacrifices, he'd visit a St. Hubertus parishioner who needed money, have them call the tip line, then wait for the authorities to arrive. God would like helping the needy. Something to think about, but not now.

AD blessed himself and prayed God would tell him how to get the word out that sin has consequences. He emptied his mind and listened.

The next time he looked at the clock, it read 7:50. He must have fallen asleep. His mouth felt like it contained cotton and sandpaper had been run along his throat. Two sips of wine helped relieve the bad feelings.

God had spoken while he napped. He could now take the oxy he craved.

Chapter 38

8:00 a.m.

Malcolm moved to the head of the war room's main conference table and looked at the thirty-or-so people who occupied chairs and stood along the walls. FBI agents, Madison PD officers, support personnel from multiple law enforcement organizations, and even a couple of local volunteer residents who had law enforcement backgrounds. He didn't know what each of them did, but knew they wanted to stop the Madison Murderer.

Having never learned the art of a shrill whistle, Malcolm clapped his hands, twice, as loud as he could. The room quieted. The only noise came from the hum of the AC.

He cleared his throat. "As most of you know, someone shot a John Doe at Tallahassee General Hospital early this morning. The shooter fired from the roof of a building across the street. Two shots struck the victim. Either would have killed him. That man was Madison Police Chief Taylor Dautry. He had only been wounded when he and Martha were ambushed Saturday night. We're pretty sure the shooter is our guy."

He paused to let his words sink in. Some people stiffened, mouths fell open, two folks blessed themselves, someone muttered, "No," and others' eyebrows rose and eyes opened wide. "Then, just a couple of hours ago, the murderer struck again. He killed a postal worker sitting in his car behind the post office. Walked right to the car window and shot Holt Steadmyer, a thirty-year employee of the post office. Shot him through the car window, the muzzle no more than a foot from the glass. Holt had a wife, who became a widow. Their two kids are fatherless, and his granddaughter will no longer have the joy of being spoiled by a doting grandfather."

He paused a couple of seconds to settle his emotions. His next words needed to be delivered in a cold, calculated way. "We're confident he's the same shooter as at Tallahassee General late last night. The same calling cards were left at both scenes. That's eight murdered men and woman. It stops here. No more. Do you hear me? No more. This sum-a-bitch must be stopped, and I don't give a rat's ass how he's stopped."

Multiple heads nodded.

"We have him on the run. He's making mistakes. We have video of him sneaking into the loading dock at Panhandle National Bank building in Tallahassee. A man walking his dog this morning reported seeing a late-model pickup with Florida tags speeding away from the post office within minutes of hearing a very loud bang that sounded like a deer rifle.

"His actions this past twenty-four hours show he's losing it, he's becoming desperate. He's no longer killing in only the rural areas. He's coming into the urban parts of Madison and right smack in the center of the state capital. People are out and about. There are security cameras everywhere you look. This man is desperate to kill, and as long as he continues to take chances like this, our odds of finding him skyrocket.

"So far, the only physical evidence we have are ballistics from the recovered bullets and shell casings where he uses Roman numerals to count his kills like notches in a gun belt. Shoe prints, tire prints are consistent across scenes, but they are products that can be bought anywhere shoes and tires are sold. A forty-word letter is the only contact we've had with him. This SOB is smart, he has planned this, but he's not perfect. We're close, so close I can smell his breath." He rolled his hands into fists. "We need a break, something, anything, that will help us find out who he is, what his name is. Trust me, and I don't say this lightly, if we get a name, the FBI will find him. You don't know the half of our capabilities to find people like him. I guarantee it."

A lady entered the back of the room with a call-center headset on. She waved her arms and made a T with her hands.

Malcolm looked at her. "You better have something important."

"I apologize, Mr. Gee. I have a man on the line who says he's the Madison Murderer and will only speak with you."

"What makes you think it's him?"

"He said"—she read from a steno pad—" 'Chief is finally dead, no markings on the last two casings.' "

Malcolm felt as though someone had punched him in the gut. Less than ten people knew both facts. "Gimme me your headset. Someone find Beverly Choo."

The crowd parted like the Red Sea. The call center lady scurried forward but stopped several feet short of

Malcolm and touched the headset's earpiece. "He disconnected."

"Can you get him back?"

"Maybe from my station." She spun and returned the way she had come.

Malcolm called after her, "I want the recording."

She gave a thumbs-up before disappearing around the corner.

All eyes remained on him. No one had spoken. He smiled. "That proves we're on his tail and he doesn't like it. He's right there"—Malcolm held his index finger and thumb about an inch apart—"right there, within reach. He's so close I feel like I can grab him." Malcolm snatched something out of the air.

Malcolm wrote on a smartboard, *What's his name?* "I only want one thing." He tapped the storyboard. "When we get his name, he'll be ours. I promise you, he'll be ours. We'll find the sum-a-bitch and stop him, one way or another, we'll stop him. A name is all we need."

He scanned the group. "It's time, folks. It's time for one of you to be a hero. Don't sit here any longer. Go find the name of the sum-a-bitch that's killed eight people. Avenge Chief, and Martha, and Scott, and Judge Harrison and all the others. Go be a hero." The same lady with the headset rushed into the empty bullpen, waving her hand. "Mr. Gee. Mr. Gee." She removed her headset and handed it to Malcolm. "It's him, he called back."

Malcolm jumped up. His stomach flip-flopped, and he threw a fist in the air. He slid the headset on, repositioned the mic, and spoke. "How do I know you're who you say you are? Tell me something only you would know."

"Ronnie Scott's fingerprints will be the only ones on the wooden chair he dragged off the road."

Malcolm nodded. "Why are you calling?"

"I thought when Taylor went to the hospital, you would take over and dig into these people's past, but you disappointed me. There's a reason each person is on my list. So, I'm going to help you a little."

Beverly Choo entered with an electronic tablet in hand. She motioned for Malcolm to continue talking.

"Um…give me a second…I need to grab something to write with."

"Nice try. I'm done talking. Oh, before I go, did you know your slut girlfriend is married? By the way, I added both of you to my list. Congratulations."

The call disconnected.

Malcolm looked at Beverly. She shook her head. "Two minutes, forty-eight seconds. Not quite long enough to pinpoint his location. He's probably using an egg timer to stay under the three-minute minimum we need. Also, I'm wondering if he was in a moving vehicle."

"Could be, he's smart."

"Don't go anywhere. I'm going to get you a new phone. I'll have the call center people route the next call directly to that phone. You can even give him the number so he'll call you directly without going through the call center."

"Um…I think it's important that all conversations are recorded."

"No problem, it'll be recorded. Plus, when the phone rings, I'll be notified and will listen in. I'll be on mute, so he won't even know there's someone else listening. Regardless of where I'm at, I'll be able to text you instructions to help us zero in on the bastard."

"I like it. I can hardly wait for the next call."

Chapter 39

12:35 p.m.

Danny, the task force scribe, pointed to the forty-inch screen mounted on the wall. "Rachel will appear in three, two, one."

The screen went black for a second, then Rachel's face appeared with a blank wall behind her.

Malcolm didn't hesitate. "Hello, Rachel, thanks for joining us on short notice. We're getting closer to this sum-a-bitch. I've—"

She waved. "Wait. He's the son of who?"

He shook his head and pursed his lips. "Sorry, Chief Dautry used to say *sum-a-bitch* instead of son of a bitch. I guess I picked it up from him or one of the locals. Back to what I started to say, I've pulled together our primary players. You know the FBI folks, Danny, Beverly, and Goose. I believe you met Acting Police Chief Jack Palmer when you were here." She nodded once. "And to Jack's left is Sergeant Charlie Wilcox from Madison PD who is Jack's second-in-command."

She asked, "Where's the other detective?"

Malcolm leaned back and his eyebrows rose. "Robert LeBeau is Chief Dautry's stepson. Robert's helping his mother who's having a hard time dealing with her husband's death and surrounding circumstances."

"Understandable. I don't have much time, let's get started." She nodded once.

"Have you kept up with progress?" Malcolm cocked his head waiting for her response.

"I review your daily reports and periodically checked the storyboards."

He gave the slightest smile and leaned forward. "Good. Based on past experience with serial killers, I've learned their victims typically have something in common. They have blonde hair, work as prostitutes, are homeless, have wronged the killer in the past, co-workers, something. If there's a commonality in this case, we haven't come across it yet."

Jack Palmer half raised his hand. "Before we get to commonalities, we have eight bodies, so we're assuming there are eight victims. Could there be more we're not aware of?"

Rachel tugged the hair bordering the left side of her face. "I believe this guy wants law enforcement to know what he's doing and why he's doing it. If he thought one of his victims hadn't been found, he'd do something to make sure it was discovered. Call in an anonymous tip, set a fire, something. He wouldn't let it pass."

Malcolm picked up. "Going back to commonality. We have six men, two women. They ranged from high school dropout to a federal judge, aged eighteen to early seventies. His victims represented all levels of socio-economic status from unemployed to hourly workers to well-paid professionals. Scott and Newton were Black. The other six Caucasian. A few lived under the radar like Newton and the Kurtz boy, others were public figures, like Scott, the judge, and Chief Dautry. Four were involved with the legal system, one a government worker, another in the medical field, a high school dropout living with his parents, and a homeless man. Does anyone see a common thread?"

Several folks shook their heads. Jack replied, "No."

Rachel straightened. "Okay, let's forget about commonality for a minute and look at motivation. By leaving the shell casings, the killer is taking credit for those kills. He wants the attention. Quite possibly he doesn't get much credit in his job, maybe a superior gets all the credit, leaving him feeling empty. Most serial killers like taunting the police. This one shows signs of that and leans strongly toward delivering a message. Normally it's a ball-buster trying to figure out what the message is. In this case he's told us they are sinners."

Malcolm rubbed his forehead. "We're already looking into counselors, therapists, social workers, and psychologists. We need to be looking at attorneys and religious people, too."

Goose shifted in his chair. "You're on to something. A rabbi, pastor, priest, minister, sadhu, lama, even a church social worker fits the definition of someone who is trusted, that people tell their troubles to." He typed furiously on his cell phone with both thumbs. Then he looked up, smiled, and spoke. "Got a list going. As soon as we get out of here, I'll get the team right on it."

Rachel cleared her throat. "I like the religious angle and sinners. Great thought there." She smoothed the hair on the left side of her face and continued to speak. "Mark my words, mistakes are a serial killer's worst enemy. Malcolm has stated a couple of times, this guy is getting desperate, he's making mistakes. He's facing a deadline, possibly self-imposed. The closer he gets to his deadline, the more risks he'll take."

"I get it," Jack offered. "It's like a football team who's trailing by six points with a minute left. They'll throw riskier passes to score before time runs out. It sounds like that's what this guy's doing."

"You're close. Some serial killers are like sledgehammers, but this guy is all about finesse. He operates with the precision of a surgeon in the way he kills: well-planned, one shot, disappears. To travel the area and not be seen, he must be local." She smiled and raised a finger. "Maybe it's not seen"—she used air quotes around seen—"maybe it's not noticed. That's it. People probably see him every day and take him for granted. They don't even realize they're looking at him. It could be the mailman, the garbage collector, the barista at their local coffee shop. Focus on the twenty-thousand-plus residents of Antler County. Your man is there, somewhere. My money says you Madison people know him."

The two Madison PD men looked at one another. Jack's brow wrinkled. Sgt. Wilcox scratched his head.

Jack thumped the table. "If he's local, we'll get him."

Malcolm redirected his attention. "Beverly, give us an update from the electronics and communications perspective."

"Sure." She thumbed through her electronic notebook and hummed something unintelligible, then stopped the scroll at what looked like a bulleted list. She looked up. "First, we're poring through video looking for any vehicles that were in Tallahassee at the time of the murder, then in Madison around the time of Holt Steadmyer's murder. Next, we have twelve call-tracker drones in the air at all times. We launch them from a farmer's field in southern Georgia, so we've got a good location and don't lose coverage when one needs a new battery. We chose that because the river serves as a natural boundary. That earlier call from the murderer came from a burner along Florida State Highway 145 between Pinetta and the state line. From what I can tell, Pinetta is a little hamlet of about a dozen houses and a general store right on 145. If it has a laundromat, they probably use clotheslines out back tied from one tree to another instead of clothes dryers. Can't do that in Chicago where I'm from unless you want it to smell of smog and have a couple bullet holes in it." She grinned.

Jack frowned and looked down at the pad of paper in front of him. Sgt. Wilcox pursed his lips and shook his head.

Malcolm tensed. "Beverly, back to your update, please."

"Oh, sure. It's about a ten-mile stretch from the hamlet to the state line. The bastard called from a moving vehicle. We couldn't tell if he was going north or south. He's smart, he knows it's more difficult to track a signal from a moving vehicle. My belief is he has a hidey-hole within a mile or two of the highway. I doubt he would cross the With…Withla…Withla Coochie-Coo or some goddamned name river. Jesus Christ, why can't they name things around here so they can be pronounced."

In unison Jack and Charlie said, "Withlacoochee

River." Charlie added. "It's easy."

Rachel asked, "Do the drones have video capabilities?"

"No video. They're Tiger drones. Model 22F. The latest greatest. This area is full of trees, road bends, and dips. I opted for the Tiger instead of Eagle Eye because they have a six-hour battery life, so less chance getting caught in a battery change."

Malcolm looked at Rachel, who nodded. "Any other questions for Beverly?"

No one spoke, so Malcolm continued. "Jack, sounds like it would be a good idea to have a couple of unmarked cars monitor that stretch looking for vehicles that appear to be driving back and forth."

"I'll have a couple of guys use their personal vehicles so they're not so obvious."

Malcolm paused for a couple of seconds. "You want to use personal vehicles?"

"We have a local agreement with three other counties where we share a pair of unmarked cars. Unfortunately, they look like unmarked cars. Besides, if the murderer is local like we suspect, he'll recognize them in a heartbeat and disappear. On the other hand, if we use personal cars, the odds are he won't know it's Madison PD personnel. And my folks want to nail this guy in the worst way. They'll do whatever is asked of them. They lost several of their own. It's like losing a family member. I guaran-god-damn-tee you they'll be jumping at the opportunity to do something proactive instead of sitting on their asses waiting for something to happen. Consider it done."

Malcolm raised his hands. "Got me convinced."

Beverly broke in. "I can set up an alert to notify

your guys when he's calling."

Jack looked up. "I'll get with you after this to sync that."

Goose pointed at Jack. "He kills between midnight and dawn, so the odds are that's when he's traveling that road. I can't imagine there'll be much traffic then, so would it be possible for your officers to help me catalog those traveling the road then?"

"Um…what do you mean catalog?"

"Get their license plate. All they have to do is take a picture with their phone and send it to me immediately. I'll build a database with the pertinent information: plate, state, date, time, and direction. It could identify a pattern and serve as supporting evidence."

The acting chief wrote and nodded at the same time, then looked at Charlie. "Can you get volunteers? We'll need four, twelve-hour shifts, two per shift. They should never be traveling the same direction, nor looking in the same direction."

"Bet your sweet ass. I may have to beat them off with a nightstick. If it's okay with you, I'll head out now and get it set up."

"Good man. Beverly, Goose, work with Charlie on the alerts. Okay?"

She gave a mock salute. "Yes, sir."

The MPD sergeant left the table, his belt of law enforcement paraphernalia creaking.

Malcolm rubbed his jaw. "Does MPD have a SWAT team?"

Jack wagged his head. "We're too small to have our own team. Besides, we've only needed SWAT once in the past twelve years that I can think of. Once again, just like the unmarked cars, the four-county area shares responsibility for SWAT. I'll coordinate with the team commander and get them staged north of town. I know a farmer near Pinetta, ex-MPD. He'll let us use his place and will keep his mouth shut."

"Anything else for Beverly or Goose or Rachel?"

Before anyone could say anything, Valerie appeared at the bullpen entrance wearing a beach coverup, flip-flops, and baseball cap. A Madison police officer stood a couple of steps behind her. Malcolm had forgotten he'd sent for her. Based on her raised eyebrows and clenched hands, it appeared she had no idea why the officer interrupted her sunbathing. "Thanks, officer, I'll take it from here."

"No problem, sir, let me know if I can do anything else." He spun on a heel and disappeared around the corner.

"We will," Malcolm called after him.

Valerie grasped the back of an empty chair, leaned forward and spoke louder than she probably realized. "What's wrong? Why am I here?"

All eyes turned to Malcolm. "Now that you're here, nothing's wrong. Bottom line is the murderer has added you and me to his hit list. You're safe as long as you're here. Take a seat." He motioned to the chair.

"What? I'm a target? When the hell did that happen? Why didn't someone tell me?"

"He called the tip line a little bit ago. I spoke to him. He's pissed and has added us to his list of targets. That's why I sent for you. As long as you're here, you're safe. So, please sit down and let us continue."

Jack and Beverly stirred. Someone mumbled something, but Malcolm couldn't tell what, or who said it. "Okay, guys, I know this is unusual, but Valerie can help us. She's the one who figured out the shell casings were marked with Roman numerals, not initials. She's also helped me understand some of the biblical stuff the killer has said. I believe she may be of assistance." He set his jaw and straightened in his chair. "Anyone have issue with her joining us?" He checked each face. No one looked at him or said anything.

He looked at Valerie. "Have a seat. Danny, please update us on what's been added since our last meeting."

"I'm going to give a short summary. If anyone has questions or needs more detail, let me know.

"First, the killer dragged the body of Kenneth Murchison, aka Crazy Kenny, a hundred and forty-five yards to the open grave. The victim weighed a hundred and thirty pounds, certainly not a heavy man, but the suspect had to drag him as opposed to carry him. Detective LeBeau, Chief's stepson, suggested maybe the suspect didn't want to get blood on himself. Our evidence response team found very little blood on the victim, so Detective LeBeau's theory doesn't seem real strong. One would think the murderer wanted to leave the scene as quickly as possible, so if he could have carried the body, he would have. The belief is the murderer didn't have the strength to carry a hundred and thirty pounds of dead weight.

"Next, surveillance video from the college shows a man carrying a rifle case, stooped over, walking across the cemetery. The figure remained on the extreme edge of the video, so they couldn't tell much. The figure appeared to be clad in black, from head to toe, including a black mask of some sort. Doing comparisons using grave markers and statues, our forensics team determined the figure to be approximately five feet eight inches, around a hundred and twenty pounds. This supports the theory he couldn't carry Crazy Kenny to the grave."

Danny looked around. "Questions?"

No one said anything. He continued. "We found the same tire and shoe marks at, or in the vicinity of, each murder, including Holt Steadmyer's. The killer's shoes are rather generic, but the forensics team is a hundred-percent confident cuts in the left shoe sole belong to the killer. Once captured, it'll be easy to tie the suspect to each scene, assuming he's wearing the shoes. The tire tread is another issue. The same tread, pattern, and gouges occur at four of the scenes. When he's captured, assuming he's in possession of a truck, they'll be able to quickly tie the vehicle to those four scenes.

"Let's move to shell casings. Police found brass .30-06 casings at each scene, standing open end up, where the murderer fired from. The only possible exception is the rooftop in downtown Tallahassee. The officers who found them can't agree if they stood erect or lay on their sides. However, the bullet trajectory to where Chief lay leaves the only possible shooter location as the rooftop. Seems pretty solid. Oh, and the casings on the rooftop did not have any Roman numerals. The working hypothesis is the killer didn't mark them because he already had left one at the Twin Pines Motel probably identified for Chief Dautry. He didn't want to double count."

Rachel interrupted. "Numbering the shell casings gives credence to him having planned each murder in advance of undertaking this insane mission. He's methodical, he's a planner, he probably uses these skills in his job." She nodded as if signaling she was done.

"I'll add those thoughts to the profile storyboard," Danny said. "Thanks for mentioning it. Continuing with new developments over the past twenty-four hours. One huge question we have about Chief's murder is how the killer knew exactly what room held Chief. Everyone believed John Doe, a gunshot victim, occupied that room. Even the Tallahassee PD didn't know whom they guarded. His hospital records didn't list next of kin, no name, no address, nothing. Only half a dozen people knew Chief's location. I've taken it upon myself to track down everyone who knew and question them, see if they might have told anyone. I'll update the storyboard with names and results by our next meeting.

"Next, I added storyboards for Malcolm Gee and Valerie Dinardo. I don't have much information to populate yet. I added them because the murderer stated he had added them to his list. We don't know how many names are on his list, nor what qualifies a person to be on the list."

Valerie slapped her hand on the table, half rose out of her chair, and pointed a finger at Danny. "Why in the hell did he add me?"

Danny's eyes got large. He swallowed, opened his mouth, but nothing came out.

Malcolm spoke. "We're not sure, but we're working on it. I'm not worried about us being on the list. I believe we'll have him in custody before he gets to us."

She plopped back into her chair and shook her head. "Okay, but I don't like this. Maybe you FBI people are used to all this death stuff, but I'm a Realtor.

I only deal with dead deals, not dead people. I don't like this. It scares the crap out of me." She folded her arms as if hugging herself.

Malcolm didn't like death either. He'd seen too much of it during his FBI time but didn't have a choice but to deal with it. Her last comment added another layer of complexity to the conversation they needed to have about him being promoted and moving to Dallas. At least, that conversation wouldn't be needed once he found out if she was married. If she was, then the Dallas decision was easy.

Danny continued. "Holt Steadmyer, postal worker, is the latest victim. Shot point-blank by a .30-06 weapon. Brass shell casing has the Roman numeral eight etched on it. We have matching shoe and tire tracks in the vicinity of the scene. No reason why the killer picked him. If the pattern holds, the killer will probably accuse Mr. Steadmyer of sinning, but we're not sure he'll actually do that, nor do we have any idea what sin, or sins, Mr. Steadmyer may have committed.

"That pretty much summarizes what's new since our last gathering. Questions?"

Malcolm turned to Goose. "Anything new to report from the social media perspective? Nine-one-one call research? Warrants and subpoenas for cell phone records? Prison releases in the last couple of years?"

"My team and I are juggling a lot of balls. Social media? Lots of chatter, lots of people talking, asking questions, but we've not seen anything that could be considered posted by the murderer. Rachel suggests the guy might be antisocial, so I'm not optimistic we'll see anything." He glanced at the screen.

Rachel nodded.

"Warrants, one cell company has provided data so far. We're parsing through what they gave us. Fortunately, the other two big companies have the data ready, they're just waiting for the paperwork to CYA themselves. We should get it tomorrow. Questions?"

He looked around, no one seemed to want to speak, so he continued. "Prison releases. We've run down every person Scott arrested who wound up in prison. There was only a handful. No apparent connections. We're working on those that Judge Harrison sent away. I know you asked for two years back, but we're doing five. We're about halfway through and nothing appears pertinent, but we're not done yet, so stay tuned. Questions?"

No one spoke.

"Last thing is video analysis. Citizens continue to contact us about their recordings. It appears a lot of people have video surveillance cameras but don't know how to retrieve the data. We've had to visit many homes and even a couple of small businesses and work with them to pull the footage. This has been really time-consuming, but we're making progress. We're almost certain the killer is driving a dark blue Ford pickup truck, at least fifteen years old. Unfortunately, we've not been able to positively identify the plate, but it looks to be a Georgia plate. It appears the mandated rear license plate illumination is not working on his vehicle so we're not able to see the plate numbers. Either he's lucky or smart and disabled the light."

Malcolm spoke. "He's smart. We've seen it ourselves, and Rachel has repeatedly told us he's a meticulous planner."

She nodded. "He'll make a mistake sooner than

later. Stay after it."

Malcolm cleared his throat. "So, in conclusion, we have three major questions. One, how did the killer know we had Chief hidden in that exact room. Two, how would the killer know what the victims did wrong to deserve being executed, or in the killer's words"—he used air quotes—"sacrificed. And three, what's common about all of them. Any final thoughts?"

Jack dropped his pen on the tablet that lay in front of him. He rubbed his forehead as if trying to ward off a headache. "I just don't understand the sin angle. Hell, I've seen almost every one of the victims at ten o'clock Mass on Sunday mornings. All of them were good, church-going people. Well, except maybe for the Kurtz kid. His folks tried, they even…"

Valerie slammed her hand on the table. All heads snapped in her direction. "That's it. They all go to St. Hubertus. The killer goes there too. Who's the only one there that would know about people's sins?"

Malcolm shrugged.

Danny said, "I'm not Catholic, no idea."

Jack straightened and slowly nodded. "I know."

Beverly poked him in the arm. "Come on, tell us what you two know the rest of us don't."

Rachel chimed in, "You're right. There's only one person who would know everyone's sins."

Jack threw his hands in the air. "Father Davidson."

Silence reigned for several seconds, then Malcolm spoke, half out of his chair. "Jack, get the SWAT team together, surround the church. I'll muster all the agents I can and meet you there."

Jack leaned back and shook his head. "He won't be there."

Malcolm's shoulders slumped and he settled into his chair. "How do you know?"

"I went to 7:00 a.m. Mass this morning. We had a visiting priest who said Father Davidson had a personal matter to attend to and wouldn't be back for several days."

Malcolm leaned back. "So, where would he be?"

Beverly stood. "Ahem. We just went over this. The two calls he made to the tip line came from burners along State Road 145 between Pinetta and the state line. He's hiding out along there somewhere. That's where we need to be looking."

Malcolm leaned forward and made the time-out signal again. "Jack, Charlie, what's that area like four or five miles on either side of the highway? Can we put boots on the ground to systematically search it?"

The Madison PD officers looked at each other and wagged their heads. Charlie spoke first. "I used to live near Pinetta. That area's full of woods, brush so thick even the deer can't get through it."

"What about drones or helicopters?"

Jack responded, "That whole stretch of road is heavily wooded, lots of huge oak trees. This guy could be in a tent, a small cabin, hell, he could be sleeping in the bed of his truck. You'd never be able to see him if he's under a tree."

Malcolm rubbed his jaw and slowly nodded. "Okay, okay." He held up an index finger. "One, Jack's going to get people to watch that stretch of road, and two"—he added the middle finger to the index finger—"we have drones that will intercept all cell calls, including burners from that area." He looked at Beverly with raised eyebrows. She nodded. "We've blanketed the vicinity. We've done everything we can for the present." Another digit rose. "Three, we need to keep researching other possibilities." All four fingers were in the air. "Four"—he looked at Jack—"notify the SWAT team commander that we're going to need their services shortly."

"Will do." Jack rose, pulled a cell phone out of a pocket, and left the area.

Malcolm called after him. "Come back as soon as you can."

With his cell phone at his ear, Jack gave a thumbs-up and disappeared around the corner.

Chapter 40

2:20 p.m.

Acting Chief of Police Jack Palmer plopped into the same chair he'd occupied earlier. "The combined SWAT teams will be assembled south of Pinetta in about two hours. Charlie Wilcox will have three officers driving that stretch in about thirty minutes. They'll rotate every hour, so Father Davidson doesn't get suspicious. We've also arranged for a citizen volunteer to sit at the border and another to hang out at the Pinetta general store. Everyone has a description of his truck and plate. If he's spotted, they'll radio the location, and we'll figure out what to do from there."

Malcolm nodded his head. "Good plan. I like it. However"—he frowned—"I don't like the idea of citizens getting involved."

"I get it, but these are members of COPs, Citizens On Patrol. They're sworn officers but don't carry weapons. They know they're not to approach him. Their only task is to watch for the truck and if they see it, call it in. Period."

"Good man."

Jack looked around. "Where did everyone go? You guys develop a plan while I was gone?"

"Everyone's off doing their thing. We talked some but agreed we need your local knowledge."

Valerie asked, "Can't helicopters see through trees somehow? Can't they fly around that area looking for his car?"

Jack shook his head. "Good idea, but not practical. That area's heavily wooded. He'll be parked under the tree canopy or a lean-to or something like that. It all shields the heat signature. If he's not driven his truck in an hour or so, it'll never register. But one of the citizen volunteers mentioned that Father Davidson drives a gray Chevy pickup, newer model. But we're looking for a dark-blue older pickup. Those two things don't jibe."

"I may have an answer for that." Goose entered, followed by Beverly. "I searched property and vehicle records in that area to see if he owned any land. Didn't find anything. Just on a lark, since it's so close, I searched the southern counties of Georgia for a Davidson owning anything. I found a lot of Davidsons, so I wrote a quick little program to do a comparative analysis and bingo! It matched Edna Davidson to Anthony Davidson, who lives in Florida. A deeper check and she owned a dark-blue Ford at the time of her death. Her will stated everything went to Anthony Davidson, her son."

"Brilliant," Malcolm said.

Goose grinned.

Valerie chuckled. "I don't think he meant you, I think he meant Father Davidson using his mother's truck registered in Georgia while functioning as the Madison Murderer but driving a silver Chevy pickup when functioning as Father Davidson, pastor of St. Hubertus church."

The grin disappeared. "Oh. I hadn't thought about that."

Valerie's eyebrows rose. "Despite that being brilliant on his part, what's that do for us? We can't wait for him to kill again. That's not an option, is it?"

Malcolm counted to himself, one-Mississippi, two-Mississippi, three-Mississippi. "Correct, that's not an option. But we now have two vehicles to be on the lookout for. Jack?"

"On it." He rose and left.

Danny typed furiously on his wireless keyboard.

Valerie leaned forward, elbows on the table, hands clasped. "Okay, Mr. Smart Guy, what if Davidson has a third vehicle?"

"I'll take care of it."

Valerie cocked her head. "And how exactly are you going to handle that?"

"I'm going to unleash a swarm of locusts."

****

AD wanted to sleep, wanted to conserve what little energy he had left, but the pain wouldn't let him. He had to act soon. He needed to sacrifice Jimmy Shiller, who dumped his parents in a retirement home and had not seen them in over a year. He'd also call on Lenny, the sleaze-bag motel owner. Secretly taping motel patrons having sex and selling the video on the internet was truly despicable. Two more tomorrow night, then the FBI agent and his harlot girlfriend the following night. That would complete the mission. He'd even give God bonus results with the last two.

Once complete, he'd find a St. Hubertus family down on their luck and have them call the Madison police. They could collect the $100,000 reward; he could prepare to meet his maker. He'd never make it to trial; he'd die before they could even set a court date.

His plan, with a couple of minor modifications, had worked.

He rubbed circles where the pain presented itself the sharpest. Initially, he used the tip of an index finger and moved it in a tiny circle, then progressively larger circles until the largest circle surrounded the pain. He knew the pain became more intense with more activity. He wanted to stay at the cabin, legs up, wine at his side. He didn't want to leave. He wanted the pain to go away. When it got really bad, he'd think of Christ being crucified, the pain he felt when they drove huge nails through the palms of his hands, the bridges of his feet. If Jesus could endure that, AD could endure pain from cancer eating his liver. He had a light at the end of the tunnel, literally and figuratively. His self-appointed mission to sacrifice twelve sinners in twelve days had almost reached its climax. Also, based on the growing pain the past two weeks, he knew he'd soon enter the eternal light of eternal life in heaven. He wondered if his parents in heaven smiled when they looked down at him. They had told him time and time again how proud he made them by becoming a priest. Certainly, they would be proud when he walked through the pearly gates, angels playing harps, serenading his every step.

He brushed a tear from his cheek. Not sure if the pain generated the tear, or if the thought of embracing his parents prompted the tear. He opted to be positive and give his parents the credit.

No matter how much rubbing and circling he did, the pain didn't lessen. If he couldn't sleep, he may as well see what FBI Special Agent Malcolm Gee had to say.

With two gulps, he finished the rosé wine, took

both sets of truck keys from the counter, and walked out the front door. Both trucks sat there waiting for him. Which one should he take? They associated the dark-blue Ford with the Madison Murderer, but that was between midnight and dawn. Did he dare take it now? *Please, Jesus, help me complete the sacrifices to honor you and your father. Point me to the truck that you will hold your hand over.*

Less than a minute later, he felt a higher power telling him to swap plates and take the blue truck. He looked toward heaven. "Hello, Mother and Father. I miss you and look forward to being in heaven with you, very soon. Thank you for all that you did for me. I'm doing everything I can to earn the opportunity to see you, to hug you. I hope you're proud of me. See you soon."

After removing the Florida plate and putting the Georgia plate on the Chevy, he entered the cab, shifted into gear, and maneuvered through the dirt track toward State Road 145. He smiled at the thought of his hunters looking for a dark blue Ford with a Georgia plate. They'd never find it, thanks to help from above. God is good.

Chapter 41

Valerie looked across the table at Malcolm. "Do you know you keep saying *sum-a-bitch* instead of son of a bitch? You pronounce it like the locals."

He rubbed his jaw and the corners of his lips turned up, but he stopped short of a smile. "The more I work with the locals, the more I seem to speak like them."

"I get it. I think it's cute."

"Not meant to be cute, just something I've learned to do over the years, try to fit in with whomever I'm working with. It makes teamwork go a lot better."

They remained silent for a minute, then Valerie asked, "What do I do now? I can't go back to the hotel, I can't lie by the pool, I can't even go shopping along Main Street. I would like to exchange this bathing suit for street clothes. In my wildest dreams I never thought I'd be held hostage in an FBI war room."

"For the time being, you're going to stay here, where you're safe. I'll figure something out later. Besides, we have a couple of things to talk about." He bellied to the table, hands clasped on the tabletop.

Her eyebrows rose. "Sounds ominous. Is there something else I should know?"

"As a matter of fact, yes. To be totally truthful, there's one thing I've not told you, and this morning I

323

learned another piece of information."

"And they both involve me?" She leaned back and crossed arms over chest.

"Yes." His stomach flip-flopped, and he felt little beads of perspiration appear on his forehead. He licked his lips. "At the end of this project, assuming it ends in a positive way, I'll be promoted to senior agent."

She uncrossed her arms and leaned on the table. Her smile warmed his heart. "I know, you told me before. I'm really, really pleased for you. I see how hard you work and are so invested in what you do. It's great that Roger sees your value. Maybe he's not the total butthead I think he is."

"Roger has a few redeeming qualities, but not many. The thing you need to know about that promotion is…"

The red cell phone Beverly had given him chirped and danced toward the table's edge. Malcolm grabbed it and looked at Valerie. She sat there with that million-dollar smile that made her so damn attractive. He wanted to wrap his arms around her and hold her tight. "Shit, bad timing." He set the phone in the middle of the table and poked the green phone icon. "Special Agent Malcolm Gee." Malcolm and Valerie leaned in and stared at the device.

"Did you miss me?" came from the phone. It sounded as though the caller were in a moving vehicle.

"Of course. It's always a pleasure speaking with you. By the way, I never got your name." He winked at Valerie. Her eyebrows rose and eyes widened.

The voice coughed. "Tsk, tsk, Agent Gee. I'm not going to fall for that."

Malcolm mouthed, *Watch this*. "If you won't give

me a name, how about I call you Father Davidson?"

No response. The car sounds continued, so Malcolm knew the caller hadn't disconnected.

Malcolm leaned even closer. "Cat got your tongue?" He felt like cheering. He'd put the sum-a-bitch on the defensive.

"I don't know how you figured out my name, but it doesn't matter. You'll not stop me."

The caller had spoken so loud Malcolm jerked back. "We will find you. Your days of killing people are over." He mouthed, *Watch*, to Valerie. "Is that a siren I hear in the background?" Malcolm grinned and held his breath. Valerie stifled a giggle.

"What? Where?" Silence other than car sounds.

"Made you look, didn't I? You had best keep looking because we're closing in on you. As sure as I'm sitting here, it won't be long, and you'll be introduced to your Miranda rights."

Valerie spoke. "How can you justify killing people? You're a priest, for God's sake." Her hands were clenched into fists, knuckles white.

"Oh, that must be your little hussy, your Jezebel. I should say it's a pleasure to meet you, but that would be a lie, and I don't lie."

"Listen to you, Mr. Hypocrite, or maybe I should call you Mr. Clueless."

"You two are the clueless ones." His volume and pitch ratcheted higher.

Malcolm smiled and gave Valerie two thumbs up. He knew emotion resulted in mistakes. Mistakes manifested themselves as a serial killer's greatest enemy. Malcolm put an index finger to his lips and looked at Valerie. She smiled and sat back.

"You two are clueless about heaven and following God's will. Luke 10: 25-27. 'You shall love the Lord, your God, with all your heart, with all your being, with all your strength, with all your mind, and your neighbor as yourself.'

"I love God more than you can imagine. I love Him enough to help Him, to cull the wanton sinners, to send them into the fires of hell. I send them to eternal damnation so they can't sin anymore. Your turn for eternal damnation is coming. Your turn to be cast into the fires of hell is coming very soon."

Valerie sat ramrod straight, clenched fists, tight jawed. "You said it yourself, Luke 10: 27, 'and your neighbor as yourself.' If you love your neighbor as you love yourself, how can you murder them? Murdering them is like committing suicide. Would you commit suicide? You know as well as I do that suicide is against the Catholic religion. If you're killing others, then you might as well kill yourself."

"Don't you lecture me, you adulteress. I'm not worried about dying. God has already given me a cancer that will claim my body before too long, but nothing can destroy my spirit. I don't have much time left to complete this mission, this crusade I've taken on. You and your boyfriend are already dead in the eyes of God." His tone became deeper and quieter when he spoke. "You're dead spiritually, and I'll see that your bodies are dead very soon."

Her face reddened and eyes bulged. She raised the phone directly in front of her mouth. "No, you won't. We'll stop you, we're smarter than you."

"Don't you get it? We're on the same side. We both want to punish those who have done wrong, but I have God on my side, that's all I need. You...you have a bunch of hypocrites on your side. And you're like all the others. Say one thing but do something totally different. You talk the talk, but won't walk the walk. You and society are in a death spiral directly into hell. I'm here to tell you that I'm trying to make a difference, trying to inform society of what happens when they sin and break the laws of God. I've told you why I sacrificed those people, they've sinned. Even if you won't publicize what they did to deserve being offered up, their sins will eventually become known. Society will see that punishment is handed out, that it is swift and sure. My prayer is that others will see what I've done. They'll undertake their own crusades, and we'll have an army of avengers taking care of..."

The call disconnected.

Valerie pounded both fists on the table and her voice cracked when she spoke. "He has it backward. The bastard can't kill because he thinks they sinned. Hebrews 9: 27, 'Just as it is appointed that human beings die once, and after this the judgment. Man must die first, then be judged.' He can't be judged before he dies. It's just not possible."

Malcolm shifted in his chair and looked away, not sure what to say. He decided it best if he didn't say anything, let her calm down.

After what seemed like thirty minutes, but was probably only two, he said, "Damn, woman. You sure do know a lot about the Bible. You quote it off the top of your head."

"I told you. I wanted to be a priest, so I studied and studied. I found it really interesting, so that helped too." She looked off into the distance, but he could tell she didn't focus on anything. "We never missed Mass on Sundays and holy days of obligation. They paid a fortune for Catholic school. I wanted to be a priest until I found out I couldn't because I used the girl's bathroom. Our pastor thought only boys could be worthy of such a position." A tear trickled down her cheek. "Many people believe Catholics are out of touch with the times. And I agree with them. But our faith is our faith. Despite being an ex-Catholic, I still believe in the Ten Commandments, the Golden Rule, and that Jesus died for our sins so an example could be set for us to follow." She wiped a couple of tears and looked at Malcolm.

"I'm not any particular denomination, but I do believe in the precepts of the Ten Commandments and the Golden Rule."

She smiled the smile that warmed his heart, that made him feel like he'd hit the lottery. "I know, that's part of why I love you." She reached across the table and put her hand on his.

"I love you too. I'm glad they didn't take you as a priest."

She rose to her feet, face reddened again, looked him in the eye and pointed a finger at him. "Don't get me started on that."

He raised his hands, surrender fashion. "Damn, I'm glad you're on my side."

Chapter 42

6:00 p.m.

Malcolm approached the twin podiums, checked his watch, then scanned the assembly. He figured at least a hundred gathered in the semicircle. Reporters and their video personnel, photographers, people holding long poles with microphones on them. He didn't remember poles yesterday; these must be in response to the podiums being out of microphone space.

Skipper Bradford stood off to the right, arms crossed, leaning against a light pole. Malcolm nodded; Skipper nodded back. The dingbat reporter who'd asked if the Madison Murderer might be a vampire stood nearby and craned her neck, presumably to see whom Malcolm nodded to. She wore a bright pink blouse, matching slacks, and shoes. She even wore a pink straw hat that vaguely resembled a fedora. She looked ready for an Easter parade.

He checked his watch again, cleared his throat, then licked his lips. Standing in front of a crowd like this and speaking to them wasn't much fun. But he didn't have a choice. With Chief gone, it fell squarely on his shoulders. Everyone looked at him for answers, answers he couldn't share at the moment. He wanted to tell the world they had figured out the murderer's name, but he couldn't. The risk of a victim's family member seeking revenge had to be avoided. A lot more good would be done if Father Davidson were taken alive. In order to do that, they needed to make sure the priest stayed hidden away until they could find him, which they would. Time to unleash the locusts.

Buoyed by the progress they had made the past twelve hours, he licked his lips once again and spoke. "Ladies and gentlemen, thanks for being here, especially in all this heat and humidity. I'm going to make this quick. There will not be any questions."

Several of the media folks grumbled. The pink-clad vampire conspiracist slapped a steno pad against a leg and pouted. Malcolm didn't care. He had work to do and needed to release the locusts to scatter throughout Antler County.

"I'd like to thank everyone who has contacted the tip line with information. We believe, as a result of someone calling in, the murderer plans to strike again, tonight."

Several reporters shouted questions.

"Who's the murderer?"

"Have you spoken with him?"

"Who's he going to kill tonight?"

"How will you stop him?"

Malcolm raised his hands and shook his head. "As I stated, I won't be taking questions. We don't know who the intended victims are, but our source tells us the murderer plans to strike again tonight. I'm asking each and every person in Antler County to stay in a safe place between midnight and sunrise. Lock your doors, turn off the lights. If you're a business owner, close no later than ten p.m. Don't open any sooner than eight a.m. I can't stress this enough: stay off the streets, stay inside. Keep you and your family safe. There will be a heavy law enforcement presence on patrol. Stay out of law enforcement's way. If gunfire erupts, you don't want to be caught in the middle. It could get pretty ugly."

He paused and surveyed the audience. More questions were shouted at him, but he ignored them. "Once again, thanks for the tips, keep them coming. I can't stress this enough, everyone, please stay off the streets. Let law enforcement do what they are trained to do, what they do best. Let them get this guy so life can return to normal tomorrow. That's it for now."

Before he left the podiums, Malcolm looked at Skipper, and the reporter gave a slight nod.

The reporters hurled a multitude of questions, but Malcolm spun on a heel and walked away. Several of the locusts followed and hounded him with questions and microphones thrust into his face. He quickened his pace and slid into the war room.

He made a beeline to the rear door where he expected Skipper to be waiting. A peek out the peephole revealed the fedora-wearing reporter leaning against a car across the street. Malcolm cracked the door open, stuck his head out, and motioned for Skipper to come over. Out of the corner of his eye, he noticed the pink dingbat reporter standing behind a bush about twenty feet away.

Skipper stopped at the foot of the steps and smiled. "What can I do for you?"

Malcolm held onto the handle to ensure the reporter didn't try to gain entry. "Thanks for the help with the chalk markings. You got it out quickly, and it paid off. That generated a call that put a lot of puzzle pieces together." Malcolm knew it wasn't the absolute truth, but it had a lot of truth in it.

Skipper's smile broadened, and he nodded. "I'll be sure to pass that along to my boss. You know we're here to help again. Tell me what you need."

"If I wanted to leak something again, would you play along?"

His grin grew. "Sure, it helps capture the bad guy, plus I look good in my boss's eyes. It's good for everyone involved."

"How many news organizations are here?"

"Not sure, but I do know there's over a hundred and fifty reporters plus video crews and cameramen. A couple of organizations have multiple crews. Like CBS has a local crew, their national people, plus I think someone from *60 Minutes*."

Malcolm whistled. "That's a lot of folks, where are they all staying?"

"None at your hotel. The FBI has that one booked. The rest stay in motels in Lee, Greenville, even as far away as Tallahassee. A bunch more stay in motorhomes parked in a farmer's cow pasture near I-10. He charges a hundred dollars per day, and another fifty when the truck comes to pump out the toilet systems."

"How's he get away with charging like that? Plus, I would think the health department would shut him down."

Skipper snickered. "You're a city fella. Things work different out here. The head of the Antler County Health Department is the farmer's son-in-law. The guy with the pump truck is his son. Go figure."

"But he'll have to report all that money. The tax

collector or the IRS will know."

"Everything's in cash. No checks. No credit cards. No invoices. Cash only. The big groups gladly pay to only be six or seven miles from the heart of town."

"Is that where you're staying?"

Skipper kicked the bottom step in an aw-shucks way. "No, my company can't afford that, but I found a friend that I share a room with."

Malcolm tilted his head toward the pink lady and raised his eyebrows.

Skipper glanced toward the bush and frowned. "Come on out, Dorothy. He knows you're there."

The pink-clad lady joined Skipper. In Malcolm's estimation they stood a little closer than mere friends would. He wondered if they had a personal relationship in addition to their professional relationship.

She held out her hand. "Dorothy Abrams, America's News Network."

Malcolm declined to extend his hand. "I remember you from the first press conference." He looked at Skipper. "What's going on? Why's she hiding behind a bush?"

Skipper hung his head and kicked the bottom step. "I told Dorothy I knew you. She didn't believe me, so I invited her along so she could see us talking. My bad."

"Yes, it is your bad. I can't trust you now."

Dorothy hugged Skipper's arm and looked up at Malcolm. "Don't be mad at Skippy. It's my fault."

"I don't care whose fault it is. It shouldn't have happened." He pulled his head in and gradually pulled the door in, waiting for Skipper to say something.

Skipper shouted, "No, wait. You wanted to tell me something, tell me."

Malcolm hesitated a couple of seconds for dramatic effect. He hated playing Skipper but would give him an exclusive interview when they caught the murderer. "I want to tell you to stay safe tonight. We know who the murderer is and who he's going after tonight. Our SWAT team is setting an ambush. Things could get ugly. Stay someplace safe."

Skipper and Dorothy straightened. She fumbled in her purse and pulled out Skipper's recorder.

A head shake from Malcolm resulted in two frowns. Skipper spoke first. "Who is it? Where's the ambush?"

Dorothy's face looked like a basset hound with sad eyes. "Yes, tell us so we know to not go around there. Right?" She elbowed Skipper in the ribs.

Malcolm wanted to laugh but held himself. "It could get bad, so I'm warning the two of you to stay safe. Whatever hotel you're staying in, stay there until sunrise." He pulled the door shut until the latch clicked, twisted the deadbolt, and leaned against the door. "Fly locusts, fly."

The cell phone in Malcolm's pocket vibrated when he entered his makeshift office. He'd forgotten he'd put it on silent prior to the press conference. A quick glance at the display made him mutter, "Shit." He settled into a chair and put the phone to his ear. "Hello, Roger, what can I do for you?"

"What the hell's the matter with you? You're going to have every frickin' reporter and media person riding around between midnight and sunrise wanting to be first on the scene. What if they become casualties? Are you trying to fuck this up? Are you trying to fail, is that what you're doing?"

Malcolm leaned back and plopped his feet on the table. "Let me explain the plan."

Before he could continue, Roger shouted, "The plan? What friggin' plan? Your promotion has been signed, I have it right here in my hand. I can rescind it if this whole goddamned mess blows up, which is what it looks like is going to happen. Not only is your ass on the line, but your whole future with the FBI. Do you understand what I'm saying?"

"I understand. Let me tell you what you don't know."

"This better be good. Thompson just became available; I'm inclined to send him in there."

"You can do whatever you want, but we'll have the killer under arrest by the time he gets here. We know who the killer is. He's the local priest. We don't know where he's at, he's hiding."

"A priest? Are you serious? Don't try to bullshit me, you're already on thin ice."

Malcom went into great detail about how they figured out it was the local priest, but he kept Valerie's name out of it. If Roger knew she had been involved, he'd blow up again and it would take Malcolm fifteen minutes to calm him down. He gave the local Madison PD folks, particularly Jack Palmer, most of the credit.

Roger remained silent for a full four minutes while Malcolm talked. It was the longest Malcolm had ever known the man to be quiet without spewing a curse, a threat, or an order.

At the end of the summary, Malcolm waited for Roger to say something,

"What happens if this priest decides to go after someone tonight?"

"That's why I told the press people about staying inside. I used reverse psychology on them. We don't have enough resources to cover the whole area, but there's enough reporters and media people here to fill a small stadium. By telling them to stay off the streets, I expect it will have the opposite effect. Every damn one of them will be out tonight, riding around, looking for the killer. The plan is that they'll keep the priest in hiding until we're able to find him. The bastard is calling us from burners. Cell drones are airborne and tracking the targeted ten-mile stretch he's been calling from. He's making more and more mistakes. He's running out of time on his own clock. Say's he has cancer and will be dead soon, so he's desperate to complete killing those on his list, which, by the way, now includes me."

"It comes with the job, Gee."

"I know. Choo will have Eagle Eye drones airborne shortly to search a sixty-square-mile sector for his truck. We're running out of light, but we'll get as much done as possible until sunset, then get going at sunrise. It's only a matter of time. If we don't get him tonight, we'll nail his ass tomorrow, I'm sure of it. But we need to protect the locals tonight. That's why I've riled up the locusts."

"Locusts? What the fuck are you talking about?"

"Chief Dautry used to call media people locusts, I suppose because they're pests and he didn't see anything good coming from them. So, that's why we refer to them as locusts."

"Makes sense. I've seen a swarm of locusts attack a stand of trees. Nothing left but a bunch of shit when they left. Same holds true for media at an event like this. We'll be reacting to shit caused by them for years, investigations, interviews, second guessers, people wanting to make us look bad."

The call disconnected.

AD and Roger must have gone to the same school of phone etiquette. Or maybe both had an egg timer. Either way, it would be good to get away from both of them. Or would he be able to get away from Roger? Valerie held the answers he needed in order to decide his future direction.

Chapter 43

10:40 p.m.

Valerie drummed her fingers on the table. "It's quiet here at night."

Malcolm kept his eyes on the laptop. "Yes, it is."

"What do we do now?"

"Wait for something to happen."

"Really, that's it? Shouldn't you be out riding around looking for the priest?"

"Nope, he'll come out of his hole, with a little luck one of the stakeout volunteers will spot his truck, and bada-bing, we'll be all over him."

"And if he doesn't come out of his hole?"

"The Eagle Eye drones will find him tomorrow. Either way, this thing's over tomorrow."

"I like your positive nature."

He sighed heavy enough to make a sheet of paper move on the table.

She frowned. "What's the matter? You don't look happy."

"I'm concerned about me and you and where this relationship is going."

She rubbed her nose. "That's a good question. I thought we've been getting along really well. I've enjoyed our time together. All this serial killer stuff is out of my element as a real estate agent, but I find it exciting. But you've been moody the past day or two. I'm not sure if this murder thing is bothering you, or if I've done something wrong, or maybe not done something you think I should have." Her eyebrows raised.

He looked away, but slowly nodded. "Roger called earlier this evening. My promotion to senior agent is signed. Once I wrap this project up, I'll have a new job."

"I know, you told me, I'm pleased they've recognized your work. Aren't you happy about it?"

"Yes and no. With this promotion comes a transfer to Dallas."

Valerie looked like someone had slapped her across the face. "Dallas? Really? That would complicate things." Her mouth hung open.

"To make matters worse, I learned…"

The red cell phone chirped, buzzed, vibrated, and turned itself sideways. He stabbed the speaker icon and set the phone in the middle of the table. "Special Agent Malcolm Gee."

"I watched your six o'clock news conference and laughed, telling people to stay inside between midnight and sunrise. It's like you've kicked the hornets' nest, people are everywhere. They're swarming all over the place like a bunch of ants after a dropped crumb. Very clever of you."

A text appeared on his personal cell phone from Beverly: *He's moving north on 145. Keep him talking.*

"Well, Father Davidson, it's a free country, and according to my religious consultant"—he winked at Valerie—"your God gave people free will, and it appears they're exercising their will. They're going where they want."

"You're not going to stop me. I'll get the rest of my list, and you'll be the last one. I'll receive pleasure when I put the crosshairs on your nose and pull that trigger."

Malcolm wanted to hang up on the sum-a-bitch but knew he needed to drag out the call as long as possible. "If you want to get me, I'm in the war room on Main Street, across from the police station. It's Johnny Robertson's old dry goods store. I'm sure you know where it is. In fact, I'll bet you have shopped in this very building. I'm here, just as big as life. Come and get me."

The car noise ceased, but the call hadn't disconnected.

"Father Davidson. Cat got your tongue?" Malcolm stood and leaned close to the phone.

A text appeared on his personal cell phone:

—He stopped, keep him talking, we almost have him.—

Valerie leaned forward. "Father Davidson, what penance would you give someone who confessed to killing eight people? Would one hundred Our Fathers, Hail Marys and Acts of Contrition be enough? More? What's the Bible say? Matthew eighteen, verses twenty-one and twenty-two, 'Then Peter came to Jesus and asked, "Lord, how many times shall I forgive my brother who sins against me? Up to seven times?" Jesus answered, "I tell you, not seven times, but seventy-seven times." ' Do you think that's enough to gain God's forgiveness?"

"Shut up, you…you…Jezebel. Don't you dare lecture me and use Bible verses to make your lame arguments. If you're so smart, let me ask this: If someone paid an enormous debt for you, wouldn't you feel obligated to repay him in kind?"

She leaned closer to the phone and spoke in a slow and deliberate cadence. "That's why God sent Jesus to earth, to pay that debt. You, sir, are not Jesus."

"You still don't get it. You hide your head in the sand. Society has become comfortable, and they've let their guard down. They've become lazy. It's like Lincoln said, we live in the greatest country in the world and if we're going to be destroyed, it'll be from within. No external force is stronger than all of us. Well, we're destroying ourselves through the laws that are being passed, the permissiveness, the internet, allowing our children to watch video games where they kill cops, and it's no wonder why there's such little respect for law enforcement." His voice increased in volume and pitch. "But what gives me the greatest anguish is that the people we put on pedestals, the people we respect are blatant sinners. Police officers, judges, medical professionals, they're hypocrites with a capital H. They think they can't be touched because of their position in society, or they mistakenly think they're doing good like Allison Newton letting people in her care die because she thought it best for them. She's not God, she doesn't get to make that choice. A wake-up call is needed. That's why I'm doing what I'm doing. I'm actually helping society and God by ridding the earth of these blatant sinners, those who knowingly violate the laws God has given us to live by."

Malcolm saw Valerie's wide eyes, clenched fists, tight jaw muscles. "Wait a minute," she said. "Who the hell are you calling hypocrites? You, sir, are a hypocrite. You, sir, willingly, with premeditation, murder people. Allison Newton is a hypocrite and you're not? I can't believe you've got the balls to even think something like that, much less say it out loud. The drugs you must be taking for your supposed cancer must be affecting your brain. You sure as shootin' are high on something."

She made Malcolm so very proud of her, her feistiness, her willingness to do verbal battle with a priest and defend innocent people. He needed a woman like her in his life. Unfortunately, she had a husband.

"You Jezebel, let's see what you think when you face Lucifer."

The call disconnected.

Valerie opened her mouth to say something but shook her head and leaned back in the chair. "Wow, that was intense. He got under my skin. I gotta calm down. Any more messages from Beverly?"

"Not yet, I'm hoping the drone got his location." He rubbed his forehead. "Any idea why he calls you Jezebel and all those other names? He's never attacked me like that."

She shook her head, ruffled brow. "Probably because I'm a woman and the Catholic church doesn't look very highly on women. We're not good enough to be deacons or priests. That's reserved for men. He probably doesn't like when a woman confronts him."

Malcolm's personal cell phone played the first few bars of "My Kind Of Town." He double-tapped the phone's face. "Did you get him?"

Beverly screeched, "Got the motherfucker. We got 'im, we got 'im, we got the motherfucker. He stopped at the intersection of Florida State Road 145 and

Coulter Road. He sat there for almost three minutes, then went east on Coulter Road less than a mile, then disconnected. According to our maps, that road's no more than a mile long, dead ends at what looks like a farmhouse with several buildings around it. Damn near the entire road is covered by trees. It's real fucking close to the river. Sunrise is 6:17 tomorrow morning. We can take him as soon as the sun pokes its head over the horizon."

"That's a big fat NFW. We're not waiting. We're going to get him tonight before the sun comes up. I don't want to take a chance on him moving. Do you have any drones you can fly over that road and look for a building with lights on?"

"You're talking to the queen bee here. I got a Stingray drone that has two heat-seeking mini-missiles. As soon as it detects a human heat signature, it'll blow the motherfucker from here to kingdom come. That cocksucker will never know what hit him."

Valerie donned a pained expression and shook her head. "What if you kill the farmer that lives there, or his wife, or family?"

"Slow down, queen bee. Valerie's right. We need to take him alive. A lot of people need closure, and a live capture will help that closure happen a lot more than a body splattered all over the forest."

"Okay, I get you. I've got a prototype drone called a mosquito. It's tiny, but capable of recognizing heat signatures. It'll tell us where possible humans are, then the grunts on the ground can then take it from there."

"Does it sting?" Malcolm asked.

The queen bee chuckled. "I like the way you think, but no, it doesn't sting. All it does is search for heat signatures and radios the coordinates. I'll set it for human so it doesn't give us car engines, air conditioners, farmers' dogs, and shit like that."

"Sounds like we have a plan. Get your mosquito to work. I'll get back to you."

Valerie bounced like a kid at Christmas, anxious to open her presents. "Oh my God, I can't wait. I've never in a thousand years thought I'd be part of a SWAT raid. This is so exciting."

"Your thousand years isn't up. You're not going to be anywhere near the action. You're a civilian. I've violated enough rules already. I'm not going to risk you getting shot. Besides, I'd be worried about you, and you'd be a huge distraction to me. I need all my focus."

"So, what am I supposed to do, stay here and wait for something to happen?" She threw her hands in the air palms up.

He closed the lid on the laptop. "No, you're going back to the hotel with me. I'm going to suit up, and you're going to pack up. It's time for you to go home."

"What do you mean suit up?"

"I need to put my tactical gear on. Let's go."

She scurried after him. "Tactical gear? Aren't the others going to do the dangerous stuff?"

He opened the car door for her. "I'll be right there with them. I need the same protection they have in case I get shot."

Day Eight—July 22nd

Chapter 44

Tuesday, 12:10 a.m.

Malcolm selected his custom 9K bulletproof vest from the hotel closet and tossed it onto the bed. Normally law enforcement officers wore a Level 2 vest for everyday duty. They were lightweight, comfortable for long shifts in a patrol car, and provided protection from most common pistol rounds such as the 9mm that he carried. A .30-06 slug from a hunting rifle carried a much more serious threat. He opted for the heavier Level 9K vest. He'd paid a small fortune to have it custom-made for maximum protection. He'd seen too many people shot and didn't want to look like them. He'd gladly take a bruise that hurt for a couple of days as opposed to a slug tearing through vital organs.

Five millimeters thick, and only a pound heavier than the Level 2 vest, it contained multiple layers of a polymer matrix laminate and would stop almost anything he'd encounter on the street, including double-aught buck-shot, blades, 9mm automatic weapons fire, and all handgun ammunition up to a .44 magnum. If the shooter got lucky enough to hit his head, arms, or legs, well, that would be the EMT or coroner's problem to deal with.

He didn't bother with the usual sport coat, but then again, he didn't have one large enough to cover the vest. Besides, no one cared what you looked like going into battle as long as you came out the victor with all your blood still in you.

Malcolm stripped off his white polo shirt and tan khakis. From one of the dresser drawers, he pulled a black long-sleeved shirt and ankle-length black workout slacks.

Valerie sat, hands clasped between her knees, and watched him methodically prepare to confront a priest who had gone off the deep end. "I've never seen you like this. It scares me. I don't like it."

He ignored her. Once dressed all in black, he slid a Beretta out of its holster, pulled the slide back, ensured the chamber was empty, then released the slide. He tossed the pistol next to the vest. Out of all of the handguns he'd worked with, he preferred the Beretta. It weighed a little over twenty-eight ounces with a full fourteen-round clip.

Valerie whimpered like a puppy who wanted to go out. "I don't like this."

"I know, that's one of the reasons you need to pack and go back to Orlando. Bad stuff might happen, and I don't want you anywhere near it."

"Is it always like this?" Tears seeped from watery eyes.

"Not always, but this is my job. This is what I do." He slid a loaded magazine into the gun that he'd tossed onto the bed and jacked a round into the chamber. He then clipped it to the left vest pocket. "You sell real estate; I find criminals and attempt to capture them. Sometimes I'm successful, sometimes not." He clipped the 9mm Beretta he normally carried in the small of his back to the right breast pocket. He had situated them perfectly for cross-handed retrieval should speed be necessary.

"Gee, I don't want to leave you. You being all alone here, it doesn't feel right. I love you and want to be here for you."

He strapped a five-inch switchblade to his left ankle, then gazed at her. "I love you too, but I'm not sure I can any longer. Do you know why the priest called you those names?"

She wiped tears off her cheeks and shook her head. "What names?"

"Jezebel, harlot, slut."

She raised her shoulders and shook her head. "I guess he was angry and lashing out."

"Because you're married. I didn't believe him when he first told me. I checked. Almost twelve years."

Her hand flew to her open mouth. "You researched me?"

"I guess I'm the fool. I never asked if you had any attachments. I assumed you would have told me up front. Guess I proved the old adage true once again—when you assume, you make an ass out of you and me."

Malcolm pulled six loaded magazines off the closet's top shelf. "You have a husband. That's why he calls you a harlot, an adulteress, and all those other names. If he hadn't said anything, I wouldn't have checked." He slid a magazine into the leftmost pocket designed specifically for it. "I suppose I should have done it sooner, but I didn't." He slid another magazine into the next pocket. "I didn't think you'd hold back that kind of information." Another magazine in another pocket. "I guess another old adage—if it seems too good to be true, it probably is—is true."

Her cheeks had become red and glistened. "Wait, it's true, I am legally married, but it's not like that. I can explain."

The fourth magazine went into its pocket. "What? You're going to tell me you and your husband have an arrangement, is that it?" The fifth magazine entered its pocket.

She stood, wide-eyed. "It's not like you think. Please, I'll explain everything and answer all of your questions, I promise." She clasped her hands in front of her chest.

The final clip slid into the sixth and final pocket. He lifted the vest with one hand, reached into the closet, and pulled out a Remington twelve-gauge pump-action shotgun with an eight-inch barrel. "Sorry, gotta go. So do you. Have a nice rest of your life."

The sound of her sobs lessened the farther he walked down the hall.

Chapter 45

2:19 a.m.

Malcolm stood behind his car parked next to Edgar Miller's barn and scanned the sky. Low-hanging clouds suggesting rain any minute stretched as far as he could see in every direction. More importantly, no moon. Perfect condition for running a night operation.

Beverly Choo, the electronics expert, self-proclaimed queen bee, attached a tactical radio to Malcolm's left collar and handed him an earpiece. He settled it into his ear and nodded. She retreated several steps and turned her back to him. "Nest to Raptor, do you copy?"

"Raptor to Nest, ten by two."

Jack jogged from around the back of the barn and stopped in front of Malcolm.

Beverly joined the two men. "The mosquito has covered four square miles and registered three heat signatures. Ninety-eight percent confident that the two in the farmhouse approximately fifteen hundred meters at the end of the road are human. Seventy-five percent confidence in one on the back porch of a small structure about two hundred meters down Coulter Road on the north side of the road. The porch appears to be on the rear of the structure, facing north, about fifty yards from Coulter Road and twenty yards from the river."

"No other signs of life?"

"Nothing human…wildlife wandering through the brush along the road…that's it."

Malcolm looked at Jack. "Give me a rundown of what personnel we have."

"I have twenty SWAT members and six of your guys. Everyone has full automatic weapons. Twelve of mine and all six of yours are night-vision equipped. All twenty of mine deer hunt in the four-county area, they know what to expect from the terrain, what to watch out for. None of yours is familiar with the area. They're city boys. I'm not sure how much good they'll be."

"Don't sell mine short. They know how to take and secure a structure. If we have to go inside, I want mine doing it. No offense, but I know the capabilities of my guys. They're very good and experienced."

"Let me ask if yours have walked through thick brush at night with bear and wild hogs in the vicinity? If not, I suggest my guys take the forward positions and yours trail in. If structure entry is warranted, yours can take the lead, mine will provide exterior support. Agreed?" Jack held out a fist.

Malcolm fist-bumped. "Good point. You'll be the logistics commander. Everything runs through you. Make sure the other side of the river is covered should he bolt and go for a swim."

"Good thought. I'll send a couple of guys with night eyes."

Beverly added, "The mosquito is overhead and will track him if he runs. In fact, there it is now." She pointed to a speck in the sky, about fifty feet away.

Jack observed, "Can't even tell it's there. By the way, part of our SWAT team is a helicopter. ETA ten minutes. I've instructed he stay a mile to the south until needed."

Malcolm nodded.

Beverly asked, "What if the small structure guy is just some guy, not the murderer?"

"We hold him, regroup, and approach the farmhouse. Any other questions?"

Jack and Beverly shook their heads.

"Okay, folks, let's get this sum-a-bitch before he gets anyone else."

****

AD leaned his head against the chair back and closed his eyes. The headache had gotten worse the longer he sat there. He wanted to scream but tried to relax. He listened for God to speak to him, to provide guidance.

The authorities knew his name, knew he had sacrificed those people. They undoubtedly knew the make and model of his truck and looked for it. The media people seemed like locusts; everywhere he looked he saw them. Too many people around for him to continue the sacrifices, at least for tonight. If he waited a couple of weeks maybe they would go away, but based on pain levels and the amount of drugs required to control them, he didn't know if he'd be able to carry through. Also, they would probably broadcast his name and picture, so he'd be recognized by Farmer Coulter or if someone saw him in public. He didn't have weeks, maybe not even days. He had become useless for over twelve hours after Holt Steadmyer. It all seemed to be coming to a head too soon. He'd turn to his hero, Jesus Christ, the son of God, who had always helped him in the past.

In order to hear what Jesus had to say, he needed to prepare himself to listen. After several deep breaths and shaking his arms and legs, he did his best to make his body limp.

Satisfied that he had relaxed his muscles as much as possible, he opened his mind and focused on his ears. He listened. He only heard thunder in the distance and an occasional bug buzzing nearby. God had created mosquitos, but they sure did annoy him. If he ever got God's ear one-on-one, perhaps he'd suggest mosquitos be removed from the earth. He couldn't think of a single benefit they brought to mankind.

He scolded himself for being distracted and refocused, so he'd hear God's word when it came.

****

Malcolm sat in the bed of Jack's pickup truck. Rain danced like jewels on the windshield of the pickup behind him. Its wipers arced back and forth in rhythm with his heartbeat. *Shhchoonk, shhchoonk, shhchoonk.*

He hated these takedown efforts. It seemed that something always went awry, like with Patrice. Not a single damn effort ever went according to plan. What would happen tonight? Would the sum-a-bitch get away? Would he even be there at all? Would more innocent people die? Would he be one of them? Would anyone mourn him like Scott's wife mourned her husband? Who would care? With Valerie no longer part of his life, he didn't have anyone. Something had to change.

The truck's headlights extinguished simultaneously with it pulling off Route 145 onto Coulter Road with a bump, jostling the five men in the bed. The following seven pickups followed suit. They parked side-by-side blocking access to Route 145. If Father Davidson managed to get to a truck, there was no way he'd be able to access the highway. They'd have him trapped. All part of the plan.

He slid over the side of the truck bed and moved to under a tree. That's when he heard the faint *whump-whump-whump* that only came from a helicopter. A quick glance south and the silhouette of a helicopter, no lights, appeared against a puffy white cloud. He texted the queen bee that he could hear faint rotor blade sounds and wanted the copter moved further away. She responded with a thumbs-up emoji.

The rain had dwindled to a mist. All the grunts, as Beverly referred to them, SWAT, and FBI had ridden in the back of pickup trucks, seemingly impervious to the moisture that fell from the sky. No one opened or closed doors, they simply slid over the sides and tailgate, barely making any noise when their feet touched the ground.

Each member of the group was grim faced, had a set jaw, flexed and clenched their hands into fists. Watching their actions and demeanor resulted in him straightening his back, pulling shoulders back, and fist-bumping anyone who came within range. The butterflies in his stomach settled.

Jack spoke to groups of two and three, giving them their instructions, sharing what their role would be. The men and women checked their equipment, silently felt pockets, pouches, and their weapon. Those with night-vision goggles pulled them on, pressed switches, and adjusted brightness knobs. Every one of them appeared resolute and ready for whatever may happen.

Jack trotted to Malcolm and whispered, "We're

ready to take the sum-a-bitch down." He nodded once.

Malcolm smiled and whispered, "Let's move out."

Jack responded with a thumbs-up. He looked like a football referee signaling a first down when he motioned to the team to move forward. They spread out into a picket line down Coulter Road, no more than four or five yards between them.

Once they stretched from Route 145 to as far as Malcolm could see, Jack motioned with both arms to begin the advance. Silently, over twenty highly trained men and women moved into the brush. Malcolm followed Jack.

He hardly noticed the cold mist that coated his bare face and neck. His adrenaline pumped so high, he probably wouldn't have noticed baseballs hitting him. Besides, Malcolm welcomed the moisture. He knew it made leaves and twigs pliable and silenced the sand from crunching when stepped on.

After about ten minutes of methodical movement, the man in front of Jack raised a clenched fist, the universal sign to stop.

Barely fifteen yards away, the dark silhouette of a cabin could be seen.

Malcolm looked left and right but couldn't see any of the others. Jack's whispered voice came into his ear. "Queen Bee, where's Marco Polo?"

"Still on the back porch."

"Heads up, everyone. Bennett, Bradshaw, Mullen, Clancy, and I will flank the cabin. We'll be between the cabin and the river. Everyone else stays low. Queen Bee, let me know if he moves even a finger."

"Ten four."

Malcolm's breath quickened. He mimicked Jack

and duckwalked forward. After just five yards, burning pain flared in his thighs. He gritted his teeth and reminded himself that he needed to resume his leg workouts, if he made it out alive. His stomach rolled, and he suddenly felt cold.

The six of them swung in an arc around the corner of the cabin until they could clearly see a dark silhouette sitting in a white chair. He caught his breath. He could actually see the man who had killed so many innocent people, ruined so many lives.

Jack whispered, "I've got eyes on him. I can confirm it is Father Davidson. Looks like he's sleeping in a chair on the porch. Alpha Team, tighten the circle. Bravo Team, take support positions as best you can."

"Ten four" came through Malcolm's earpiece twice.

"Queen Bee, are there any heat signatures in the structure?"

"Unknown. The only one that registers is on the back porch. If someone's inside, they're covered by a blanket or under furniture, something that would squelch the mosquito recognizing heat."

"Ten four, Queen Bee. Foxtrot, you are clear to enter the structure. Slow and easy. No need to hurry. Once you clear the structure, exit the rear door, take him from behind."

"Ten four."

Malcolm's heart raced at the sight of four shadows emerging from the brush and moving toward the front of the cabin.

****

Something hard and cold nudged the side of AD's head. "Wake up, Father Davidson."

355

Simultaneous with the voice, six high-powered flashlights bathed AD in light that blinded him. "What? What's happening?" He squinted and raised a hand to shield his eyes.

"Don't make any sudden moves. I have the muzzle of my weapon against the back of your neck. One trigger squeeze will send thirty rounds of lead that will sever your skull from your spine."

"But what's happening, I don't understand. Who are you?"

"I'm Sergeant Charles Wilcox, Madison Police Department. You called me Charlie when I served as an altar boy at ten a.m. Mass. Put both hands on top of your head."

Jack, followed by Malcolm, ascended the three steps onto the narrow porch and flanked the priest.

"What do you want?" Father Davidson asked.

Jack took the lead. "You're under arrest for the murder of eight citizens. Please stand, slowly, keep your hands on top of your head."

Malcolm realized he had been panting instead of normal breathing. He took a deep breath and slid the Berettas into their holsters on the front of his vest. He and Jack took an arm apiece and helped Father Davidson to his feet. Charlie Wilcox lowered his AR-15 to point at Father Davidson's back, or center mass, as Malcolm recalled from training.

"Please accompany us down the steps. Keep your hands where they are."

"Why? I've not done anything wrong." Father Davidson's head swung back and forth, almost as if clearing his mind to comprehend his circumstances.

"I'm not going to ask again. If you won't do as I

request, I have thirty officers who will gladly assist you. With that many helping hands, you may accidentally fall and get hurt, so I suggest you go of your own volition."

Malcolm tightened his grip on the priest's arm. Jack maintained a grasp on the other arm as they descended the steps. At the bottom, Jack instructed, "I'm going to pull your left hand to behind your back. Do not resist. Do you understand?"

"Why are you doing this?"

"Last time, Father Davidson, if you resist it will end very badly for you."

"Okay, okay, just don't hurt me."

Jack extracted a zip tie from his weapon belt and pulled the left hand down.

The *whoomp-whoomp-whoomp* of the helicopter could be heard overhead. Its searchlight came on with a hum and centered on Father Davidson. He looked like an actor illuminated by a spotlight on stage.

AD stiffened. "Go ahead, put the handcuffs on. They arrested Christ, too, even beat him. But his word got out and still exists to this day. I may not be able to sacrifice any more sinners, but I'll have a lot to teach the world before I ascend into heaven."

Jack pulled the other hand down and cinched the zip ties. "Father Davidson, you are under arrest for the murders of Chief Taylor Dautry, Martha Osgood, and six others. You have the right to remain silent. Anything you say can and will be used against you in a court—"

AD smiled and shrugged. "You bet I'm going to say things, and I'm not going to wait until court. I'm going to tell the whole world what a bunch of hypocrites this town is. I'm going to—"

"Father Davidson, I'm advising you to shut up," Jack muttered through clenched teeth.

AD shook his head. "I'm going to tell the world what every one of you hypocrites has done to violate God's laws. Why, you ask? Jesus saved us by the blood of his cross…I'm saving the world by the blood of those being offered up. Recall Mark 2:17, 'Those who are well do not need a physician, but the sick do. I did not come to call the righteous but sinners.' "

Jack shook his head and waved his free hand. "Father, you're supposed to watch over the parishioners of St. Hubertus. You're supposed to protect your flock. How could you kill the people you're supposed to protect? We're all Catholics. We're supposed to be brothers and sisters."

Father Davidson grinned. "The people I sacrificed were Catholic in name only. Their actions didn't fulfill or demonstrate Catholic teachings. You're right, I'm a shepherd, I guard my flock." He looked around at the shadowy figures surrounding him. "Who among you wouldn't put down an animal that preyed on your flock, those that you're supposed to protect?" He nodded at individuals. "You would, you would, and you would." He swung his head in an arc. "Everyone one of you would. Well, how does that differ from what I've done, what others will do once the word gets out? I offered up those who had wantonly sinned. They preyed on the flock that I'm supposed to protect."

Jack tried again. "Father Anthony—"

He threw his head back and proceeded in a loud voice. "When the world finds out the sins of these supposedly God-fearing, church-going people, it'll ignite a crusade like no other. I'm going to—"

He stopped and looked cross-eyed at a red dot that appeared on his left nostril.

The dot climbed to the top of his nose and centered between his eyebrows.

Simultaneously, a loud *bang* and flash occurred.

A black hole replaced the dot.

Father Davidson's head jerked back. He appeared to look into the helicopter light, as if it came from heaven. The smile remained on his face.

Only the *whoomp-whoomp-whoomp* of helicopter blades could be heard until Father Davidson's body hit the ground.

Malcolm drew the Berettas and pointed them at Chief Dautry's stepson. "Drop it, Robert, or there will be two bodies for the coroner to haul away."

Robert grinned and lowered his handgun. Holding the weapon with thumb and index finger, he crouched and laid it on the ground. He raised his hands and stood erect.

A nearby SWAT team member stepped behind Robert, pulled one arm behind his back, then the other, and zip-tied them together.

Jack approached his fellow detective. "Christian, make sure those ties are tight. It's wet out here, and I don't want him slipping out."

"Ten four." The SWAT team member gave an extra tug that caused Robert to wince, but he didn't stop smiling. After patting Robert's chest, arms, pockets, and legs, Christian declared, "He's clean."

"Thanks." Jack faced Robert. "What the hell are you doing?"

Robert continued to grin. "Don't you get it? If he

lives, he'll tell some reporter everything he heard in that stinking confessional. My mother already feels overwhelming shame about Chief's infidelity. Personally, I don't give a shit that he's dead. He always treated me like an idiot. But what he did to that sweet woman, running around behind her back all those years, telling her one bullshit story after another. She believed him, she trusted him. And he did that to her." Robert wagged his head and frowned. "Not good, not good at all."

Jack licked his lips. "But you knew, we all did."

"But my mother didn't. She had a happy, contented life. Now that this piece of shit—" He kicked Father Davidson's leg. "—has made it known to the whole world what an asshole Chief was and how he duped his wife, that's not right. An eye for an eye, is what the Bible says."

"Robert, you're no better than him. You became judge, jury, and executioner, just like him. Only God can do that." Jack stomped.

"And a tooth for a tooth. He'll not ruin any more lives, or cause any more embarrassment by repeating what we all told him in the confessional. He's supposed to maintain confidentiality, not discuss anything he hears in that damn little box. Did you tell him things you don't want others to know about?"

"Well, yeah, but trust is part of being Catholic."

"I guarantee you if he'd stayed alive and gone to trial, he'd be singing like the choir about everyone's sins. I couldn't let that happen. I couldn't let him heap mountains of shame on Madison's citizens. It would have smothered this whole community."

Malcolm approached and looked Robert in the eye.

"Did you do it to keep from disgracing the town, or did you kill him so he wouldn't humiliate you?"

The grin returned. "Guess you'll never know."

Jack looked at Christian. "Read him his rights and book him for the murder of Father Anthony Davidson."

Day Nine—July 23nd

Chapter 46

Thursday, 2:10 p.m.

Malcolm had ignored Roger's phone calls and emails for the past two days, maybe three, depending on how one counted. His boss couldn't be avoided any longer. He turned from the hotel room window, snatched his phone off the desk and called Roger. *Maybe it'll roll to voicemail, and I can just leave a message.*

Roger answered on the second ring. "It's about God damned time I hear from you. I didn't get a report last night. Why the hell not? I don't have much time, give me a quick update."

Good old Roger. Never happy. Couldn't even offer congratulations. Just busting my balls on not sending a frickin' report. He's making the Dallas offer look pretty damn good. "Here's everything in a nutshell. Chief's stepson, Robert LeBeau, is in solitary in the county jail. He's lawyered up and not talking. Our facilities people are dismantling the war room. Everything should be loaded and headed back end of day tomorrow. There's nothing more for me to do here, so when I finish packing, I'll be headed out. I'm taking two of the six weeks of vacation I've accrued. Now you're caught up."

"Why the hell did LeBeau kill the priest? He's in

law enforcement. He knows he's either getting the needle or he'll rot in prison for the rest of his life."

"He killed him so the priest wouldn't create any more problems by telling residents' sins. Sorta taking one for the team." He moved to the window and watched the traffic on the highway.

"One of your reports said he'd taken time off to attend to his mother. How did he know what you were doing, and how the hell did he get close enough to kill the priest? Didn't you have a perimeter set to keep unwanted people out of the zone?"

That son-of-a-bitch, he's always looking to find fault. Why can't he just be satisfied that the Madison Murderer has been stopped? What's it matter who or how? Malcolm spun on a heel and paced toward the door. "He remotely monitored the storyboards. When he saw the priest's name come up as the murderer and heard where we were headed, he got there shortly after we left the staging area. He followed us through the brush and trees. It had just rained, so everything was wet and didn't make any noise. No need to set a perimeter in the middle of nowhere in the middle of the night. Besides, if someone had seen LeBeau, they'd have assumed he was part of the team and not challenged him. He's almost as well-known as Chief Dautry."

Roger remained silent for a couple of seconds. "There are plenty of eyewitnesses who saw the shooting, right? You won't have any trouble getting a conviction, right?"

Malcolm turned at the door and paced toward the window. "There are fourteen eyewitnesses, including me. All law enforcement. The Florida Department of

Law Enforcement shouldn't have a problem."

"I didn't know FDLE was involved. You never mentioned them in your reports."

He reached the window and turned back toward the door. "They weren't involved until LeBeau shot the priest. They investigate all law enforcement officer shootings."

"Oh, right. What's this bullshit about taking vacation? I didn't authorize it. You can take a couple of days, but I expect you to be available next Monday."

Malcolm stopped at the closet, grabbed an empty suitcase, and tossed it onto the bed. *I'm not playing his bullshit game anymore.* "I'm exhausted. If I don't get some real rest, I'm going to be worthless on another project. Roger, I'm taking two of the six weeks I've accrued. Besides, I've got to figure this Dallas thing out. Am I going, am I staying, just what I'm doing. And I can't do that while I'm pushing paper in the office."

He tucked the phone between his shoulder and ear and started throwing clothes from a drawer into the open suitcase. He didn't care whether they wrinkled or not, he needed to get the hell away from Madison and Roger, especially Roger.

"All right, I'll authorize it, but keep your phone handy in case me or the Madison people need something."

He pushed the top dresser drawer closed with a knee and opened the middle drawer. Valerie's white nightshirt with monarch butterflies sat alone in the drawer. His breath caught.

"Gee. You still there?"

"I'm here." He lifted the shirt and inhaled deeply. It smelled like her perfume.

"I said, keep your phone handy in case the Madison people or I need to reach you. Do you fucking understand?"

He plopped onto the bed. "Yeah. Whatever. I gotta go. We'll talk in a couple of weeks." Malcolm pressed the disconnect icon and set the phone on the desk next to his briefcase. *There, you son-of-a-bitch. How do you like it when someone hangs up on you?* He extended his middle finger toward the phone.

Malcolm sat for almost a minute with the nightshirt cradled in his hands. "It was good while it lasted, but I don't fool around with married women. Never have, never will." He balled the shirt up and dropped it in the trash can next to the desk. .

Thirty minutes later, luggage cart loaded to the max with a pair of suitcases, four file boxes, and half a dozen equipment cases with his weapons and tactical gear, Malcolm took one last look around.

Bathroom empty. Closet empty. Nightstand drawers empty. Dresser drawers empty. Desk drawer empty.

Then he noticed Valerie's butterfly nightshirt in the trash can and hesitated. He looked at his reflection in the mirror. "I really thought she might be The One."

He settled onto the desk chair, pulled the shirt out of the can, and placed it in his lap.

It seems a shame to toss her shirt. She liked it. Maybe when I get home, I should send it to her. After a long sigh, Malcolm rose.

With Valerie's shirt tossed over his shoulder, he pushed the luggage cart down the hall toward the elevator.

A word about the author...

Henry James Kaye is the award-winning author of the Malcolm Gee Mystery Series and the Stesti Mystery Series novels. He's also had numerous mystery short stories published in various anthologies. He and his wife live in New Smyrna Beach, Florida, along with their menagerie of dogs and birds. Twelve Sinners is the first novel in the Malcolm Gee Series.

HenryJamesKaye.com

Thank you for purchasing
this publication of The Wild Rose Press, Inc.

For questions or more information
contact us at
info@thewildrosepress.com.

The Wild Rose Press, Inc.
www.thewildrosepress.com